OUTSTANDING PRAISE F[illegible]

SANO ICHIRŌ THRILLERS

Red Chrysanthemum

"A careful, beautiful portrayal of a dangerous time in Japanese history. . .compelling and lively."

—*Dallas Morning News*

"A blend [of] political intrigue and barbed sexual commentary." —*Entertainment Weekly*

"A page-turner...Rowland matches her talent for storytelling with her ability to render convincing historical detail." —*Publishers Weekly* (starred review)

"Rowland's historical detail and graceful prose enhance another solid mystery." —*Kirkus Reviews*

"Rowland puts her own spin on the multiple storytelling tactics invented five decades ago in the movie *Rashomon*, adding an extra dimension to her long-running series. . . . The tension leads to a corker of a denouement—one that opens up new doors for future series offerings."

—*Baltimore Sun*

The Assasin's Touch

"Sano may carry a sword and wear a kimono, but you'll immediately recognize him as an ancestor of Philip Marlowe or Sam Spade." —*The Denver Post*

"Evocative detail and suspense...Rowland's characters remain fresh." —*Publishers Weekly*

"A welcome breath of fresh air." —*Booklist*

"Elegantly told and interspersed with delicious bits of history." —*Kirkus Reviews*

More...

The Perfumed Sleeve

"Deftly combining a classic whodunit with vivid period detail, Rowland raises the stakes for her next book with an unexpected twist at the end that promises to present her dogged but fallible hero with even more difficulties in the future."

—*Publishers Weekly*

"Think James Clavell meets Raymond Chandler."

—*San Francisco Chronicle*

The Dragon King's Palace

"Rowland's masterful evocation of the period enables the reader to identify with the universal human emotions and drives that propel her characters while absorbing numerous telling details of a different culture and era."

—*Publishers Weekly*

"A lively dissection of the samurai code of honor, sexual dishonor, palace infighting, and ancient Japanese mores."

—*Kirkus Reviews*

The Pillow Book of Lady Wisteria

"This series just keeps getting better and better."

—*Booklist*

"Delicate prose and a plot full of the overtones and undercurrents that shade real life push Rowland's latest historical beyond the standard whodunit. All the animosity and fear in this seamless work is put forth in demure language that perfectly suits the culture Rowland portrays."

—*Publishers Weekly*

Black Lotus

"Well-developed characters, a complex, absorbing plot, and rich historical detail should help win the author a place on mystery bestseller lists."

—*Publishers Weekly* (starred review)

"Laura Joh Rowland's richly detailed books about a 17th-century Japanese samurai-warrior-turned-detective are... packed with plot narrative." —*Chicago Tribune*

The Samurai's Wife

"As a fan of *Shogun*, it's easy to say that *The Samurai's Wife* provided me with the same sense of place and culture that was so invigorating in James Clavell's epic yarn. . . . Rowland's a pretty terrific storyteller." —*Chicago Tribune*

"Rowland delineates the distinctions of her characters with subtlety and pulls together the strands of her multifaceted plot with enviable grace." —*Publishers Weekly*

"An authentically detailed and wonderfully involving historical novel." —*Library Journal*

The Concubine's Tattoo

"Rowland's understanding of the society she depicts shines through, and she succeeds in presenting Sano as an intriguing combination of wiliness and decency, making this a good bet for fans of historicals as well as of mysteries past." —*Publishers Weekly*

"Rowland is deepening and broadening her distinctie series in interesting ways. She expertly evokes an exotic world—in its difference and brooding darkness—that can be confused with no other. . . . Both author and detective come through with colors flying." —*The Times-Picayune*

"A fascinating, well-researched, and action-filled costume adventure." —*Library Journal*

"Rowland offers fascinating glimpses into the culture of medieval Japan." —*Booklist*

ALSO BY LAURA JOH ROWLAND

Red Chrysanthemum

The Assassin's Touch

The Perfumed Sleeve

The Dragon King's Palace

The Pillow Book of Lady Wisteria

Black Lotus

The Samurai's Wife

The Concubine's Tattoo

The Way of the Traitor

Bundori

Shinjū

The SNOW EMPRESS

Laura Joh Rowland

St. Martin's Paperbacks

This is a work of fiction. All of the characters, organizations, and events portrayed in this novel are either products of the author's imagination or are used fictitiously.

THE SNOW EMPRESS

For information address St. Martin's Press, 175 Fifth Avenue, New York, NY 10010.

Library of Congress Catalog Card Number: 2007027693

ISBN: 0-312-94535-3
EAN: 978-0-312-94535-0

Printed in the United States of America

St. Martin's Press hardcover edition / November 2007
St. Martin's Paperbacks edition / November 2008

St. Martin's Paperbacks are published by St. Martin's Press, 175 Fifth Avenue, New York, NY 10010.

10 9 8 7 6 5 4

In memory of Fat Boy, 1988–2007

Ezogashima

Genroku Period

Year 12, Month 9

(Hokkaido, October 1699)

Prologue

She hastened along a narrow, winding path illuminated by the full autumn moon that shone upon the forest. Her feet, clad in high-soled lacquer sandals, stumbled over the rough terrain. Branches reached out from the darkness and snagged her long hair and her flowing silk robes. A chill wind stripped leaves off boughs that waved and creaked. Wolves howled.

Having grown unaccustomed to physical exertion, she panted, inhaling the odors of pine and dead leaves tinged by smoke. Her heart beat faster with anger. She had better things to do than ramble through the cold night! She hated the forests; she shrank from the eerie voices of the spirits that inhabited the wilderness. If she had her way, she would never venture outdoors again. She didn't belong here, even though her ancestors had called this land home since the beginning of time. How much better to relax in a warm, lit, comfortable room than to bother with this foolish business!

Huffing in exasperation, she peered ahead through the whispering shadows. But she saw no one, heard no footfalls nor breaths except her own. Her tongue brimmed with scathing words. She quickened her pace, eager to settle matters for good.

Against her shin pressed a line of tension, as if from a vine grown across the path. She tripped. At the same time, she heard a loud snap. Instinctive fear seized her. She recognized that sound. As she pitched forward, arms flung wide to catch herself, a whizzing noise cleaved the night, rushing through the forest toward her. A hard thump struck her chest below her right breast. Sharpness pierced deep between her ribs. She fell, screaming in terrified pain. Her hands and knees smacked the ground. The impact punched the breath from her lungs. She groped at her breast, searching for the source of the agony.

She found a long, thin, rounded wooden shaft. The end embedded in her flesh was made of iron. The opposite end had two bristly ridges of feathers. It was an arrow.

Blood spilled from the wound, gleaming black in the moonlight, warm and wet on her fingers. The pain was cruel as a hungry animal savaging organs and sinews. It tore gasps and whimpers from her. But she knew that worse was yet to come. She knew what she must do if she wanted to save her life.

She closed her hands around the shaft and pulled. The arrowhead ripped through tissue already torn, scraped bones on its way out. Her shriek blared through the forest. The arrow came free in a gout of blood, dropped from her hands. Black stars coalesced in her vision, obliterating the moonlight. Faintness weakened her. Moaning, she fumbled at her sash. But she'd long ago ceased the habit of carrying a knife. She clawed desperately at her breast, tearing the skin that encircled the wound. Bits came off under her fingernails; all the while more blood poured out.

Yet she realized it was no use. The arrow had gone too deep, touched her innards, planted destruction. Dizziness and chills attacked her. The moon blazed as bright and hot as the sun. A choking sensation clenched her throat; nausea embroiled her stomach. The spirits of the forest rose up and whirled around her, cawing like carrion birds.

She lurched to her feet and down the path the way she'd come. She called out for help, but the one who might have rushed to her aid did not. Everybody else was too far away to hear, let alone rescue her. Convulsions shuddered through her, knocked her to the ground. She keened in anguished protest.

She heard the spirits laughing and exclaiming triumphantly: *Now you'll never leave us.*

A world away, in the city of Edo, the autumn moon shone upon Zōjō Temple. Warm, mellow light gilded the pagoda. Conversation and laughter rose from the crowd gathered in the garden to view the moon on this summery night. Fashionably dressed samurai and ladies reclined on the grass, composing poetry. Servants poured wine and passed out moon-cakes. Children ran and squealed in delight. Samurai boys fought mock battles, their wooden swords clattering, their shouts loud above the boom of temple gongs. Incense smoke spiced the air. Flames in stone lanterns chased the darkness to the perimeters of the garden, where pine trees shadowed the landscape.

Chamberlain Sano Ichirō and his wife, Lady Reiko, sat amid friends and attendants, laughing at silly poems they recited. But although Sano was enjoying this rare time away from the business of running the government, he couldn't relax completely. Too many years as a target for political plots had taught him caution. Now the hour was late, and Sano's party had a long ride back to Edo Castle, through city streets where rebels marauded.

Raising his wine cup, he announced, "One last toast to our good fortune! Then we must go home."

Amid groans of disappointment, his attendants prepared to depart, calling farewells to nearby groups. Sano said to Reiko, "Now if only we can find that son of ours."

Masahiro was eight years old; independent and grown-up, he preferred to rollick with friends his age rather than sit sedately beside his elders.

"I'll fetch him." Reiko walked through the crowd to the boys playing war. "Masahiro! Time to go."

There was no answer. He probably didn't want to leave the fun, Reiko thought. Her gaze darted among the running, yelling boys. She didn't see Masahiro with them. Less worried than impatient, she moved toward the garden's edge.

Perhaps he was hiding in the woods. Then she spied an object that lay on the ground near the pine trees.

It was Masahiro's toy sword. A replica of a real samurai weapon, it had a hilt bound in black silk cord, a brass guard decorated with his flying-crane family crest, and a wooden blade. Reiko's impatience turned to alarm because her son would never run off and leave behind his most prized possession.

"Masahiro!" she cried, frantically scanning the other children, the gay crowd, the temple. Dread invaded her heart. "Where are you?"

Edo

Genroku Period

Year 12, Month 10

(Tokyo, November 1699)

Chapter One

A gray, clouded twilight befell Edo. Thin drizzle glazed the capital's tile roofs and subdued the crowds trudging through the wet streets. The cold vapors of late autumn floated on the Sumida River. Mist rendered Edo Castle almost invisible upon its hilltop and drenched the lights in its guard turrets.

Seated inside his office in his compound within the castle, Sano saw Detective Marume, one of his two personal bodyguards, standing at the threshold. He paused in the middle of a letter he was dictating to his secretary. "Well? Did you find him?" he demanded.

The sad expression on the burly detective's normally cheerful face was answer enough. The hope that had risen in Sano drowned in disappointment.

Masahiro had been missing for almost two months, since the moon-viewing party. Sano still had troops out searching, to no avail. The possibility of kidnapping had occurred to him, even though no ransom demand had come. He had suspicions about who might be responsible, but he'd investigated all his enemies and come up with no clues that tied Masahiro's disappearance to them; in fact, no clues at all. Every day Masahiro was gone Sano grew more desperate to find his beloved son, and more afraid he never would.

"I'm sorry," Marume said. "The sighting was another false lead."

False leads had taunted Sano from the beginning. At first he and Reiko had thrilled to each new report that a boy who fit Masahiro's description had been spotted in this or that place. But as the hunt had gone on and on, as their hopes were cruelly dashed time after time, Sano had come to dread new leads. He couldn't bear to tell Reiko that this last one had come to naught, to see her suffer.

The only hardship more terrible for them than another day without Masahiro was not knowing what had happened to him.

"Don't worry, we'll find your boy," Marume said, as if anxious to convince himself.

Fighting the idea that despite all his power, his troops, and his wealth he couldn't bring Masahiro back, striving to remain optimistic, Sano said, "Any new information?"

Marume hesitated, then said, "Not today."

The only thing worse than false leads was no leads at all. Sano felt his endurance crumbling under a wave of grief, but he couldn't fall apart. Not only his wife but the Tokugawa regime depended on him. "Keep the search going. Don't give up."

"Will do," Marume said.

A manservant came to the door. "Excuse me, Honorable Chamberlain. There's a message from the shogun. He wants to see you in the palace right away."

Sano was reminded that the disappearance of his son was only one of his troubles.

Sano found the shogun in his bath chamber. Tokugawa Tsunayoshi, the military dictator of Japan, sat naked in the sunken tub of steaming water. A blind masseur rubbed his withered shoulders. The shogun's favorite companion, a beautiful youth named Yoritomo, lounged close to him in the tub. Guards and servants hovered nearby. Lord Matsudaira, the shogun's cousin, crouched next to the door. He was sweating in his armor, his stoic expression not hiding his resentment that he must dance attendance on his cousin or lose influence over him and control over the regime.

"Greetings, Chamberlain Sano," he said.

Five years ago, Lord Matsudaira had set out to take over

the regime because he thought he would be a better dictator than the weak, foolish shogun was. His first step was to eliminate the former chamberlain, Yanagisawa, who'd been the shogun's lover and ruled Japan from behind the throne. Lord Matsudaira had defeated Yanagisawa on the battlefield and exiled him. But Lord Matsudaira had had a harder time maintaining power than achieving it. Now antagonism toward Sano iced his polite manner. Sano felt his guard go up against this man who'd become his personal enemy.

"Are you surprised to see me?" Lord Matsudaira asked.

"Not at all." Sano was displeased to find Lord Matsudaira here but had expected as much. Lord Matsudaira was always around when Sano saw the shogun, the better to prevent them from getting too close.

"Perhaps, then," Lord Matsudaira said, "you're disappointed that I'm still alive after last night's incident."

Sano guessed what was coming. *Not again,* he thought in dismay. "What incident?"

"A firebomb was thrown into my villa on the river while I was hosting a banquet there," said Lord Matsudaira.

"Dear me, how terrible," murmured the shogun. "It seems as if this sort of thing is, ahh, always happening to you."

Although Lord Matsudaira had purged the regime of Yanagisawa's allies, subjugating some and banishing or executing others, Yanagisawa still had underground partisans fighting Lord Matsudaira with covert acts of violence. And Lord Matsudaira was so insecure in his power that his relations with his own supporters had deteriorated. He harshly punished them for the slightest hint of disloyalty while forcing them to pay large cash tributes to prove their allegiance. He'd created such a climate of fear and disgruntlement that there were many people in his camp who wouldn't have minded seeing him dead.

"I'd have thought that you of all people would have known about the bombing." Lord Matsudaira glanced at the shogun, who looked puzzled trying to catch the drift of the conversation, then fixed an accusing stare on Sano. "Perhaps in advance."

"You're mistaken," Sano said, exasperated because this was the third time in as many months that Lord Matsudaira had accused him of something he hadn't done. He wasn't responsible for the bombing even though the man had reason to think so.

Last year the folks who'd put Lord Matsudaira on top had started casting about for somebody to take him down. Sano had found himself pushed to the head of the line.

At first he'd rejected the idea of challenging Lord Matsudaira because his duty and loyalty to the shogun extended to the entire Tokugawa clan. But Lord Matsudaira treated him so badly, always criticizing him, accusing him of treason and corruption, threatening him and his family with death. Sano had faced a choice between leading a movement against Lord Matsudaira and bowing down and giving up his post, his self-respect, and his samurai honor.

That was no choice at all.

Lord Matsudaira now regarded Sano with hostility, believing him guilty of the attack no matter what he said. "You might be interested to know that my guards caught the man that threw the bomb. Before they killed him, he told me who sent him."

"I'm sure that by the time you were finished with him, he would have said anything you wanted," Sano said, denying that the bomber was one of his men. Now he had his own bone to pick with Lord Matsudaira. "If you're so determined to lay blame, then consider the attack a retaliation."

"For what?" Lord Matsudaira said, disconcerted.

"Some troops were ambushed and fired at by snipers eight days ago." Aware of the shogun listening, Sano kept his speech circumspect; he didn't say that the troops were from his own army or that he thought Lord Matsudaira responsible.

"This is the first I've heard of it."

Although Lord Matsudaira sounded genuinely surprised, Sano didn't believe him any more than he'd believed Sano. "You may be interested to know that the snipers were seen by witnesses before they ran away. They were wearing a certain family crest." *Yours,* his look told Lord Matsudaira.

Outraged incredulity showed on the man's face. "The witnesses are lying. Why would one send men on a sneak attack labeled with one's own crest?"

"Because one didn't expect anybody would live to tell," Sano said.

As he and Lord Matsudaira stared each other down, Sano felt a sense of momentum careening out of control, as if they were two horsemen tumbling down a hill while they fought together. He'd expected Lord Matsudaira to meet his opposition with due force; Sano had armed himself with a long-term strategy of building support and had hoped for a painless takeover, but the attacks were propelling them toward outright battle. His samurai spirit filled with bloodlust. He could taste both victory and death.

"I don't know what you're arguing about," the shogun interrupted, peevish because Sano and Lord Matsudaira had excluded him from their conversation. "Settle your differences elsewhere. Chamberlain Sano, I brought you here to discuss a very important matter."

"What would that be, Your Excellency?" Sano said.

"It's a report that you sent me." The shogun fumbled at some scrolls beside the tub. "Now which one is it?"

Yoritomo reached over, picked out a scroll, and handed it to his lord and lover. He shot a nervous glance at Sano, who pitied him. Yoritomo was a son of Yanagisawa, the former chamberlain. Although Lord Matsudaira had exiled Yanagisawa and his family, the shogun had insisted on keeping Yoritomo. Yoritomo had Tokugawa blood—from his mother, a relative of the shogun—and rumor said he was heir apparent to the dictatorship. Sano had befriended Yoritomo, who seemed alone and lost at court, a decent young man who deserved better than to be a political pawn and a target for Lord Matsudaira's schemes.

The shogun opened the scroll and jabbed a wet finger at the characters. "I am concerned about this, ahh, situation you mentioned." Lately, he'd begun taking an interest in government affairs instead of leaving them to his subordinates. Perhaps he sensed how much control he'd lost and wanted to snatch it back, at this late date. "The one that involves Ezogashima."

Ezogashima was the far northernmost island of Japan, sometimes referred to as Hokkaido, "Northern Sea Circuit." A vast, sparsely populated wilderness of forests, mountains, and rivers, it consisted of two domains. The largest was Ezochi, "barbarian place," inhabited by the Ezo, primitive tribal people scattered among tiny villages. The other was Wajinchi, "Japanese place," squeezed into the southwest corner, a remote outpost of the Tokugawa regime and its foothold in alien territory.

"You say there is a problem with the Matsumae clan," the shogun said.

The clan were his vassals who governed Ezogashima, their longtime hereditary fief. In the rigidly organized world of Japan, their status was ambiguous. They weren't traditional landholders like the *daimyo,* feudal lords who ruled the provinces. There was little agriculture in Ezogashima, no income from farming. Rather, the Matsumae derived their wealth and political power from their monopoly on trade with the Ezo. They took a share of the money made on furs, gold, wild game, fish, and other products exported to the south. They were looked down upon by samurai society because they blurred the line between warrior and merchant.

Squinting at the inked characters, which had begun to run, the shogun said, "Remind me what the problem is, Yoritomo-*san.*"

"Lord Matsumae didn't show up for his attendance this year," the youth said in a quiet, deferential tone.

"He was due in the summer," Sano clarified.

The Matsumae came to Edo to visit the shogun about once every three years, less often than other lords, who came annually. This was not only because of the long distance from Ezogashima but also for political factors. Lord Matsumae was supposed to be busy defending Japan's northern frontier, and he was so removed from the power plays of Edo that he was considered not much of a threat to the Tokugawa, which therefore kept him on a loose rein. He didn't even have to leave his wife and children in Edo as hostages to ensure his good behavior. However, he did owe respect to the shogun. His failure to appear was a serious violation of protocol.

"Even more disturbing is the fact that there's been no communication at all from Ezogashima in two months," Lord Matsudaira said, obviously familiar with the situation. There was a sly smile on his face that Sano didn't like.

"What have you done about this, ahh, matter?" the shogun asked Sano.

Sano had to pause and think. Masahiro's disappearance had made it hard for him to concentrate on anything else. "I sent envoys to find out what's going on. They never returned."

"Worse and worse," Lord Matsudaira muttered, but he sounded pleased for some strange, private reason.

"What could be the cause of this?" the shogun asked.

"Perhaps an Ezo uprising has prevented Lord Matsumae from leaving his domain or sending communiqués," Sano said.

From time to time the barbarians warred against the Japanese, invariably over trade disputes and Japanese intrusion into Ezo hunting and fishing territory. The last war had occurred some thirty years ago, when Ezo chieftains had banded together, attacked the Matsumae clan, and attempted to drive them out of Ezogashima. More than two hundred Japanese had been killed before the Matsumae finally subdued the barbarians. But another war with the Ezo wasn't the most dire possibility.

"Maybe the Manchurians have attacked," Lord Matsudaira said.

The regime had long feared an invasion, via Ezogashima, by the Manchurians from the Chinese mainland. The Matsumae clan was Japan's buffer against them. Sano imagined war raging in Ezogashima, the Matsumae defeated, then enemy legions conquering Japan province by province before anyone in Edo knew. As everyone contemplated such a fate, fear opened the shogun's mouth. He reached for Yoritomo, who held his hand.

"Something must be done," the shogun said to Sano.

Sano knew what was coming. Even if instinct hadn't alerted him, Lord Matsudaira's sly smile would have. He hurried to head it off. "I'll send a battalion of troops to Ezogashima today."

"That's not good enough." The shogun pointed a dripping, withered finger at Sano. "I want you to go yourself."

A sense of injustice flared up in Sano. That the shogun still treated him like an errand boy, ordering him here and there on a whim, even now that he was second-in-command! Yet he knew he had no right to be angry even though a trip to Ezogashima was the last thing he needed. He was just as much at his lord's disposal as the lowliest foot soldier was; he owed the shogun unstinting duty without expectation of reward. That was Bushido, the Way of the Warrior, the code of honor by which he lived. And he knew that sending him to Ezogashima wasn't the shogun's idea. Sano glared at Lord Matsudaira.

Lord Matsudaira met his gaze with bland indifference before saying, "That's a wonderful idea, Your Excellency. I'm sure Chamberlain Sano will straighten everything out for us."

While Sano was gone, Lord Matsudaira would steal his allies and build up his own power base. Then there would be no place left at court for Sano. If he went to Ezogashima, he might as well never come back.

"I'm eager to be of service, but if I go, who will help you run the government, Your Excellency?" Sano said, appealing to the shogun's self-interest.

That ploy usually worked, but this time the shogun said, "My dear cousin has assured me that he will, ahh, fill your shoes in your absence." He smiled gratefully at Lord Matsudaira, who smirked.

But Sano had another, more urgent reason besides politics for wanting to get out of the trip. Desperation drove him to beg for special consideration even though he never had before. "Your Excellency, this is a bad time for me to leave Edo. My son is missing."

"Ahh, yes, I recall," the shogun said, diverted. "Poor little boy. How terrible for you and Lady Reiko."

Sano hastened to press his advantage: "I have to be here to lead the search for him."

The shogun wavered but then turned to Lord Matsudaira. "What do you think?"

"I think that perhaps his wish to find his son gives Chamberlain Sano all the more motive to go to Ezogashima," Lord Matsudaira said in a portentous tone. "Before you argue anymore, Chamberlain Sano, I have something to show you."

He stood, reached under his sash, pulled out an object, and handed it to Sano. It was the hilt of a miniature sword, the wooden blade broken off. As Sano gazed at the flying-crane crest stamped on the brass guard, recognition and puzzlement stunned him. The hilt came from one toy sword of a pair he'd given Masahiro. The sword was the mate of the longer one that Reiko had found at the temple. Masahiro had worn both weapons that night.

"Where did you get this?" Sano demanded.

Shrugging, Lord Matsudaira smiled, his expression innocent. "I think you can guess."

Sano pictured Lord Matsudaira's soldiers emerging from the woods at the temple, grabbing Masahiro. He saw Masahiro struggle to defend himself, his blade breaking. The soldiers smuggled Masahiro away from town, under the cover of darkness, careful to leave no trail. Revelation confirmed what Sano had suspected from the start despite a lack of evidence.

Lord Matsudaira had kidnapped Masahiro.

Such rage beset Sano that a shrieking noise blared in his ears and blood crimsoned his vision. Lord Matsudaira had taken his son, put him and Reiko through two months of hell.

"You!" Sano lunged at Lord Matsudaira.

The shogun exclaimed in fright. The guards dragged Sano away from Lord Matsudaira, who was unfazed. Sano fought them, shouting, "What did you do to him? Where is he?"

"What's going on?" the shogun cried.

Sano drew a breath to say that Lord Matsudaira had kidnapped his son as yet another move against him in their ongoing strife, to tell the shogun, at long last, that his cousin was after his place at the head of the dictatorship.

"Beware, Chamberlain Sano," Lord Matsudaira cautioned, shaking his head, his voice ominous, his smile gone. "Speak, and you'll hurt yourself more than me."

Prudence grappled with anger in Sano and won. He exhaled his intentions in a gust of air, because he knew Lord Matsudaira was right.

The shogun was still unaware that his cousin had seized control of Japan and Sano was contesting Lord Matsudaira. No one had told him, and he wasn't observant enough to have noticed. Sano and Lord Matsudaira enforced a nationwide conspiracy of silence because if he did find out, the precarious balance of power could tip in a direction that favored neither of them. Their rivalry could become a three-way civil war if the *daimyo* on their sides shifted their backing to the shogun, who had the hereditary right to rule. They would see the advantage of grouping together under one leader versus dividing their strength between two. The shogun could emerge the victor in spite of his personal shortcomings. And defeat would be worse for Sano than Lord Matsudaira.

Even if Lord Matsudaira lost his domains, his army, and his political position in a war, his blood ties to the shogun could shield him from execution for treason. He could live to fight another day. But Sano, an outsider, would be put to death, as would his family and all his close associates.

Now Sano's tongue was silenced, his hands chained. He could only stare with bitter hatred at his foe who'd struck him the lowest blow in his most vulnerable spot.

"I won't forget this," he said in a voice so harsh, so threatening, that Lord Matsudaira flinched.

"Forget what?" the shogun piped up timidly.

"Where is he?" Sano demanded again.

Lord Matsudaira recovered his swagger, his smile. "In Ezogashima."

Although Sano was stunned by fresh shock, he realized he shouldn't be. The news of where Lord Matsudaira had sent his son had a feeling of inevitability. All the strands of conflict and misfortune in his life had braided together. This whole discussion had been leading up to this moment.

"In Ezogashima," Lord Matsudaira repeated, "where trouble is waiting for you to investigate." His eyes shone with evil triumph. "He should have arrived in the castle town of Fukuyama City a month ago. You mustn't lose any time getting there."

If you want to rescue your son, said his unspoken words. The ransom for Masahiro was Sano's mission to Ezogashima, his absence from Edo. Despite the circumstances, Sano felt the burden of his misery lighten. At last he knew where Masahiro was. Lord Matsudaira could be lying, but Sano's samurai instincts told him otherwise. His political instincts said that although Lord Matsudaira could easily have had Masahiro killed, that wasn't the case, because Masahiro was too valuable alive, as a hostage.

Now Sano's mind shifted focus away from the present scene, to his top priority of retrieving his son. The people around him seemed to shrink as if viewed from the far end of a spyglass. His new sense of mission dwarfed even Lord Matsudaira. Sano would deal with him later.

"If you'll excuse me, Your Excellency," Sano said, bowing to the shogun, "I must prepare for a trip to Ezogashima."

"Ahh, are you going, then?" The shogun sounded relieved. All he'd gleaned from their conversation was that Sano had decided to obey his orders. Yoritomo gave Sano a strange, tormented, apologetic look, as if he thought himself to blame for Sano's whole predicament. "Well, ahh, have a good voyage."

Sano was already out the door. He would rush headlong up north, as if he were a dog and Lord Matsudaira had thrown a stick for him to fetch.

Chapter Two

The waterfall cascaded from a high cliff top. The setting sun gilded the water spilling past the twisted pine trees that shaded the damp, eroded rocks. Cold water splashed onto Hirata, who sat immersed up to his waist in a pool in a forest so remote that few ever ventured there.

His naked body was numb beneath the pool's surface; he couldn't feel his buttocks, legs, or feet. His upper half shivered in the freezing wind, and his teeth chattered despite his clenched jaws. His skin was as pale as ice, his lips and fingernails blue. His hair was plastered to his head; his muscles and veins stood out like iron cords beneath his taut flesh. His closed eyelids quivered as he tried to ignore his physical distress.

This was a ritual necessary to reaching the next level in mastering the secrets of *dim-mak,* the ancient mystic martial art that he'd been studying for four years.

During his last lesson, he'd fought his teacher, the old priest Ozuno, in a practice match that had begun at dawn. They'd wielded swords, staffs, knives, bare hands, and magic spells at each other. It was afternoon when Ozuno finally knocked Hirata to the ground and held a blade to his throat. They'd both collapsed on the ground, exhausted.

"I hate to admit it, but you almost beat me," Ozuno said grudgingly. But his pride in his pupil and his own teaching showed on his stern face. Beneath his unkempt gray hair, his shrewd eyes twinkled. "You're ready for your ordeal by waterfall."

Hirata groaned. "What good will it do me to freeze my rear end for ten days?"

"What good will this do, what good will that do?" Ozuno mimicked him. "For once in your stupid life, can't you accept instructions without questioning them?" But he explained, "Your body is a prison that holds your mind captive. To be truly at one with the cosmos and the wisdom there, we must set our minds free. We do that by overwhelming the senses, by subjecting the body to a state of near death. Then the spirit can move to a higher level of enlightenment."

"What does true enlightenment feel like?" Hirata asked.

"It can't be described, only experienced," Ozuno said. "You'll know when you achieve it."

Now Hirata was locked in a struggle to slow his heartbeat, to confine the flow of blood to his vital organs, to shut down his bodily processes to the minimum functioning required for survival, as Ozuno had taught him. Finally the cold, the sound, and the deluge of the waterfall receded from his consciousness. His spirit poised on the narrow line between life and death. The borders between himself and the environment dissolved. His mind floated in pure, liberated tranquility.

He sensed the people in distant villages. He felt himself climbing up and up, beyond the vast human world that echoed with a million voices, thoughts, and emotions. Stars and planets appeared at the far reaches of his inner vision. Faster and faster he ascended. His spirit soared with the certainty that it verged on a breakthrough to a higher plane of consciousness.

Suddenly his propulsion shuddered to a halt. Sensory manifestations intruded. Flashes of the water spilling down on him and pangs from the chill in his bones pierced his tranquility. Stars and planets winked out like snuffed candles. Then he was falling, his mind a rock dropping from a great height toward the body that shivered in the pool. Disappointment crushed Hirata.

The breakthrough had eluded him. His perceptions were too limited. His spirit lacked some unknown, crucial dimension.

As he plummeted into the human world, one pattern of thought and emotion among legions snagged his mind. He hung suspended long enough to recognize that pattern, that unique life-energy. He knew the man to whom it belonged. It resonated across space to him. At the same moment that his mind reinhabited his body, realization flashed through every cold, wet, trembling fiber of him.

Sano is in trouble.

Hirata staggered up from the water. Frozen and dripping, he clambered onto the bank. Sano, his master whom he was honor-bound to serve, who'd generously released him from his duties so that he could pursue his martial arts studies, now needed him. Hirata couldn't resist the summons even though it was an involuntary cry for help that he'd sensed, not a direct order from Sano. No matter how much he desired enlightenment, it would have to wait.

The path he must follow was the road to Edo.

Evenings were the hardest times for Reiko. Each one ushered in the end of another day without Masahiro. Ahead of her stretched many long, dark hours before morning brought new hope that he would be found. Now, as she knelt in the lamplit nursery with her one-year-old daughter on her lap, she sank into despair. Not even her baby could comfort her. Akiko squirmed and bawled. She wouldn't stop even though Reiko rocked her and sang to her. Her little face was bright red with temper, her mouth wide, her eyes squeezed shut and streaming tears.

"Shh, Akiko, it's all right," Reiko murmured.

But Akiko cried harder, for no apparent reason. She was a fussy child who gave Reiko not a moment of peace. Reiko often wondered if certain troubles she'd experienced during her pregnancy were to blame. Akiko was so unlike her brother, who'd been a lively yet much easier infant.

The thought of Masahiro as a baby provoked such anguish in Reiko that she moaned as if physically struck. She knew she should be thankful to have one child left, but her heart was so full of pain that there was no room for gratitude.

"Please stop crying, Akiko!" she wailed.

Her friend Midori hurried into the chamber. "Let me have the baby." She knelt, took Akiko in one arm, and enfolded Reiko in the other. "Don't worry," she said. "They'll find him."

"But it's been so long!" Weeping quaked Reiko. Every time she thought she'd run out of tears, she rediscovered that the well was bottomless. Akiko bawled louder, and Reiko knew that her own distress was worsening her child's, but she couldn't stop crying. "I'm so afraid I'll never see him again."

"Of course you will," Midori said, forceful and certain. "He'll be back soon." She hugged Reiko. "But I don't know how he'll recognize you. You're so thin I can feel your bones. Have you eaten today?"

Reiko shook her head. When she put food in her mouth, her throat closed up; she could hardly swallow. The flesh had melted from her body. She was as emaciated and weak as she'd been plump and healthy while pregnant with Masahiro. It was as if she were now pregnant with grief.

"You have to keep up your strength," Midori said. "I'll bring you some soup."

"No thank you." Reiko gulped while tears bled down her face. She wiped them away with a skeletal hand. Once she'd been full of vitality, practicing martial arts and traveling around town to help people in trouble in a manner unheard of for any woman, let alone the wife of a high official. Now she felt fragile and vulnerable, as if when she went outside she would fall and break her bones or be run down by a galloping horse. But although it was grief that debilitated her body, it was terror that consumed her spirit.

"Oh, Midori-*san*," she cried, "what if Masahiro is—what if he's—?"

She couldn't speak the awful word.

Midori turned and said, "Here's Chamberlain Sano."

Reiko looked up to see her husband standing in the doorway. The baby stopped crying; she thrust out her little arms at him. He entered the chamber and took her from Midori.

Akiko adored her father. She cooed and played with his topknot. Reiko's sobs paused while she searched Sano's face, as she did every day, for a sign of good news. She braced herself for another disappointment.

This time she saw his familiar concern for her as he knelt before her, but his eyes were bright with elation. The tears dried on Reiko's cheeks. Her heart began to pound furiously.

"What is it?" she asked, breathless with hope.

"I know where Masahiro is," Sano said.

A gasp choked Reiko. She pressed her hand to her chest. "Merciful gods!" Her spirits skyrocketed from the depths of misery to the heights of joy.

"That's wonderful!" Midori exclaimed. "Oh, Reiko-*san,* I'm so happy for you."

Reiko wept so hard with relief that a moment passed before she realized that Sano hadn't actually said he'd found Masahiro. "Where is he?" she said, jumping to her feet. "Why haven't you brought him to me?"

Sano reached for her hand, drew her back down to the floor. "He's in Ezogashima."

"Ezogashima?" Puzzled surprise arrested Reiko's joy in midflight.

"How in the world did he get there?" Midori asked.

"Lord Matsudaira had him kidnapped." Anger suffused Sano's features. "That's where he's been taken."

As he elaborated, Reiko experienced two reactions that rushed upon her like waves coming from opposite directions. The first was gladness that her son was alive and she knew where. The second was horror that he was so far away, that such a thing had been done to him, that he was in terrible danger. She imagined Masahiro attacked by bandits on the highway or pirates at sea while he was under the dubious protection of Lord Matsudaira's men, who would steal a little boy in order to further their master's political aims.

"You have to rescue him!" Reiko said, clutching at Sano.

"That's exactly what I'm going to do," Sano said. "As soon as I can outfit a ship, I'll sail for Ezogashima."

Reiko wasn't satisfied. "I'm going with you."

Sano looked as if he'd expected this but was resistant. "That's out of the question. There are serious problems in Ezogashima." He described the breakdown in communication and the possible reasons. "It's too dangerous for you to go."

"Not any more for me than for Masahiro," Reiko said. Her maternal urge to be with her son overrode all concerns for her own safety.

"It's a difficult journey even at the best of times. The winters are harsh up north," Sano warned.

"I don't care!"

"I'll bring him back. Trust me. You'll be better off waiting here."

"For how long?" Impatience agitated Reiko. "A month? Two? Three?"

"Under the circumstances, I can't say," Sano admitted. "Before I come back, I have to fix whatever's wrong in Ezogashima, which could take more time than finding Masahiro."

"Then I can't wait. I can't just sit here wondering when you'll be back." The idea of such unendurable suspense! Reiko insisted, "I must go. I have to see Masahiro the moment you find him, not later. Besides, he'll need me."

The baby in Sano's arms let out a plaintive squeal. She'd noticed her parents ignoring her, and she didn't like it.

"Akiko needs you," Sano said. "You have to stay home."

As if she knew her mother wanted to leave her, Akiko started bawling again. Reiko felt stricken by guilt because she would abandon her daughter for the sake of her son. She loved them both with equal passion, yet her firstborn had the strongest claim on her heart. This shamed Reiko, but she couldn't deny it.

"I'll take care of Akiko for you." Midori gave Reiko a look of painful, understanding sympathy.

Reiko remembered that Midori knew what it was like to have a husband go off without her, without a hint of when he might return. Hirata had been gone a year, with no word from him. Midori was offering to free Reiko so that at least one of them could be happy.

"Thank you," Reiko said with fervent gratitude, then turned to Sano. "If I don't go, I might not live to welcome you and Masahiro home."

Their gazes met.

Hers said she'd made up her mind.

His appraised her frail body and said he wouldn't argue, even though he was concerned about her safety, because he feared the wait would kill her.

He slowly, reluctantly, nodded his assent.

It took Sano eight days to locate a seaworthy vessel, bring it to Edo, and equip and man it. Now, on a bright, unseasonably warm morning, the war junk floated at dock on the Sumida River. Made of cedar, it had two masts with multiple white sails, a complex web of rigging, and banners bearing the Tokugawa triple-hollyhock-leaf crest. A dragon figurehead snarled. The deck bristled with cannons. Oars protruded from below deck, where rowers sat ready to propel the ship down the river to the sea. Detective Marume supervised porters lugging provisions up the gangplank. Sano's other personal bodyguard, Detective Fukida, peered down from the crow's nest at the two smaller ships that would carry troops and servants. The junk's cabin was a house with a curved roof, like a miniature temple. Inside, Reiko paced amid bedding and chests of clothes. She peered out the window, eager to be off.

She felt better than she had since Masahiro had disappeared. She breathed the heady air of hope that revived her appetite and strengthened her muscles. The wait was almost over. Restless with energy, she watched impatiently for Sano.

He strode up the gangplank, accompanied by a man of such odd appearance that spectators gathered outside nearby warehouses pointed and laughed. Reiko recognized him as an acquaintance known as the Rat. He was short, with a thick, shaggy beard and mustache that were rare in Japan.

He carried a bundle on his back. His feral face wore a look of misery.

"The Rat doesn't like Ezogashima even though it's his native land," he said. "That's why I left. I hope you know what a big favor I'm doing you by coming along with you."

"Favor, nothing," Sano said. "I'm paying you handsomely."

"As well you should," the Rat said. "I'm the only one of my kind in town. Who else can serve as your guide and interpreter in Ezogashima?"

The sailors hauled up the gangplank behind Sano and the Rat; they raised the anchor. Reiko's heart beat fast while anticipation reverberated through her spirit. Soon she would be with Masahiro. The captain shouted to the rowers. From below deck rose their chanting as their oars propelled the junk away from the riverbank. The spectators waved and cheered.

"Wait!"

The cry came from the dock. Reiko saw a man running along it toward the ship. The two swords at his waist marked him as a samurai. His long, ungroomed hair, his worn cotton garments, and the pack on his back suggested that he was an itinerant *rōnin,* a masterless warrior. At first Reiko wondered who he was and what he wanted. Then, as he neared her, she noticed his slight limp. She recognized his familiar features masked by whisker stubble. Exclaiming, she ran outside onto the deck, where Sano beheld the man in surprise.

"Is that who I think it is?" Sano said.

"Hirata-*san*!" Reiko called, waving at him.

He reached the edge of the dock. The ship had moved some twenty paces out into the current, but Hirata took a running leap. He sprang higher, farther, than Reiko had thought possible. He landed crouched on the railing, then hopped aboard. Sano and Reiko laughed with pleasure as they welcomed their friend.

"Don't think I'm not glad to see you," Sano said, "but what are you doing here?"

"You called me," Hirata said. He'd changed, Reiko observed; there was a new maturity and seriousness about him.

"I did?" Sano said, puzzled.

"Whether you meant to or not," Hirata said. "By the way, where are we going?"

"To Ezogashima," Sano said as the fleet sailed down the river.

Chapter Three

For eleven days the fleet sailed north along the coast. The weather turned steadily colder. Sano, Reiko, Hirata, the detectives, and the Rat spent most of the journey in the cabin, huddled around charcoal braziers. The skies remained clear until they reached the Strait of Tsugaru, which separated barbarian territory from Japan proper. Dressed in quilted cloaks and boots, they stood on deck while falling snow obscured their first glimpse of Ezogashima's coastline. Wind whipped the snow into swirls and howled around the ship.

"I've never seen such a blizzard," Sano said, as he and his companions hurried into the cabin.

"Get used to it," the Rat said glumly. "I hate to tell you, but you haven't seen anything yet."

Waves slammed the ship. It pitched and rolled, flinging everyone off balance. Wind blew the shutters in with violent snaps. Snow and spray exploded into the cabin. Outside, the sailors fought to hold the ship steady. The ocean topped the deck behind Hirata, the last one to enter. He shut the door against water that poured across the floor.

"This ship had better not sink," the Rat said. "I'm not a very good swimmer."

"We can't sink!" Terrified, Reiko gripped Sano's arm so tight that he felt her fingernails dig through his padded sleeve. "We have to rescue Masahiro."

Detective Marume struggled to close the shutters and

fight off sliding baggage and furniture. "Merciful Buddha, if you're not too busy, please save our miserable lives."

The rigging strained and creaked. Below deck, oarsmen screamed for help as water flooded them. Yells arose from the sailors: "Men overboard!" A sudden, enormous crash assailed the ship. Sano and Reiko catapulted forward, tumbling into the others. Everyone shouted in alarm. A crack like thunder preceded a loud scraping sound that rasped under them. The ship tossed wildly, then canted nose down and shuddered to a halt.

"We've run aground!" Sano yelled.

"Welcome to Ezogashima," the Rat said. "Pretty soon you'll understand why I never wanted to come back."

Sano heard his detectives muttering prayers of thanks and Reiko moaning in relief. He barely had time to be glad himself that they'd survived, before they all hastened out of the cabin. Snow fell in thick veils and had already coated the ship—or what was left of it.

"Hey! Where's the other half?" Marume exclaimed.

The stern had broken off behind the cabin. Snowflakes blasted into Sano's eyes as he looked out at the gray ocean, which was a mass of whitecaps, curtained by the blizzard, and empty as far as he could see. "Gone," he said, "with the crew and the fleet."

No one could survive in that icy water. Sano's heart ached for the many lives lost. And now he and his few comrades must face the trouble in Ezogashima alone.

"Where are we?" Fukida asked.

"Your guess is as good as mine," Sano said. A snow-covered beach and forested slope stretched before them. The white terrain was barely distinguishable from the white sky. "We may have drifted off course from Fukuyama City."

He noticed the atmosphere darkening: Night came fast in the north. Now he had more pressing concerns than how he would find his son, solve the problems in Ezogashima, or return home afterward. "We'd better get off this wreck and find shelter before we freeze to death."

Everyone gathered a few possessions, climbed over the railing, and splashed through the freezing shallows while the blizzard keened and tore at them. They huddled together on the beach. Sano turned to Reiko. "Are you all right?"

"I'm better every moment." Her face was red and pinched from the cold, but her smile shone with happiness. "We're close to Masahiro. I know; I can feel him. Can't you?"

"Yes," Sano said, although he only wished he could. What he felt was dire uncertainty about their prospects. Straining his eyes toward the forest, he said, "Maybe there's a village up there. Let's go."

Hirata led the way up the slope, outpacing his companions, barely conscious of the cold, the snow, or their predicament. From the moment he'd set foot in Ezogashima, he'd sensed an indefinable strangeness in the atmosphere. It vibrated with sounds at the edge of his range of hearing, like alien music. He perceived a soft yet powerful pulse emanating from the landscape. It resonated through him and called to some deep, uncharted place within him. He realized that this trip wasn't an abandonment of his mystic martial arts studies but a continuation of his quest. Here he would find the enlightenment he sought.

His master's involuntary call for help had brought him to this land of his destiny.

As he neared the forest of leafless oaks and birches, his nerves tingled alert to human presences other than those of his comrades behind him. Three figures suddenly emerged from between the trees, into the windswept snow. Hirata stopped in his tracks as the men blocked his path. He stared in amazement.

They were the tallest men he'd ever seen; they stood half a head higher than Detective Marume, the biggest man in his group. Coats and leggings made of animal skins clothed their strong physiques. Geometric patterns with curves, spirals, and cusps decorated their hems, sleeve edges, and neck bands. Thick fur that trimmed their mittens, covered the calves of their fish-skin boots, and lined their leather hoods gave them a bestial aspect. They were obviously not Japanese. They must be Ezo, northern barbarians.

They looked like giant, uncivilized versions of the Rat. Their coarse beards and mustaches were even longer than his. Under bushy brows that grew straight across the bridges of their prominent noses, their eyes were narrow as if permanently squinted against the wind and snow. Their complexions were tanned and creased, their expressions as harsh as the climate.

The one in the middle addressed Hirata in a gruff barrage of syllables that sounded nonsensical. Although the Ezo and the Japanese had engaged in trade for centuries, the Ezo were forbidden to learn the Japanese language. This was a law enforced by the Matsumae clan to protect its trade monopoly. If the Ezo could speak Japanese, they could trade independently with merchants from Japan and bypass the Matsumae middlemen. Now the barbarian made a gesture that meant the same thing in any language: *Go away!*

Hirata saw the daggers they wore in carved wooden sheaths at their waists. He instinctively grasped the hilt of his own sword. Sano caught up with him.

"It's time for you to earn your pay," Sano called to the Rat. "Talk to them. Find out what they're trying to tell us."

The Rat gulped and reluctantly obeyed. His eyes lost their characteristic bold gleam as he spoke to his countrymen in their language. He seemed to shrink smaller. Hirata realized that the Rat hadn't left Ezogashima solely because he wanted to make his fortune in the city; he'd been a misfit among his own kind.

After a brief conversation with the barbarians, the Rat turned to Sano and Hirata. "They say we should go home."

"I gathered that much," Sano said. "But why?"

"They say that we're in danger."

"From what?"

The Rat conveyed the question to the barbarians. Frowning, they muttered among themselves. The spokesman, whose strong, not unhandsome features distinguished him from the others, repeated his same words in a louder voice, as if that would make Sano heed them.

"We want to go to Fukuyama City," Sano told the barbarians. "Can you show us the way?"

Again the Rat translated. The Ezo leader looked disturbed. He conversed with the Rat, who told Sano, "He says to stay away from Fukuyama City. If we want to live, we should go before they find out we're here."

"Who are 'they'?" Hirata asked.

He could see from their eyes that the barbarians understood the gist of his question, but the leader only repeated the same warning in a more forceful manner.

"We can't go on like this," Sano said to Hirata. With an obvious effort to quell his irritation, he addressed the barbarians: "Would you please give us shelter for the night, or take us to someone who will?"

When the Rat translated, they shook their heads at one another. The leader stepped boldly toward Sano, flung out his arm, pointed at the sea, and shouted a command in a voice both authoritative and laced with desperation.

" 'For your own good, go back where you came from,' " the Rat translated.

"We can't," Marume said. "Our ship is wrecked." He advanced on the barbarians, who ranged themselves against him. "Either help us or get out of our way."

The Ezo responded with pleas, warnings, or threats. Marume and Fukida drew their swords. The barbarians stood their ground, and even though fright shone in their eyes, they drew their daggers.

"Back off!" Sano ordered his men. "We need these people whether they want us here or not. Don't hurt them!"

He tried to appease the barbarians while the Rat frantically translated. Somehow, at last, the weapons went back into sheaths; tempers subsided.

"Throw us on their mercy," Sano instructed the Rat. "Tell them that unless they take us in, we'll die."

The Rat spoke. This time, as the barbarians discussed what they'd heard, Hirata perceived resignation in their tones. Primitive though they might be, they didn't lack human compassion, whatever their reason for wanting to chase off newcomers. They nodded, and the leader spoke to Sano.

" 'Come with us,' " the Rat said with a sigh. As he and the rest of Sano's group followed the barbarians into the forest, he muttered, "I hope we won't be sorry."

The barbarians led the way along a path that paralleled the coast. The trees screened the view of the ocean and served as a windbreak. Hirata was glad the natives had decided to cooperate. The farther he walked into Ezogashima, the stronger he felt its pulse, the more compellingly sounded its call.

A clearing appeared in the forest, and Hirata saw what he first took to be huge, pointed mounds of snow. As he moved closer, he realized they were huts. Pungent wood smoke drifted up from chimney holes. Smaller outbuildings, some elevated on stilts and accessible by ladders, stood nearby. Hirata didn't so much as hear voices inside the huts as feel conversation stop when he and his party approached. Thatch curtains lifted to reveal doorways. Barbarians peered out, gazing suspiciously at the strangers.

Their escorts made straight for the largest hut at the center of the settlement. The leader entered for a brief time, then reemerged. He beckoned and spoke to Sano.

"He says to come in," the Rat said.

The pull that the island exerted on Hirata was stronger near the hut. "Shall I go first and make sure it's safe?" he asked Sano, who nodded. Hirata cautiously ducked under the thatched doorway curtain that the leader held up for him.

He found himself in a cramped entryway, where he dusted the snow off his clothes and removed his boots. The leader ushered him under another thatch curtain and into a room filled with smoky, flickering orange light from a fire that burned in a square pit at the center. An Ezo sat near the pit, hands folded in his lap, on woven reed mats that covered the floor. His long hair, mustache, and beard were white with old age, but his frame was strong, his posture erect. His hands and face were so weathered and deeply lined that he seemed made of gnarled wood. Silver hoops with dangling black beads pierced his ears. He wore a blue robe patterned with the same designs as on the other barbarians' clothes. Hirata had assumed that the man who'd done the talking on the beach was their leader, but now he knew this man held the authority.

His eyes, which scrutinized Hirata from beneath thick, white brows, reflected the firelight and gleamed with dignified, calm intelligence. As their gazes met, a thought flashed through Hirata's mind.

Meeting this man is crucial to my destiny.

The Ezo inclined his body in a bow that indicated familiarity with Japanese manners. He spoke in a deep, resonant voice and spread his hands in a universal gesture of welcome.

Hirata hesitated a moment, shaken by his revelation. Then he called through the doorway to Sano and his other comrades, who were waiting outside. "It's all right."

Everyone crowded into the hut, knelt around the fire pit. The air steamed with the snow melting on their garments. Hirata sat on one side of their host, Sano on the other. Although Hirata was transfixed by the old barbarian, he hadn't lost his samurai habit of always taking note of his environment. He tore his attention away from the Ezo long enough to glance around the hut.

Fishnets, hunting weapons, kitchenware, bedding, and household miscellany were piled against dirt mounds that insulated the walls. Thatch curtains covered windows. Pots and tools hung from a shelf suspended from the ceiling above the fire. Additional light and fishy-smelling smoke came from wicks burning in scallop shells filled with oil. In a corner stood a stick, its bark shaved down from the top and hanging in a mop of curly strands. Hirata felt an aura shimmering in invisible waves around it. He intuited that it was a sacred object, the repository for a divine spirit.

"Introduce us," Sano told the Rat.

The Rat bowed to their host, gave what seemed to be a polite greeting in Ezo language, and reeled off speech in which Hirata recognized only the names of his party. The barbarian elder nodded, replied briefly, and bowed to the assembly.

"He says his name is Awetok, and he's the chieftain of the tribe," the Rat explained.

The other barbarians stood by the doorway. "Honorable Awetok, why did your men try to chase us off?" Sano asked.

The Rat translated. The chieftain answered, "To save you."

"From what?" Sano said. "Or whom?"

"Those that control Ezogashima."

"And they are . . . ?"

Hirata could feel Sano wondering whether the chieftain meant Japanese in the persons of the Matsumae clan, or invaders from China who'd occupied Ezogashima.

Caution glinted in Awetok's eyes as the Rat interpreted. He spoke, removing two objects tied to his sash and holding them up. One was a metal tobacco pipe such as one might find anywhere in Edo. The other was a bearskin pouch. Awetok opened it and revealed a quartz flint, a fragment of iron that served as a striker, a piece of charcoal for tinder, and dried tobacco leaves inside. The habit of smoking was apparently as popular among Ezo as among the Japanese.

"He's offering us a smoke," the Rat explained unnecessarily, adding, "It's a hospitality ritual."

"He's stalling," Sano commented to Hirata, "but we'd better play along."

The pipe was filled, lit, and passed. Everyone took a puff whether they smoked or not. Reiko stifled a cough. The atmosphere in the hut grew thicker, acrid. Sano said, "Whoever are the powers that be, why are they a threat to us?"

"Because all outsiders are banned from Ezogashima."

"I'll ask him who says," the Rat volunteered.

After he spoke, the chieftain answered, "We're forbidden to discuss the matter."

"By whom?" Sano's growing impatience inflected his voice.

"I've already told you more than I should."

Sano said, "I'm the shogun's second-in-command. I have a right to know what's going on here. I order you to explain."

"That ought to shake it out of him," the Rat said. But when he'd passed on the order, the chieftain's response came in words so adamant that Hirata understood their meaning despite the language barrier. "He says he's sorry to inform you that your rank means nothing here, and your rules don't apply."

Carefully studying the chieftain, Sano said to Hirata, "I think he's afraid to talk."

Hirata had to nod, even though he'd seldom seen anyone look less afraid. Awetok's face was impassive, but Hirata sensed the unmistakable vibrations of his fright. He caught Awetok's eye. Something less than camaraderie toward Hirata yet more than indifference showed in it. Fascination took root in Hirata as he realized why he'd met the Ezo chieftain.

When one is ready to learn, a teacher will appear.

So went an important premise of the martial arts.

Although Hirata now knew who could help him in his quest for enlightenment, he had yet to discover how.

"What will happen if you tell me what's going on?" Sano said, oblivious to the conversation's undercurrent, focused on his immediate problems.

"The same thing that will happen to you and your comrades if you don't leave before you're discovered. My people will be put to death."

"How are 'they' going to find out that you talked?"

"They have their ways."

Hirata imagined that even in this wilderness, those in power had spies and informants.

"Well, that settles that," Sano said to his group. "We can hardly force these people to talk at the cost of their lives."

"What are we going to do?" Reiko asked, her face tense with her fear that their missions were doomed.

"In any case, we're stranded here. Our first step is to survive." Sano addressed the chieftain: "We humbly beg you to give us shelter and food."

When the Rat conveyed this plea, controversy erupted among the Ezo. The younger three protested to the chieftain, clearly begging him to refuse.

"They say that taking us in would endanger them," the Rat said, wringing his hands. "Oh, I wish we'd never come!"

Chieftain Awetok raised his hand, silencing his men. He spoke to Sano.

"He says he can't turn helpless folk out in this weather no matter the danger to his own people," the Rat said. "He'll feed us and make room for us in the huts." The three younger men accepted the pronouncement with ill will, glowering at Sano's party. The Rat said darkly, "I have a bad feeling about this."

But the others in the party exchanged relieved glances. Sano said, "A million thanks for your generosity, Chieftain Awetok." And Hirata was fervently glad that they had a foothold, no matter how precarious, in this alien land.

Chapter Four

A flash of light and a cold draft on her face awakened Reiko. As she stretched under the heavy bed covers, she opened her eyes to the same thought that had been first in her mind every day for now more than two months: *Masahiro is gone.* The same grief sank her heart. But as the cloud of sleep cleared, her second thought was, *Where am I?*

In the dim, warm space that smelled of wood smoke, embers glowed in a fire pit near the thick, lumpy mat on which she lay. Other human forms slept beneath fur blankets. Then she remembered the shipwreck on Ezogashima. This was the hut where the barbarians had put up her and Sano and their fellow refugees. Her next thought accompanied a spring of joy.

Today we'll find Masahiro!

Reiko reached for Sano, but he was gone from their bed. She'd felt the sunlight and wind when he went out the door. Now she became aware that her bladder was uncomfortably full. She scrambled out from the blankets. No need to dress; they'd all slept in their clothes. Careful not to wake the men, she found her shoes in the entryway. She lifted the mat over the exterior door and stepped into a world born anew.

The sky was the brightest, clearest blue she'd ever seen. Snow quilted the trees, huts, and ground, sparkling in rainbow crystals in the sunshine, deep violet in the shadows. The light dazzled her eyes so much they watered. The air was so cold that inhaling froze her nose. Dogs barked and cavorted in an open space, wolflike beasts with rough black and brown pelts. An Ezo man flung down meat for them. They gobbled and fought over the food. The man spied Reiko and pointed into the forest.

She followed a path to three small thatched sheds. She went inside one, raised her robes, and squatted over the pit. It took only a few moments, but she was shivering and her bottom felt like ice when she'd finished. Outside, she met Sano.

"Good morning," he said with a smile. "I'm sorry if I woke you. I tried to be quiet so you could sleep a little longer."

"That's all right," Reiko said. "I was ready to get up. When can we go find Masahiro?"

"As soon as I can persuade our hosts to give us breakfast and point us toward Fukuyama City."

When they returned to the settlement, they found Ezo men gathering firewood from piles, filling buckets with snow to melt for water, and fetching food from raised storehouses. Suddenly they all froze motionless, as if on some silent command. Then Reiko heard what their keen ears already had—the distant barking of dogs, coming closer.

The dogs in the settlement growled in reply. Reiko heard crashes, rustles, and a scraping, whizzing noise from the forest. Down a path came ten hounds, each harnessed to a wooden sled. On each sled sat a samurai, driving his dog like a horse. The men wore swords at their waists, bows and quivers full of arrows on their fur-clad backs, and leather helmets. At first Reiko was glad for this sign of Japanese civilization, but as the dogsleds burst into the camp, Sano reached for his sword. Hirata, the detectives, and the Rat rushed from their hut, alarmed because they'd sensed a threat. The Ezo men grouped together, bracing for an attack.

"I have a feeling that getting to Fukuyama City isn't our biggest problem," Sano said.

The riders were youths in their late teens, led by one who wore deer antlers on his helmet. Sano supposed they were Matsumae soldiers who'd found the wrecked ship on the beach, and they'd come looking for survivors. The riders steered their sleds up to Sano's party and reined in their dogs, who halted and panted, muzzles dripping icicles, teeth sharp.

"There's too many of them to take back to the castle and execute," Deer Antlers said as he and his comrades jumped off their sleds. "Let's kill them here."

Sano realized that the trouble in Ezogashima had come straight to him. "Stop right there," he said.

They ignored his order and advanced on him. Detective Marume said, "It's been a while since I've had a good fight."

He drew his sword. Fukida and Hirata followed suit. The samurai aimed bows fitted with sharp, deadly arrows at them.

"Drop your weapons!" Deer Antlers said. He had thick features set in a cruel, hungry grin. "Line up in a row. Prepare to die."

Reiko moaned softly, but she held her dagger in her hand. Sano knew that although he and his comrades could probably take these men, there were many more where they'd come from; he'd better stop the fight before it started. He said, "I'm the chamberlain of Japan. Put down your bows and kneel."

Deer Antlers aimed at Sano and said, "Shut up! Do as I said." But his friends gaped at Sano, exchanged glances of dismay, and lowered their bows.

"Hey, what do you think you're doing?" Deer Antlers said. "We have our orders. Shoot them!"

"Orders from who?" Sano asked.

"Lord Matsumae."

"I outrank him. You'll follow my orders, not his." Sano spoke with all the authority he could muster.

Nine bowstrings went slack. Deer Antlers said, "Don't listen to him!"

His friends objected: "He's too important to kill." "We'll get in trouble."

"I'm here on the shogun's business," Sano said. "Hurt me or anyone with me, and you're dead."

"We'll get in trouble if we don't kill him," Deer Antlers said, his arrow trained on Sano. "Lord Matsumae will kill us."

One of his men said, "Then *you* shoot him. When he doesn't come home, when the shogun's army comes up here to see what happened to him and finds out he's been killed, we'll say you did it."

Deer Antlers hesitated, torn between murder and fear of punishment. His eyes shifted, seeking a compromise in which he wouldn't lose face.

Sano said, "Let's go to Fukuyama Castle and sort this out."

"All right." Deer Antlers scowled. "But hand over your weapons first."

Although Sano hated to be disarmed, he nodded at his group. Carrying their possessions in bundles, they marched along the road, the ten samurai riding the sleds behind them, dogs panting at their heels. Gaps between the trees showed glimpses of the ocean, brilliant blue and crusted with ice at the shoreline. The clear air was bitterly cold despite the sun, but Sano began to sweat from trudging through the deep snow. Reiko lagged, and he pulled her along. At least the exercise kept them warm.

"You'll all be sorry we came," the Rat muttered.

Sano wondered what was waiting for them at Fukuyama Castle. There was no plotting strategy without some idea of the circumstances. "Why does Lord Matsumae want us dead?" he called over his shoulder.

"Shut up," came Deer Antlers' peevish voice.

"What's the matter with him?"

"Just keep moving."

More questions brought Deer Antlers riding up close behind Sano. Dogs leaped on Sano's back and knocked him into the snow. Hirata helped him to his feet and dusted him off.

After almost an hour, Fukuyama City came into view. It was built on a harbor where ships stood in dry-dock near warehouses. Wisps of smoke rose from what looked like a small, fortified Japanese town. Snow-covered buildings clustered around the castle that squatted on a rise. Beyond town spread Ezogashima's vast forests, the distant mountains fading blue into the sky. Southward, the ocean stretched, blank and boundless.

Their escorts goaded Sano and his group past a military checkpoint. The abruptness with which they entered town unsettled Sano. The distance had seemed greater—a strange illusion. Along a main street, dingy wooden buildings contained shops. Merchants shoveled snow off their doorsteps. Sano didn't see any women; they were few in these parts. He heard a gong tolling nearby, then realized that the sound came from a temple he could barely see perched on a high, faraway hill. An unusual quality of the air warped sound as well as sight. It gave Sano a disquieting sense that nature's usual rules didn't apply in Ezogashima.

"Everyone here is Japanese," Reiko commented softly.

"The law bans Ezo from the city," Sano explained.

Samurai patrolled on foot, outnumbering the commoners, who kept their heads down, fearful of attention. Sano had the impression of a city clamped down even tighter under martial law than at home. He thought to wonder what the Ezo he'd met were doing around here at all. The Ezo came from their villages in the interior to live in the settlement during the trading season, spring through autumn only. Here was another strange circumstance.

The procession mounted the rise to the castle. It was similar to Edo Castle, enclosed by a high stone wall topped with covered corridors and a guardhouse built over the ironclad gate, but on a smaller, lower scale. Its few peaked roofs seemed to sag under their weight of snow. Pine trees and a keep rose above them. Deer Antlers ran up to the two guards pacing outside the gate. They argued about what to do with their prisoners, until a guard said, "Take them to Lord Matsumae."

Marched through the gate, Sano found himself in a courtyard facing run-down barracks. More samurai guards loitered outside. As Deer Antlers led the way through a gate to the inner precinct, he called to a guard and pointed at Reiko.

"Take her to the women's quarters."

Reiko looked aghast at the thought of being separated from her group. Sano said, "No. She stays with us."

"One more word out of you, and I'll cut you even if you are the chamberlain." Deer Antlers told the guard, "Take her."

Sano felt helpless as he was led in one direction and Reiko another. He sent up a silent prayer for her safety. He never should have let Reiko come.

A garden of snow-mounded shrubs and boulders surrounded the palace. Servants were clearing paths bordered by snow from earlier falls. Shaggy evergreens almost hid the half-timbered walls. More guards let Sano, his comrades, and his escorts in the door. Deer Antlers led them along a corridor almost as cold as outside. They entered an audience chamber. Its smoky heat from many charcoal braziers and glowing lanterns was a relief. But Sano felt something bad in the atmosphere even before he saw its occupant.

Lord Matsumae crouched on the dais. He sprang to his feet as his men pushed Sano, Hirata, the Rat, and the detectives to their knees before him. An old, faded black robe that hung loose on his emaciated figure gave him the look of a crow. His face was gaunt and shadowed by whisker stubble, his shaved crown sprouting tufts of hair. His eyes were sunken, bloodshot, and burned with a strange light.

Sano had met him once, during his attendance in Edo three years ago. He remembered Lord Matsumae as an intelligent man with sensitive features, refined manners, and impeccable grooming. The change in him shocked Sano. When Lord Matsumae moved to the edge of the dais and loomed over him, Sano smelled a foul stink of unwashed body. His robe was blotched with stains. What had happened to him?

"Honorable Chamberlain." A sneer twisted Lord Matsumae's voice. "This is such an honor, that you've come all this way to see me." His mockery turned to rage, and he shouted, "Now what in hell are you doing in my domain?"

Sano realized that Lord Matsumae had gone mad. Whatever the reason, he was the source of the trouble in Ezogashima. And madmen were dangerous, especially when they commanded an army. Hirata and the detectives looked at Sano, angered by Lord Matsumae's rudeness to him and expecting him to put the man in his place. But Sano thought it wiser to be cautious.

"The shogun is concerned about you because you didn't show up for your attendance," Sano said, his tone deliberately mild. "He sent me to find out if you're all right."

"Why, I'm perfectly fine." Sudden tears glistened in Lord Matsumae's eyes. Half his attention focused on Sano; half aimed inward, at something dark.

"Then why didn't you come?" Sano said.

"I had more important things to take care of."

There shouldn't be anything more important to a samurai than obeying his lord's law. "Such as?"

Emotions jerked Lord Matsumae's face into tics.

"Why have you closed Ezogashima?" Sano said, impatient as well as fearful because this man in the throes of a mental breakdown held the power of life and death over him and his comrades. "Why have you cut off communications?"

Lord Matsumae crouched face-to-face with Sano. His stink nauseated Sano; his teary eyes blazed. "For the sake of justice. That's something you should understand very well, Honorable Chamberlain. You, who have a reputation for seeking justice yourself and stopping at nothing to get it." He laughed at the surprise on Sano's face. "Oh, yes, I know about you. We in the far north aren't such a bunch of isolated, ignorant brutes as you think. I am simply following your fine example."

Sano was dismayed that he could have inspired Lord Matsumae's bad behavior, even unwittingly. "Justice for whom?"

Lord Matsumae dropped to his knees. He whispered, "Tekare."

Sano felt Deer Antlers and the other guards hold their breath, a signal that the conversation had entered dangerous territory. "Who is Tekare?" Sano asked.

"She was my mistress." Grief clenched Lord Matsumae's face. His tears spilled. "My dearest, beloved mistress. She's been dead almost three months now."

Glad that they seemed to be getting somewhere at last, Sano said, "What happened to her?"

"She was—" Lord Matsumae gulped. Tremors shook his body. "—murdered."

This, the loss of his woman, was the cause of his breakdown and the reason for everything that had followed. Love and grief had deranged him. Then he'd used his power to act out his madness and put himself in bad odor with the regime.

"I'm sorry to hear that. My sincere condolences." However, Sano couldn't quite believe that mourning was all that ailed Lord Matsumae. He'd never seen it cause such a spectacular transformation of character. There must be more to Lord Matsumae's troubles, although Sano couldn't imagine what. Again he had the disorienting sense that things were different here, the people as well as their environment subject to strange phenomena. "But I don't understand why you closed off Ezogashima. What was that supposed to accomplish?"

"I want to know who killed my Tekare," Lord Matsumae said. Sardonic humor glinted through his misery. "You may think you're a great detective, Honorable Chamberlain, but I've spent twenty years ruling this domain, and I know something about police work. What do you do with a murder suspect?

"You lock him up and interrogate him until he confesses. Well, I have a whole city of murder suspects, all the people who were in the area when Tekare died. I've locked them all up. I've been busy interrogating them. I don't want anybody from the outside to come in and interfere. And I won't stop until one of them confesses to killing Tekare."

Holding the domain hostage was a clever albeit extreme plan for a murder investigation, but it didn't seem to have worked. "No one's confessed?"

"Not yet. But somebody will. They can't hold out much longer."

A cold, ominous sensation trickled through Sano as he remembered the fear in the townspeople's faces. "What have you done besides interrogate them?"

Lord Matsumae laughed. "Come now, Honorable Chamberlain. Certainly you're aware of means of making people talk."

Torture, Sano thought; legal although not always effective. "I'm aware that they often produce false confessions."

"No matter." Lord Matsumae's hand flicked away the legions who must have suffered at it. "And no matter that some of the suspects couldn't withstand my interrogation."

"How many died?" Sano said, all the more disturbed.

Lord Matsumae's expression turned deliberately vague, mockingly innocent. "Did I say anyone died? But if they did, then their example should encourage someone who knows the truth about the murder to inform on the culprit."

If Lord Matsumae didn't kill everybody first. Sano's ominous feeling turned to dread. "I sent some envoys to you a while ago. They never returned. What became of them?"

The darkness inside Lord Matsumae emanated from him in almost visible waves. "Ask them. You'll be seeing them soon."

Sano was horrified for another reason besides his certainty that Lord Matsumae had murdered them and intended to kill him, too. "Lord Matsudaira had my son kidnapped and brought here." Lord Matsudaira couldn't have known what the trouble in Ezogashima was; by sheer luck he'd sent Masahiro, and Sano, into peril beyond his wildest imagining. "What's happened to him?"

Chapter Five

The women's quarters of Fukuyama Castle had winged eaves shading a railed veranda and wooden bars over the windows. A garden that might have been beautiful in summer was bleak with deep snow, bare trees, a frozen pond, and a deserted pavilion. The guard escorted Reiko inside, opened a sliding door, and thrust her into a room.

"Here's a visitor," he announced to the people inside, then pointed a finger at Reiko. "You stay put. Or else."

After he left, Reiko looked at the five women who sat around a *kotatsu*—a frame with a table on top, a fire underneath, and a quilt spread over it and their legs. As she and the women exchanged bows, Reiko had an unsettling sense that she'd walked into any lady's chamber back in Edo. They wore silk kimonos, white face powder, and red lip and cheek rouge, just like at home. Their eyes measured her from beneath shaved, painted-on brows. Chopsticks, tea and food in lacquer bowls, and porcelain spoons on the table completed the illusion.

"Welcome," the oldest woman said in a strangely flat, toneless voice. "I am Lord Matsumae's wife." She was in her forties, her upswept hair streaked with gray. Her face was pretty, but dark shadows of fatigue showed through her makeup. Her features sagged in a misery so strong that it tugged down Reiko's own spirits. "May I ask who you are?"

As Reiko gave her name, she noticed things about the scene that were different from home. The floor wasn't tatami but native woven mats, the same kind that insulated the walls. The women's robes were lined with fur that showed at the collars and cuffs, and they wore gloves. Reiko had an even stranger sense of Japanese culture grafted unnaturally onto Ezogashima, like a peach growing from a thorn bush.

"I'm the wife of Chamberlain Sano from Edo," Reiko said.

The other four women looked surprised, but Lady Matsumae's sad, tired expression didn't change. "Please join us."

Everyone shifted to make room at the *kotatsu.* Reiko sat beside the youngest woman—a girl in her teens, who had a round face, hair worn in a long braid, and thick, pursed lips. She helped Reiko cover her legs with the quilt. Lady Matsumae introduced her other three companions. They were her ladies-in-waiting, wives of her husband's retainers, all in their thirties. They murmured polite greetings. They seemed so much alike that Reiko promptly forgot which was whom. Lady Matsumae didn't introduce the girl, who was evidently a maid. Her flowered robe was cotton, not silk. She wore no makeup; her face was naturally pale with rosy lips and cheeks. She flashed bright, curious glances at Reiko.

Lady Matsumae offered food and drink. Reiko politely refused twice, then let herself be persuaded. There'd been no time for breakfast before the soldiers came to the Ezo camp, and she was starved. She drank hot tea and ate rice gruel with pickled vegetables and bits of fish. It tasted wonderful.

"What brings you here?" Lady Matsumae said as if she couldn't have cared less.

Her eyes seemed to look right through Reiko, who thought that if she waved her hand in front of them, they wouldn't even shift. "My husband has business with yours. Also, we've come to fetch our son, Masahiro. He was kidnapped in Edo and sent here." Reiko's urgency heightened with the hope that rose in her. "Have you seen him?"

"I'm afraid not." Lady Matsumae spoke so promptly and indifferently that it was obvious she hadn't bothered to think before answering.

"He's eight years old and tall for his age," Reiko persisted. "Are you sure you don't know where he is?"

"I'm sure."

Reiko turned to the other women. "What about you?"

The ladies-in-waiting murmured polite apologies. Their callous attitude chilled and mystified Reiko. The maid gave her a sympathetic look but shook her head.

"He may be inside this castle," Reiko said. If Masahiro and his escorts had reached Fukuyama City, they would have come here, wouldn't they? Reiko tried not to remember that the troops had almost killed her and Sano at the Ezo settlement. She resisted the fear of what might have happened to Masahiro. "I need to look for him. Will you help me?"

Lady Matsumae had been eating her gruel while Reiko talked. She sipped her tea before she said, "I'm sorry, but that's not my business."

She sounded less afraid of getting in trouble than too lethargic to lift a finger. The ladies shook their heads. The maid silently poured Reiko more tea.

"I haven't seen Masahiro in almost three months." Reiko's eyes filled with tears. "He's such a good boy. He's smart; he works hard at his studies. He's going to be a good sword-fighter, too." Reiko knew it was rude to brag about one's own child, and she saw disapproval on the women's faces, but she couldn't stop herself. "I miss him so much. Please, won't you help me find him?"

The ladies-in-waiting looked at Lady Matsumae. A tremor crossed her face. It might have been from annoyance or stomach indigestion. She said, "That's impossible."

"Why?" Reiko cried.

Lady Matsumae sighed. "You ask too much."

Reiko couldn't believe they could be so heartless. *What's wrong with you?* she wanted to shout. Instead she said, "I know I'm a stranger. I know you don't owe me anything." Even worse, she sensed that someone in this room did know something about Masahiro. She could smell it in the air. But why this conspiracy of silence? Desperate, she appealed to whatever compassion they had. "Do you know what it's like to lose a child? Do you have any children of your own?"

Lady Matsumae jerked as though Reiko had stabbed her. Pain shattered her indifference. "How dare you—you shouldn't—you have no idea—," she stammered. An upheaval of anger broke through the flat surface of her eyes.

Puzzled by her reaction, Reiko said, "I'm sorry. What did I say that disturbed you?"

There was a creaking noise, as if weight on the floor had shifted someplace nearby but out of sight. Lady Matsumae seemed to forget about Reiko. The anger congealed on her face as she whispered, "What was that?"

"Your son?" Lord Matsumae's gaze turned cagy. The audience chamber went still, the air thick with tension, as he narrowed his eyes at Sano. "I don't know anything about him."

"You're lying!" Furious, Sano leaped to his feet, but Deer Antlers and another guard dragged him down.

"I never saw him," Lord Matsumae said, suddenly defensive. "He must not have gotten here."

"Tell me the truth!" Sano demanded as terror shot through him. Had Masahiro been killed while Sano searched for him? Had he been dead while Sano and Reiko were traveling north? "What have you done to my son?"

He lunged at Lord Matsumae. Two guards seized him as Lord Matsumae jumped backward, avoiding his clutching hands. Rage and grief stained Sano's vision so dark that he could hardly see. He lashed out blindly.

"Stop!" ordered Lord Matsumae.

Hirata, Marume, and Fukida jumped the guards who held Sano. Deer Antlers and the other guards hurried to restrain them. Sano hit, kicked, and cursed at anyone who came near him. Hirata attacked the guards, who shrieked in pain from his strikes, flew through the air, and crashed bleeding and motionless. The Rat cowered fearfully in a corner. Lord Matsumae backed against the wall behind the dais as Sano went charging at him.

"Help!" he shouted.

Sano fell upon Lord Matsumae and seized him by the throat. "Where's my son? What have you done to him?"

Lord Matsumae gurgled and coughed while Sano choked him. His hands clawed at Sano's. Soldiers exploded into the chamber. They pulled Sano off their master. Three wrestled Sano to the floor. So many more pinned down Hirata that he barely showed under them. Others held Marume and Fukida. Around the room lay the broken, dead bodies of eight guards that Sano and his men had killed with their bare hands.

Sano panted, exhausted and bathed in sweat. The hot red tide of temper receded, stranding him in cold despair. His son must surely be gone forever. At this moment Sano didn't care what happened to himself.

"Take them outside," Lord Matsumae told his men. "Execute them all."

"My pleasure." Deer Antlers glared at Sano. His mouth was swollen and bloody. He told his friends, "Get the chamberlain's wife. She dies, too."

The thought of Reiko aroused Sano's survival instinct. Self-discipline returned. He had to act despite the terrible temptation to give up.

"Go ahead and kill us, Lord Matsumae," he called over his shoulder as the guards hauled him and his men away. "But don't think you can get away with it."

Hirata and the others resisted fiercely. Sano saved his strength to push words out past the weight of misery on his heart. "If you know so much about me, then you know I've got an army back in Edo. When I don't come home, they'll come looking for me. And there'll be too many of them for your army to hold off. They'll kill you and your entire clan to avenge my death. So unless that's what you want, we'd better talk."

He was almost out the door when Lord Matsumae said, "Wait. Bring them back."

Muttering curses, the guards hurled Sano and his comrades onto the floor in front of the dais.

"Talk about what?" Lord Matsumae was apparently not so insane that he'd lost his entire sense of self-preservation.

"You made some mistakes," Sano said, "but it's not too late to undo the damage."

Lord Matsumae crooked his neck. He again reminded Sano of a crow, this time uncertain whether to fly for cover or peck out his adversary's eyes. "I'm in so much trouble that I don't see any way out except to get rid of you and your people."

Sano nodded. Lord Matsumae realized that having witnesses to this situation would only make things worse for him with Lord Matsudaira and the shogun. He couldn't hide from their wrath forever. They would wipe his clan off the map. He couldn't afford to let Sano live, even if killing him would mean retaliation from Sano's army.

Improvising for dear life, Sano said, "There's a way around every problem."

"Such as what?"

"I propose a deal," Sano said.

Eyeing Sano with a mixture of hope and suspicion, Lord Matsumae said, "What kind?"

"I'll find out who killed Tekare for you," Sano said.

"Can you?" Distracted from his predicament, Lord Matsumae leaned forward and clasped his hands. He practically salivated with his hunger for truth and vengeance.

"Yes," Sano said, even though he didn't think much of his chances of success investigating a murder that was already three months past, in unfamiliar territory.

Doubt crept into Lord Matsumae's expression. "What do you ask in return?"

"That you let me, and everyone in my party, go free. That you stop breaking rules and killing people, and you bring things back to normal in Ezogashima."

"No." Lord Matsumae was obstinate. "Even if I do that, I'll still be in trouble for what I've done. You have to save me."

"I will," Sano said. "I'll talk to the shogun and Lord Matsudaira. I'll convince them to excuse you."

Sano had no idea whether he could, but he would promise the Nihonbashi Bridge and jump off it when he came to it. As Lord Matsumae vacillated, Sano said, "Well? Do we have a bargain?"

He hadn't brought his son into the negotiation even though Masahiro was more important than his own life. Sano didn't want to ask about the boy again and hear Lord Matsumae admit he'd killed Masahiro. He didn't want to believe it. Sano meant to look for Masahiro while investigating the murder, and find him alive. He refused to consider any other outcome.

"I don't know." Lord Matsumae's gaze skittered between suspicion of trickery, desire for justice for his mistress, and fear of punishment.

Sano saw that logic had inadequate sway over his madness. Impulses to wreak more havoc and violence were stronger. They seemed native to Ezogashima. Sano waited with an anxiety that he could barely conceal. He felt Hirata and his other men willing the balance to tip in their favor.

"I'll think about it," Lord Matsumae said at last. He told the guards, "In the meantime, take the Honorable Chamberlain and his people to the guest quarters. Lock them in."

Reiko watched Lady Matsumae tiptoe across the room and fling open a sliding door hidden by woven mats. On the other side stood five women of such bizarre appearance that Reiko couldn't hide her shock.

They were as tall as men, clothed in brown, coarsely woven robes with geometric designs embroidered on the hems, sleeve edges, and collar bands. They wore fur leggings and slippers. Their black hair was long, loose, and wavy. Reiko realized they were Ezo women. Strands of blue beads and brass medallions hung around their necks. Gold hoops pierced their ears. But most startling were their tattoos, which looked like blue mustaches painted around their mouths.

She barely had time to wonder what they were doing in the castle, where Ezo supposedly weren't allowed. Lady

Matsumae shouted at them, "Were you eavesdropping? How dare you!"

She marched up to a woman who seemed younger than the rest, her features pretty in spite of the disfiguring tattoo. Lady Matsumae spat in the woman's face. "Whore! Animal! Filthy barbarian!"

Her fists swatted the young woman's stomach and breasts. The woman raised her hands to protect herself, but although she looked strong enough to knock Lady Matsumae down, she didn't fight back. She uttered muffled noises of pain while she took the beating. Nor did the four other Ezo women defend her. They looked on, unhappy but silent. The ladies-in-waiting sipped their tea as if their mistress's behavior were nothing out of the ordinary. But Reiko was too appalled to stand by and watch.

"Stop!" She hurried over to Lady Matsumae and pulled her away from the Ezo woman.

Lady Matsumae shrieked, "Let go of me!"

She turned on Reiko like a wildcat. She kicked Reiko, clawed at her. The Ezo women huddled together, hands over their mouths. So did the ladies-in-waiting. The maid ran out of the room. Reiko grabbed Lady Matsumae by her wrists. She said to the Ezo women, "You'd better go."

They fled. Lady Matsumae screamed and fought while Reiko struggled to control her. The maid hurried back with two guards, who dragged Reiko and Lady Matsumae apart.

"Why were you so mean to her?" Reiko asked Lady Matsumae. "What's your trouble?"

Lady Matsumae's eyes were red and crazed, her hair disheveled. "None of your business," she said in a voice harsh with rage. "Don't interfere with things you don't understand."

She turned her back on Reiko and told the guards, "Get her away from me."

The Fukuyama Castle guest quarters were in a building connected to the palace by a covered corridor. Shaded from the sun by dark fir trees, with snowdrifts halfway up its walls, the building looked desolate and forbidding. The guards marched Sano and his men into a dank, cold set of rooms. Servants came to pad the walls with woven mats, to stoke and light the charcoal braziers.

"Home away from home," Detective Marume said.

"Don't try anything," Deer Antlers warned Sano as he and the other guards left. "We'll be watching you."

"Do they feed the prisoners in this jail?" Detective Fukida said. When more servants brought in trays of rice balls, smoked salmon, pickled radish, and tea, he said, "I don't care much for Lord Matsumae's manners, but he does right by his guests."

"After he's decided to postpone killing them," Marume said.

As everyone ate, Sano worried about what had happened to Reiko, until two guards brought her.

She ran to Sano, knelt by him. "I'm so glad to see you!"

"Thank the gods you're all right." Sano held Reiko's cold hands. "Where have you been? What happened?"

"With Lady Matsumae." Reiko described how she'd stopped Lady Matsumae from beating the Ezo woman, and how Lady Matsumae had then attacked her. "Isn't that strange?"

"It is." Sano couldn't help thinking that Reiko had been at the castle less than an hour and already gotten into a fight. He told himself he should be glad nothing worse had happened. At least so far.

"What's even stranger," Reiko said, "is that Lady Matsumae and her attendants and maid absolutely refused to help me look for Masahiro. I think they know something, but they wouldn't talk. They don't care. I never met such cold-hearted women." She said eagerly, "What happened with Lord Matsumae?"

That was a topic Sano would rather not discuss. "He sent us food. There's some left. Are you hungry?"

"I've already eaten. Did you find out what the trouble is? Did you ask him about Masahiro?" She looked at the other men, who avoided her gaze. In the silence she asked, "What's wrong?"

Sano couldn't hide the facts from her no matter how much he wanted to protect her. He told her as gently as possible about how the murder of his mistress had driven Lord Matsumae mad, how he claimed Masahiro had never reached the castle but Sano didn't think he was telling the truth.

Reiko's eyes went round with shock and horror as she understood that Lord Matsumae might have killed their son. But she only nodded; she didn't fall apart. She never did during a crisis. Sano loved her for her bravery.

"Masahiro is alive," she said with quiet conviction. "If he weren't, I would know."

If it helped her endure, Sano wouldn't contradict what he feared was wishful thinking. He found himself heartened by her words in spite of himself. "We'll keep looking for him."

"But how?" A note of discouragement crept into Reiko's voice. "There are soldiers outside. They've locked us in. We're prisoners."

"I'm hoping that will change," Sano said, and told her about the deal he'd proposed to Lord Matsumae. "If I investigate the murder, I should have free run of this place."

His hope lit Reiko's face like a ray of sunshine. "Do you think he'll agree?"

Who knew what a madman would do, Sano thought. But he said, "Oh, yes. We just have to be patient."

And wait until Lord Matsumae decided whether his desire for justice was stronger than his reason to kill them.

Chapter Six

They spent the rest of the day idle in the guest quarters, keeping warm by huddling under blankets or pacing the floors. They ate the meals brought to them and took turns bathing in a tub filled by servants lugging pails of hot water. The night was the longest and coldest Sano had ever known.

Japanese architecture couldn't match the Ezo huts in protecting humans against the weather. Drafts blew through the guest quarters. The charcoal braziers gave off inadequate whiffs of heat. Pressed close to Reiko under piled quilts, Sano couldn't sleep even though she did, and his men snored across the hall. He missed the human noise of Edo Castle: the troops patrolling, music from parties, temple gongs ringing. Here he heard wolves howling in the forest. It was almost dawn before he fell asleep.

A short time later he was jolted awake by the presence of a stranger. Sitting up, he blinked at the figure that stood in the doorway.

"Honorable Chamberlain." The voice was male, gritty. "Lord Matsumae wants to see you."

Sano hoped this meant good news. "Give me a moment to dress."

He told Hirata to come with him and the other men to stay with Reiko, who was still asleep. When he and Hirata stepped outside the building into another day of bright, eye-watering, bitter cold, the man greeted them and said, "I'm Matsumae Gizaemon. Lord Matsumae's uncle."

About sixty years old, he looked like a cross between a Japanese and an Ezo. He wore a deerskin coat and mittens lined with fur, and fish-skin boots. His face was as weathered and lined as the barbarians', his brows bushy; the eyes beneath them squinted as if from a lifetime spent looking at sun on snow. But his bare head had its crown shaved and its gray hair gathered in a topknot, samurai-style. At his waist hung the customary two swords.

Sano introduced Hirata. As they walked along the covered corridor to the palace, three guards fell into step behind them. Gizaemon said, "Sorry I wasn't around to meet you yesterday." He had the quick, agile gait of a much younger man. "I was away on business for Lord Matsumae."

"What do you do for him?" Sano asked.

"Help him manage his domain. I'm his chief aide." Gizaemon reached in his coat, took out a toothpick, and chewed it vigorously. Sano smelled the sweet, spicy odor of sassafras bark. "I inspect the trading posts. Keep the Japanese merchants in line. The Ezo, too."

"You must know Lord Matsumae fairly well," Sano said.

"Known him since he was born. His father was my older brother. Left his education to me. I practically raised him. He's like my own son." Affection and concern crept into Gizaemon's voice. He was clearly troubled by the turn Lord Matsumae had taken.

"What's the matter with him?" Sano asked. "Surely not just that the death of his mistress has upset him?"

"No," Gizaemon agreed. "He's possessed by her spirit."

"You're not serious?"

"Yes, I am." Gizaemon laughed dryly. "It's obvious that you think spirit possession is just a myth. Well, maybe that's so in Edo. But not here. I've seen spirits take over people's bodies, make them speak in tongues and jump off cliffs." Seeing Sano's skeptical look, he said, "Don't believe me? Just wait till you've been in Ezogashima a while longer."

"Did Lord Matsumae tell you about our meeting?" Sano asked.

"Some." Gizaemon sounded angry, but not with his nephew. "Hell of a guest you are, coming in here and killing our men."

"Excuse me, but Lord Matsumae isn't exactly blameless," Sano said evenly. "Are you aware of what he's done?"

"Here we are," Gizaemon said, dropping the subject of his nephew's crimes.

"Has Lord Matsumae made a decision about my offer?"

"You'll have to ask him yourself." Gizaemon spat his toothpick into the snow below the corridor, then opened the palace door.

Lord Matsumae received them in his private chamber. It was furnished with the same built-in cabinets, lacquer furniture, and study alcove as any samurai official's, with no native décor except the wall mats. Sprawled amid quilts rumpled by a restless night, he looked like a man suffering from a malignant illness. In each of his cheeks burned a spot of fever.

"Greetings, Honorable Chamberlain." He lifted a bowl of herb tea; his hands shook as he drank. "I've thought about what you said yesterday. And I've decided to accept your offer."

"Good," Sano said, relieved. "My men and I will begin investigating the murder right away." And look for Masahiro.

"Not so fast!"

The voice that came out of Lord Matsumae was high-pitched, not his own. Sano felt every hair on his body rise in a shivering tingle. He was astounded to see Lord Matsumae's face alter. It seemed to grow younger, female.

"You can't just go off wherever you want." The voice had a strange accent, with inflections that Sano had heard in the Ezo language. "Why should we trust you? How do we know you can find out who killed me?"

Shocked, Sano and Hirata looked at Gizaemon.

Gizaemon's dour smile said, *I told you so.* "Better answer the question."

Sano said, "I was once the shogun's detective." He was so fascinated by the stranger looking at him through Lord Matsumae that he hardly knew what he was saying. "His Excellency trusted me to solve murders for him." The presence of the spirit infected the atmosphere. Atavistic fear crept through him. "He was satisfied with my work."

Lord Matsumae's face reverted to its own aspect; he spoke in his own voice: "You will tell me everything you're going to do and get my permission in advance. You and your men won't go anywhere without an escort."

"Those conditions weren't part of the deal," Sano said, disturbed not only because he now had two taskmasters, one a figment of the imagination or a real ghost. The constraints would allow him little freedom to search for his son as well as hinder his efforts to find the killer.

"Take it or leave it!" Lord Matsumae said. Two intense lights burned in each of his eyes, from two souls.

"Very well," Sano said, astonished into conceding.

Pacified, Lord Matsumae said, "What is your first step?"

"I would usually examine the body of the murder victim," Sano said. But so much time had passed; the corpse must be long cremated and buried. "Since that's not possible, maybe you could just tell me what happened—"

"It's possible," Lord Matsumae said, turning to his uncle. "Take them to see Tekare."

As Gizaemon gestured Sano and Hirata toward the door, his eyes glinted with sardonic humor at their surprise. "Right this way."

Alone in her room, Reiko climbed out of bed. It was so cold she could see her breath. She washed, dressed, and groomed herself as fast as possible and ate the meal that a servant brought her. She opened the window shutters, pushed aside the paper panel, and peeked outside.

Matsumae troops loitered on the veranda. She was desperate to look for Masahiro, but if she tried, would they stop her? Sano and Hirata had been escorted away by other troops who'd seemed not about to let them stray. Was she under the same arrest? In Edo, the rules were clear-cut. Here she felt marooned in a lawless, senseless nightmare.

There was a tap on the door. "Come in," Reiko called.

It was the maid from Lady Matsumae's chamber. She carried in a bundle of leather and fur. "Pardon me, Honorable Lady," she said, bowing, "but I thought maybe you'd like these." Her speech was carefully polite. Kneeling, she laid a fur-lined deerskin coat and hood, fish-skin boots, and leather mittens in front of Reiko.

"Thank you," Reiko said, grateful for the maid's kindness. She put on the garments. They were roughly made, similar to what the maid wore, and smelled gamy, but they were much warmer than the clothes Reiko had brought from Edo.

"I didn't think *she* would give you anything," the maid said. "Not after what happened yesterday."

She could only be Lady Matsumae. Reiko studied the maid, whose raised brows and tentative smile indicated eagerness to gossip. "Can you stay a while?"

"Yes." The maid went breathy with delight. "A thousand thanks."

"What is your name?" Reiko said.

"Lilac."

Her eyes reminded Reiko of bright, quick butterflies looking for sweet flowers. Lilac sidled over to the dressing table and caressed Reiko's silver comb, looking glass in the lacquer frame with jade inlays, and matching box of makeup. Awe parted her sensuous, pursed lips.

"Does Edo have lots of shops where people can buy nice things like these?"

"Yes," Reiko said. "Haven't you ever been there?"

"No. I was born here in Ezogashima, and I've never left it. My family are servants of the Matsumae clan. But I wish I could go to Edo." Passion swelled Lilac's voice. "More than anything in the world."

She stepped over to the cabinet, where Reiko had stored the few clothes she'd rescued from the ship. "May I look?" she said boldly.

Reiko nodded because they'd struck an unspoken bargain that granted permission for the girl to snoop. Lilac opened the cabinet and lifted out a silk kimono patterned with a blue and silver landscape.

"So beautiful!" she exclaimed, holding it up to herself. Then she sighed. "Even if I had clothes like this, there's no place to wear them around here. And there's nobody worthwhile to see me. How I wish I lived in the big city."

It was time for Reiko to exact her half of the bargain. "Maybe you can answer some questions for me."

"I'll do my best." Lilac gave the kimono a last caress, put it away, and knelt by Reiko.

There was a brazenness about her that put Reiko off, but Reiko was in no position to be choosy about her companion. "First, who are those Ezo women?"

"They're concubines."

Reiko was startled because the barbarians seemed so strange that she hadn't imagined sexual relations between them and the Japanese. "Lord Matsumae's?"

"No, they belong to his retainers."

That explained why the women were in the castle even though Ezo were prohibited. "Why did Lady Matsumae get so angry at them?"

"She hates them. And I'll tell you why."

Lilac glanced at the open door. Across the hall, other maids were sweeping the men's rooms. They giggled while Marume, Fukida, and the Rat flirted with them. Lilac beckoned Reiko to lean close and whispered, "She and her ladies-in-waiting think the Ezo concubines are inferior, like animals. They're jealous because the men want them. They punish them whenever they get a chance."

Because they couldn't punish the men, they took out their jealousy on the concubines, Reiko realized. And the concubines couldn't fight back because if they made trouble, they and their people would be punished. Reiko began to pity the Ezo.

"But Lady Matsumae started treating them even worse when her daughter died."

Comprehension stole through Reiko. "When was this?"

"Last spring."

"How old was her daughter?"

"Eight years."

The same age as Masahiro. "Has she any other children?"

"No." Lilac added, "Lord Matsumae adopted a cousin as his heir. She's too old to have any more."

At last Reiko understood why Lady Matsumae had reacted so violently when asked whether she had any children and if she knew what it was like to lose one. Reiko had unintentionally touched a raw wound. Now she pitied Lady Matsumae; she regretted her own words and the fact that she'd provoked Lady Matsumae's cruelty toward the helpless Ezo concubine. She wondered how Lady Matsumae's daughter had died, but shied from talking about a child's death while her own son was missing. And she had more pressing concerns.

"I want to find my son," she said. "Can you help me?"

Lilac drew back from Reiko. Her eagerness to please dissolved into worry.

"You know something, don't you?" When Lilac wouldn't meet her eyes, Reiko pleaded, "Tell me!"

"I think I saw him," Lilac said reluctantly.

Dizzied by hope, Reiko said, "When was this? Where?"

"About a month ago. Here at the castle. A little boy, with three soldiers. I'd never seen them before."

It had to have been Masahiro escorted by Lord Matsudaira's men, Reiko thought. The hesitation in Lilac's speech made it clear that she didn't want to tell this story because the ending wouldn't please Reiko, but Reiko had to know the truth. "What happened?" she demanded.

Lilac sighed. "Lord Matsumae's troops brought them inside the palace, to Lord Matsumae's chambers."

Lord Matsumae had lied when he'd told Sano he didn't know anything about Masahiro, when he'd claimed the boy had never reached Fukuyama City.

"I don't know what happened in there, but . . ."

"Go on," Reiko prompted, even though dread filled her.

"After a while, the troops brought out the soldiers. They had ropes wound around them, and gags in their mouths.

The troops took them to the courtyard. They made them kneel down. And then—" Lilac gulped. "They cut off their heads."

Reiko felt a terrible darkness crowding out all the light in the world. There was no reason to think that Lord Matsumae had spared her son after killing his escorts. "What about the boy?" She forced the words out past the breath caught inside her.

"I don't know," Lilac said. "He wasn't with the soldiers."

A fragile, tenuous relief seeped through Reiko. If Masahiro hadn't been killed during the execution Lilac had seen, perhaps he was still alive. "What happened to him?" she almost didn't dare to ask.

"I don't know. He never came out of the palace, at least not that I saw."

He could have been killed inside by Lord Matsumae, who's mad enough to murder the chamberlain's child. The voice of her common sense taunted Reiko. *Lord Matsumae lied because he didn't want Sano to know he'd killed Masahiro. He was sane enough to be afraid of punishment.* But Reiko's spirit refused to believe it.

"Have you seen him again?" Reiko demanded.

Lilac recoiled, frightened by the intensity of Reiko's gaze. "No."

"Could he still be in the castle?" Reiko sat very still, her ears pricked, her eyes wide, mouth open, every sense straining to detect her son's whereabouts.

"He could," Lilac said, but she sounded more as if she wanted to please Reiko than as if she thought so.

One of the other maids peeked in the door. "Lilac! Lady Matsumae wants you."

"I have to go," Lilac said, rising.

Reiko clutched her arm and whispered, "Can you find out if my son is here? Will you look for him for me? Please!"

Sly satisfaction glittered through the sympathy in Lilac's eyes. "I'll try."

As she hurried off, Reiko knew that she'd put herself right where Lilac wanted, in her debt. Reiko didn't trust someone who would take advantage of the mother of a kidnapped child, but she would deal with all the gods of evil to find Masahiro. At least now she had more hope than before, something else to wait for besides news from Sano. But the waiting grew even harder to bear. With every moment that passed, Reiko's patience stretched beyond the limits of frustration.

The other maids came to sweep her room. When they finished, they fastened their fur-lined coats and pulled their leather hoods over their heads, preparing to go out into the cold. Inspiration flashed through Reiko as she looked at their clothes, then at her own that Lilac had given her. She quickly tagged after them. People took servants for granted, didn't pay them much attention. The maids were chattering together and didn't seem to notice Reiko. She kept her head down, and the guards at the door didn't look twice at her as she walked past them out the door.

Chapter Seven

Gizaemon and the guards led Sano and Hirata outside, to a tea ceremony cottage with a thatched roof, plank walls, and a stone basin by the door for washing hands before entering. This symbol of Japanese high culture looked out of place in the alien north. Sano felt more unsettled than comforted by the familiar sight, as if he'd flown to the moon only to discover trappings of home. He had thought that after what he'd already experienced here, nothing else could shock him, but when he stepped inside the cottage with Hirata and Gizaemon, he found out how wrong he'd been.

The corpse lay in a pine coffin set on the tatami floor, between the gnarled wooden columns that supported the ceiling. Strewn around it were gold lotus flowers and brass incense burners. Tekare wore a lavish gold silk brocade kimono embroidered with darker gold water lilies. Her thick, wavy black hair fanned across the pillow under her head. Her eyes were closed, her arms laid at her sides. Lord Matsumae had enshrined his beloved's remains. The cold had semipreserved her, although her face was withered, sunken. At first Sano thought the bluish discoloration around her mouth was decay, but then he realized it was a tattoo such as Reiko had described seeing on the Ezo concubines.

"Lord Matsumae's dead mistress was an Ezo woman," Sano said.

As he and Hirata stood gazing down at the corpse, he noticed the flattened silk cushion beside Tekare's head. Lord

Matsumae must spend hours kneeling beside her. Mourning her. Worshipping her. Sano thought about the scene in Lord Matsumae's chamber. His intellect couldn't accept what he'd seen, heard, and felt. Surely the dead Tekare hadn't taken over Lord Matsumae; surely his madness made him act out her persona. But spirit possession appeared to be the prevalent belief about what ailed him, and Sano—his prisoner—didn't have much choice except to operate under the same assumption.

"Taking Ezo women as concubines is common in these parts," Gizaemon said. "Not enough Japanese women, and some men have a taste for native meat."

Sano raised his eyebrows at the crude remark. "You don't approve?"

"Only because of the trouble it can cause. Which you've seen with my nephew."

"Didn't you like Tekare?" Hirata asked.

"She was as good as any of them."

"Is it Ezo in general you don't care for?"

Gizaemon shrugged. "They have their uses. If not for them, my clan would be foot-soldiers for the shogun instead of ruling a trade monopoly."

Hirata exchanged glances with Sano as they noted Gizaemon's attitude. Sano asked, "Can you tell me how she died?"

"She was shot with a spring-bow. Ever seen one?" When Sano shook his head, Gizaemon explained, "It's for hunting, a bow and arrow rigged with a string that's tied across a path. When an animal trips the string, the bow lets loose. Except in this case, it wasn't a deer that the arrow hit."

He took the front of the woman's robe between his thumb and forefinger and gingerly pulled it open. Her flesh was grayish, her breast shriveled. Between her ribs was an ugly wound, the tissue blackened with blood and rot.

"A good, clean shot," Gizaemon said.

The satisfaction in his voice repelled Sano. "Why does Lord Matsumae think Tekare was murdered? Couldn't her death have been accidental? She walked into a trap set for deer?"

"Not a chance," Gizaemon said scornfully. "Nobody hunts game on that path. There isn't any so close to town. Make no mistake, this wasn't an accident."

He added, "It wasn't just the arrow that killed her. The head was poisoned with *surkuay.*"

" *'Surkuay'?"* Sano frowned at the unfamiliar word.

"A native potion made from monkshood plant, tobacco, stingray spines, and other poisonous things. You hit a bear anywhere on his body with it, and he can walk only about two hundred paces before he dies. You follow him until he drops. There's only one cure. Immediately cut away the poisoned flesh and wash out the wound. As you can see she tried to do."

"With her bare hands," Sano said as he and Hirata studied the claw marks around the wound.

"Little good it did," Gizaemon said callously.

Sano thought his negative view of Tekare equaled fertile ground for the murder investigation. "Who do you think killed her?"

"Had to be an Ezo." Gizaemon sounded certain.

"What makes you say that?"

"The spring-bow is an Ezo weapon. The poison is Ezo. One plus one equals two."

"You sound as if you want the killer to be an Ezo," Sano said. "Why?"

Amused condescension flickered across Gizaemon's weathered face. "Let me explain the situation here in Ezogashima, Honorable Chamberlain. Relations between Ezo and Japanese have always been tense. They don't like us keeping them confined in their own territory, controlling their trade with the outside. They'd rather come and go as they please."

"If they sell their goods directly to customers in Japan, they can set their own prices and cut the Matsumae middlemen out of the deals," Sano said. "I know. What's your point?"

"So far we've had a compromise. The Ezo behave themselves. We let them choose their own leaders, rule their own villages, keep their traditions. But it doesn't always work."

"There have been Ezo uprisings.

"Right. Even though the Ezo will never drive us out, they'll keep trying. Who needs the trouble? Much better to get them under our thumb for good."

His words conjured up a vision of the Ezo subjugated by warfare, their territory annexed to Japan. Sano thought of the men who'd saved him and Reiko and their companions yesterday. Now he saw the murder case in the larger context of politics. It had dimensions far beyond the matter of justice for one dead woman. If an Ezo had killed Tekare, that would give Lord Matsumae an excuse to subjugate the barbarians, even though she'd been one of their own. The survival of an entire people hinged on the outcome of this investigation.

But Sano felt enormous pressure to solve the crime whatever way he could. His own fate, his wife's, his son's, and his dearest comrades' depended on his success. He couldn't shy away from incriminating the Ezo, and perhaps one of them was guilty.

"Why would an Ezo have murdered Tekare?" Sano asked.

"Who knows? Some squabble. Who cares?" Gizaemon's tone said all personal relations between the barbarians were trivial.

"I promised Lord Matsumae I would find Tekare's killer," Sano said. "I doubt he would be satisfied with pinning the murder on her people in general. Knowing why she died might lead me to who did it."

"Well, I'm not the person who can tell you why," Gizaemon said. "Better talk to the Ezo themselves."

"I intend to," Sano said, "but first I must talk to you, about my son."

Resistance immediately hardened Gizaemon's face.

"What happened to him?" Sano prodded. "Where is he?"

Gizaemon shook his head.

"Do you mean you don't know or you won't tell me?"

"I mean you can't force me to say anything that can be used against my nephew," Gizaemon said with the obstinacy of a samurai loyal to his master.

Sano's anger at Lord Matsumae expanded to include

Gizaemon, who he suspected did know Masahiro's fate. "This is an innocent eight-year-old child who's at stake. How can you do nothing?"

Offense drew together Gizaemon's bushy eyebrows. "I'm trying with all my might to keep order in Ezogashima and minimize the damage that Tekare does through my nephew. Wouldn't call that 'nothing.' Imagine yourself in my place. One lost boy would be the least of your concerns."

That logic didn't diminish Sano's need to find Masahiro or his determination to enlist the aid of Gizaemon, who seemed the only person here with any sense even if he was a good murder suspect. "You don't have to betray your nephew. Just let me search for my son."

"Can't do. You're supposed to be solving the crime. My orders are to help you with that and nothing else."

"Lord Matsumae won't have to know."

Gizaemon chuckled harshly. "I'm not going to help you, and neither is anyone else here. You want to get off this island alive, you'd best forget your son, cut your losses, and march in step."

Although Sano realized how even more serious the situation was than he'd thought at first, and how prudent was Gizaemon's advice, he said, "In case you don't realize it, your nephew has put you in a bad position. He'll eventually be held accountable for his actions. Do you really want to go down with him?"

"It's my duty to go wherever my lord goes." Gizaemon sounded ardently pledged to that duty; he wasn't just paying lip service to Bushido. "I gladly bow to his wishes."

"Cooperate with me, and I'll help you later," Sano persisted.

"Forget it."

"If my son is here, at least ask Lord Matsumae to give him to me. Use your influence to save him."

Sadness in his gaze said that Gizaemon wasn't as heartless as he seemed, but he shook his head. "I have no influence with Lord Matsumae anymore. Nobody does, except Tekare."

Sano tasted the bitterness of defeat yet refused to swallow it. There was always more than one path to a goal. For now he said, "I'll talk to the Ezo. Can you bring me the ones who were around town the night of the murder?"

"That I can do."

Reiko darted around the corner of the guest quarters and crouched among some bushes. Her heart fluttered with exhilaration because she'd made her escape. But where should she go first? How long before the guards discovered she was gone?

Thankful for her fur-lined boots, Reiko trudged through a snowy garden. Fukuyama Castle seemed bigger than it had yesterday, with more buildings. Her heart sank at the amount of ground she had to search for Masahiro.

If he was here at all.

If he was still alive.

Reiko shut those thoughts out of her mind. As she skirted the palace, she heard male voices coming toward her. She ducked behind a tall stone lantern. Two guards passed her. She saw others patrolling everywhere. Security was even tighter here than in Edo Castle. Eventually she would run smack into someone who would realize she wasn't one of the maids. She slipped through a gate and found herself in a compound of dingy outbuildings.

Some were storehouses with fireproof plaster walls, iron doors, and tile roofs. Smoke and food odors identified others as kitchens. Reiko heard voices shouting over a din of chopping, banging, and sizzling inside. Servants carried in coal, came out and dumped slops. Reiko hurried past them, face averted. She darted out another gate.

An uproar of barking startled her. Four huge, fierce dogs charged at her, their teeth bared. Reiko screamed and flung up her arms in self-defense.

A voice called a command in Ezo language. The dogs halted close to Reiko, their eyes glaring, hackles bristling, and growls thrumming, but didn't attack. Reiko looked beyond them and saw an Ezo woman standing outside an open shed that contained sleds and harnesses. She was the concubine Reiko had tried to protect from Lady Matsumae.

She spoke to the dogs, who turned and trotted to her, docile and tame as pets. She rubbed them behind their ears and smiled at Reiko in a shy but friendly fashion. Understanding leaped across the barrier of experience and culture that separated them. Reiko had stood up for her, and she wanted to return the favor. Reiko smiled, too. Here was an ally more trustworthy than Lilac. But how could Reiko communicate what she needed?

The Ezo woman looked around furtively, as if to check whether anyone was observing them. She beckoned to Reiko. "Come," she whispered in Japanese.

Chapter Eight

Gizaemon sent men to fetch the barbarians and told Sano and Hirata, "You can interrogate them in the trade ceremony room."

This was a chamber where Lord Matsumae and his officials received the Ezo when they made their yearly visits to Fukuyama Castle. Its décor told Hirata that the ceremony had evolved from a mere striking of deals into a demonstration of Japanese supremacy and Ezo submission. The chamber was furnished with hanging curtains that bore huge Matsumae crests and a display of armor, lances, guns, and cannons.

"Doesn't hurt to show them who's in charge," Gizaemon said.

Sano said, "I'll need my interpreter."

"I speak Ezo language. I'll translate for you."

"I'd rather use my own man," Sano said.

Hirata knew he wanted someone he could trust more than the kin of the madman who was holding them captive. And he had other reasons to distrust Gizaemon besides his association with Lord Matsumae.

"Suit yourself." Gizaemon's indifference said he didn't think much of Sano's chances of solving the crime no matter what interpreter he used.

The Rat was summoned. He came wearing a look of doleful resentment.

"Have a seat," Gizaemon said, pointing Sano and Hirata to the dais.

The guards brought the seven barbarians who'd sheltered

Sano's party. Hirata was disconcerted by the change in them. Instead of their animal skins they wore silk robes printed with Chinese designs, apparently intended as ritual costume. They held hands like children and walked with a hunched-over, mincing gait. Hirata supposed this protocol was meant to degrade them. He felt a stab of outrage on behalf of the old Ezo chieftain Awetok, who bore his humbling with stoic dignity. Awetok glanced at Hirata, and although his face showed no recognition, Hirata sensed the same affinity between them.

The Ezo knelt on the lowest level of the multitiered floor, emphasizing their inferiority. Seated in the position that symbolized Japanese power, Hirata gazed at the man he'd marked as his destiny, his teacher, across an even wider separation of rank and culture than ever.

"Tell them to recite their names and titles," Gizaemon ordered the Rat. "That's standard procedure."

The Rat obeyed; the Ezo men spoke, and he translated. The chieftain's companions turned out to be men from his village. The strong one with the blue bead necklace was named Urahenka. He behaved as docilely as the rest, but Hirata read resentment in his fierce eyes, the clench of his jaw.

"I'd like to speak to them in private," Sano said to Gizaemon. "Would you and your men wait outside?"

"Our duty is to watch you," Gizaemon said. "And after yesterday, you bear watching."

Hirata could tell how little Sano liked being treated like a dog on a leash, forced to conduct the investigation on the terms of a madman, when all he wanted was to find his son. But Sano bowed to the Ezo and said, "Greetings. Your presence is appreciated." Hirata knew he was trying to make up for their poor treatment, in the hope of willing rather than forced cooperation. "I am investigating the murder of Tekare, who was Lord Matsumae's mistress. I need you to answer some questions."

After the Rat translated, the chieftain's shrewd glance flicked from Sano and Hirata to the Matsumae guards stationed around the room. Awetok clearly understood that the newcomers were under some kind of duress even if he didn't know the details. He spoke, his voice steady. "As you wish," the Rat said, and the process of questions and translations, answers and more translations, began.

"Did you know Tekare?" Sano asked.

Nods all around. The chieftain said, "She was from our village."

"Why were you in town when Tekare was murdered? Wasn't trade season already over by then?"

"We came to rescue her."

"Rescue her?" Sano frowned in the same puzzlement that Hirata felt. "From what?"

While the chieftain spoke at length, Hirata sensed anger behind his calm tone, building inside the other barbarians. "Lord Matsumae stole Tekare from us. He turned her into a slave for his pleasure. As if it isn't enough that he forces us to sell our goods to his clan for ridiculously low prices, he helps himself to our women."

Offense darkened Gizaemon's face. He rapped out an order to Awetok. The Rat said, "He told him, 'Watch your mouth. Any more criticism of Lord Matsumae, and you'll be beaten.' "

"Tell him he has my permission to speak frankly," Sano said. As the Rat conveyed his words, Sano turned to Gizaemon. "Whether or not you approve of my investigation, Lord Matsumae wants it. It may be his best chance of regaining his sanity. Your interfering won't help him." Sano paused for an instant. "Or maybe it's not him that you're trying to help?"

"Of course it is," Gizaemon said, annoyed. "I've served him since he was born."

But people didn't stand in the way of justice unless they had something to lose, Hirata knew from years of detective experience. And Gizaemon had already given him and Sano enough reason to be suspicious of him. They should have a little talk with him later.

"Tekare was only one of many Ezo women who were mistresses to Japanese men," Sano reminded the chieftain. "Why did you want to rescue her in particular?"

"She was the shamaness of our village."

Sano leaned forward, intrigued by this new fact about the murder victim. Hirata's own interest quickened at the introduction of Ezo spiritual tradition, which might relate to the mystic martial arts and his own quest. "What does a shamaness do?" Sano asked.

"She diagnoses and cures diseases with potions, rituals, and exorcisms. She's our conduit between the spirit world and the human world. Without her, we cannot call upon the spirits to help us and protect us. So you can understand why we want her back."

Apparently Lord Matsumae had worsened the hostilities between the Ezo and the Japanese by taking a most important person from her tribe as his sex slave.

"Aside from being important to the village," Sano said, "what kind of person was Tekare?"

"She was a strong, capable woman."

Even though Hirata didn't know what Awetok was saying until it was translated, he sensed that Awetok was deliberately speaking of the dead in the most general, uncritical terms. He also perceived the mental energy that the chieftain gave off while Sano asked questions.

"What did you think of her?" Sano said.

"I thought very highly of her abilities. She was the most powerful shamaness I've seen in my lifetime."

"And you?" Sano addressed the other men.

They echoed the chieftain's opinion. Evasions all around, Hirata noted. Either they couldn't think for themselves, they didn't want to contradict their leader, or they hadn't cared for the woman.

Sano then asked each man what relation he had to her. The chieftain was her uncle by marriage, one man her brother-in-law, another her cousin. The Ezo village evidently consisted of several interrelated families. Urahenka identified himself as her husband. *Well, well,* Hirata thought as the blue-beaded strongman rose to the top of the hierarchy of Ezo suspects.

"Were you on good terms with Tekare?" Sano asked him.

Urahenka spoke with bitter resentment. "We were on no terms at all. I hadn't seen her in almost three years. Not since she was taken from me."

Hirata imagined how would it be to have his own wife stolen and forced to be somebody else's mistress. He felt a twinge of guilt because he'd neglected Midori while studying martial arts. He missed his sweet, loyal wife, and he sympathized with Urahenka in spite of himself.

"Was your marriage satisfactory before she was taken?" Sano asked.

"Yes. I loved her. I wanted her back. But now she's gone. I'll never see her again in this life."

He emphasized his words by pounding on his heart, grasping the air with his hands, then letting them drop while his shoulders sagged in grief. The language barrier and his foreignness made gauging his truthfulness difficult. Hirata focused on the field of mental energy that surrounded him. It hummed with contradictory vibrations.

"Where were you the night Tekare died?" Sano asked.

Urahenka glared at Sano. "Do you mean, did I kill her?"

Gizaemon barked out a command in Ezo language, obviously ordering Urahenka to answer, not ask questions.

"I didn't!" Urahenka balled his fists, more angry at the tacit accusation than fearful of punishment.

"That's what he's been saying all along," Gizaemon muttered. "That's what they've all been saying."

"Maybe it's true," Sano said, his tone even. He addressed the young barbarian: "If you expect me to believe you're innocent, then tell me where you were the night of the murder."

"I was at the camp."

When asked individually, each Ezo, including the chieftain, said they'd all been at their camp, together, the whole night.

"That alibi's worth nothing," Gizaemon said disdainfully. "The bastards always lie for each other."

Chieftain Awetok raised his hand. Sano nodded permission for him to speak. "The Matsumae soldiers were guarding our camp. We couldn't have left without them knowing. We were there. Ask them."

Sano turned a questioning look on Gizaemon.

"Hard to keep track of the bastards. They move through the forest like ghosts, there one moment, gone the next," Gizaemon said. "Could have sneaked out and back in, nobody the wiser."

Urahenka shouted angry words. Gizaemon snapped at him.

" 'If you want to find out who killed Tekare, you're looking at the wrong people,' " the Rat interpreted. " 'Don't speak until you're spoken to.' "

Sano's chest swelled with a breath of vexation. Hirata could tell how tired he was of Gizaemon getting between him and the suspects, how helpless he felt to do anything about it while a prisoner, and how desperate he was to look for his son instead of indulging a madman. But when Sano addressed Urahenka, his manner was patient, controlled.

"Which people do you suggest I look at?"

"Japanese!"

Nobody needed the Rat to translate that. Sano said, "But Tekare was shot with a spring-bow, an Ezo hunting weapon."

"It was a trick by a Japanese. To make us look like we killed her."

Urahenka let loose a stream of imprecations. Gizaemon stalked over to him and shouted at him.

"He's insulting the Matsumae clan," the Rat explained. His feral eyes shone with nervousness. "Gizaemon is telling him to watch his mouth."

Chieftain Awetok spoke words of caution that Urahenka ignored. Urahenka sprang to his feet. He and Gizaemon yelled into each other's faces.

" 'You Japanese want to stamp us out. You started by killing my wife, and you won't stop until we're all gone and you can take over our land,' " the Rat interpreted. " 'Show some respect, you animal, or you'll be the next to die.' "

The other men stood, rallying around Urahenka, their furious voices joining his. Hirata surmised that they belonged to a faction of Ezo that wanted to fight Japanese domination. As they argued with Gizaemon, he shoved them. They shoved back. The guards went rushing to support Gizaemon, swords drawn.

Dismay gripped Hirata because he realized that a war could start here, in this very room. Sano leaped up and shouted, "Stop! Everyone back off!" Hirata called upon the mystical power within himself. A strong, calming energy flowed from him over Gizaemon, the guards, and the barbarians. Chieftain Awetok uttered a warning. His lips kept moving after the sound from them stopped. He flexed his hand, as though casting a spell.

Later Hirata couldn't have said which tactic had worked, or whether all of them together had. But the guards sheathed their weapons and retreated. Urahenka and the other Ezo men dropped to their knees. Gizaemon squatted, surly but tamed, near the dais. All the combatants looked relieved but confused; they didn't know what had happened, either. But the tension had been diffused.

As Sano and Hirata resumed their seats, Hirata sent Chieftain Awetok a curious gaze. The chieftain sat silent and impassive, but Hirata detected a sly glint in his eye. Hirata felt more strongly than ever that the old Ezo man possessed abilities that he couldn't fathom but were far beyond his own, and knew things Hirata needed to know.

"Just a few more questions," Sano said. He fixed his solemn attention on the Ezo, measuring each man. "Did you kill Tekare?"

Each shook his head and said a word that clearly meant "No." Their gazes met Sano's as the chieftain spoke. "We are innocent."

Sano gave no hint of whether he believed them, although Gizaemon snorted. "Then who do you think did?"

Chieftain Awetok answered. The other Ezo nodded. "If I were you, I would talk to a Japanese named Daigoro. He's a gold merchant who lives in Fukuyama City. He's known for mistreating our women."

This wasn't the first time Hirata had seen people point the

finger toward others and shift suspicion away from themselves. But at least he and Sano had a new lead to follow. And Hirata was inclined to believe that the Ezo were innocent. He realized he'd chosen sides with the barbarians against his own Japanese countrymen.

"Thank you for your assistance," Sano said, as courteous as if the Ezo had given it voluntarily.

Chieftain Awetok spoke a question. Gizaemon said, "Of all the nerve. The bastard is asking you for a favor, Honorable Chamberlain."

With an obvious effort, Sano ignored Gizaemon. "What is it you want?"

"A proper funeral for Tekare, according to the traditions of our people. Without one, her spirit can't cross over to the realm of the dead. It lingers in this world, haunting Lord Matsumae."

"I'll see what I can do," Sano told the chieftain.

Awetok bowed in thanks. Once more Hirata felt the shape and texture of the chieftain's mental energy. Now he knew what it meant. When Sano spoke to him, the chieftain understood. Awetok knew Japanese.

A group of guards rushed into the room. "Begging pardon for the interruption, but there's bad news," said the one with the deer antlers on his helmet.

"Well, what is it?" Gizaemon said.

"The honorable chamberlain's wife is missing."

Chapter Nine

"How come you know Japanese?" Reiko asked.

"I live in castle . . ." The Ezo woman raised three fingers.

"Three years?"

Nodding, she touched her ear. "I listen."

They stood in the shed together. It was cold, dim, and smelled of the dogs, who sniffed and wagged their tails around Reiko. Reiko felt safe, hidden from Lord Matsumae's troops.

"What's your name?" Reiko asked.

"Wente." She pointed at Reiko, shy and inquisitive.

"Reiko."

They smiled at each other. Wente bowed, humble as any Japanese peasant, and said, "Many thanks."

Reiko nodded, aware that Wente was expressing gratitude because Reiko had stepped in to protect her yesterday. "I'm sorry for how Lady Matsumae treats you."

Wente made a gesture of resignation that said volumes about what the Ezo endured from the Japanese. She studied Reiko as if curious about this rare Japanese who wasn't cruel. "Yesterday. In Lady Matsumae's room. I heard." She groped for words, then cradled her arms, the universal sign language of a mother holding a child, and pointed at Reiko. Pity darkened her eyes. "I sorry."

This was the first sign of genuine caring about her kidnapped child that anyone in Ezogashima had shown Reiko. It broke down Reiko's self-control. Tears burned down her cold cheeks. Wente stood by, awkward and embarrassed.

"I sorry. I sorry," she repeated, almost as though she were personally to blame and asking forgiveness.

"I don't know what to do anymore." Reiko's tears froze as she wiped them away. A dog licked her hand. Its dumb, animal comfort jolted a sob from her. "Nobody will help me."

"I help you."

"How?" A glimmer of light pierced Reiko's grief.

Eyes shining with gladness at being able to offer salvation, Wente said, "Boy here."

Caution warred with the joy that leaped inside Reiko. "But—but Lord Matsumae's troops killed the men who brought my son. They must have killed Masahiro, too."

"No, no." Wente shook her head, adamant.

"How do you know?" Reiko said, desperate to believe.

"I listen. I see." Wente beckoned Reiko to the door of the shed and pointed upward, at the white tower of the keep, which rose beyond and above the palace. "He there."

"How did Lady Reiko get out?" Gizaemon demanded.

"I don't know," Deer Antlers said. "One moment she was in her room. The next time we checked on her . . ." He spread his empty hands.

"You idiot, Captain Okimoto! Letting a woman trick you!" Gizaemon turned in one direction, then another, so upset he was almost literally beside himself.

Sano was alarmed that Reiko had escaped, but not exactly surprised. He knew how determined she was to find Masahiro, and how clever about finding ways to go places she shouldn't. "Does Lord Matsumae know?" Gizaemon asked.

"No," said Okimoto. "We haven't told him."

"If he finds out, there's no telling what *she'll* put him up to." Gizaemon was much less concerned about Reiko than about protecting Lord Matsumae from the evil spirit of Tekare. He mumbled to himself, "I've been trying to save him day and night, for three months. How much longer can this go on?"

He told Captain Okimoto, "I'm joining in the hunt. You fools take the barbarians back to their camp." Pointing at Sano and Hirata, he added, "Lock them up."

"No!" Fear for Reiko stabbed Sano. He leaped off the dais. "I'm going with you."

When Gizaemon started to object, Sano said, "I can help you find my wife."

"The last thing I need is you running around loose." But Gizaemon hesitated, torn between his fear for his mad nephew, his distrust of Sano, and his wish to catch Reiko.

"I know how she thinks, the kind of places she would go," Sano said. "She'll hide from you, but she'll come out for me."

"Very well," Gizaemon said reluctantly on his way out the door. "But Okimoto will keep a tight leash on you."

Sano suddenly understood why Gizaemon was anxious to control him: He had secrets to hide. Did they have to do with Masahiro, the murder, or both?

Captain Okimoto scowled, but said, "Yes, master." As he led Sano from the room, Hirata followed. "Hey. Where do you think you're going?"

"With you," Hirata said.

"Oh no, you're not."

"I need you to talk to the gold merchant," Sano told Hirata. They mustn't delay the investigation. If they didn't produce results for Lord Matsumae, the gods help them.

"Well, he can't do that, either," Okimoto retorted. "He's not supposed to wander around by himself. Lord Matsumae's orders."

"Then send somebody with him," Sano said. "Lord Matsumae gave us permission to investigate the murder where we need to as long as we're escorted."

"Lord Matsumae also said everything you do has to be cleared with him in advance."

"Fine," Sano said. "Ask him if it's all right for Hirata-*san* to go into town and interview a suspect." Impatient because he must find Reiko before anyone else got to her, Sano added, "Come on, stop wasting time!"

"All right, all right." Okimoto told two men to take Hirata to Lord Matsumae and the others to accompany him and Sano. "But don't let Lord Matsumae know that the woman's escaped or that Chamberlain Sano is looking for her instead of the killer."

Sano realized that Lord Matsumae's men were terrified of him even though they carried out his insane, cruel orders. Rarely had samurai duty seemed so perverted, so destructive.

"As for you," Okimoto said to Sano and Hirata, "you'd better not try anything funny."

As Reiko gazed up at the keep, memory cast her back to a time when a different madman, who'd called himself the Dragon King, had imprisoned her in a tower on another remote island. A sense of déjà vu sickened Reiko. Now her son was the captive.

"I must rescue him!"

She started outside, but Wente ran after her. "No can go! Dangerous!"

"I don't care!"

Wente blocked her path. "Soldiers there." Her pretty face was stricken with alarm. "They catch you. Hurt you."

"Not if I can help it." Looking around the shed, Reiko saw tools hung on a wall—hammers, knives, awls, hatchets. She snatched down a sturdy knife with a wooden handle and a long, sharp steel blade.

"In case I don't see you again, I'll thank you now for helping me find my son," Reiko said. "If there's anything I can do for you in return, I will."

"No," Wente pleaded. Her mouth worked inside its blue tattoo as she fumbled for words. "You don't know how go. You get lost."

Finding her way to the keep didn't appear difficult to Reiko, who'd navigated around huge, labyrinthine Edo all her life. "Good-bye."

The dogs jumped in front of her. They barked and snapped. Rather than attacking her, they seemed anxious to protect her. She cried "Get away from me!" and waved her knife.

Wente uttered a command in Ezo language. The dogs retreated. She hesitated, frowned, and bit her lip. "I go with you. I show you."

"All right," Reiko said.

As Wente led her by the hand through the castle grounds, Reiko felt thankful to have a guide. Wente knew how to walk as if invisible. Maybe it was an Ezo talent developed while hunting game in the forests. Maybe she'd just had practice hiding from the Japanese in Fukuyama Castle. She and Reiko flitted from behind one building, tree, boulder, or snow pile to another. They avoided servants and officials who passed near them along the paths and covered corridors. Wente seemed to anticipate where the patrol guards would be. Reiko saw many across courtyards and gardens, but never near her and Wente. She felt invisible, as if Ezogashima had many different dimensions and they moved through one hidden from other humans.

Skirting the palace, they slipped through a gate and emerged into a compound. On a low hill at the center stood the keep. Seen at close range, the square tower wasn't white but dingy gray, the plaster on its surface cracked and weather stained. Gulls swept down from the brilliant turquoise sky and perched on the tiled roofs, whose upturned eaves protruded above each story. Bars covered the small windows. Reiko squinted against the sun at them, and although she couldn't see inside, her whole being tingled with the sense that Masahiro was there. She wanted to hurl herself at the keep.

A flight of steps led up the hill to it. The snow had been shoveled off them. At the top, the ironclad door of the keep opened. The sound of coughing drifted down to Reiko. Two young soldiers stepped out the door. They carried buckets whose liquid contents they dumped onto the snow. As they went back inside and shut the door, Reiko's hope of rescuing Masahiro stalled like a bird shot in flight.

"No can get in," Wente whispered.

"There must be a way," Reiko whispered back, even as

she saw another soldier walk around the corner of the keep and go inside. That Masahiro was so close, yet out of reach! She could barely stand the agony.

Wente tugged at her arm. "Must go. Before men see us."

"Wait! No!"

Reiko couldn't leave. She felt as if an invisible chain connected her to her son inside the keep and anchored her to the ground. But storming the keep was out of the question. Even though she'd been trained in combat and won fights before, she was one woman with a knife against heaven knew how many armed guards. Getting caught would do Masahiro no good.

She let Wente tear her away. Her every heartbeat was a throb of pain as they moved from hiding place to hiding place through the castle. Reiko could hardly breathe past the sob caught deep in her lungs. The invisible chain dragged harder at her with every step.

They'd reached the garden outside the guest quarters when five soldiers appeared. Wente yanked Reiko to the ground behind a snowdrift. They lay on their stomachs, holding their breath and listening to the soldiers' voices.

"She can't have gotten out of the castle."

"And she can't hide forever. We'll find her eventually."

"You three stay here and watch the chamberlain's men. The last thing we need is more prisoners on the loose. We'll keep looking for her."

Footsteps crunched through the snow near Reiko and Wente. Reiko was horrified to realize that the guards had discovered she'd escaped. She lost all hope of sneaking back into the guest quarters undetected. With her chin pressed into the icy snow crystals, she thought fast and hard.

"What you do?" Wente whispered.

Giving herself up wasn't an option. The guards would lock her in and watch her more closely than before. Reiko would sit in her room, helpless. This was her one chance to reach Masahiro. She couldn't waste it.

"I'm going back to the keep," she told Wente.

Although her expression said what a rash plan she

thought this was, Wente gamely accompanied Reiko. But search parties swarmed the castle. Reiko and Wente dived behind bushes, darted around buildings, narrowly evading one patrol after another. They circled the keep from a distance, like a moon orbiting a planet, never getting any closer. Out of breath, gasping with fatigue, they paused in the shadow of a storehouse to rest.

Its door burst open. A soldier came out and spotted Reiko. "There she is!" he shouted.

Reiko fled. Too late she noticed that Wente had run in a different direction. Separated from her guide, on her own now, Reiko ran for her life.

Chapter Ten

Granted permission to interrogate the gold merchant, Hirata headed into town with the soldiers assigned to guard him. They were two samurai about eighteen years old. Filled with youthful masculine gusto yet insecure about their abilities, they were anxious to prove themselves superior to other men, including Hirata, their closest target.

"Try to get away from us," one said, as they escorted him along the road down the hill from the castle. He had a round, pimpled, mischievous face. "Come on, try."

"We'll give you a head start." The other was tall and lanky with an overbite, hopping in his eagerness for a fight. "But you won't get very far."

Hirata kept silent and kept walking.

"Of course he won't," said the first guard. "Look at him. He limps."

"What happened? Did you fall and break your leg?" the second guard asked.

Even though they must know that Hirata had killed several of their fellows yesterday, they felt safe teasing him because his comrades back at the castle were hostage to his good behavior. When he didn't answer, the first man jeered "Cripple!" and shoved him.

Hirata, trained to stay in equilibrium under any conditions, let the energy from the shove pass through and out of his muscles. His step didn't even falter. The guard gave him another, harder shove. This time Hirata flashed its energy back at his tormenter. The guard went reeling as if struck. He landed on his buttocks on a patch of ice and slid.

"Hey!" he cried.

He and his companion lunged at Hirata. Hirata dodged so fast that he seemed to vanish from the place he'd been standing. They collided and fell facedown. Scrambling up, they stared at Hirata with expressions now sober and frightened. Snow clung to their cheeks like sugar on cakes.

"If you try any more nonsense, I'll have to hurt you," Hirata said. "Understood?"

They proceeded into town without further incident.

Fukuyama City was a poor excuse for a capital. Along the main street, people fought a losing battle with winter, shoveling the snow from two days ago off their roofs. The stores were identified only by names carved on plaques, and when the few customers passed through the doors, Hirata could see nothing inside except dim lantern light. Wolfish dogs prowled, leaving yellow marks in the snow. Down the side streets nearest the castle, walls surrounded mansions that must belong to Matsumae officials. Farther away; fences enclosed houses where the rich merchants probably lived. The whole place had a shut-in, unwelcoming aspect. Men with what Hirata now recognized as the typical weathered, prematurely aged Ezogashima complexion loitered outside a teahouse, smoking pipes. They regarded Hirata with suspicious curiosity.

His escorts led him to a storefront that took up an entire corner and looked more prosperous than the other businesses. Thick pillars supported the eaves over the veranda. The chimney spewed smoke. Iron filigree lanterns hung on either side of the door. Inside was a Japanese shop modified for the northern climate, its walls lined with the ubiquitous woven mats. A large, square fire pit in the center held burning logs. Around the fire, three clerks sat at tables strewn with coins, *soroban* for counting money, brushes, ink, and paper for recording transactions. One customer emptied a pouch of gold nuggets in front of a clerk. They haggled about the exchange rate. The other clerks and their customers bargained over debt payment schedules. Daigoro was evidently a banker and money-lender as well as a gold merchant. Two samurai, who looked to be *rōnin* hired to guard the shop, lounged nearby, playing cards. As everyone looked up at Hirata, business and talk ceased.

One of Hirata's escorts announced, "This is Hirata-*san,* chief retainer of Chamberlain Sano from Edo. He wants to talk to Daigoro-*san.*"

A clerk went through a passage hidden by a mat at the back of the shop. Soon he returned and said, "He'll see you in his private office."

"You wait here," Hirata told his escorts.

He went down the passage. At the end was a door covered by another mat. He stopped short of it, revolted by a powerful sense of death. Below the faint stench of decayed flesh vibrated the echo of pain and violence.

When Hirata cautiously entered the room, a man seated behind a desk near a fire pit bowed and said, "Greetings."

Small, thin, and some forty years old, he wore a lush brown fur coat. His features were neat and well-proportioned, but the gleam in his eyes, the flare of his nostrils, and the wetness of his lips expressed pure avarice.

"At your service, master," Daigoro said.

Hirata felt an odd, plushy texture under his feet. Glancing down, he saw a bear pelt, complete with claws. He looked up at the head mounted on the wall alongside a stuffed eagle. Other, smaller creatures—rabbits, foxes, and otters—stared at Hirata with eyes made from black beads. Antlers attached to fur-covered bits of skull branched over them. No wonder Hirata had sensed death. This office was a tomb for slain animals.

"What a collection," Hirata said.

"Oh, it's nothing," Daigoro said modestly.

"Is this a local custom, displaying them like trophies?"

"No, I thought up the idea." Daigoro sounded proud of his originality.

"Did you kill them all?" Hirata pictured the merchant setting a spring-bow, felling a woman instead of wild game.

"Of course not. I buy them from the Ezo. But I do stuff them myself."

The very idea repulsed Hirata. The man totally lacked the traditional concern about cleanliness and purity. He seemed more feral than Japanese, more barbarous than the Ezo.

"I don't just collect animals." Rising, Daigoro pointed to an exhibit of wands with shaved tassels at the ends, such as Hirata had seen in the Ezo chieftain's hut. "These are *inau*—the barbarians' messengers to their gods. Those are *ikupasuy*." He showed Hirata some sticks carved with geometric designs, animal figures, and strange symbols. "Prayer sticks, used in Ezo religious rituals. And look here."

He opened a cabinet. On a shelf inside lay what looked like belts made of multiple woven cords cinched with black twine at different intervals. Attached to them by black cords were square black cloth tabs in varying numbers.

"These are *kut*—chastity bands," Daigoro said, "worn by Ezo women under their clothes. It shows what family line they belong to. A woman can't marry a man whose mother wears the same type. That prevents inbreeding. *Kut* are supposed to be secret. Men aren't allowed to see them. Women who take them off, or wear them to commit adultery, are clubbed."

"How did you get these?" Hirata asked.

Daigoro laughed, an insolent chuckle. "When people need money, it buys anything from them."

Hirata was even more revolted by the man's collection of relics than by the animal trophies. Daigoro had plundered the most sacred, personal items from the native culture. Hirata's sympathies swung even further toward the Ezo.

"I travel all over Ezogashima, surveying the gold mines, prospecting for new ones," Daigoro said. "I've been to all the villages, picked up whatever I liked there."

"Did that include a woman named Tekare?" Hirata asked.

A knowing look brightened the dirty gleam in Daigoro's eyes. "Ah, we're getting down to business now. I assume you're helping Chamberlain Sano investigate the murder of

Lord Matsumae's mistress. A clever man, your master. Buying his life with a promise to solve the crime."

"How did you know?"

Daigoro tapped his forefingers near the corners of his eyes, then on his ears. "I have these everywhere."

People at the castle who owed money to Daigoro would be willing to exchange news for a reduction in their debts, Hirata supposed. "You didn't answer my question."

"Yes, I found Tekare during a prospecting trip. The villages in that part of Ezogashima are known for their beautiful women. I've sampled quite a few. But she was the best."

Hirata had never thought to criticize men he knew for taking their pleasure with women from the Japanese lower classes, but the Ezo women seemed even more helpless, and their exploitation by Daigoro cruel instead of condonable. "So you collected her the way you collected these things?" Hirata gestured to the dead, preserved animals.

The merchant frowned at the disapproval in Hirata's tone. "Judge me if you want, but with all due respect, you have no idea what life is like in Ezogashima. I can tell you, because I've been here twenty-two years, since I was just a boy.

"I was convicted of raping the three daughters of the man who owned the shop in Osaka where I worked. That's not a crime, but the magistrate felt sorry for the girls. He sentenced me to be exiled here." He didn't deny what he'd done, but he clearly thought his punishment excessive. "I was dumped off a ship and left to fend for myself. Have you ever mined for gold?"

When Hirata shook his head, Daigoro said, "You walk along streams, filtering water through a sieve. If you find gold nuggets, you divert the stream and expose the bottom. Then you dig under the sand and rock until you find the gold deposits. It's long, hard work. And I did it for thirteen years, until I struck a big lode and made my fortune. I deserve a little enjoyment."

"At the expense of the Ezo women," Hirata said.

"Not always." A strange note crept into Daigoro's voice.

"With the other women, maybe, but not Tekare. She was different."

"You mean you didn't force yourself on her?" Hirata said skeptically.

"No. That is, it might have seemed that way. I followed her into the woods, and I took her. But it wasn't." Daigoro's face acquired the same dumb, beaten expression as the stuffed animals on the wall. "It was as if *she'd* taken *me*."

Eager to make Hirata understand, Daigoro said, "Tekare wasn't like the other Ezo women. She wasn't content to go on hunting trips with her husband. That's how the Ezo do it, you know. The husband shoots the game. The wife carries his gear, sets up camp, does the cooking. That's why strong women are the ones the men want to marry. But Tekare was more than just the usual beast of burden.

"She thought she deserved more. When I first met her, she'd given herself to all the traders, miners, and fishermen who passed through her village. In exchange, they gave her Japanese trinkets. Other Ezo women are simple, humble, and virtuous. Not her." Disgust and admiration mingled in Daigoro's laugh. "Tekare played men for all she was worth. She put on such airs, her nickname was 'The Empress of Snow Country.' "

This description of Tekare challenged Hirata's view of the murder victim. At least according to Daigoro, she hadn't been a downtrodden sex slave to the Japanese, but an ambitious climber out for herself. Daigoro's version of her jibed with the vindictive spirit that inhabited Lord Matsumae.

"After a while she wasn't satisfied with porcelain tea sets, lacquer boxes, and jade figurines. What good did they do her, when she was stuck in the middle of nowhere? She wanted to live like a fine Japanese lady. She started looking for someone who could take her away from her village." Daigoro pointed at his chest. "That sucker was me."

Hirata thought of the courtesans in Edo's Yoshiwara pleasure quarter. They were usually poor peasant girls sold into prostitution or sentenced to it as punishment for petty crimes.

Some managed to use the men who used them to win fame, wealth, and independence. Tekare must have been their sister under the skin.

"She hung around my camp. She flirted with me, drove me wild. One night, when she walked back to her village, I went after her, but that was what she wanted. She rode me like a horse. She was the most exciting woman I've ever known." The memory of passion suffused Daigoro's eyes. "I couldn't get enough of her. I fell in love. When I came back to Fukuyama City, I brought her with me."

"So Lord Matsumae didn't steal her from her village," Hirata said. "It was you."

Daigoro laughed, bitterly this time. "Nobody stole Tekare. I was her passage to civilization. I put her up in my house, gave her servants, Japanese clothes, whatever she wanted. But pretty soon she realized that even though I'm rich, I'm not the biggest man around. That's when Lord Matsumae came into the picture."

"Who introduced her to him?" Hirata said.

"Me, fool that I was." Daigoro grimaced. "I loved her, I was proud of her, I wanted to show her off. I invited Lord Matsumae to a banquet at my house. He took one look at Tekare, and he was smitten. She took one look at him and saw her fortune. The next day he sent for her. She moved out of my house and into the castle. She didn't even thank me."

Indignation swelled Daigoro. "After all I'd done for her!"

"So you were angry at Tekare," Hirata said.

"You bet I was."

"You wanted to punish her." Hirata thought Daigoro had much more cause for murder than did the Ezo men, who'd wanted to rescue their shamaness even if she didn't want rescuing.

"What are you getting at?" Daigoro regarded Hirata with narrowed eyes.

"Where were you the night she was killed?"

"At home, asleep in bed. Ask my servants."

Hirata figured they would lie for their master, upon whom

their livelihood depended. He didn't think much of Daigoro's alibi. "You'd have liked a little revenge on Tekare, wouldn't you?"

"If you're asking me if I murdered her, no, I didn't," Daigoro said. "I didn't need to. Someone else did it for me."

He smiled, a dirty smile of private, satisfied reminiscence. "Do you want to know what I think happened?"

Hirata's distaste toward the man grew as he saw that here came Daigoro's attempt to divert suspicion away from himself onto somebody else. "I suppose you're going to tell me."

"I wasn't the only one with a grudge against Tekare. She was a troublemaker, caused bad feelings wherever she went. You should be looking among her own people."

"Which ones?" Hirata was dismayed to see the wind of suspicion blown back at the Ezo.

"Her husband, for a start. He knew exactly what Tekare was doing, and he hates the Japanese. He didn't like being married to a whore who sold herself to them."

I loved her. I wanted her back, Urahenka had said. Hirata wondered against his will if the man had been lying.

"The day before Tekare left the village with me, he ordered her to stay and threatened to kill her if she didn't. She disobeyed. He shows up here, and a few days later she's dead." Daigoro raised an insinuating eyebrow.

Hirata thought how easy it was to visualize Urahenka setting the spring-bow for his wife, then chasing her along the path until she triggered it. It was as easy as imagining Daigoro doing it, wishing he could mount Tekare on the wall beside his other trophies. Who was the more likely killer, the exiled criminal or the cuckolded husband?

"But don't stop with her husband," Daigoro said. "Nobody in that village liked Tekare. Maybe they thought she was a disgrace to their tribe. Or maybe they were just jealous." He grinned, showing jagged teeth that looked strong enough to dig gold out of riverbeds. "And what do you know? There were other Ezo who came into town with Tekare's husband. If he didn't do it, one of them could have."

And they included Chieftain Awetok, whom Hirata had marked as the man who could lead him to his enlightenment. A man whom Hirata should not balk at incriminating if he must, to solve the crime and save Sano, Reiko, and his comrades.

Chapter Eleven

"If you're in there, come out!" Captain Okimoto banged his gloved fist against the door of the stable.

"Keep your voice down," Sano said angrily. "Shouting like that will only scare her off." He called, "Reiko-*san,* it's me."

The hunt for Reiko had gone on all day. Now the early winter dusk descended upon Fukuyama Castle. The western sky glowed with the cold orange flames of sunset, the trees and buildings black against them, the snowdrifts colored deep blue by the encroaching night. The temperature had dropped from cold to lethally cold. And still Reiko was missing.

Standing with his guards outside the stable, Sano heard other search parties crunching through the snow and calling to one another. Their lanterns flickered in the distance. Their desperation to capture Reiko vibrated the air like drumbeats. Earlier, Lord Matsumae had noticed his men rushing about the castle and demanded to know what was going on. He'd forced them to admit that one of his prisoners had escaped, then he'd announced that if she wasn't found by dark, he would pick a soldier at random and burn out his eyes with a hot poker. Sano feared that if Lord Matsumae made good on his threat, the friends of the unlucky scapegoat would take out their anger on Reiko when they found her.

If she didn't freeze to death first.

Okimoto flung open the stable door and stalked inside. His two comrades followed, pushing Sano in front of them, holding up their lanterns. Horses neighed in the stalls. The smell of manure filled air warmed by coal braziers. Okimoto hurried along the stalls, opening them and looking inside, as if Reiko were stupid enough to hide behind a horse that could trample her, as if they hadn't already searched the whole castle.

The guards at the gates swore that Reiko hadn't gotten out, and the walls were too high for her to climb. She must be still inside, running from one hiding place to the next, a few steps ahead of her pursuers. Sano could feel her fright even though he couldn't see her.

At the end of the stable stood a huge pile of hay. Okimoto drew his sword and began hacking at the hay, shouting, "Come out from under there! You can't hide!" His men joined in. "I'm going to get you!"

"Stop!" Sano yelled, horrified because if Reiko was under the hay, they would stab her. They were all so young, so cruel in their thoughtlessness.

He grabbed Okimoto, restraining his arm that wielded the sword. The other guards fell upon Sano. In the tussle, one dropped his lantern. It set fire to the hay. Flames leaped, crackled, and spread.

"Fire!" cried Okimoto as smoke filled the stables. The horses whinnied, reared, and pounded their hooves on the doors of their stalls. "Put it out!"

As he and his men stamped on the flames, they forgot to watch Sano. Sano knew that if Reiko were hiding in the stable, she would have come out by now rather than risk burning to death. She wasn't here. Sano slipped out the door.

The sky had faded to dull copper along the horizon. Stars and a crescent moon winked in the onrushing ultramarine night. Sano heard barking, excited and bloodthirsty. They'd set the dogs after Reiko. He plunged across the snow, away from his guards. Ahead loomed a group of outbuildings. Sano didn't see any lights there; other searchers must have already tried them. Maybe Reiko had slipped inside after they'd gone. He trudged down an icy path between two storehouses. Their doors were open, revealing straw bales of rice stacked on pallets.

"Reiko-*san*?" he called.

Snow crunched under stealthy footsteps behind him.

He whirled and saw a blur of motion down the path, in the gap between the storehouses. At the same instant his mind registered a human figure hurling an object, something struck him. Sano cried out as pain jabbed between his shoulder and elbow. Stumbling, he skidded on the ice and fell. He grasped the place that hurt. A knife protruded from it. The blade had cut through his heavy coat and pierced his flesh. If he hadn't turned, it would have struck him in the back and killed him.

Sano yanked out the knife. Even as he grunted in pain and felt warm, slick blood pour down his skin under his sleeve, he lurched to his feet, yelling, "Stop!" Brandishing the knife, he ran after his attacker.

But complete darkness had fallen in the last several moments. Lights flashing from distant lanterns illuminated dark buildings and empty snow. There was no sign of whoever had thrown the knife. From all around, Sano heard footsteps beating the snow, men yelling, dogs barking. The assassin had blended in with the search parties.

"There he is!" said a familiar voice.

Captain Okimoto and his two friends surrounded Sano. Their relief turned to alarm as they saw the knife in his hand. "Hey!" Okimoto exclaimed. "Put that down!"

The guards drew their swords. Sano said, "Wait. Let me explain."

"You were running away," Okimoto accused.

"I was running after an assassin. He threw this at me." Sano held up the knife.

That provoked yells and sword-waving from the guards. "Put it down, put it down!" Okimoto screamed.

Sano dropped the knife. The guards pounced on it, dug it out of the snow. "There's blood on it," one of them said. "He's already killed somebody."

"That's my blood," Sano said, his hand clasped over the wound. "I was hit."

Suspicious and wary, the guards shone their lanterns on him. The blood had soaked through his coat, staining it red. "I guess you were," Okimoto said, surprised. "Who did it?"

"I don't know. I didn't get a good look. He's gone."

"We'll take you to the physician," Okimoto said. "Lord Matsumae doesn't need to know about this, but he probably wouldn't want you to bleed to death."

"No," Sano said, even though his arm was sore and throbbing and he was afraid he'd already lost a lot of blood. "I have to find my wife."

"Forget it! Shut up!"

In the physician's chamber, Sano eased his injured arm out of his kimono. It was covered in blood. The physician, an old man dressed in the dark blue coat of his profession, peered at Sano's wound. He soaked a cloth in warm water and bathed off the blood that still oozed from the cut.

"How bad is it?" Gizaemon asked. He and the men with him seemed less concerned about Sano's fate than worried about how it would affect their own.

"Not too deep," the physician said. "The honorable chamberlain was fortunate. His coat protected him. The wound should heal perfectly."

Sano was relieved that his sword arm wouldn't suffer permanent damage.

"But it needs to be sewn up." The physician threaded a horse-tail hair through a long, sharp steel needle.

The sight opened a pit of dread in Sano's stomach. "Fine. Do it," he said, trying to act as though he didn't care.

"This must be the work of an intruder who broke into the castle." Gizaemon turned a fierce stare on Captain Okimoto and the other two guards.

"No one got past us, I swear," Okimoto protested.

"How would you know?" Sano said. "You were too busy setting the stable on fire to notice a whole army of invading assassins."

"Go search the whole castle," Gizaemon told the men.

After they'd left, Sano said, "I doubt they'll find any outsiders. I don't think I was attacked by one."

"Then who did attack you?" Gizaemon said. "And why?"

Sano couldn't answer the first question, but he had a hunch about the second. "Maybe because of my investigation."

The physician produced a ceramic jar of brownish green jelly, which he dabbed around Sano's cut. It smelled a little like mint, but acrid and bitter.

"What's that?" Sano asked suspiciously.

"Native balm," the physician said. "To dull the pain."

Sano said to Gizaemon, "My guess is that whoever threw the knife at me doesn't want me to find out who murdered Tekare, and tried to kill me because he's afraid I'm getting too close to the truth."

Gizaemon's squinty eyes narrowed further at Sano. "Are you getting close? What have you learned?"

"That the Ezo could have killed Tekare."

"Well, that's what I told you. But then some people have to figure things out for themselves. I'll tell Lord Matsumae. He'll be eager to get his hands on those bastards."

The needle pierced Sano's skin. It didn't hurt as much as he'd expected, maybe due to the balm, but he had to steel himself against the pain. "Wait," he said, alarmed by Gizaemon's premature rush to judgment. "The Ezo had the opportunity to set the spring-bow, but that doesn't mean they did. When I spoke to them, I wasn't convinced they're guilty. And now there's a good indication they're not."

"Oh? What?"

In and out went the needle. The thread tugged Sano's flesh with every stitch. Sano couldn't look. "If it was the killer who attacked me, that clears the Ezo." Sano drew deep, controlled breaths, fighting the waves of faintness that washed over him. "They weren't in the castle at the time. You sent them back to their camp. If my theory is correct, then they weren't involved in Tekare's murder."

"Then who was?"

Sano heard skepticism in Gizaemon's voice. His body

flinched involuntarily as the physician sewed. "I'll need to question all the Matsumae retainers who were in the castle when I was attacked."

"Our retainers?" Gizaemon scowled, both puzzled and offended. "You think one of them threw the knife?"

"They knew I was out there. Any one of them could have followed me."

The physician knotted the thread and snipped it with a razor. He bound Sano's arm with a white cotton bandage, then left. Sano stifled a groan of relief.

"You're saying that one of our retainers killed Tekare?" Gizaemon looked dismayed at the suggestion. "But how could they do that to Lord Matsumae? And why?"

"Those are good questions for them." Sano paused, then said, "Also for you."

The moment had come for the confrontation that they'd been moving toward all day. As their gazes locked, Sano felt the antagonism between him and Gizaemon turn as sharp as the needle that had stitched his wound.

"You think I did it." Gizaemon's tone made the phrase half question, half statement.

"Evidence against you keeps cropping up," Sano said. "You hate the Ezo; that includes Tekare. You know all about spring-bows and native poisons."

"So do most of the men in Ezogashima. And so what if I hate the barbarians? So do plenty other Japanese."

"You're constantly pointing the finger at the Ezo. What better reason than to divert me from you?"

"For your own good!" Gizaemon seemed exasperated by what he considered Sano's foolishness. "And for the sake of my nephew. I'm trying to help you solve the crime, so that he'll get well."

After ten years as a detective, Sano knew better than to accept at face value even such a logical explanation from a suspect. "Where were you when I was attacked?"

"Searching for your wife in the servants' quarters. Which are across the castle grounds from where you were."

"Was anyone with you?"

Instead of answering, Gizaemon picked up the knife from a table and examined it. The blade was about as long as his hand, attached to a short, smooth wooden handle. He turned it over, looked for markings, and said, "No identification on this. It's not mine, and you can't prove it is."

"I doubt that you'd have used a weapon marked with your name."

Gizaemon jammed a toothpick into his mouth. "I'm starting to wonder if there really was an attack on you. The troops told me they got there after it happened. We have only your word that it did."

"Then how do you explain this?" Angry at being accused of lying, and at having the interrogation turned on him, Sano pointed to his wound.

"You could have done that to yourself. Wasn't a fatal cut, was it? And you could have found that knife lying around someplace."

"Why would I cut myself?" Sano said, on the defensive and more vexed than ever.

"So you could accuse me of murdering Tekare and make it look like I tried to kill you to keep you from finding out," Gizaemon said. "But I didn't kill Tekare. I didn't attack you. And I don't have to take any more accusations from you." He called to guards outside the room: "Take Chamberlain Sano back to his quarters." Then he bowed, insolently courteous, said "Good night," and walked out the door.

Sano didn't miss the fact that Gizaemon had not named a witness to furnish him an alibi for the attack on Sano.

Chapter Twelve

"What happened to you?" Hirata asked when the guards brought Sano back to the guest quarters.

As Sano explained, they huddled around the charcoal braziers with detectives Marume and Fukida and the Rat. The room grew colder with the deepening night; icy drafts puffed the mats that covered the walls. More concerned about Reiko than himself, Sano said, "Is there any news about my wife?"

"I'm sorry to say she's still missing," Hirata said.

A sense of helplessness threatened to drag Sano into a black whirlpool of despair. He hoped that at least the murder investigation had made progress. "Did you question the gold merchant?"

"Yes," Hirata said. "You'll be happy to know that he's quite a good suspect."

"What did you find out from him?"

"For a start, he had plenty of reason to kill Tekare. He admits he was angry at her because she left him for Lord Matsumae. Then his alibi for the night of the murder is weak." Hirata explained: "Even if it's true that he was at home when Tekare died, he could have set up the spring-bow in advance. Besides, he's an odd character with a taste for death." Hirata described the trophies Daigoro had collected. "Maybe Tekare was his latest."

This sounded promising to Sano, but he spotted a problem. "Exactly when did you talk to the gold merchant?"

"A couple of hours ago."

Sano told Hirata and the other men his theory about the attack on him. "If Daigoro was with you then, he couldn't have sneaked into the castle and attacked me."

"Daigoro needn't have thrown the knife himself," Hirata said. "He admits having spies inside the castle. I suspect that some Matsumae retainers owe him money, and they repay him with information. And maybe other services, like getting rid of the man who's investigating a murder that he committed."

"My assassination ought to be a big enough service to get any debt excused." Sano saw the arrow of suspicion point away from Lord Matsumae's uncle to his troops, who'd had as good an opportunity to kill him.

"That's not all I learned," Hirata said. "According to the gold merchant, Tekare wasn't exactly the most popular woman around." He described her ambitions, how she'd used and discarded men, created jealousy among both the Japanese and the Ezo, and fomented trouble everywhere. "Not that I would believe everything that comes out of Daigoro's mouth, but this could explain why someone wanted Tekare dead."

Sano pondered the new information about the murder victim. " 'The Empress of Snow Country.' I wonder how she got to be a shamaness. If she really was a universal troublemaker, then she'd have made enemies in the castle."

"Maybe she played the same game with Lord Matsumae's retainers as she did with the miners, fishermen, and traders," Fukida said.

"If she did, they wouldn't have needed Daigoro the gold merchant's orders to kill her," Sano said.

"How many Matsumae retainers live in or near Fukuyama Castle?" Hirata asked.

"Too many," Sano said as he saw the pool of potential suspects expand.

"We'll have to interrogate them all," Hirata said.

"Which won't be easy while they're our jailers." Sano wondered how long the investigation would last. Would he solve the crime before Lord Matsumae's patience gave way to his madness?

Servants brought dinner, and the men dug in with hearty appetites. "This isn't bad," Marume said. "What is it?"

"Lily root dumplings," the Rat said as he gobbled his meal. "Salmon stew made with ferns, garlic, and butterbur. Wine brewed from millet. Traditional Ezo food. Even the highest-ranking Japanese here have to eat it at least some of the time, or starve. There's not enough Japanese food."

Sano ate to keep up his strength, but he wasn't hungry. Another day was ending, and he had yet to find his son. Another night stretched before him, long and cold. And where was Reiko?

He heard the exterior door open down the passage, the guards' voices, and a scuffle along the corridor. Okimoto marched Reiko into the room. Relief gladdened Sano, but her appearance shocked him. She wore a fur-lined deerskin coat, mittens, and boots that were too big for her. She was streaked with black grime, her hair disheveled, her eyes wild.

"We found her hiding in the coal shed," Okimoto said. "Keep her in here from now on, I'm warning you."

He shoved Reiko at Sano, then left. Sano gathered Reiko into his arms. She was shuddering with cold and fright. He seated her by a brazier, put a bowl of hot wine in her hands. They trembled so much that he had to help her drink. He wiped her soot-stained cheeks with a napkin. Gradually the wine warmed the color back into them.

"Where have you been?" Detective Marume asked.

"We were so worried about you," Fukida said.

"I went looking for Masahiro," she said, her teeth chattering.

That didn't surprise Sano; but just the same, he was upset. "You shouldn't have gone. Lord Matsumae threatened to blind his men if they didn't capture you. They were so afraid of him that they went berserk. They might have killed you by accident."

Reiko spoke over his words, which she seemed not to hear. "I found out what happened to Masahiro." She poured out a disjointed tale of how their son had arrived in Fukuyama City and Lord Matsumae's troops had put his escorts to death. "The maid saw. But the Ezo concubine says he's alive, in the keep."

Sano was amazed that Reiko had apparently managed to locate their son. Even after nine years of marriage, her daring, her abilities, and her luck never failed to surprise Sano. And praise the gods, Masahiro was alive!

"But I couldn't get to him," Reiko said, her voice breaking. "There are guards at the keep. And then they started chasing me." Eyes fever-bright, she tugged at Sano. "We have to go to Masahiro. Can't you get us out of here?"

Sano himself was frantic to rescue their son now that he knew, at long last, where and how close Masahiro was. He wanted to fight his way to the keep with his bare hands. Instead he told Reiko how little freedom he had and explained the situation with Lord Matsumae. "One step out of line could push him over the edge. He could kill us all. And Masahiro would be an orphan alone in this hell."

Reiko nodded unhappily; she knew he spoke the truth.

"The best thing to do is solve the crime," Sano said. "Maybe then Lord Matsumae will come to his senses—or the spirit of Tekare will leave him, whatever the case may be—and he'll set us all free, including Masahiro. Then we can all go home."

Reiko didn't ask when that might be; nor did she protest. She sat perfectly still, her knuckles pressed against her mouth, her eyes unfocused. Sano could feel her desperation and her struggle to contain it so that it wouldn't burden him. Embarrassed in the presence of her grief, the other men slipped out of the room, leaving Sano and Reiko alone. He could see how close she was to breaking. He had to give her some hope, and something else to concentrate on besides the thought of their son a prisoner, unreachable, and in who knew what condition.

"Reiko-*san,* listen," he said.

Dropping her hands, she turned on him a gaze so brimful of pain that he could barely stand to meet it.

"The faster I solve the crime, the sooner everything will be all right," Sano said. "I need your help."

"Help?" Reiko's one word conveyed that she had none to give, and bewilderment that Sano should expect her to care about the investigation at a time like this.

"Yes," Sano said. "You've always helped me with investigations. Do you remember when we were first married? And our wedding was disrupted by the murder of the shogun's favorite concubine?"

Reiko stared as if she'd forgotten because her present-day woes had blotted out happy memories from the past.

"You wanted to help me find out who the killer was. I said no, because I didn't think it was a woman's place to investigate murders and you wouldn't be any use." Sano smiled, his heart warmed by the thought of a younger, willful, passionate Reiko. "Well, little did I know. You proved I was wrong."

Did a ghost of a smile alter Reiko's tragic expression? Encouraged by this real or imagined sign that he was reaching her, he said, "Without you, I wouldn't have solved that case, or the others that followed. No matter the trouble or the danger, you were always brave, always ready to go anywhere and do anything. I could always count on you."

Sano took her hands in his. They were clenched into fists, all hard, cold bone. "Can I count on you now?"

Reiko averted her gaze. Sano could feel in her exactly what he'd felt when he'd thought Lord Matsumae had killed his son—the temptation to give up, the lack of the strength to cope anymore. But he also felt the stubborn spirit in Reiko that refused to be beaten down. After a long moment passed, she said, "What do you want me to do?"

Relief broke through Sano. "Before you came in, Hirata and I were discussing what we've learned about the murder so far." He summarized it for Reiko. "It appears that Tekare had many enemies. Some could be right here inside the castle. And there's a group of possibilities that you should have better luck investigating than I would."

Reiko lifted her eyes to him. He was gratified to see a glimmer of interest in them. "The women?"

"Yes," Sano said. "They would have known Tekare, and they'll probably be more willing to talk to you than to me."

This was Reiko's strength as a detective: the ability to get close to the women associated with crimes and elicit the most private facts from them. She said, "I already know that the Japanese ladies hate Ezo concubines. And maybe the Ezo concubines didn't get along with one another." Her natural curiosity revived. "If one of those women killed Tekare, I'm going to find out."

"Good," Sano said, knowing what a monumental effort she was making for his sake and their son's.

"But how will I talk to them if I'm locked in here?"

That seemed a minor obstacle compared to others they'd already surmounted. Sano said, "I'll find you a way tomorrow."

Chapter Thirteen

Morning dawned gray and quiet. The air was warmer, its sharp edge blunted by the clouds massed over Fukuyama City. As Sano, Hirata, the detectives, and Gizaemon headed across the castle grounds, smoke from the chimneys dissolved into heavens the same color. The muted light rendered trees and buildings in stark monotones. The snow looked dull and soft, without brilliance or shadow. Sano could smell more coming, its scent like dust, ready to chill, oppress, and conceal.

"How's the arm?" Gizaemon asked Sano.

"Better," Sano said, although it ached and the stitches burned. "How is Lord Matsumae?"

"Worse." Gizaemon's rough features were etched with concern. "Bad idea to bother him now. Advise you to wait."

"That's not possible." The investigation must continue. Everything depended on it. Every step of it required approval from Lord Matsumae, and Sano wasn't going to tolerate obstruction from Gizaemon, a suspect.

Gizaemon shrugged. "Your funeral."

Opening a gate, he ushered them into a forest preserve. Through the evergreen foliage and bare branches Sano saw a tall, square, half-timbered building. Piercing shrieks came from it.

"Lord Matsumae is inspecting his hawks. This is where he keeps them," Gizaemon said.

He led Sano and Hirata inside the building. The shrieks blared at Sano. He saw some thirty birds of prey tethered to perches, enormous eagles and smaller hawks and falcons. Some screamed incessantly, their curved beaks opening and closing, their wild eyes glaring. Others wore leather hoods over their heads; they sat still and quiet. Huge wings flapped, stirring air laden with the pungent chicken-coop smell of bird dung and the stench of decayed meat.

Lord Matsumae stood in the center of the room, berating three samurai. "These mews are filthy. You've been neglecting my precious hawks."

The men mumbled apologies. Gizaemon said close to Sano's ear, "The keepers have been busy guarding the ports, as he ordered them to do. This is the first attention he's paid his hawks since that woman was murdered."

"You two clean this place up at once," Lord Matsumae said, pointing at the men. He was as untidy as the mews, his whiskers growing into a straggly beard, his hair long and uncombed; he wore a tattered fur coat and muddy, scuffed leather boots. "And you help me inspect the hawks."

The two samurai began sweeping up dung, feathers, and castings. The other trailed Lord Matsumae, who headed toward Sano. "What do you want?" Lord Matsumae asked.

Sano was disturbed to see two pinpoints of light in each of his eyes, one from his own soul, the other from the spirit that possessed him. "To tell you my plans for today."

"Very well," Lord Matsumae said with an agreeability that Sano didn't trust. "We can talk while I inspect my hawks."

The keeper flung a heavy cloth over a sleek gray falcon and lifted her off her perch. She snapped at Lord Matsumae as he examined her talons, beak, eyes, and plumage.

"Clean these talons," he said. "Fix these broken feathers. She's my gift to the shogun. She has to be perfect."

He seemed to have forgotten that he was in trouble for neglecting to send the shogun any gifts. Sano could feel Tekare's watchful, menacing presence in him. The keeper put the falcon back on her perch. Lord Matsumae tossed the bird a mouse from a bucket full of dead rodents. She gulped it down.

"I'd like Hirata-*san* to interview the Ezo again," Sano

said. "We ask your permission for him to go to their camp this morning."

Gizaemon said, under his breath, "Finally someone's looking for the killer in the right place."

"Permission granted," Lord Matsumae said as he and the keeper grappled with another hawk that struggled under the cloth and screamed. But he immediately spoke again, in Tekare's accented voice, sharp with suspicion: "Why would you let him go after my people?"

He replied in his own voice, "They might have killed you."

"So might your people have. Would you let them get away with my murder?"

"No, my beloved." Lord Matsumae's manner alternated between masculine and feminine. "I just want to be sure not to miss anything."

Sano listened, appalled. Now Lord Matsumae was not only speaking in Tekare's tongue, he was carrying on a conversation with her spirit, which had gained a stronger hold on him.

Gizaemon whispered, "I warned you." He ordered three guards to take Hirata to the camp and said, "He causes any trouble, you'll be posted to the far north."

"Take Marume and the Rat with you," Sano said to Hirata.

Hirata went off with his escorts. Sano said, "Lord Matsumae, I would like permission for my wife to visit yours."

"I advise against that," Gizaemon said.

"Oh?" Lord Matsumae scraped dirt off a hawk's talons with a knife. "Why?"

"Lady Reiko might try to run away again. She should be confined to her quarters, where we can watch her."

"She's promised me that she'll behave herself," Sano said.

"It's still not a good idea," Gizaemon said. "Lady Matsumae is in mourning. She won't want to be bothered with entertaining a guest."

His concern for Lady Matsumae seemed to Sano more an excuse to keep her and Reiko apart than motivated by genuine sympathy for the bereaved woman. "Perhaps my wife's company would cheer up Lady Matsumae," Sano said.

"I think not," Gizaemon said. "Better forbid this visit, Honorable Nephew."

Sano wondered whether Gizaemon had guessed that Reiko was working with him on the murder investigation and intended to pump Lady Matsumae for evidence. Sano's suspicions toward Gizaemon increased.

"What do you think, my beloved?" Lord Matsumae said. He replied in Tekare's voice, "I think it's a good idea," then said in his own voice, "I'll grant permission for Lady Reiko to visit my wife."

Now Sano wondered if he—or Tekare—suspected that Lady Matsumae had been involved in the murder.

Intent on the falcon he was examining, Lord Matsumae gave no sign that Sano could see. "Just make sure the guards stay near her at all times, Uncle."

"As you wish." Gizaemon's dark look said how much he hated being overruled by a ghost although not by his nephew.

The birds were calmer now. Only the largest, a magnificent eagle with gold plumage, still shrieked. Lord Matsumae slipped a gauntlet on his left hand and whistled. With a great flap of wings, the eagle leaped onto his fist. He rewarded the eagle with a dead mouse. Sano thought how barbaric seemed the ancient sport of falconry. Since Buddhism had taken root in Japan some eleven centuries ago, hunting had fallen into disfavor because Buddhist doctrine forbade eating meat. Most samurai kept falcons as a mere bow to tradition. But Ezogashima was a world apart from mainstream Japanese society. Here, blood sport flourished. But Sano was more interested in a different kind of hunt: the search for a killer.

"What else are you going to do?" Lord Matsumae asked.

"Detective Fukida and I will examine the scene of the murder," Sano said.

"That's a waste of time," Gizaemon scoffed. "There's nothing left to see."

"I still need to have a look." Sano wondered what Gizaemon didn't want him to find.

"That's fine with me." Lord Matsumae unfastened the tether that tied the eagle to its perch. "And me," echoed Tekare's voice. He cast the bird off his fist. It flew in circles while the other birds shrieked and flapped as if envious of its freedom. "Anything else?"

"I have a request from the Ezo," Sano said. "They ask permission to hold a funeral for Tekare."

"A funeral? To bury her in the ground?" Lord Matsumae exclaimed in horror. "You want to take her away from me!" He clutched his arms as if embracing his dead mistress in them. "Her remains are all I have left of her. How can you ask me to give them up?"

"The Ezo say a funeral will help her cross over to the spirit world," Sano said. "She'll stop haunting you."

"But I don't want her to cross over. I don't want her to leave me!"

Lord Matsumae waved his arms. One struck the eagle as it flew by him. Confused or frightened, it screeched and flew straight at Sano.

"Look out!" Detective Fukida said.

The eagle came so near Sano that he could see the luminous flecks in its golden eyes. Ducking, he felt wings brush his head. Lord Matsumae guffawed and cackled. Sano dodged the eagle as it dived repeatedly at him while the other falcons set up a din of screeches. Fukida ran after the bird and yelled. It swooped toward him, then Sano again. Hands raised up to protect himself from its talons, Sano said, "A funeral could reveal the truth about Tekare's murder."

"Nonsense," Lord Matsumae began, then said in Tekare's voice, "Wait, my lord. He may be right."

"But I don't want you to go to the spirit world, my beloved. I don't want you to leave me."

"I won't. A funeral can't take me away. I want to know who killed me."

Clasping his hands, Lord Matsumae beseeched the empty air around him: "Do you promise?"

"I promise. Now let the honorable chamberlain live so he can finish what he's started."

"All right, my beloved."

Lord Matsumae held up a scrap of meat and whistled. The eagle alighted on his fist. It gulped the meat and folded its wings. Sano was relieved and amazed that he'd been saved by a ghost.

"The funeral will be held tomorrow morning," Lord Matsumae decided. "In the meantime, Chamberlain Sano will continue his investigation. Take him to the scene of the murder, Uncle."

Gizaemon scowled, unhappy to be overruled yet again. "All right, Chamberlain Sano." *You win this time,* said his tone. "Let's get it over with."

The way to the murder scene lay out the back gate of the castle, down the hill through stands of trees, and along a trampled path that divided into a fork. One branch led farther downhill, toward town. The other led along a ridge edged by bare trees. Following Gizaemon onto this path, Sano could see the ocean, gray and dull like beaten steel.

"Not that I wouldn't like to get rid of that corpse in the teahouse, but you shouldn't have mentioned a funeral to my nephew," Gizaemon said. "That always sets him off."

"You could have told me," Sano said.

"Next time listen when I warn you to stay away from him."

The path inclined gently into forest that was thick enough to shut off all sight of Fukuyama City, and quiet except for an occasional bird's squawk. Sano could imagine himself in the wild heartland of Ezogashima instead of a short walk from civilization. "What was Tekare doing out here?"

"There's a hot spring up ahead." Gizaemon chewed a sassafras toothpick. Sano smelled acid as well as the spice in his breath. He must have indigestion and need the sassafras to calm his stomach. "Women in the castle like to bathe in it."

"They come all the way out here to take a bath?" Sano said, puzzled by what seemed a strange custom.

"Takes a long time to heat water in the winter. But there are springs all over Ezogashima, naturally full of hot water all year round. The women can come here whenever they want a bath. They don't have to wait for the tub to warm up. And the water has healing powers."

Glancing at the snow on the path, Sano saw his footprints and Gizaemon's overlap other, smaller ones. The spring got a lot of use even though it was a cold walk from the castle. He smelled its moisture and warmth, and a whiff of sulfur.

"Where was the spring-bow set?" Sano asked.

"Up there." Gizaemon stopped and pointed to a patch in the forest where broken stumps remained from trees that had fallen. It lay along a clear line of shot to the path.

"The trip-string was tied to that," Gizaemon said, indicating a pine beyond the path's opposite side.

Sano and Fukida examined the trunk of the pine. They moved on to the place where the murder weapon had stood. The snow there looked untouched, except for a few tiny animal tracks.

Gizaemon said, "I hope you're satisfied. I told you this was a waste of time."

Sano was disappointed nonetheless. He'd hoped for any clue that might help him solve the case. As they returned to the path and resumed walking, Fukida said, "Where is the spring-bow now?"

"Lord Matsumae hacked it apart with an axe and burned the pieces. He needed something to punish."

So much for examining the murder weapon for clues. Sano said, "Where was the body found?"

Gizaemon paced some twenty steps farther. Sano and Fukida marched alongside him, stopped when he did. Gizaemon grinned. "Right where you're standing."

Sano looked down and saw a mental image of the woman now enshrined in the tea cottage. Tekare lay, her black hair fanned out, against ground covered with pine needles and leaves. Her body was robust, youthful, and ripe instead of withered. Her face was smooth and beautiful instead of decayed. The blood from her wound gleamed red, newly spilled, dotting the path between her body and the place where she'd tripped the spring. The image was so vivid that Sano could feel the essence of the woman, passionate and tempestuous. He blinked. Her image disappeared. He was gazing at blank snow.

"That's where she fell," Gizaemon said. "She was strong, to get this far before the poison on the arrow killed her."

"Who found her?" Sano asked.

"You're talking to him," Gizaemon replied.

Now we're getting somewhere, Sano thought. "How did you happen to be the one to find Tekare?"

"That morning, Lord Matsumae wanted her company. She wasn't in the women's quarters. Her bed hadn't been slept in. We looked for her all over the castle, no sign of her. I led the search party that checked this path."

"Why was it your party that came out here?"

Gizaemon shrugged. "Just lucky, I guess."

But the person who discovered the body often turned out to be the murderer. Maybe Gizaemon had known where to find Tekare because he'd set the spring-bow for her. Maybe he'd wanted to be first on the scene to see if his trap had worked. If he was the killer, that would explain why he wanted to prevent Sano—or Reiko—from finding evidence. But if he wasn't, then he was an important witness.

"Tell me what you saw when you found Tekare," Sano said.

"The spring-bow, the loose string." Gizaemon pointed at the places he'd seen them. "The arrow lying on the ground where she left it after she pulled it out of herself. A trail of blood leading to her body."

"Was there anyone around?"

"Not that I saw." Gizaemon regarded Sano with disdain. "The killer could have set the trap at any time before she came along the path. That's the advantage of the spring-bow. You don't need to be there to bring down your prey."

"Some killers like seeing their victims die," Sano said.

"Well, if that was the case, he could have watched and been long gone by the time I came," Gizaemon said. "Tekare's body was cold and stiff. She'd been dead since the night before."

The circumstances of the murder troubled Sano. "You indicated that other women besides Tekare used this spring?"

"That's right."

"Then the trap could have been set for someone else."

"Maybe," Gizaemon said, "except that she liked to come here at night. But even if she wasn't the person meant to die, what does it matter? You still have to find out who killed her."

"True," Sano said, but it did matter. If Tekare hadn't been the intended victim, then he'd wasted yesterday on inquiries related to her. If a different woman was the killer's actual target, there were motives, suspects, and clues he had yet to discover. Even worse, what if the killer hadn't had a particular victim in mind? What if he was like a hunter who didn't care which deer he bagged as long as he got one? How could logical detective work solve such a random crime?

But Sano thought it best to proceed under the theory that Tekare had been the intended victim, unless he found out otherwise. With all the enmity and strong passions Tekare had inspired, she seemed the perfect target for murder.

And the man beside Sano seemed a perfect suspect. "How did you know that Tekare liked to bathe in the hot spring at night?"

"General knowledge."

"But maybe you knew Tekare's habits because you watched her. Followed her. Stalked her like game in the forest."

"After me again, are you?" Gizaemon said, irritated. "I told you I didn't kill Tekare. But if you're so good at making up theories, explain this: Why would I kill the woman Lord Matsumae loved? He's the most important person in the world to me." His expression filled with proud, fierce tenderness. "How could I hurt him?"

Sano didn't have an answer. That was the biggest weakness in his case against Gizaemon.

Gizaemon laughed. "I thought so. Maybe now you'll

believe me when I tell you that it was an Ezo who killed Tekare."

"If I believe you, that would give you more than an excuse to subjugate the natives and take over Ezogashima."

Gizaemon ignored Sano's hint that he was guilty and diverting the blame for the murder onto innocent people in order to avoid punishment himself. "They're a shifty, dishonorable people. The opposite of samurai." Fukida rolled his eyes at Sano: They'd met too many samurai who were a disgrace to the Way of the Warrior. "And they don't respect Japanese law. One of theirs misbehaves, they take care of the problem in their own fashion. That rule applied to Tekare."

"The Empress of Snow Country?" Sano said. "The wife who sold her favors to men in exchange for gifts, then left her husband to come to the city as a mistress to Japanese men?"

Sardonic humor wrinkled the leathery skin around Gizaemon's eyes. "I see that Hirata-*san* got an earful from the gold merchant. You should listen, Honorable Chamberlain. It'll lead you to her killer."

"Urahenka?" Sano said, recalling the young Ezo's passionate claim that he'd loved his wife, wanted her back, and had come to Fukuyama City to rescue her. His angry denial that he'd murdered her had seemed more credible yesterday, before the gold merchant had shown Tekare in a bad light.

"Not him. He doesn't have the authority to act on his own. The chieftain's the one I mean."

"Why would he have killed Tekare? She was the village shamaness. He wanted to bring her home for the good of the tribe."

"If you believe him, then I'll sell you the hot spring to take back to Edo." Gizaemon turned and stalked down the path the way they'd come. "No, he wanted to punish her."

"Punish her for what?" As Sano kept pace with Gizaemon, he felt lost in this land of unfamiliar customs.

"For everything she did wrong. The Ezo believe that the shamaness keeps the village in balance with the cosmos. If she's a good girl, fortune will smile upon them. If not, the spirits will send them sickness, famine, and death. Tekare had upset the natural order. The only way for the Ezo to restore it was to destroy her. And that was the chieftain's duty."

Sano frowned. Chieftain Awetok had impressed him as straightforward and honest, but maybe Sano was misjudging the man due to his ignorance about the Ezo. Maybe he was viewing them as savages who didn't have motives or relationships as complicated as Japanese had. Maybe he was too ready to think them incapable of subterfuge. Were they hiding secrets behind the barrier of cultural differences? Understanding the Ezo might be critical to solving the crime, but Sano understood his fellow Japanese very well. Gizaemon behaved like a decoy soldier planting false tracks for enemy troops to follow.

"You said Tekare upset the natural order. Did she do that here? Did she cause trouble for you?" Sano said.

Gizaemon snorted as they walked down the path. He seemed to imply that a mere Ezo woman was too trivial to bother him. "She didn't know her place in the world. But that wasn't my business. She was the barbarians' problem. And their chieftain dealt with her."

Trying to pin Gizaemon down was like trying to nail an eel to a board while it slithered repeatedly out of one's grasp. Sano said, "You seem to know a lot about the Ezo."

"I should. I've spent most of my life in their territory."

"That would include knowing how to use Ezo weapons," Sano said, "like the spring-bow."

Gizaemon halted at the spot where the string had been stretched across the path. Exasperation colored his tough face. "For the last time, I didn't kill that woman. For your own good, you'd better stop trying to pin her murder on me. When Lord Matsumae gets tired of waiting for you to solve the crime and puts you to death, don't say I didn't warn you."

Refusing to be intimidated or sidetracked, Sano said, "Where were you the day Tekare died, before she sprang the trap?"

"Nowhere near it. You won't be able to prove I was."

"Have you ever used a spring-bow?"

Gizaemon's manner turned condescending. "If you want to know about the spring-bow, let me explain something to you. There's no trick to using a spring-bow. That's the whole point of it. You don't have to be a good shot. You just set it up, aim it in the right direction, and tie the string. You walk away and wait. Then—"

His fist socked his palm. "Anyone with a little strength and the slightest intelligence can score a hit. Even a woman."

Chapter Fourteen

At the entrance to Lady Matsumae's chambers, the guard said to Reiko, "We'll be waiting right here. Don't try anything."

Reiko bowed her head meekly even though rebellion seethed in her. If she wanted to find Masahiro, she must lull the guards into trusting her, the better to escape again later.

Inside the chamber she found Lady Matsumae, her attendants, and the maid Lilac. Lady Matsumae knelt at a table spread with sheets of paper, a writing brush in her hand. The attendants mixed and poured out ink for her. Their actions had the solemn air of a religious ritual. Lilac fanned the coals in a brazier. She gave Reiko a furtive smile. The other women bowed politely.

"Good morning," Lady Matsumae said.

The few syllables conveyed that she was anything but happy to see Reiko again. Reiko saw that if she wanted information from Lady Matsumae, she had serious amends to make.

Kneeling and bowing, Reiko said, "I'm sorry about your daughter. I shouldn't have spoken so insensitively yesterday. Please accept my condolences."

"They are much appreciated." Lady Matsumae seemed to relent a little. "It was wrong of me to treat an honored guest so discourteously. Please forgive me."

In spite of this apology, Reiko felt a new aversion to Lady Matsumae. Now that she knew Lady Matsumae had lost a child, she didn't want to be near the woman. She had an irrational yet potent fear that Lady Matsumae's bad luck would rub off on herself. But she mustn't let Lady Matsumae sense her feelings.

"There's nothing to forgive," Reiko said, forcing compassion into her tone. "I understand."

"My daughter was my only child." Lady Matsumae inked her brush and drew lines on a page—practicing calligraphy, Reiko assumed. "She was only eight years old when she died."

Reiko sympathized with her need to speak of her daughter, but she didn't want to listen because she felt a terrible kinship with Lady Matsumae. There wasn't enough distance between a woman whose child was missing and a woman who'd lost hers forever. Reiko could imagine herself speaking similar words: *Masahiro was my only son. He was only eight years old when he died.*

Lady Matsumae was watching Reiko, awaiting some response. Reiko had a nightmarish idea that their positions had reversed and it was she telling her story of tragedy to Lady Matsumae. She stammered, "May I ask your daughter's name?"

"Nobuko." Lady Matsumae lingered on the word as if it were a spell that could resurrect the dead.

"She was such a beautiful little girl," said one of the ladies-in-waiting.

Yesterday Reiko hadn't paid them much attention and they'd seemed identical. She'd forgotten their names, but now she noticed that they were in fact very different in appearance. The one who'd spoken was as slender as a bamboo rod, intelligent of expression, her movements precise as she ground more ink for Lady Matsumae.

"And so good and charming," twittered the lady who mixed the ink with water. She had a rounded figure and a sweet, vacuous face like a pansy.

"Nobuko was very accomplished," said the third. Sitting idle, nearest to Lady Matsumae, she had a strong, thick build and features. If she shaved her crown and wore a suit of armor, she could pass for a soldier. "She played the samisen, wrote poetry, and embroidered. Her honorable mother brought her up as well as any young lady in Edo."

"It was nothing," Lady Matsumae murmured as she set aside her finished calligraphy and started a fresh page. "She was just an ordinary girl."

Despite this obligatory disclaimer, she smiled, her spirits lifted by the praise. Then she saddened again. "The climate in Ezogashima is very harsh on children. Last winter Nobuko took ill. The fever and cough wouldn't go away. She lost all her appetite." Lady Matsumae frowned over her writing. "Even though the physician did his best to cure her, it was no use. Soon she was too weak to get out of bed."

Each spurt of pain Lady Matsumae vented stabbed a bleeding wound in Reiko's heart. *The political climate in Edo is very harsh on children. Last autumn, my husband's enemies kidnapped our son. We searched for him all over Japan, but it was no use.* Reiko wanted to clap her hand over Lady Matsumae's mouth to stop the flow of disaster-bearing contagion.

"When spring came," Lady Matsumae said, "Nobuko seemed to rally. The cough wasn't as bad. She ate; she grew stronger. But then—"

A long, peculiar hush fell upon Lady Matsumae. She trembled as if possessed by emotions that threatened to shatter her. She whispered, "I held Nobuko in my arms as her spirit passed from this world to the next. I said good-bye to her, and I prayed that we will be reunited when I die."

Her hand gripped the brush, which splattered ink droplets. Reiko felt as though it were her own blood staining the white paper. *I held Masahiro's body in my arms, but I was too late to say good-bye. His spirit had already passed from this world. May my death someday reunite us.* Reiko knew that thinking like this was bad luck, but she couldn't stop.

Lady Matsumae scrawled on page after page, writing with manic intensity, then said to Lilac, "I'm ready."

Lilac removed the iron grating from atop the brazier. Lady Matsumae picked up a page and dropped it in.

"You're burning your writing?" Reiko said, startled.

"It isn't writing."

Lady Matsumae held up the other pages for Reiko to see before feeding each one to the fire. They were rough, unskillfully drawn sketches—a kimono printed with flowers, a little house, a pair of sandals, a fan, and a baby doll. "Here are some things for you, my dearest," Lady Matsumae murmured. "Your mother loves you."

The fire curled and blackened the pages; smoke swirled heavenward. Lady Matsumae was following the age-old custom of sending gifts to the spirits of the dead. The elaborate miniature wooden models usually burned must not be available here. Reiko saw herself as an old woman, sending toy swords and horses to a son who'd never lived to grow up, whose death she'd never ceased mourning. She couldn't bear this conversation any longer. She had to change the subject, get the information she needed, then leave.

"There's something else I should beg your pardon for," she said. "Please excuse me for interfering between you and the Ezo woman yesterday." Although she didn't regret it, especially now that Wente was her friend, she pretended she did and said, "I'm sorry. I didn't understand."

Some of the initial hostility crept back into Lady Matsumae's expression. "And you think you do now?"

The temperature in the room seemed to drop below freezing. The ladies-in-waiting eyed Reiko with reproach. Lilac flashed Reiko a warning glance.

"Two days on Ezogashima, and already you are an expert," Lady Matsumae said disdainfully. "That's the same mistake outsiders always make. They believe they know about the ways of this place when they don't at all."

Her antagonism roused Reiko's own ire, like sparks from flint striking tinder. Lady Matsumae knew the pain of losing a child, yet wouldn't help another mother save hers. Dropping the social niceties, Reiko said, "What do you have against the Ezo concubines?"

"They're ugly and grotesque. Those horrible tattoos! And

they're dirty." Lady Matsumae scoured her brush with a sponge. "They smell."

"They carry diseases," said the lady-in-waiting that Reiko thought of as Lady Smart. "My husband got one from his Ezo concubine. He gave it to me. That's why I'm barren."

"They're sorceresses," said Lady Pansy. "They cast evil spells that—"

The mannish Lady Soldier cleared her throat. Lady Pansy shut her mouth at once. She sneaked a frightened glance at Lady Matsumae. Reiko understood that Lady Pansy had trespassed on another sensitive area. Communication in Ezogashima was as fraught with pitfalls as a pond covered with thin ice.

"Now that you're in Ezogashima, you'd better watch out," Lady Soldier told Reiko. "If your man lies with a native girl, you could give birth to a monster."

"That's all you need to know about the Ezo," Lady Matsumae said crisply. "My advice to you is to stay far away from them."

Reiko felt a kind of abhorrence toward these women that she'd never felt before. Their hatred of the Ezo seemed different from ordinary prejudice against Japanese people from lower classes. It was a blanket castigation of an entire race, based on dubious notions. Lady Matsumae's attitude didn't endear her to Reiko, particularly in view of the fact that an Ezo woman had helped Reiko while Lady Matsumae had refused.

Emboldened by anger, Reiko deliberately raised the issue that she figured was the most sensitive of all. "I heard that an Ezo woman was recently murdered," she said. "Who was she?"

The ladies-in-waiting sucked air through their pursed lips. Lilac waggled her eyebrows at Reiko and mouthed, *Not now!*

"Tekare." Lady Matsumae spat the name as if it were bile.

"Did you know her?" Reiko said.

"I could hardly not have known her." Lady Matsumae

worked so hard to remove the ink from her brush that she frayed its hairs. "She was my husband's mistress." Her voice was as frosty as the Ezogashima winter. "He gave Tekare chambers next to mine. He treated her as if she was his wife. She thought she was the lady of this castle instead of me!"

"She did whatever she pleased," Lady Pansy said, eager to weigh in on this interesting topic now that it had been broached. "She had parties in her room, with the other Ezo women, late at night. When Lady Matsumae told her the noise was keeping her awake, she just laughed."

"Lord Matsumae gave Tekare lots of things, but it wasn't enough for her," Lady Smart said. "She helped herself to Lady Matsumae's best clothes."

"There's a pavilion in the garden where Lady Matsumae likes to sit when the weather's nice," Lady Soldier said. "Tekare took it over for herself. When Lady Matsumae ordered her to move, she wouldn't."

"I scolded her. I told her she had to learn her place and show me some respect. I slapped her face. And she slapped me back!" Lady Matsumae touched her cheek as if she could still feel the blow. "The nerve of that witch!"

Her attendants murmured in disapproval. "Normally I handle problems in the women's quarters myself," she said, "but I was helpless against Tekare. So I went to my husband. I told him how badly she was treating me, but he took her side. He said no one was allowed to interfere with anything she wanted or anything she did. Then he beat me and threw me outside in the rain. He said I could stay there until I was ready to accept the way things were. He warned me that if I ever laid a hand on Tekare again, he would divorce me and send me back to my family in disgrace."

Lady Matsumae shuddered at this outrage. She laid down her brush and wrapped her arms around herself, as if to keep from falling apart. "Well, I spent three days outside. My husband never relented."

"Nobody was allowed to go near her," Lady Pansy said, "not even to give her food or a blanket."

"She caught such a bad cold and was so miserable that

she finally had to give in," Lady Smart said. "And from then on, Tekare ruled us all as if she were an empress."

The Empress of Snow Country. Reiko recalled Hirata's description of how Tekare had earned her nickname. Tekare had certainly fomented trouble in the women's quarters as well as among the men she'd used.

"What did you do?" Reiko asked Lady Matsumae.

With a bitter laugh, Lady Matsumae said, "What could I do? I put up with the situation. I had no choice."

"You'd think Tekare would have been satisfied because she'd won," Lady Pansy said, taking a coy delight in this gossip. "You'd think she would have left well enough alone. But not her. She ordered our poor lady to kneel and bow down to her whenever they happened to meet."

"And our lady had to do it or be cast out." Lady Smart's serious manner didn't hide her relish of the drama.

"My husband didn't care," Lady Matsumae said. "He didn't protect me. Not even after our daughter became ill and I was beside myself with worrying about her. Instead, he—"

Her throat visibly contracted as she swallowed. She lowered her eyelids; tears leaked from under her dark, spiky lashes. Her attendants sat in hushed sympathy. Reiko sensed secrets permeating the silence. She glanced at Lilac, who puffed her cheeks to express that she was bursting with tales but didn't dare speak.

"What happened?" Reiko asked.

Nobody answered. History on Ezogashima was as deep and opaque as the sea around it. Reiko decided to go fishing. She said in a quiet, confidential manner, "Your life must be easier now that Tekare is dead. She stole your husband's affections. If you took revenge on her, I wouldn't blame you. I'd admire you for having the courage to do what many women in your position only wish they could."

Lady Matsumae's head snapped up. She and the ladies-in-waiting stared at Reiko in apparently genuine shock. "You think I killed Tekare?"

"You can tell me." Reiko smiled a conspiratorial smile,

woman-to-woman against the world of men. "I can keep a secret."

"You haven't the slightest idea what you're talking about. I did not kill that woman, no matter how much I would have liked to." Lady Matsumae spat the words at Reiko's face. "You may be the chamberlain's wife and a guest in my house, but I am utterly insulted by your accusation."

Reiko was chagrined that her ploy had failed. She shouldn't have pushed Lady Matsumae so hard so fast.

"Of course she didn't kill her," Lady Smart declared.

"She's too gentle, too good," Lady Pansy said indignantly.

Lady Soldier folded her arms and fixed an insolent gaze on Reiko. "You seem to know a lot about our business, but maybe not as much as you think. Did you know that Tekare was shot with a spring-bow?"

"So I've heard," Reiko said.

"Who told you?" Lady Smart asked.

"My husband."

Comprehension flashed across Lady Smart's plain features. "I've heard about your husband's deal with Lord Matsumae. He finds out who killed Tekare, and Lord Matsumae will set him and you and your friends free. If he fails, you all die. You're trying to help him by putting the blame on our lady."

So much for covert detective work, Reiko thought. "We're only trying to discover the truth."

"The truth is that our lady is innocent," Lady Pansy said with staunch, childish loyalty.

Lady Soldier picked up Lady Matsumae's hands, peeled the gloves off them, and held them up. "Can you imagine these setting a spring-bow?" The fingers were tapered and soft, typical of a high-class woman who'd never done any physical work in her life.

An alternative had become clear to Reiko. "You wouldn't have had to do it yourself," she said to Lady Matsumae. She turned a significant gaze on the ladies-in-waiting. But instead of being frightened because her suspicion had turned to them, they smiled.

"Well, I suppose I know how to set a spring-bow," said Lady Smart. "My father is a trade official, and my family spent a lot of time in Ezo country while I was growing up."

"The same with me," Lady Soldier said.

"I knew that Tekare liked going to the hot spring at night," Lady Pansy simpered.

"We could have plotted to kill her," Lady Soldier said, "and punish her for hurting our lady. But even if we did, you'll never be able to prove it. And we'll never tell."

Her smug smile was reflected on the faces of her two friends. Lady Smart said, "I'm afraid this visit with us has been a waste of your time, Lady Reiko. You came after one person you thought might have killed Tekare. Instead, you found four of us. Are not too many suspects as bad as too few?"

Reiko experienced the same weird disorientation as when she'd first met the women. On the surface they were as familiar as any at home, but inside they were infected with savagery native to Ezogashima. Violence and murder were in their blood, under the veneer of civilization.

Lady Matsumae beheld Reiko with an expression of hard, humorless triumph. "I think it's time you left."

Chapter Fifteen

The sound of angry voices came from the Ezo camp as Hirata and his companions approached it. He and Detective Marume, the Rat, and their guards arrived to find the barbarians facing off against three Matsumae troops. The barbarians had bows and quivers slung over their shoulders; they wore snowshoes made of bent wood and leather straps. Two of their dogs were harnessed to a sled. Barbarians and troops shouted at one another in Ezo language.

"What are they saying?" Hirata asked.

The Rat looked especially miserable this morning. He sniffled and coughed. His eyes were bleary, and frozen mucus matted his whiskers. "The Ezo want to go deer hunting. The Japanese won't let them."

Hirata had never been hunting, even though the idea had always intrigued him. The Buddhist religion prohibited slaying animals as well as eating meat. So did Tokugawa law, upheld by the shogun, a devout Buddhist. But there were exceptions to law and tradition. People weakened by illness or injuries were given meat stews and broths to cure them. Edo had a flourishing wild game market for that purpose. Here in Ezogashima, the barbarians hunted in order to survive, and the Japanese usually allowed them—but not today.

"The Japanese say the barbarians have to stay in camp. Lord Matsumae's orders," said the Rat.

Urahenka, the onetime husband of Lord Matsumae's mistress, raged at the troops, who retorted. Hirata jumped into the fray. "Let them go," he said.

Both sides looked at him in surprise. The lead Matsumae soldier said, "You don't give orders around here."

"I'm investigating the murder," Hirata said, "and I have Lord Matsumae's permission to question the barbarians. I can talk to them while they hunt."

"You want to go hunting with them?" The leader and his men were flabbergasted. The barbarians muttered among themselves, trying to figure out what was being said—except for Chieftain Awetok, who watched Hirata with unmistakable comprehension.

"Yes." Hirata wanted a new experience as well as a chance to speak with the Ezo away from their masters.

"Well, we're not letting you," the leader said. "If they run away, we'll be blamed."

"I won't let them," Hirata said. "My men and I will bring them back."

"That's what you think. You don't know these sneaky devils. As soon as they get to the forest, they'll give you the slip. You'll be lucky if you find your way home before you freeze to death."

"Please listen to him," the Rat said with a loud sneeze. "He's right."

"We'll compromise," Hirata said. "I'll take just those two"—he pointed at Urahenka and Chief Awetok—"if they'll promise to be good." He turned to the Rat. "Tell them what I said."

The Rat obeyed. The two Ezo nodded. Urahenka looked wary, Chieftain Awetok curious.

"I'll leave the others behind. If their friends don't come back, you can take it out on them," Hirata said to the soldiers. "Well? What do you say?"

As the soldiers exchanged glances, sly grins crossed their faces. They liked the idea of giving their superior from Edo a taste of northern life. "Suit yourself," the leader said, and conveyed the information in Ezo language to the barbarians.

Chieftain Awetok pointed at Hirata's, Fukida's, and the Rat's feet. He spoke a terse sentence.

"He says that if we're going hunting, we'll need snowshoes," said the Rat.

"Well, Honorable Chamberlain, it looks as if you've taken your investigation as far as it can go," said Gizaemon.

"Not quite," Sano said.

Snow had begun falling, and as they and Detective Marume trudged from the scene of the murder to the castle, swirling white flakes filled the sky and landscape. The footprints they'd left on their way out were almost filled. Sano could barely see the castle, its walls and turrets dissolved into a white blur. They reached it to find the sentries absent from the gate. Gizaemon muttered in disapproval.

"They should know better than to desert their post. As soon as I can get somebody to let us in, I'll take you to Lord Matsumae. He'll be wanting to hear what you've found out, even though it's nothing." He stalked to the base of one of the turrets that flanked the gate. "Hey! Anybody up there?"

Sano spoke in a low voice to Marume: "It's time for a talk with Lord Matsumae. He's the next step in our investigation."

Marume gave Sano a look of surprise. "You can't be thinking he's the killer."

"The killer is often the person who was closest to the victim." Sano spoke from years of experience as a detective. "In this case, it's him."

"But he was in love with the woman," Marume said.

"Love can be a stronger motive than hate. Particularly when the loved one had a talent for stirring up jealousy."

"But he's letting you investigate the murder. Would he do that if he were guilty?"

"Maybe." Who understood what went on in the mind of a madman apparently possessed by the victim's evil spirit?

A soldier popped his head out a window in the turret. Gizaemon told him to open the gate. Soon Sano, Marume, and Gizaemon were inside the castle. Snow blanketed the courtyard, and the air seemed colder here than outside. As they walked through passageways, the castle seemed deserted, a ghost village. The palace had the air of a beast hibernating.

"I would prefer to see Lord Matsumae alone," Sano said.

Gizaemon looked weary of arguing. "Fine. Your man and I will wait nearby."

Lord Matsumae was seated in his private office, poring over ledgers by the light of a lantern hung from the ceiling. Heat simmered up through grilles in the floor, from charcoal braziers underneath. When he saw Sano at the threshold, he said in a loud whisper, "Come in. Please sit down. I'm reviewing the account books. They seem to have become disordered."

Surprised to find him so calmly and productively occupied, Sano entered, knelt, and glanced at the ledgers. Even reading upside down, he could tell that the entries for the past few months were sketchy, the writing almost illegible. Lord Matsumae's officials must have been too busy coping with him to keep the books.

"I'm sorry to admit that I've been neglecting the affairs entrusted to me," Lord Matsumae said ruefully. "I can only hope the shogun will forgive me."

His remorse seemed genuine, his state of mind normal. But Sano detected something in the air around him, like the smell of a sick person who has only temporarily rallied from an illness.

"But my work can wait," Lord Matsumae said, folding his hands atop the ledgers. "Have you found out anything new?"

"Not yet," Sano began.

"Shhh!" Putting a finger to his lips, Lord Matsumae whispered, "Keep your voice down. Tekare is asleep. Don't wake her up."

Sano's flesh crawled at the thought of her spirit coiled inside Lord Matsumae like a dormant snake. He said quietly, "I must ask your help with my investigation."

"Of course I'll help," Lord Matsumae said readily. Now

Sano noticed a strange quality about his breathing. It rasped softly, like a woman's gentle snores. "What can I do?"

Sano knew he'd better proceed carefully. Lord Matsumae and Tekare weren't the only ones inclined toward violence. Sano was furious at Lord Matsumae for holding Masahiro prisoner and refusing to admit it. Hiding his fury, Sano forced himself to concentrate on the investigation.

"For me to solve this crime, I need to understand Tekare. I'd like a little background information on her. Could you please give me your impressions of her?"

Grief and nostalgia colored Lord Matsumae's features. "Tekare was like the iris that blooms wild in the far north. So bright, so beautiful, so fresh. So untouched by the evils of society that pollute Japanese women. A truly gentle, innocent spirit. She was rare even among Ezo women. The others are eager to take whatever they can from Japanese men. They always want food, clothes, jewels, and gold in exchange for their favors. But not Tekare. She never asked me for anything. When I gave her presents, I practically had to force her to accept them. She always said that all she wanted was me. All she asked was the privilege of making me happy."

Lord Matsumae leaned forward, his eyes moist with tears and gratitude. "Can you imagine how wonderful it was, to have a woman want me for myself, not for my status or for what I could give her? To know that she loved me as much as I loved her?"

Sano could imagine that Tekare had used the same ploy as did the most popular courtesans in Edo. They pretended to fall in love with their clients. They made a show of refusing gifts, which made the men heap even more upon them. They were consummate actresses. And so might Tekare have been, if she'd hidden from Lord Matsumae a mercenary side she'd revealed to the gold merchant and her other lovers.

"I understand that she was special to you," Sano said tactfully.

He also understood that he now had four very different portraits of the murder victim. Shamaness, social climber, innocent spirit, vindictive ghost—which was the real Tekare? Lord Matsumae seemed to believe his version of her. Love could be spectacularly blind. If that were the case for Lord Matsumae, there went his potential as a suspect.

"Did anyone have any quarrels with Tekare?" Sano said.

"Not that I know of," Lord Matsumae said. "And she had none with me. We agreed on everything."

During his time as a detective, Sano had learned that there was a point at which one couldn't break a witness or suspect without provocation, threats, or physical force. He knew he'd reached that point with Lord Matsumae. Push too hard, and risk another violent episode.

"That's all I have to ask you for now," Sano said. "Thank you for your cooperation."

Gizaemon and Detective Marume appeared in the doorway: They'd listened to the whole conversation and heard it ending.

"If there's anything else you need, just let me know," Lord Matsumae said.

"There is," Sano said. "I'd like to look around the castle." Not only did he want to search for clues and witnesses, he wanted to find out if his son was in the keep, as the Ezo woman had told Reiko, as Sano was desperate to believe.

"Why?" Gizaemon was quick to challenge Sano.

"Standard procedure, I suppose," Lord Matsumae said. "It's all right. We've nothing to hide." A shadow moved behind his gaze. "But you'll confine your exploring to the palace. My uncle will escort you."

As Sano was led away, he heard Lord Matsumae whisper, "Don't worry, my beloved, I didn't tell him any of our secrets."

Now Sano knew that Lord Matsumae did indeed have something to hide. And he was sure it included Masahiro, imprisoned in the keep, as well as information about the murder.

Chapter Sixteen

Walking in snowshoes was harder than Hirata had expected. As he plodded along a trail through the forest north of Fukuyama City, he tried to imitate the two barbarians, who moved as easily as across bare, solid ground. But his shoes scooped up and dug into the snow. The old leg injury that hadn't pained him in years began to ache. He and Detective Marume lagged farther and farther behind the Ezo men, their dogs and sled, and even the Rat, who'd remembered the snowshoeing techniques he'd learned in his youth. Hirata climbed out of a thigh-deep drift, shook snow off his shoes, and paused to rest. Breathing hard, sweaty despite the cold weather, he cursed as he recalled the soldiers' warning that the Ezo would shake him off and escape.

"If we go back to Fukuyama City without them, the soldiers will laugh at us," Marume said, panting and doubled over beside Hirata. "Sano-*san* will be angry because we lost two of his murder suspects. And heaven knows what Lord Matsumae will do."

"Come on," Hirata said grimly.

They slogged onward until they caught up with the group. Urahenka spoke, and the Rat translated, " 'What took you so long? You're slowing us down.' "

Hirata had no chance to retort, because Chieftain Awetok said in clear, fluent Japanese, "Now we are far enough from the city that you can ask me things that you could not before."

"Now we're far enough from the city that we can quit pretending you don't speak my language," Hirata said with a smile.

"He speaks Japanese?" the Rat exclaimed. "And you knew?" Indignant, he said, "You dragged me all the way out here, when you don't even need me to translate! Well, I'm going home."

He huffed down the trail, but Hirata snagged his arm. "Oh, no, you don't. We still need an interpreter." Awetok wasn't the only barbarian Hirata needed to talk with. "And if you tell anyone he speaks our language, I'll wring your scrawny neck."

Hirata walked with the chieftain, who slowed his pace for the Japanese. Detective Marume brought up the rear, but Urahenka forged ahead.

"What did you want to ask me?" Chieftain Awetok said.

Hirata had many questions about the barbarians' world and spiritual practices as well as the murder. "There's an energy in Ezogashima, like a pulse. I sensed it as soon as we landed here. What is it?"

The chieftain glanced at Hirata, as if surprised that he'd noticed something which the Japanese usually didn't. "It's the heartbeat of Ainu Mosir."

"Who is that?" Hirata said, wondering if the chieftain meant some barbarian god.

"Ainu Mosir is our name for this place. It means 'human land.' *Ainu*—human—is what we call ourselves. It's you who call us barbarians and our home 'Barbarian Island.' "

"Oh."

Hirata hadn't realized how insulting was the Japanese word for the natives. He was ashamed because he hadn't known that they minded, or that they didn't think themselves the wild, half-animal creatures that the Japanese did.

"Why does . . . Ainu Mosir have a heartbeat?" From now on he must avoid using the words *Ezo* and *Ezogashima* in the presence of the natives. "I've never felt one in any other land."

"Ainu Mosir is alive," said Chieftain Awetok. "She hasn't been killed by men who cut down forests, plow land for farms, and build cities." *By the Japanese,* implied his tone, *in your own land.*

"The heartbeat is growing stronger." It vibrated in Hirata's bones, behind his eyes.

"The Matsumae have driven Ainu Mosir's spirit away from the coast. Her interior is where it is most powerful."

It tantalized Hirata, beckoned him, promised him secrets. He wanted to learn more about it, but snow had begun falling. A few flakes sifting to earth rapidly became thick white veils. The hunting party would have to get to work fast or return home empty-handed. And the murder investigation was Hirata's first priority.

"I've heard some things," he began.

"People will tell you many things," Chieftain Awetok said. "That doesn't mean you should believe them."

That was wise enough advice, if not the kind Hirata ultimately wanted from the man. "What I heard was about Tekare." Although the chieftain didn't react, Hirata felt his guard go up. "She seems to have been a bad woman."

He described what the gold merchant had told him of Tekare's ambitious, conniving nature. "Is that true?"

"The truth has many faces," Awetok replied. "A man may see only one because his prejudices blind him to the others."

Hirata noted that the chieftain could be as deliberately inscrutable and obstructive as Ozuno, his mentor. Must his fate always lie in the hands of old men who made younger ones work hard for every scrap of information doled out? Impatient, Hirata said, "Did Tekare in fact give herself to men, then climb over them to her position as Lord Matsumae's mistress?"

"In fact, yes," Awetok admitted. "But there is more to truth than fact. There is more to knowing Tekare than knowing what she did."

"What else is there?"

Awetok gazed through the veils of snow. Ahead of them, the Rat and Urahenka were barely visible, shadows in a whitening landscape. "Life is dangerous for our women.

Japanese men like the gold merchant invade our villages and help themselves to the girls. When Tekare was fourteen years old, a band of traders caught her in the woods while she was gathering plants. She was missing three days before we found her, badly beaten and left for dead. It took months for her body to get well. Perhaps her mind never did."

Hirata pondered this story and its relevance to the murder. "I don't understand. If Tekare was mistreated by Japanese men, why would she want anything more to do with them? How could she bear to have them touch her? Wouldn't she have wanted revenge instead of sex with them?"

"There is more than one kind of revenge."

Tekare had apparently taken hers by driving the Japanese wild with her charms, extorting gifts from them, then enjoying their pain when she dumped them. But there was something else Hirata didn't understand. "Was Tekare's behavior considered acceptable by the Ezo—I mean, the Ainu?"

"Not at all." The chieftain frowned, as though Hirata accused his people of condoning immorality.

"Then how could she be your village's shamaness? Isn't that too important a position for a woman like her?" In Hirata's opinion, that would be akin to making a courtesan the abbess of a nunnery. "I should think you'd have chosen someone of better character."

"We do not choose our shamaness," Awetok said. "The spirit world does."

"Oh? How?"

"Early in life, a girl who's destined to be a shamaness will show a sign that the spirits have chosen her as their vessel. When Tekare was young, she caught a terrible disease. She was unconscious for a long time. But she survived. That was the sign. While she was unconscious, her soul left her body and joined with the spirits. They agreed to speak through her and none other in our village."

Skeptical, Hirata said, "Yes, well, then, didn't the spirits mind that she was a troublemaker? Didn't that upset the equilibrium of the cosmos?"

Chieftain Awetok gave him a thin, sidelong smile. "I see you're still ready to believe everything you've heard about us from those who would slander our people. But, yes, Tekare's behavior did put our relations with the spirit world in danger."

"And it was your job, as chief, to bring her back to the village and make her behave properly?"

"Yes."

"Or to get rid of her when she wouldn't cooperate?"

Awetok's smile hardened into a grim fissure in his weathered face. "By 'get rid of,' I suppose you mean 'kill.' You misunderstand our traditions. We Ainu have no penalty of death for crimes."

Unlike you Japanese. Hirata heard the message behind Awetok's words: *Which of our races is more barbarous?*

"I would have performed an exorcism, to drive out the evil spirits that had possessed her," the chieftain said.

"And what would that involve?"

"A ritual, not a spring-bow trap."

Hirata wanted to believe the chieftain was innocent, but he wasn't sure a ritual could cure a habit of causing trouble. And he mustn't forget what Awetok had said: *People will tell you many things. That doesn't mean you should believe them.* That advice applied to the chieftain as well as anyone else.

"Suppose you had performed this exorcism on Tekare," Hirata said. "Does that mean everything bad she'd done in the past would have been forgiven?"

"All would have been forgiven," Awetok said. "That is our custom."

But Hirata doubted that a ritual could erase years of bad feeling. Forgiveness didn't come that easily, and Hirata could think of one Ainu whom Tekare must have hurt the most. He peered through the snow at Urahenka. The young man had trekked so far ahead and was so covered with white flakes that he was almost invisible. Hirata sensed that Urahenka was less eager to reach the hunting grounds than determined to avoid conversation. Hirata called to him, "Hey! Wait!"

Urahenka reluctantly turned and stopped. When Hirata and the Rat caught up with him, he began walking faster, to shake them loose. He grumbled, and the Rat said, "He wants to know what you want."

"To talk about your wife." Hirata tried not to pant as he struggled to keep pace. Chieftain Awetok and Detective Marume had already fallen behind.

"I already told you everything yesterday."

"Not everything," Hirata said. The path had disappeared, and they were forging through dense woods. The slope of the terrain rose into the hills. Hirata had a sense of moving deeper out of his own element. "You said Lord Matsumae stole your wife from you. But that's not true, is it? You didn't tell me that she went to him voluntarily."

A terse, defiant reply came from Urahenka. "He stole her."

"She not only went to live with Lord Matsumae, but she had many other Japanese men before him," Hirata said.

When the Rat translated, Urahenka didn't answer. His mouth compressed behind his whiskers.

"Tekare left you," Hirata goaded him. "She preferred Japanese men because they gave her more than you could. She whored herself to Lord Matsumae, the highest bidder."

Snowflakes pelted Urahenka's forehead and disappeared, as if vaporized by the heat of his anger. But was his anger directed at his dead wife or toward Hirata for insulting her memory? At last he began speaking rapidly. "I have nothing else to say about Tekare. It's time to hunt now. Be quiet or you'll scare away the deer."

Primitive didn't equal stupid, Hirata noted; refusal to talk was a good way for a suspect to avoid being trapped into admitting guilt, and Urahenka obviously knew it.

The chieftain and Detective Marume joined them. The Ainu men left the dogs with the sled, then led the way farther into the forest. "Stay behind us so you don't get shot," the chieftain told Hirata, Marume, and the Rat.

He and Urahenka carefully placed one snowshoe in front of the other, easing down their weight. Hirata and his comrades followed suit as best they could. The Ainu men aimed their bows and arrows from side to side, scanning the landscape for prey. The forest was so quiet that Hirata could hear the snow patter on a dead leaf here, plop onto the ground from a branch there. He watched and listened for movement, but the trees and the dense curtains of snow obscured his view. The land seemed empty, lifeless.

Suddenly the Ainu men froze. They simultaneously released their arrows, which zoomed into a stand of pines. Hirata heard thumps as the arrows struck wood. A deer with a silvery pelt bounded out from the trees and scampered away unharmed.

Urahenka muttered what sounded like a curse. Chieftain Awetok merely drew another arrow from his quiver. Amazed, Hirata said, "I didn't even know the deer was there. If it had been a man, I would have sensed his presence." His mystic martial arts training had taught him to detect the energy that people gave off. Nobody could sneak up on him.

Awetok chuckled. "You samurai focus too much on the world of humans. You ignore the world of nature, which is just as important. Until you learn to pay attention to what nature has to show you and tell you, you are as good as blind and deaf and crippled."

A sense of revelation struck Hirata. Was nature the dimension missing from his awareness? Did it hold the key to enlightenment? The idea seemed too simple, yet alluring. Was oneness with nature and the entirety of the cosmos what he'd come to Ainu Mosir to learn from the chieftain?

As the hunt resumed, Hirata strayed away from the other men. He inhaled and exhaled deep, slow breaths in the meditation technique that he'd learned from Ozuno. Fresh, wintry air flowed through every fiber of him, stimulating yet calming. He let his thoughts drift up into the gray sky. The cold whiteness of the landscape and the sting of snowflakes on his face overwhelmed his senses, liberated his spirit. A trance possessed him.

His spirit inhabited the body trudging through the woods yet floated in a dimension free of himself. He felt his awareness expand as though his mind's energy had burst out of his skull that confined it. He had a terrifying, awesome perception of the world as much vaster, richer, and more complex than he'd ever dreamed. Around him and through him flowed the spirit of Ainu Mosir. Her heartbeat drummed powerfully in rhythm with his own. The forest became animated with forces he hadn't noticed before—the life dormant in the leafless trees and in the animals hibernating in burrows, the energy bound up in rocks, earth, and ice. Nature clamored at Hirata in voices beyond the range of normal hearing, in languages he didn't know. Arms spread, face lifted to the sky, he grasped for comprehension.

A human presence suddenly intruded upon his awareness. His trance shattered. The voices were silenced. Nature's dimension withdrew from Hirata as fast as a hermit crab scuttling into its shell. His spirit snapped back into the iron cage of his body. A premonition of danger blared through Hirata's mind. He whirled in the direction from which it came.

Urahenka stood amid the trees some ten paces away. He held his bow vertical, string pulled back, sighting along the arrow aimed at Hirata. As their gazes met, Urahenka grinned. Hirata was looking death straight in the face.

Triumphant shouts startled them both. The Rat came thrashing through the trees. "Hey!" he yelled. "The chieftain's shot a deer!"

Urahenka quickly lowered his bow and arrow.

"It's a big one," the Rat said happily. "We can go home now, thank heaven." He looked from Hirata to Urahenka and frowned. "What's going on?"

Urahenka gestured at Hirata and spoke. Hirata didn't need to know Ainu language to understand that the man was saying, "He got lost. I found him."

Hirata stared at Urahenka as he walked past him. Urahenka met his eyes, innocently bland. Had he intended to warn

Hirata off investigating him and the chieftain? Or had he really meant to kill Hirata—then claim it was an accident—because he was guilty of murder and eager to prevent Hirata from finding out?

Chapter Seventeen

Reiko sank to her knees in her chamber, exhausted from her visit with Lady Matsumae.

In the past she'd held her own against bigger, tougher adversaries who'd threatened and attacked her, but this encounter had battered her emotions. She'd had her heart rubbed in her worst fears about her son. Although she'd promised to help Sano with the murder investigation, and she knew that solving the crime was their best hope of freeing themselves and Masahiro, she didn't think she could bear to go on with it.

She looked at her hands: They were shaking. Even though the room was freezing cold, her clothes were damp with sweat. A headache pounded in her temples, and nerves twisted her stomach into a tight, nauseous coil.

Lilac added coal to the braziers. "It'll be warm soon."

"Thank you," Reiko murmured. Sick and dizzy, she doubled over to keep from fainting.

"What's the matter?" Lilac asked. "Don't you feel good? I'll get you something." She hurried from the room and returned with a ceramic jar and cup. Kneeling, she poured amber-colored liquid. "Here. Drink this."

Reiko took the cup and sniffed. Alcoholic fumes stung her nostrils. "What is it?"

"Native wine. Made from millet and rice. It'll make you feel better."

It could hardly make her feel any worse. Reiko drank it down. The liquor was tart and strong. It burned her throat, but her nausea abated, and a calming, sedative relief crept through her. "Thank you."

Lilac beamed, happy to be of service. As she took the cup from Reiko, their fingers touched. "Your hands are like ice. Here, let's warm them up." She pulled a brazier close to Reiko.

"You're very kind," Reiko said, gratefully holding her hands over the heat.

Yet she still didn't care much for Lilac. She felt the pressure of an ulterior motive behind the girl's kindness. But if the girl wanted to be useful, Reiko would give her the opportunity.

"What do you have to tell me that you couldn't when we were with Lady Matsumae?" Reiko asked.

Lilac's eyes sparkled with eagerness, but she hesitated. "I don't know if I should say."

"Why not?"

"I'll get in trouble if I talk about Lady Matsumae."

That was an understandable fear for a servant at the mercy of her mistress, but Reiko suspected a less admirable reason behind Lilac's sudden reticence. "In that case, I'd like to be by myself," she said, not in the mood for games. "You're dismissed."

As Lilac rose, she seemed torn between her need to keep quiet about what she knew and her wish to stay with Reiko. She said slowly, "Lady Matsumae wasn't jealous about her husband. That's not why she hated Tekare."

Reiko motioned Lilac to sit. "Why did she?"

Lilac obeyed, although Reiko could see her calculating how to make the most of the least that she could tell. "It was what happened to her daughter."

The last thing Reiko wanted was to hear another story about Lady Matsumae's dead child, but it might illuminate a possible motive for the murder. "What happened?"

"When Nobuko got sick, the Japanese doctors couldn't cure her. Lady Matsumae was desperate. Tekare was a shamaness. She was supposed to be able to cure diseases with magic. Lord Matsumae said to let her try to cure Nobuko.

Even though Lady Matsumae doesn't like the natives, she agreed. So Tekare performed a spell."

Lilac paused. Thoughts creased her brow. Reiko prompted, "What kind of spell?"

"A spell to drive off the evil spirit that was causing the sickness. Tekare burned a branch of spruce. She beat on a drum and sang prayers. She wrapped Nobuko with bulrush cords. Then she cut them off with a knife. She said that would cut the spirit's power, so it couldn't hurt Nobuko anymore. And she gave Nobuko a potion to drink, to make her strong again."

"But she didn't get better," Reiko finished.

"She died the very next day. Tekare said it was because the spirit had too strong a hold on Nobuko. Lord Matsumae believed her. But Lady Matsumae didn't. She said Tekare had put poison in the potion. She accused Tekare of murdering Nobuko."

Surprise jarred Reiko. No wonder Lady Matsumae had laughed at the suggestion that she'd killed Tekare because the native woman had stolen her husband's affections. It was so far off the mark—if Lilac was telling the truth.

"Ask the other servants," Lilac said, noticing Reiko's distrust. "They'll tell you that's what happened."

"But why would Tekare have killed Nobuko?" Reiko asked.

"You've seen how Lady Matsumae treats the Ezo women. Maybe Tekare wanted to get even with her."

"Badly enough to poison the child?" Incredulity filled Reiko.

"Tekare wasn't a nice person," Lilac said. "She didn't put up with Lady Matsumae or anybody else being mean to her. She could have done it."

"But to kill Lord Matsumae's daughter?" Reiko couldn't believe Tekare had dared kill the child of a man who was not only her lover but the ruler of her land.

Then she remembered another woman who'd tried to murder a child of another powerful man because of her cruel, sick hatred for the child's mother. A shiver rippled through Reiko, as it always did when she thought of Lady Yanagisawa, now exiled to Hachijo Island with her husband, the former chamberlain. She felt the same rage as on the day that Lady Yanagisawa had almost contrived Masahiro's death. Lady Matsumae's belief that Tekare had poisoned her daughter gave her a far better cause for murder than did sexual jealousy.

"Lord Matsumae thought Nobuko was going to die anyway," Lilac said. "Tekare knew he wouldn't have blamed her. And he didn't. He thought she could do no wrong."

Reiko shook her head, deploring the idea that Tekare had been a woman capable of such an atrocity, that Sano and Reiko were trying to get justice for a victim who hardly deserved it. "What was in that potion?"

"Native plants, I guess. Ezo shamanesses keep that kind of thing secret."

But even if Lady Matsumae was the murderer, how could Reiko prove it? She contemplated Lilac. "You spend a lot of time with Lady Matsumae, don't you?"

"Yes," the girl said. "She works me practically to death."

"Has she said anything to indicate that she killed Tekare?"

"Not that I heard. She's careful about talking in front of the servants."

But Reiko suspected that Lilac was adept at spying. "Did you see her do anything that looked suspicious?"

"No."

"On the day that Tekare died, did Lady Matsumae leave the castle?" Reiko said. To set the trap, she would have had to go to the path before nightfall.

"I don't know. But I wasn't with her that whole day. I remember she sent me out shopping in town."

Perhaps to rid herself of a nosy witness, Reiko thought. Or perhaps to cover for someone who'd set the trap for her. "What about her ladies-in-waiting? Did they go out?"

"I don't know."

Frustration slid Reiko's spirits downward. Even though she'd discovered a new, strong possible motive for the murder, she was back where she'd been when she'd left

Lady Matsumae—with four suspects and no evidence. Even though somebody in the castle might have seen one of them sneaking outside, spring-bow in hand, how could Reiko search for a witness while she had such limited freedom?

She said in desperation, "Lilac, do you know anything else?"

The girl's gaze slithered away from Reiko.

"What is it?"

Thoughts flitted across Lilac's face. She toyed with a patch on her coat. The threads were coming loose.

"Tell me!" Reiko ordered, bursting with impatience.

"Suppose I do." Lilac put one word slowly after another, as if giving herself time to think. She watched Reiko from the corners of her eyes. "If I tell you, what will you do for me?"

Here it was, the real reason Lilac had at first balked at revealing the story about Lady Matsumae: She wanted to barter her knowledge for personal gain. She didn't want to throw it away for the mere sake of helping Reiko. Although Reiko disapproved of the girl's attempt at extortion, she was in no position to resist.

"I'll do anything you ask," she said. "Just name it."

A smile twitched Lilac's mouth as she sensed her fondest wishes within reach. "I want to get out of Ezogashima. I want to go to Edo, to live in the big city. Maybe you need a maid? When you go home, you'll take me with you?"

Under any other circumstances, Reiko wouldn't hire such a shifty character as Lilac, but now she said, "Yes, if that's what you want."

Lilac turned to her, eyes agleam. "It would be better if I didn't have to work. Maybe I could be your companion instead?"

At the girl's mercy, Reiko said, "All right."

"Someday I'd like to marry a rich samurai. Could you find a husband for me?"

The nerve of her! Reiko's jaw dropped.

Obviously sensing she'd overstepped herself, Lilac said,

"Yesterday I told you I'd look around for your son. What if I know something about him, too?"

"Do you?" Reiko gasped with hope even as she hated Lilac for playing on her vulnerability.

"I might," Lilac said, crafty and enjoying her power over Reiko. "But if you want me to tell you what, you'll have to make it worth my while."

"All right. Yes!" If the girl helped reunite her with Masahiro as well as solve the murder, Reiko would marry Lilac to the shogun himself. "Tell me!"

She saw how eager Lilac was to grab the prize. The girl's hands curled into little grasping claws. Dimples bubbled in her cheeks. But her gaze measured Reiko. "How do I know that if I tell you, you'll keep your end of our bargain?"

"You can trust me," Reiko assured her.

Just then, the door opened and two guards peered in, checking on Reiko. Lilac started guiltily. They both waited in taut silence until the guards shut the door and left.

"I can't talk now," Lilac whispered. "Not here."

"Then where? When?" Reiko pleaded in an agony of frustration.

"Tomorrow," Lilac said.

"But—"

Before Reiko could protest any further, Lilac jumped up, bowed hastily, and ran from the room.

Chapter Eighteeen

Escorted by Gizaemon and a squadron of troops, Sano and Detective Fukida inspected offices, a guard room, and reception chambers that contained nothing of interest. At last they arrived in Lord Matsumae's private quarters. Gizaemon leaned in the doorway while Sano and Marume looked around the bedchamber.

The lacquer tables, screen, iron chests, and silk cushions were aligned parallel to the walls. The alcove held a jade vase that contained a branch of scarlet berries and a scroll with calligraphy so stylized that Sano couldn't read it. The décor could have been lifted from any fashionable samurai house in Edo. The servants had neatened the room during Lord Matsumae's absence, but Sano could still smell his stale body odor, which had soaked into the mats on the floor and walls.

"What are you looking for?" Gizaemon asked.

"I'll know when I find it," Sano replied.

Gizaemon snorted and chewed a sassafras toothpick. "This shouldn't take long."

Fukida opened chests that held dishware for serving tea and sake, playing cards, a chessboard and pieces. Sano went to the cabinet. Inside he found clothes, shaving equipment, a toiletry kit with mirror, brush, and comb, and pairs of shoes. The compartments for bedding were empty; it had probably been taken away for washing. Not only did Sano not know exactly what he was looking for that might implicate Lord Matsumae in the murder, he hadn't much hope that he would find it here.

"Excuse me, Gizaemon-*san,* may I speak with you?"

A samurai official appeared at the door. While Gizaemon turned to talk to him, Sano continued searching the cabinet. On the floor stood a wooden trunk, stained black and inlaid with ivory designs that resembled the spiral patterns Sano had seen on Ezo clothing. It looked out of place among Lord Matsumae's other, Japanese-style possessions.

"There's disease in the castle," the official said.

"What kind?" Gizaemon sounded concerned.

"Fever, chills. Aching head and muscles. Weakness."

Sano knelt and opened the trunk's clasp, which was fashioned from an iron loop and the fang of a wild animal. He lifted the lid. Inside the trunk he found a ceramic jug sealed with a cork; cloth drawstring pouches; a silver tobacco pipe; a writing set with brush, ink-stone, and water jar; strips of willow wood bound together with a leather lace; a knife with a carved wooden hilt and sheath, such as the Ezo men carried; and iron fishhooks strung on cords. The ends were tipped with what looked like dried blood.

"Sounds like northern plague. How many have taken ill?"

"Eight last night, seven this morning. All soldiers, except for two servants who work in the barracks. It broke out there."

Sano picked up the jug and shook it. Liquid sloshed inside. He removed the cork and sniffed bittersweet, alcoholic fumes. He resealed the jug and opened the pouches. They contained dried leaves, roots, and seeds. On the bottom of the trunk, under the other items, lay two books—one large and square, the other a small, slim rectangle—bound in coarse taupe fabric and tied with frayed reeds.

"Has the physician been called?" Gizaemon asked.

"Yes. He's with the patients now."

Sano barely heard the conversation. His heart pounded with excitement because he sensed he'd made an important discovery. He opened the larger book and turned the pages. They were paintings done in ink, crudely executed, featuring a samurai engaged in sex with a tattooed Ezo woman. They coupled in contorted positions that exposed their naked genitalia. Each was stamped with Lord Matsumae's signature seal. He'd chronicled his intimate relations with Tekare in a "spring book," a collection of erotic art.

The pages of the smaller book were covered with calligraphy that was precise and elegant in the beginning, then deteriorated into scrawls. Flipping through them, Sano noticed one set of characters repeated over and over. They were syllables in phonetic writing. *Tekare.* This book appeared to be Lord Matsumae's diary, a series of entries without dates, separated by lines, about his mistress.

"Have you quarantined the sick men?" Gizaemon asked.

"Yes."

"Well, when the physician is done with them, have him examine everybody else in the castle."

"Right away."

Instinct warned Sano not to let Gizaemon know what he'd found. He tucked the diary under his coat, closed the trunk, and shoved it back in the cabinet. He stood and turned just as Gizaemon entered the room and said, "Well? Find anything interesting?"

"No," Detective Fukida said.

"No," Sano lied.

Gizaemon gave them an *I told you so* look. "Still want to search the rest of the palace?"

"Yes." Anxious to read the diary, Sano thought of the one place where he could have some privacy. "But first I need to visit the Place of Relief."

The Place of Relief was a privy shed attached to the palace by an enclosed corridor. Inside, Sano stood in the corner, as far as possible from the malodorous hole cut in the floor. The privy was freezing cold, but he opened the window to admit light and fresh air. Snowflakes drifted in. Conscious of Gizaemon waiting nearby, Sano began reading the diary.

From the time I was a young boy, it was my dream to experience true, eternal love. But as years passed, I grew certain I never would. I didn't lack for women—a man of my position can have as many as he wants. But each affair ended in boredom. Women provided me nothing more than momentary physical release. Some essential ingredient was missing. I resigned myself to yearn forever for a woman with whom I could share a deep, spiritual affinity.

But tonight, a wondrous miracle happened. I went to a banquet given by Daigoro the gold merchant, one of his usual ornate, vulgar affairs designed to show off his wealth and ingratiate himself with his betters. In the midst of the music and feasting, I went outside on the veranda. The spring night was lovely, the flowers fragrant, the moon full. I composed some lines of poetry and spoke them aloud. Then I realized I was not alone.

An Ezo woman stood at the far end of the veranda. That was the first time I saw Tekare. She looked like an apparition from another world. I was stunned by her beauty. I desired her at once. But as our gazes met, I felt more than physical attraction. Something in her reached out to the yearning, lonely part of me. Then she smiled, such a sweet smile. And I knew she was the woman I'd been searching for all my life.

I have taken Tekare from the gold merchant and brought her to the castle. At first I thought I must bed her at once. But she is so shy, so nervous. When I come near her, she trembles, and she speaks only in soft, polite whispers. She seems like a bird wounded by too many men, who would die if I laid a hand on her. Thus, I have forced myself to be patient. I write and read poetry to her. I have given her the finest clothes, the finest rooms in the castle, everything she could want. I must court her until she falls in love with me, as I already have with her. Yet how can I bear to wait? Oh, the longing, the torment!

At last my patience is rewarded, and oh, the joy! Yesterday Tekare said to me, "Master, will you please come to my room tonight?" All day I could hardly keep my mind on my work. When finally the sun set, I went to Tekare. Her room was lit by a hundred lamps made of scallop shells and whale oil. She sat, dressed in the silk robes I'd given her, on a bed covered with a bear pelt. She looked like a native goddess.

"Master, I have been waiting so many nights for you," she said in a voice filled with the same longing that I felt. "I love you so much."

Overwhelmed by gladness, I sank to my knees before her like a worshipper. This was what I'd dreamed of, yet I was too in awe to touch her. It was Tekare who led the way to my heart's desire.

"Please let me show you the Ezo wedding night ceremony," she said.

She gave me wine to drink, and a silver pipe to smoke. Soon my head was light, my senses dizzied. Weird music echoed around me. Tekare seemed to float amid the lamp flames. Chanting spells, she undressed me and wrote mysterious symbols on my naked flesh. The brush caressed my manhood. I almost swooned with pleasure. When finally I entered her, I felt our spirits touch. Mine melted into hers in such radiant warmth as I had never before experienced. Tekare and I were truly one.

In the past, my feelings for a woman would always cool after I made love to her. Familiarity would set in. I would have my fill of her and seek excitement elsewhere. But that didn't happen with Tekare. She was always as much a mystery as when we'd first met. The day after the wedding ritual, she was again shy, aloof. I had to begin courting her all over again, plying her with more gifts, more love poetry. At last she relented, smiled, and welcomed me into her chamber. This happened many times. I was always uncertain of her feelings for me, always her suitor rather than her lord. My love and need for her only increased.

And no matter how often we coupled, I could never get enough of Tekare. We always began with the wine and the pipe filled with native herbs, but each time brought some new, thrilling ritual. One night she tied me up and whipped me with a flail made of willow boughs. Another night she inserted fishhooks in my nipples and pulled on cords attached to them. She taught me that pain intensifies sexual excitement. As I bled and cried, my release was pure ecstasy. I learned the pleasure of submitting to my beloved.

I can think of nothing except Tekare. When I'm not with her, I daydream about her. The wine and smoke leave me in a constant stupor. When I should be working, I instead paint pictures of myself and Tekare together. I hardly listen to what anyone says to me, because her voice is inside my head, chanting her love spells. I neglect my duties, my appearance, and my health while I live in a dream-world. This obsession is not normal. But how can something that feels so wonderful be wrong? I am truly in love for the first time in my life. Everything I do with her seems sacred. As long as Tekare is mine, I will be content.

Exactly when did I begin to fear that I will lose her? I do not remember. I only know that the fear tortures me. I notice how other men look at Tekare. Does she smile at them? Do their eyes hold a moment too long? I am so dazed, my body and mind so weakened, that I cannot trust my impressions.

Sometimes Tekare says she does not feel well and needs to rest alone. One night, consumed by suspicion, I hid outside her window. I heard her voice and a man's, whispering. I saw shadows moving together. Agony twisted my heart. Eventually the light in the window went out. A door opened. Onto the veranda stepped one of my soldiers, a young, handsome fellow. He strolled away in the darkness, whistling to himself.

Later I confronted Tekare. I accused her of being unfaithful to me. She denied it, said I'd imagined what I'd seen. And perhaps I did, for I can hardly distinguish between dreams and reality. I must believe that Tekare is true to me.

My worst fears have been realized. Last night, after Tekare and I made love, I fell into a deep slumber. I was awakened hours later by cries and moans. The scallop-shell lamps were burning. In the light of the dancing flames, I saw Tekare and the young soldier. They were naked. She had her back against the wall, her legs around his waist, while he plunged into her. They dared to couple right in front of me, as if I were not there!

I tried to protest. I tried to rise and stop them. But I could neither move nor make a sound. My gaze caught Tekare's. She smiled. She smiled at me as I lay helpless and horrified and she made love with another man!

This time, when I told Tekare what I'd seen, she didn't deny it. She laughed. All her sweetness disappeared. She turned into a cruel stranger. She said that if she wanted another man, she would have him, and she didn't care if I was jealous.

I raged at her. I lifted my hand to strike her, but she pushed me away, and I was so weak that I fell. I called her ungrateful. I told her she wouldn't get any more gifts from me. She said she wouldn't give me any more fun.

Fun! That is what she called our sacred lovemaking!

I threatened to put to death any man she dallied with. She said that by the time I was done, I would have no retainers left. I threatened to send her back to her tribe unless she behaved herself. But she said that if I did, I would never see her again. And I know that my threats are no good. I am at her mercy.

What am I to do? I now fear and revile Tekare as much as I love her. She has cast over me an evil spell that has reduced me to a pathetic shadow of myself. I must break free of her, but how?

After much thought, I have realized that I must destroy her before she completely destroys me. At night I lie awake, plotting her death. If I take my sword to her, she will overpower me before I can strike her down. Perhaps I can cut her throat while she sleeps. But I cannot bear to watch her die. I must attack her on the sly, when she least expects it, when she cannot stop me. Perhaps I should poison her food. Or set a spring-bow trap along a path she walks. But whatever I do, it must be soon, while I still have a chance for salvation. May the gods give me the will to act!

As Sano deciphered the final passage in the diary, he experienced such shock that he barely noticed the snow falling through the window onto his sleeve, the stench inside the privy shed, or the fact that his hands were frozen stiff. But he had no time to ponder the significance of what he'd read, because there came a loud banging on the door.

"Honorable Chamberlain, what's taking you so long?" said Gizaemon. "Come out, or I'll break the door down."

Chapter Nineteen

Reiko awakened suddenly from a thick, dark sleep induced by the strong wine that Lilac had given her. She felt someone in the room with her, sat up, and saw Wente, the Ezo woman, crouched near her.

"How did you get in here?" she said.

Wente put a finger to her lips. She beckoned Reiko.

"What—?"

"Hurry!" Wente whispered, sidling out of the room.

"Wait a moment." Reiko ran to the cabinet and dragged out her futon. Wente helped her arrange quilts on it so that if someone looked in on her, it would look like she was taking a nap. They tiptoed down the corridor and out the door. Snow was falling heavily, mounding the castle's walls, turrets, and roofs, coating the trees. Not a single distinct edge existed in this new white landscape. Not a soul did Reiko see.

"Where are the guards?" she asked.

"Sick," Wente said.

Reiko surmised that disease had befallen the men, who'd left their posts. Her depression evaporated like fog dispelled by a radiant dawn. Now Wente could take her to rescue Masahiro.

They hastened toward the keep, its white shaft almost lost against the white, dissolving sky. The snow quickly coated their garments, camouflaging them. The route looked so different that Reiko didn't recognize it. She was glad to have Wente guiding her, and Wente might be able to help her in more ways than this.

"Did you know the woman who was killed with a springbow?" Reiko asked.

Wente's head snapped around toward her. Fear flashed across her tattooed face. Walking faster, ahead of Reiko, she muttered something in Ezo language.

"What did you say?" Reiko hurried to catch up.

"Sister," Wente said, her voice slurred, her face distorted by grief. Snowflakes melted in the tears that wet her cheeks.

"Tekare was your sister? I didn't know. I'm sorry." Reiko didn't like to upset her friend by talking about the murder, but Wente was the only person she'd met here, except for Lilac, who'd been willing to help her. And Reiko trusted Wente more than she did the servant girl.

"Do you have any idea who killed Tekare?" Reiko asked.

Wente shook her head so hard that her fur-lined hood slipped off. She pulled it up, shoulders hunched, as they tramped through a courtyard. She uttered a phrase in her own language, then said, "It was mistake."

"Mistake? Do you mean an accident? She just wandered into a trap set for deer?"

Again Wente replied in Ezo language, words that she didn't translate for Reiko. When upset, she seemed to lose her ability to speak Japanese.

"Lord Matsumae thinks Tekare was murdered," Reiko said.

"No." Wente sobbed.

Perhaps it was too painful for her to believe that her sister had been deliberately killed. Reiko said, "Do you think Lady Matsumae did it?"

A few garbled words came from Wente. Under other circumstances Reiko would have pressed her for information. Under other circumstances Reiko would have questioned Wente about her relationship with Tekare, for Reiko knew that a murder victim's kin were potential culprits. But Wente seemed honest, decent, and truly grief-stricken by Tekare's death. And now she was leading Reiko up the hill toward the keep.

Anticipation sped Reiko's pace so fast that she stumbled

climbing the steps. She half-crawled the rest of the way. Gasping, she looked up at the keep's dingy plaster walls, protruding roofs, and barred windows. Snow pelted her face. Vertigo and hope dizzied her. She reached the ironclad door, which was unguarded. Wente helped her tug it open. Cautiously they stepped inside.

A dim, quiet anteroom enclosed them. The cold air stank of urine and feces. Wooden studs showed through gaps in the plaster on the walls. Reiko saw wooden benches, braziers filled with ash, and mops that stood in pails of water. The water was a dirty reddish brown. Instinctive fear bit deep into Reiko. Holding their gloved hands over their noses, she and Wente stole through a doorway that led farther into the keep. They found a maze of cells with metal bars across their fronts. Soiled hay had been swept into corners. The walls were smeared, streaked, and blotched with blood. Red-stained rags littered the floors. Reiko stared in horrified comprehension.

This was where Lord Matsumae had imprisoned the outsiders who'd arrived in Ezogashima during his madness. Here they'd been tortured and killed. The troops she'd seen here yesterday had been trying to clean the place up, probably in case Sano should see it. But the troops had taken ill, leaving their job unfinished and the truth plain as day to Reiko.

She was standing in a slaughterhouse.

A slaughterhouse to which her son had been brought.

"Masahiro!" she cried, running through the maze, peering in the cells. All were empty but for signs of carnage.

"Here!" Wente pulled her up a staircase that led to a square hole in the ceiling.

They emerged into the keep's second story. Light came from gaps around the shutters and chinks in the plaster. Reiko rushed through unfurnished rooms partitioned by sliding walls. In the last one she found a strange object, a big, square box with a wooden top and bottom, and sides made of crisscrossed iron bars. It was a cage for a large animal—or a small human. But no one was inside. Reiko let out a cry. She saw an image of Masahiro huddled in the cage, his eyes filling with joy as he recognized his mother who'd come to save him. She flung herself at the cage.

The image vanished. The cage was empty again except for hay, the door open. Nearby lay a quilt stained with blood.

"No!" Reiko wailed.

She snatched up the quilt and pressed her face to it, inhaling the sweet, earthy, little-boy smell of Masahiro and the ranker odor of his blood. She wept, assailed by a terrible vision of troops beating him to death.

Wente knelt beside her, patted her back, and murmured words of sympathy in Ezo language. She reached inside the cage, removed something from the hay, and put it in Reiko's hand. It was a leather drawstring pouch that contained a figurine carved from wood, a brightly painted horse clad in battlefield armor. The horse belonged to a set of toy soldiers that Reiko and Sano had given Masahiro. Reiko held it to her heart and sobbed harder. This was all she had left of her son.

He was gone.

She was too late.

Sano had spent all day searching the rest of the palace and questioning the Matsumae clan members, officials, troops, and servants. He'd found no clues, but then he hadn't really expected to; the crime wasn't the kind that would leave evidence such as wounds on the culprit or blood-stained clothes in his possession. A vial of arrow poison was easily disposable, and nobody had left a written confession.

Except Lord Matsumae.

Sano's interviews had also turned up nothing. The witnesses were nervous and reluctant to talk. Gizaemon had listened in on all the conversations, even though Sano had repeatedly asked him to stand out of earshot. Maybe the witnesses didn't want to say anything that would incriminate him, Lord Matsumae, themselves, or their friends. Sano and Detective Fukida returned to their quarters at dusk empty-handed.

Except for Lord Matsumae's diary.

The blizzard had stopped, and the sky was dark, but the snow gave the landscape a spectral luminescence. A lantern over the door spilled a golden glow over high white drifts piled up against the guest quarters. Gizaemon left Sano and Fukida with the lone guard stationed in the entryway. The northern plague must have sent the others to bed.

"See you at the funeral tomorrow, Honorable Chamberlain," Gizaemon said.

After he and Fukida had removed their shoes, Sano went to the chamber he shared with Reiko. Her blanket-covered figure lay in bed in the darkness. He decided to let her sleep. She needed rest, and he didn't have any good news for her. He joined his men in their room; Hirata, Marume, and the Rat had returned. They'd spread their coats upon drying frames over the charcoal braziers. Sano added his to theirs. The room was steamy and redolent of wet fur. Marume poured hot tea and laid out a dinner of cold rice balls, dried salmon, and soup with seaweed and boiled lotus roots. As he and the other men tore into the food, Sano forced himself to eat. Fear for Masahiro chased through his anxiety about the investigation. He felt the snow weighing upon the roof, suffocating him.

Fukida explained about the plague. "Now would be the time to cut and run, while the troops are sick and there aren't so many around. But we don't exactly have anyplace to go. Too bad, because we aren't making much progress on this investigation." He asked Hirata and Marume, "What about you?"

"We went hunting with the Ainu," Hirata said.

"The what?"

"Ainu. That's what the natives call themselves." Hirata added, "They saved our lives. We owe them at least the courtesy of using their proper name."

He sounded defensive on their behalf, Sano observed. His interest in the Ezo—or Ainu—seemed to have been strengthened by the hunt. "Did you get anything?"

"One deer," Hirata said.

"I meant information pertaining to the murder," Sano said.

"Oh. Well." Hirata told how Chieftain Awetok had explained his way of disciplining his people and his ritual for driving out the evil spirits that made them behave badly. "He said he didn't kill Tekare. I think he's telling the truth."

"What about her husband?" Sano asked.

"The same with him."

But Hirata looked into his tea instead of at Sano. Now Sano knew something more had happened on the hunt besides a talk about native customs and shooting a deer. Something that incriminated one or the other native, that Hirata didn't want to tell Sano. Hirata's loyalties had become divided.

"Well, I've found a clue," Sano said, "although it's not exactly what I wanted."

He produced the diary. Hirata read it first, then the detectives. They all reacted with surprise.

"This is the most incriminating evidence we've got against anyone," said Hirata.

"Especially that last part about the spring-bow," Marume said. "It sure sounds like Lord Matsumae is our killer."

"It may be proof of intention, but not of deed," Sano said. "The diary doesn't say whether he actually carried out his plan to murder Tekare."

"Do you really think he did?" Fukida sounded doubtful. "Then pretended to think someone else had killed her? Held the whole island hostage? And agreed that you should investigate the crime that he committed himself? It sounds insane."

"Which Lord Matsumae is," Hirata said.

A new idea occurred to Sano. "Sometimes a disturbed mind hides painful things from itself. And Lord Matsumae's mind seems to have been disturbed long before Tekare died." Sano opened the book and read aloud the passage about the wine and the pipe filled with native herbs. "I wonder what those herbs were? And what was in that wine?"

"Poisons that made him forget he killed Tekare and made him think he's possessed by her spirit," Marume suggested.

Sano wondered if enslaving and ruining Lord Matsumae had been another form of Tekare's revenge against the Japanese who'd mistreated her. "Maybe they also drove him to all the other violent acts he's committed since her death."

"Supposing he did kill her," Fukida said, "why would he have let you search the palace and find his diary?"

"Maybe a part of him wants to be caught and punished," Hirata said, "and leaving his diary for you to find is his way of confessing."

"I wonder what the spirit of Tekare would do to him if she found out that he killed her," Fukida said.

"What do we do next?" Marume asked.

Sano had been pondering that question ever since he'd found the diary. He'd delivered many criminals to justice, but never one who'd been holding him prisoner. "Lord Matsumae won't take kindly to my telling him that he's the killer I've been commissioned to catch. Particularly if he doesn't remember killing Tekare and believes he's innocent."

"We could arrest him," Marume said.

Nobody laughed at his joke. The time might come when they must try to take Lord Matsumae by force. The samurai code of honor didn't excuse them from suicide missions.

"I'm not willing to move against Lord Matsumae based on this alone," Sano said, holding up the diary. "Not when there are still other suspects." And not while he needed to stay alive to rescue his son.

"Where should we look for evidence against them?" Hirata asked.

"The funeral is a good place to start. Some if not all of the suspects should be there. Let's watch how they behave."

A tapping noise caught Sano's attention. Puzzled, he got up, walked to the wall, and lifted the mat. Underneath was a window. He opened the panel of paper panes and the shutters.

Reiko stood on the veranda. "Let me in!" she said in a loud, urgent whisper.

Sano hauled her through the window and closed it. "I thought you were in bed. Where have you been?"

She was trembling violently, her eyes red-rimmed, face crusted with mucus, lips white. Sano brushed the snow off her, hung her coat and gloves over a drying frame, and helped her remove her boots. He seated her and himself by a brazier. Hirata offered her hot tea, but she pushed it away.

"I went to the keep." Her voice quavered. "Wente took me. This time we got inside. But Masahiro wasn't there. All we found was an empty cage and a blanket with blood on it. And this." She gave Sano a leather pouch she'd been clutching in her hand.

Sano opened the pouch and saw the toy horse painted to resemble the real horse that Masahiro had been learning to ride. His worst fears solidified into reality. Hope withered like burnt-out ashes.

"Masahiro is dead!" Reiko began to cry with violent, wracking howls. "He probably has been since before we came here. We were too late from the beginning!"

Sano held her. Her sobs shook them both. He wanted to break down and weep with Reiko. All along he'd seen the signs that their son was dead and tried to ignore them. He couldn't now.

"Maybe Masahiro escaped," Hirata said.

"Yes, why not?" Marume said. "He takes after his mother. She's pretty good at getting out of tight spots."

Their efforts to cheer up Sano and Reiko failed. Sano had tried not to wonder why Lord Matsumae and Gizaemon wouldn't just give him back his son; what harm could it do them? The reason was that they knew Masahiro was dead because they'd killed him. They didn't want to admit it to Sano for fear of eventual consequences. But at this moment Sano was devastated beyond craving retribution. All sense of meaning and purpose drained from his existence. His son was dead. Nothing mattered anymore.

"Let me die," Reiko moaned in Sano's embrace. "Let my death reunite me with Masahiro. Masahiro! My baby, my firstborn, my dearest child!" Her frantic cries resonated through the hollowness inside Sano. "Just let me see him again!"

As the other men watched with stern pity, Sano ceased to care about the investigation, about whether he ever found out who'd killed Tekare. He no longer cared whether Lord Matsumae set him and his comrades free or put them to death. If he and Reiko died on Ezogashima, at least their earthly remains would be near their son's.

Through all the past dark times, Sano had always believed a brighter day lay ahead of him, that he would not only survive but triumph.

Not this time.

Life as he knew and cherished it had ended tonight.

Chapter Twenty

The morning of Tekare's funeral was clear and bright. Reiko stood lost among the mourners and guests convened outside the palace's main reception hall. It seemed impossible to her that the sun was shining, the sky brilliant turquoise, the snowdrifts pure, fresh, and beautiful. The light hurt her eyes, which were swollen from weeping. How incredible that the world should go on, indifferent to her sorrow; that she was still alive when her heart had been torn out of her; that she should attend a funeral for a stranger while she grieved for her son.

She hadn't wanted to come, but Sano had said, "Lord Matsumae's ordered everyone in the castle to go. You must."

He'd acted calm and strong, although his eyes had an expression that she'd seen in them once before, while he convalesced after he'd been beaten almost to death by an assassin. Then he'd looked as if his body had been tortured to the very limit of survival. This time he looked as if his spirit had. They'd spent the night clinging to each other in bed, but although they'd conceived Masahiro together and should have taken comfort from sharing their loss, Reiko had felt utterly alone in hers. She now felt as distanced from Sano as if he were on the moon, even though he stood beside her.

The funeral party entered the hall, led by Lord Matsumae, his uncle Gizaemon, and their officials, clad in formal black ceremonial robes decorated with gold crests. The native men and concubines followed, wearing their usual animal-skin clothing and bead jewelry. Reiko saw Wente, but Wente was watching the native men. A small, thin, male commoner strode in after them, bundled in a luxurious fur coat. Reiko heard Hirata say to Sano, "That's Daigoro, the gold merchant."

Lady Matsumae and her three attendants, all in lavish silk robes, minced up the stairs. Reiko was surprised that her mind continued functioning despite her grief. She noted that Lilac was absent. She remembered that Lilac had promised her information about Masahiro, about the murder, today.

Troops resplendent in full armor ushered Sano, Reiko, Hirata, the detectives, and the Rat last through the door. Inside the hall, a fire burned in a native-style hearth. The corpse lay north of the hearth, on a woven mat, amid brass bowls from which rose yellow, acrid smoke.

"It's the native custom to burn sulfur, to mask the odor of decay," the Rat whispered.

Reiko smelled its vicious stench despite the sulfur. The natives hugged one another, hands positioned on shoulders or under armpits, in a gesture of mutual condolence. Lord Matsumae and his men knelt along the north wall. His face was hollow-eyed and drawn with misery, theirs stoic. The strong, handsome native that Reiko remembered from the beach squeezed in beside Lord Matsumae, who was nearest to the corpse.

"You don't belong here," Lord Matsumae said, offended. "Sit somewhere else."

The native blurted out angry speech. The Rat whispered, "Urahenka says that as Tekare's husband, he's the most important mourner, and he, not Lord Matsumae, should sit in the place of honor."

The troops stood over Urahenka. He slunk off to join the other native men along the east wall. Wente's solemn gaze clung to him. Sano and his comrades took places along the south wall, the women along the west. Kneeling in the gap that separated the Japanese ladies from the native concubines, Reiko got her first good look at the corpse.

Tekare wore leggings, fur mittens, and an ocher-colored

robe with black-and-white designs on the collar band and sleeve hems. These covered her shrunken body, but her face showed in all its gruesome mortality. The blue tattoo around her mouth melded with the discolored adjacent skin that had sunken at the eye sockets. Outlines of her teeth showed through it. Silver earrings hung with black, turquoise, and red beads pierced lobes that looked like dried gristle. Disgust nauseated Reiko. She thought of Lilac, who'd somehow avoided the funeral, and a spark of new emotion kindled within her grief.

It was anger toward Lilac. Reiko was certain that Lilac knew Masahiro was dead. She'd strung Reiko along, teasing her with false hopes, wangling for a new life in Edo. Such despicable cruelty!

Servants brought trays containing a feast—dried salmon, deer stew with vegetables, fish roe, chestnuts, cakes made from millet, and water vessels. They placed one tray beside the head of the corpse, offerings to the gods. The other trays were laid before the assembly. The natives and the local Japanese began to eat, slowly and ceremonially, with their fingers. "You have to eat," the Rat hissed at the Japanese from Edo. "You'll be cursed if you don't."

Reiko nibbled at a millet cake, forced herself to swallow a few crumbs, and washed them down with water. Sano, Hirata, and the detectives did the same. Lord Matsumae sobbed.

"Tekare!" he wailed, then said in an eerie female voice, "I'm here with you, my lord. Be strong."

Weeping broke out among the natives, a low, collective wail. "It's the custom to weep at funerals, no matter how you felt about the person who died," the Rat explained.

The natives chanted, *"O-yoyopota! O-yoyopota!"*

The Rat said, "That means, 'Oh, how dreadful.' Everybody should join in."

Everybody did, except Lady Matsumae, who wore a faint smile. Under the cover of the noise, Reiko said to Lady Smart, who sat beside her, "Where is Lilac?"

"She must have sneaked out of the castle. The bad girl!"

Lord Matsumae rose, walked to Tekare, and knelt by her head. So did Urahenka. "Go away," Lord Matsumae said, shooing the man away as though he were a dog.

Sulky and defiant, Urahenka held his position. A servant brought a cup of water, which he and Lord Matsumae both grabbed for. It spilled. Another servant hurried over with two cups. They drank the ritual toast, glaring at each other, then retreated to their places.

"Where did she go?" Reiko asked Lady Smart.

The woman shook her head, but Lady Pansy spoke across her: "To the hot spring."

The chanting continued. The chieftain began to speak, apparently prayers to the gods. The natives moved forward one by one to bow and weep over the corpse. Sulfur smoke and fury choked Reiko. That Lilac had sneaked off to cavort in the hot spring while she suffered! After scheming to exploit her!

At last the chieftain ended his prayers. The native women wrapped Tekare in the mat upon which she lay. They bound the mat with plaited black-and-white strands of hemp. The men tied it to a long pole. Lord Matsumae grasped one end of the pole, but he was too weak to lift Tekare's weight. Captain Okimoto hefted the pole onto his shoulder. Lord Matsumae laid his hand on it, reverently as if touching his beloved's flesh. He ignored the native man who took up the pole's other end. The assembly rose as the bearers angled the wrapped, suspended corpse feet-first toward the door.

Wente, carrying a small lacquer water vessel, led them out of the hall. The officials followed with a lacquer chest. Urahenka trudged after them, a walking stick in his hand, a lumpy bundle on his back. The other native men followed, laden with more paraphernalia. The troops herded the Japanese and native women, then Reiko, Sano, and their comrades, outside.

The sun was at its dazzling zenith, the snow glittering with jeweled reflections. The procession filed through the castle grounds to a back gate. As she realized that they were leaving the castle, Reiko saw her chance to settle a score.

The procession moved down the hill, along a path plowed for easy walking two or three abreast. The natives chanted. Reiko lagged behind Sano. He turned toward her, but a soldier said, "Don't look back, sideways, or down!" He prodded Sano with his lance. "That'll invite evil spirits to possess us!"

Sano marched face-forward, as did everyone else. Reiko silently thanked the gods for native superstition. She fell into step with Lady Smart and whispered, "Which way to the hot spring?"

Lady Smart frowned and shook her head.

"Please!"

"Take the right fork in the path."

When they reached it, Reiko peeled away from the group, which marched right past her. She sped off in pursuit of Lilac.

The graveyard was located on a plateau above the city. Towering cedars surrounded and cast deep blue shadows on open snow studded with wooden burial posts. These marked the graves of natives who'd died in the Japanese domain. Some of the posts had pointed tops; the rest, elongated holes.

"Spears for men, sewing needles for women," the Rat said.

This lesson on native customs glanced off Sano. He felt like a vestige of himself, as though Masahiro's death had amputated his spirit from his body. But the Way of the Warrior kept him stoically going through the motions of life. Bushido was like a skeleton that held him up. He still had his duty to his lord to fulfill, and he came from a long line of samurai who'd marched from one battle to the next, bleeding from their injuries, to fight until they dropped.

Four Ainu men cleared snow off the ground and began digging a hole. Sano watched Lord Matsumae shambling amid his entourage. Centuries of instinct stirred in Sano. His samurai blood flamed with the age-old desire for vengeance. Lord Matsumae was responsible for Masahiro's death. Never mind the deal they'd struck—Lord Matsumae's days were numbered.

The gravediggers finished. They lined the rectangular hole with matting. At its west end they placed two bowls of earth. Wente poured water from her vessel into these. Lord Matsumae moaned, clutching at his heart, while the native men lowered the corpse into the grave. Urahenka opened his bundle. It contained a robe, a spindle, needles and thread, a bowl and a spoon, a knife, a cooking pot, and a sickle. The officials opened their chest and brought out a silk kimono, Japanese lacquer sandals, and hair ornaments.

"Grave goods," whispered the Rat. "For the deceased to use when she gets to the spirit world."

Urahenka raised his walking stick and struck his grave goods repeatedly. He shattered the bowl, dented the pot, and ruined the other items. A soldier handed Lord Matsumae a lance. He wept and staggered while he hacked at the things his men had brought.

"They have to be broken to release their spirit to the service of the dead," the Rat explained.

The pieces were dumped into the grave. The natives and Lord Matsumae picked up handfuls of dirt. Urahenka flung the first handful onto his wife's corpse. Lord Matsumae dropped in his own dirt from fingers that shook with the sobs that wracked him. Sano longed for a sword, longed to feel his blade cut through Lord Matsumae's flesh, to spill blood for blood. But he was patient. He came from a long line of samurai who pursued their enemies to the end of the earth, for as long as it took.

The gravediggers filled in the hole, placed the needle-shaped burial post. The native women brushed the covered grave, one another, and their men with willow switches. "To purify them," said the Rat.

The group prepared to depart. Sano recalled that he'd hoped that the funeral would provide information useful to his investigation, that something would happen to unmask the killer. So far it hadn't.

Suddenly Chieftain Awetok spoke in a tone of command.

Everyone paused, turning to him in surprise. He raised his hand, spoke again. An excited murmur swept through the natives.

"He says to wait," the Rat said. "He wants to perform a special ritual."

"What kind of ritual?" Sano asked.

The chieftain spoke. Gizaemon said, "A trial by ordeal. It's the Ezo custom when one of them is murdered. They dip their hands in boiling water." The native men set an urn on the hot charcoal brazier they'd brought. "If they're guilty, they get scalded. If they're innocent, the spirit of the victim protects them, and the hot water doesn't burn them."

A buzz of disapproval arose among the Japanese officials. Lord Matsumae regarded the Ainu with skepticism and hope. "Can this really determine who killed Tekare?"

"Of course not," the gold merchant said scornfully.

"It's just barbarian foolishness," Gizaemon said. "Don't allow it, Honorable Nephew."

The native men began protesting. "They say they've been unjustly accused," the Rat said. "They want a chance to prove their innocence. And they want everyone else to be tested, to find out who's guilty."

Urahenka stood beside the brazier. He flung off his right mitten and held up his bare hand.

Sano said, "I order the trial to proceed." Not that he believed in magic rituals, but he was amenable to anything that might shed light on the crime that he'd taken responsibility for solving. And if Lord Matsumae took the test and scalded himself, so much the better.

"You're not in charge here, Honorable Chamberlain," Gizaemon said. "And I, for one, won't play along."

"Neither will I," said Daigoro.

Lord Matsumae vacillated, besieged by doubt, confusion, and what might have been fear, then spoke in Tekare's voice: "I want to find out who killed me. Let there be a trial."

Chapter Twenty-One

Reiko trudged through the forest. Icicles hung like sculpted fangs on the pine boughs and snow covered the path. She stepped in footprints that had earlier broken the white crust. As the terrain inclined uphill she panted with fatigue, but she hurried faster, anxious to reach the hot spring before the Matsumae folk noticed her absence from the funeral procession. Her anger at Lilac kept her going.

Anger was a distraction from grief, a temporary antidote for pain. Now past the first shock of Masahiro's death, Reiko wanted to punish someone for it. She was powerless against Lord Matsumae, and she couldn't strike out at Lord Matsudaira, who had sent her son to Ezogashima but was far out of reach, but she had a convenient target in Lilac, who had deceived her. By the time she smelled the sulfurous odor of the hot spring, she was ready for combat.

She rounded a curve, and the path ended at an irregularly shaped pond about fifteen paces wide and twenty paces long, set in a wide clearing. Rocks jutted up from the earth around the pond, forming a low, craggy wall. A cloud of steam hid the water that Reiko heard percolating beneath the pond's surface. The heat had melted the snow off the rocks. Near a gap between them lay folded clothes beside a pair of boots.

"Lilac!" Reiko called. "I want to talk to you."

There was no answer, no sound except the burbling water. Maybe Lilac was playing games, teasing Reiko again. Infuriated, Reiko moved to the pool's edge. She crouched in the gap between the rocks, fanned at the steam with her hand,

and saw a dark object partly submerged in the water nearby. It was the top of a head. Long black hair floated from it.

"There's no use hiding," Reiko said. "You'll have to come up for air eventually."

A moment passed. Lilac didn't move. Reiko grabbed Lilac's hair and pulled. Steam obscured her vision. She felt the heavy weight of the girl dragging through the warm water that lapped onto her gloves. The motion disturbed the steam, which thinned enough for Reiko to see the pale, long body floating on its stomach beneath the surface. Lilac's head butted up against the rocks. Reiko was puzzled because Lilac didn't resist. With an effort that strained her muscles and splashed water onto herself, she turned Lilac.

The girl rolled face-up. Her skin was a bright, unnatural pink. Waves bobbed her limbs. Her mouth gaped, filled with water that vaporized in the cold air. Her open eyes had a cloudy, blank appearance, like those of a steamed fish. She was dead. The hot water had begun to cook her.

Reiko screamed, recoiled, and lost her balance. She fell backward onto the hard, slick ice around the spring. Her horror was mixed with shame for her vindictive thoughts toward Lilac. No matter how venal Lilac had been, she hadn't deserved to die.

The wind stirred the pines. Icicles rattled like bones, fell, and stabbed the snow. Panic launched Reiko to her feet. She ran away from the hot spring as fast as she could go.

At the graveyard, the water in the urn began to boil. Chieftain Awetok removed his right glove. He and Urahenka plunged their hands into the urn. The assembly gasped. Urahenka tried to suppress a cry but failed. The chieftain didn't react at all. He spoke a command; he and Urahenka pulled their dripping, steaming hands out of the water. Six times they performed this torture. Urahenka shuddered. Involuntary tears ran down his tanned face. But Awetok's remained calm; he appeared impervious to the pain. At last he and Urahenka extended their hands to the audience. He spoke, eyes flashing.

" 'The spirit of Tekare has proclaimed us to be innocent of her murder,' " the Rat translated. " 'Come and behold the proof.' "

Everyone rushed forward to inspect the natives' hands. Sano was amazed to see that they appeared perfectly normal. Exclamations of awe arose.

Urahenka shouted triumphant words. The Rat said, " 'We told you that we didn't kill Tekare. Do you believe us now?' "

"It's a trick," the gold merchant huffed.

"How did they do it?" Hirata quickly challenged him.

"Some native potion on their hands, maybe."

Sano couldn't imagine any potion would protect flesh from boiling water, and he knew that humans were capable of wondrous feats. Martial arts history was full of examples. Maybe the Ainu had discovered a mental discipline for controlling their bodies and resisting injury. Or maybe their unmarred hands were in fact proof that Chieftain Awetok and Urahenka were innocent.

"It doesn't mean anything," Gizaemon said. "Trial by ordeal isn't recognized by Japanese law."

But Lord Matsumae beheld the Ainu as if the miracle had shaken him to his bones. Tekare's aspect cloaked his features; her voice said, "If they didn't kill me, then who did?"

Urahenka beckoned and hurled a loud verbal challenge at the audience; he pointed at the boiling water.

Appalled glances flashed from person to person. Sudden piercing cries sounded from a distance. Everyone turned to see Reiko burst out of the forest. She ran to Sano and collapsed, moaning, in his arms.

"Where have you been?" he asked, upset because he hadn't noticed she was gone. His thoughts of vengeance had crowded even Reiko out of his mind. "What's wrong?"

The funeral party crowded around them. Reiko blurted, "Lilac is dead."

Sano had to think a moment before he remembered that Lilac was the maid who'd befriended Reiko. Shock appeared on the faces of the Japanese, who understood what

Reiko had said, and on those of the natives because they sensed it meant trouble had struck again.

"How?" Sano said as possible implications occurred to him. "Where?"

Reiko pointed. "At the hot spring."

The trial by ordeal was forgotten as the funeral party hurried from the cemetery. Hirata and the native men reached the hot spring first, Gizaemon and the soldiers next. Lord Matsumae shambled up the path in their wake. Sano stopped Reiko short of their destination, while the other women trailed behind them. He left her with the detectives, said "Look after her," then joined the scene at the spring. Hirata and Urahenka hauled Lilac from the pool and laid her on the ground. Water ran off her, hissing as it melted the snow. Her body steamed like a boiled lobster.

"Looks like she drowned," Gizaemon said.

Hirata looked into the pool. "How deep is this?"

"Not very, but that doesn't matter," Captain Okimoto said. "I know of a man who drowned in water that was only knee-high."

The women arrived. One lady-in-waiting fainted. The others fussed over her. Gizaemon said, "Get them out of here," and the troops bustled them to the fringes of the action.

Sano knew how to determine whether a death was due to drowning: Cut open the lungs and look for water inside. But Tokugawa law forbade autopsies, and if Sano tried one even this far from Edo, he could expect severe opposition. Crouching by the body, Sano noticed the snow under Lilac's head turning red.

"Let's turn her over."

He and Hirata rolled Lilac onto her stomach. She was limp and floppy, not long deceased. The back of her head was thick with blood. Sano saw white bone fragments caught in her tangled hair, and brain tissue that had oozed from her shattered skull.

"She didn't drown," Sano said. "She was killed by a blow to her head."

"She probably fell against the rocks." Gizaemon's tone expressed contempt for Lilac's carelessness. "Knocked herself out, slipped under the water."

Hirata walked around the spring, inspecting the rocks. "No blood on these."

"A fall couldn't have done this," Sano said, examining Lilac's wound. "This was murder."

Sano heard a small sound like a strangled whimper, but couldn't discern who'd made it. It was quickly overlaid by murmurs and exclamations of shock from both the Japanese and the Ainu. The native men and women drew together, segregating themselves from the Japanese. Lord Matsumae hunched over Lilac, wringing his hands.

"First my Tekare is murdered, now this poor girl." He turned on Sano. "You promised to find out who killed Tekare. So much for your promises! And now there's been more blood spilled." His finger pointed at Lilac. "Who did this?"

"The same person must have committed both murders," Sano said. "Two murders of two young women from the castle, in the same vicinity, within a few months, can't be a coincidence."

Captain Okimoto scoffed "How would you know?" and turned to Lord Matsumae. "He's not familiar with the ways of Ezogashima. But I am, my lord, and I can tell you who killed this girl. It was them!"

He pointed at the natives. They stepped back in unison, clearly aware of what accusation he'd leveled at them. Chieftain Awetok uttered a vehement denial. His comrades seconded it. The Japanese guards cried, "Yes, you did!" "Murderers!"

Sano hastened to dash the cool influence of reason onto igniting tempers. "How do you know they killed Lilac?" He stepped between the two sides and faced Okimoto. "Did you see them do it?"

"Well, no," the captain blustered, "but it's obvious."

"Why?"

"One of their women was murdered. So they killed one of ours."

"A life for a life," Gizaemon said. "That's barbarian justice."

"I seem to recall you tried to convince me that they're responsible for Tekare's murder," Sano said. "If they are, why would they need revenge? You can't have it both ways."

"No, but they can. They're savages. Logic means nothing to them."

Lord Matsumae sidled into the argument. "Can this be true?" Wonder and fury united in his voice. "They killed my Tekare, and now they've attacked a Japanese?"

The Rat was busy translating for the natives. They shouted contradictions that the Japanese guards angrily shouted down. Sano raised his voice over theirs: "We don't know who's guilty yet. There's no evidence to prove that the natives were involved. A Japanese could have killed both."

But Lord Matsumae ignored Sano and railed at Chieftain Awetok, "You owe your position to me. None of you tribal lords rule without permission from my clan. We've given you authority over your people and fair prices for your goods. And this is how you repay us? By slaying our folk?"

"I appreciate your generosity," Chieftain Awetok replied through the Rat. "I would never repay it with violence. Neither I nor my people had anything to do with either death."

"Don't listen to him, my lord," urged Okimoto. "He's lying."

"You ungrateful, treacherous monster!" Spittle flew from Lord Matsumae's mouth like daggers toward the chieftain.

Awetok endured the insult with dignity. "If you seek the girl's killer, look among your own kind." He pointed at the Japanese men and women.

Incensed, Lord Matsumae drew his sword. "How dare you accuse us?" He lunged at the chieftain.

The native men pulled their knives. There was a tussle so brief that Sano didn't see what happened. Lord Matsumae let out a high-pitched cry. The natives scattered. He knelt on the ground, dropped his sword, and pushed up his left sleeve. A gash on his forearm dripped blood.

"You cut me!" he howled at the natives. "How dare you?"

They looked as surprised as he. Urahenka spoke. The Rat translated, " 'You attacked us. We were only defending ourselves.' "

"I don't care!" Lord Matsumae shrieked. "I declare war on you and all your kind." He ordered his troops, "Kill them!"

Chapter Twenty-Two

Yowling with bloodlust, Captain Okimoto and the other troops drew their swords and charged the natives. Sano was appalled because the tensions between the natives and the Japanese had been ignited by unproven accusations and Lord Matsumae's minor injury. He, Hirata, and the detectives grabbed the troops in an attempt to stop the fight. The troops fought them off. The women scattered in fright; the Rat dived into the forest. Okimoto shoved Sano, yelling, "Stay out of this!"

Sano skidded on ice and collided with a soldier. The soldier punched his jaw. Sano went reeling. Marume and Fukida brawled with other troops. Hirata exploded into action, a blur of flying punches and kicks. Troops fell away from him, but others attacked the natives, whom they outnumbered at least ten to one. Chieftain Awetok barked orders at his men. All except Urahenka turned and ran. He and Awetok crouched, knives raised, prepared to fight and give their comrades time to escape.

"Stop!" Sano threw himself between the two sides and spread his arms. "This is insane!"

Troops barreled past him. They drew bows and fired arrows at the fleeing natives, hacked at them with swords and cut them down as they ran. Three soldiers grabbed Sano. Captain Okimoto shouted, "Hey, Hirata-*san*!" He held the point of his sword to Sano's throat while Sano struggled against the men holding him. "Quit that, or I'll kill your master!"

Hirata spun to a halt amid the bodies of the soldiers he'd downed. Chieftain Awetok and Urahenka fought; swords battered knives. Amid curses in Ainu language and Japanese, the combatants lunged, struck, retreated, and lunged, trampling Lilac's dead body.

Afraid that Reiko would be caught in the battle and killed, Sano frantically looked for her. He saw a few troops gather her up with the other women and hurry them all away. From the forest came cries of agony as the troops slew the natives. Lord Matsumae jumped up and down, waved his sword, and cackled with gleeful excitement.

In a desperate attempt to restore order, Sano called to him, "We haven't yet found out who killed Tekare. Don't you want to know?"

"We do know. It was them!" Lord Matsumae pointed at the chieftain and Urahenka, who were fighting for their lives.

"Maybe it wasn't," Sano said. "They passed the trial by ordeal. They could be innocent."

Lord Matsumae shifted his attention from the battle to Sano; he stopped cackling. Captain Okimoto pricked Sano with his blade. "Shut up!"

Sano's flesh recoiled from the sting of cold steel. "If you kill them now, you'll never know for sure. Neither will Tekare. She'll never be certain she's had her revenge."

A vestige of rationality tinged Lord Matsumae's frown.

"Her murderer may still be out there," Sano said.

Impulsive as ever, Lord Matsumae shouted, "Stop the battle!" He kept shouting until the troops backed away from Chieftain Awetok and Urahenka, who stood panting, knives clutched in their hands, bleeding from cuts. "Everybody come back here!"

His army rushed out from the forest. At first they were too busy hooting in triumph to notice that everyone else was at a standstill. A soldier roared, "They're all dead. We got every last one of the barbarians."

Then they looked around in puzzlement, halted, and quieted. One said, "What's going on?"

"The war is postponed until we get to the bottom of things." Lord Matsumae pointed at Awetok and Urahenka, the sole surviving natives, and said, "These are our prisoners of war. Bring them back to the castle."

The funeral procession turned into a wild, raucous march home from battle. At its head Lord Matsumae walked in a daze, accompanied by cheering soldiers. Gizaemon followed, grimly triumphant. More troops escorted Chieftain Awetok and Urahenka. The two native men wore stony expressions, held their heads high. Behind them walked Sano, Hirata, and their comrades, also escorted by guards, little more than prisoners themselves. Then came a hooting mob of the youngest soldiers, carrying the severed heads of the slain natives. Blood dripped from the grisly trophies.

Trailing the march was another, quiet procession of servants. They carried Lilac's body, wrapped in their coats. The girl whose death had precipitated a war was all but forgotten.

As Sano trudged along, he felt ill with horror about the massacre. Detective Marume said, "I've met samurai bullies in my time, but these boys are the worst."

"They're like a wolf pack," Fukida said.

The Rat moaned, "Merciful Buddha, transport me back to Edo!"

Hirata's face was set in tight lines of anguish and fury as he watched the chieftain prodded and tormented along. Through Sano's horror rang guilt. If he'd solved the murder sooner, he might have prevented the massacre. Now he must do something to forestall more senseless slaughter.

At Fukuyama Castle, sentries at the gate greeted the troops like returning heroes. They mounted the severed heads on pikes outside the castle wall. The army cheered Lord Matsumae: "Hail to the future conqueror of Ezogashima!"

He smiled but looked perplexed, as if he didn't quite understand what had happened. Sano rushed over to him. "Lord Matsumae, please call off the war. Even if Chieftain Awetok or Urahenka did kill Tekare, their people had nothing to do with it."

"They're guilty by association," Lord Matsumae said.

"Japanese law says that a criminal's kin must share his punishment," Gizaemon added.

"Only his immediate family and close associates," Sano said. "It would be unfair to kill the other tribes."

"These bastards are all related as far as we're concerned," Gizaemon said.

If reason wouldn't get through to them, maybe threats would. "The shogun won't want a war. You're already in trouble with him for disrupting trade with the natives. A war will stop it altogether. He'll throw your clan out of Ezogashima and turn you all into masterless samurai."

Another cheer regaled Lord Matsumae. He raised his arms, beaming. Gizaemon said, "Trade will be better than ever after we wipe out the barbarians. We'll open up Ezogashima to every Japanese who wants to hunt game or mine for gold. There will be more wealth for the shogun."

"Ezogashima's a huge place. Your troops will be spread thin. You'll need reinforcements from the Tokugawa regime, from other samurai clans. That won't make Lord Matsudaira happy. He needs everybody to help him fight the rebels who are trying to depose him."

"We'll win a fast victory." Gizaemon sounded confident. "Lord Matsudaira will thank us for bringing him more riches to pay his army and his allies."

The castle gate opened. Troops swarmed through, carrying Sano in on the tide of their uproar. He fought to stay near Lord Matsumae and Gizaemon. "The practical details are against you. There's a plague among your men. And winter is no time to launch a military expedition. If there's this much snow here, how deep is it in the far north?"

"We won't go there yet," Lord Matsumae said. "We'll attack the nearest villages and save the others for spring." He cried, "Let's drink to our future victory!"

"At least wait until I finish investigating the murder," Sano pleaded.

"You are finished." Sudden anger enflamed Lord Matsumae. "I put my faith in you, and you've let me down. I'm taking back charge of the investigation. I'll find out who killed Tekare by persuading our prisoners to tell the truth."

"Best idea I've heard in a long time," Gizaemon said. "I'll help. Let's go."

Horror struck Sano because he knew what they intended. Hirata said "No!" and rushed forward to save Urahenka and Awetok from the troops herding them like animals.

Captain Okimoto said, "I wouldn't do that if I were you, Hirata-*san*." Rowdy, grinning soldiers aimed bows at Sano. One loose finger could end his life. Hirata stared in frustration and rage.

"Let Hirata-*san* and me come with you," Sano said to Gizaemon. Maybe he could keep things from getting out of hand. Maybe he was a deluded fool.

"All right," Lord Matsumae said. "I'll show you how an interrogation is done."

At the women's quarters, the troops locked the native concubines in their rooms. Reiko found herself thrown together with the Japanese ladies in theirs. Maids stoked braziers and brewed tea. The ladies-in-waiting fussed over Lady Matsumae. They removed her coat, wrapped her in quilts, and rubbed her cold hands and feet. No one paid any attention to Reiko. She knelt in a corner, spent by the day's events.

Discovering Lilac dead and learning that she'd been murdered had been bad enough. Reiko was aghast that it had led to a war. How many of the natives had been slaughtered? Reiko feared for Sano. Would he be killed in the fight? Would she lose her husband as well as her son?

Guilt filled Reiko. She'd been so immersed in her own loss that she'd done nothing to help Sano. If they never saw each other again, this separateness would be her last memory of him. Reiko felt such a debilitating exhaustion and despair that she wanted to lie down and sleep through whatever happened.

Lady Matsumae retched into a basin and vomited while the ladies-in-waiting held her head. "The sight of that girl was just awful," she groaned. "So was the fight. All that blood! I can't get it out of my mind."

Lady Smart offered her a cup of herbal tea. "Drink this. It'll settle your stomach."

"I can't." Lady Matsumae gagged and shivered. "I feel so cold. I feel dirty from being around death all day. It's rubbed off on me."

"A hot medicinal bath will help you," Lady Pansy said.

Reiko experienced a renewal of the anger that had sent her looking for Lilac. Now that the girl was beyond reach and Reiko could forgive her, the anger found a different focus. Such terrible things had happened, and all Lady Matsumae did was make work for other people. Reiko's earlier resentment toward Lady Matsumae deepened into hatred. She had no sympathy left for this woman who'd lost her daughter. Reiko had lost her son, and her own daughter, Akiko, was too far away to be any comfort. Lady Matsumae didn't deserve special consideration or the right to behave selfishly. Lilac had at least given Reiko warm clothes. Lady Matsumae had offered nothing whatsoever. And Reiko wondered if Lady Matsumae was at fault for more than that.

Her attendants helped Lady Matsumae out of the room. Reiko followed them down the corridor, stood outside the door of the bath chamber, and listened. Water splashed while the attendants washed Lady Matsumae. When they left her alone to soak in the tub, Reiko sneaked into the chamber.

It was a small room with a raised floor of wooden slats. Mats on the walls had a pattern of leafy green plants woven into them, for visual warmth. In the center was a round, sunken tub. Lady Matsumae sat submerged up to her chin. Her head lolled; her eyes were closed. The water steamed up in clouds that smelled of sweet, pungent herbs. Reiko had a sudden image of Lilac dead in the hot spring. For an instant she felt Lilac's inert flesh, saw the boiled-fish eyes staring sightlessly at her. The sensations nauseated her and fueled her anger.

"Wake up, Lady Matsumae," she ordered.

"Uh?" Lady Matsumae's head jerked up. Her eyes snapped open. She looked older without her makeup, her complexion sallow, mottled, and loose, her mouth pale and puffy. Hostility focused her bleary eyes. "What do you want?"

"To talk."

"Well, I don't want to," Lady Matsumae said peevishly. "Go away." She lay back, shut her eyes, and compressed her lips.

"I'm not leaving." Reiko had ideas about what had happened to Lilac, and she had bones to pick with Lady Matsumae. She dipped her hand in the tub and splashed water in Lady Matsumae's face.

Chapter Twenty-Three

Chieftain Awetok and Urahenka knelt on the dirt floor of an empty storehouse inside the castle. They were stripped to the waist, hands and ankles tied. Their fierce faces gleamed with sweat raised by a crackling wood fire whose flames gilded the thick hair on their bodies and cast their shadows toward Gizaemon, Lord Matsumae, and Captain Okimoto. Okimoto held a leather whip that bristled with metal barbs.

"This is your last chance," Lord Matsumae said, shrill with manic excitement. "Admit you murdered Tekare."

Gizaemon relayed the order to the natives in their language. Near the door, eight soldiers guarded Hirata and Sano. Hirata had never felt so helpless. If he tried to save the Ainu, the Matsumae folk wouldn't punish just Sano but also Reiko and their other comrades. He watched with impotent rage as the chieftain and Urahenka spoke, denying the accusation.

"They say their trial by ordeal proves they're innocent," Gizaemon said.

Lord Matsumae laughed. "Let's see if you can withstand my kind of ordeal!"

Okimoto cracked his whip, striking the chieftain and Urahenka across their chests. They held themselves rigid, jaws clenched. Bloody lash marks appeared on their skin. Sano wore the intense, somber expression that Hirata knew meant he was thinking hard, formulating and discarding strategies.

"What do you say now?" Lord Matsumae asked the natives. Each uttered denials. "Well, if you want to suffer, by all means do."

Again the whip cracked. Again the natives stoically bore the punishment. Chieftain Awetok's body was so tough with sinew and leathery skin that he looked as if he could endure the whipping indefinitely. But Urahenka was shivering; the sweat rolled down his face.

Tearful with frustration, Lord Matsumae hurled more accusations and demands for confessions at the natives. But Gizaemon had an air of enjoyment. Sano said to him, "You're eager for them to confess, aren't you?"

"You bet." Gizaemon relished chewing a sassafras toothpick. "It'll help my nephew, make him well again."

"I think your reason is more personal than that," Sano said. "If they confess, that lets you off the hook."

Gizaemon glowered. "That's enough from you."

Sano persisted even though the troops pressed their spears into his coat: "Before Lilac died, she told my wife that she knew something about the murder." He raised his voice above Lord Matsumae's angry shouts. "Was it about you?"

Hirata understood what Sano was trying to do—draw suspicion away from the natives and focus it on Gizaemon. And he could tell that Gizaemon knew.

"Lilac seems to have had a habit of bartering information for favors," Sano said. "But maybe you already know that, from personal experience."

"I'm warning you," Gizaemon said.

"Did she tell you that she saw you set the spring-bow trap for Tekare?" Hirata joined in. "Did she threaten to tell Chamberlain Sano unless you gave her money?"

Gizaemon didn't answer, and Lord Matsumae was too busy ranting to hear the suggestion that his uncle could be the murderer. The natives continued to resist him until their torsos were crisscrossed with bloody lines punctuated by deeper wounds where the barbs had dug in. Both were breathing hard now, both in obvious pain. Hirata looked away in shame. He couldn't bear to see the chieftain whipped to death while he stood by.

Suddenly the chieftain blurted an exclamation. "Wait," Gizaemon told Okimoto, who'd raised the whip again. "He says he's ready to give in."

Alarm beset Hirata. He didn't think the chieftain was a murderer; Awetok must have simply reached the limits of his endurance. But Hirata's confidence wavered in spite of himself. Maybe the chieftain was guilty. Maybe Awetok had been deceiving Hirata, luring him with promises of knowledge, to win an ally.

"At last you've come to your senses," Lord Matsumae said with relief. "Let us hear the truth."

The chieftain spoke. Gizaemon's expression turned foul. "The bastard says he'll talk only under one condition. That we call off the war."

Awetok was sacrificing himself to protect his people. Hirata admired the man's nobleness even as he continued to wonder if Awetok was the killer. Hirata knew two things for sure: The chieftain had held out this long to increase the value of his confession and use it as leverage to save the Ainu, and he would be executed whether he deserved it or not.

"You're in no position to bargain," Lord Matsumae said. "Talk now, and we'll make a deal later."

As Gizaemon relayed these words to him, Awetok nodded in resignation. He uttered a statement that sounded final.

"He admits that he killed Tekare," Gizaemon said with a smug look at Sano.

Sano's mouth curled with disgust. "This is as false a confession as I've ever seen."

Lord Matsumae ignored Sano, exulting, "At last I know who the culprit is. At last I will have justice for my Tekare." He beckoned Okimoto. "Take him to the execution ground."

Urahenka began yelling. The chieftain rapped out a command at him, but he yelled louder.

"What's he saying?" Sano asked.

"That the chieftain didn't kill Tekare," Gizaemon said,

annoyed by the interruption. "He says the chieftain only confessed to protect him. He's the killer, and he wants to prove it to us, with his own confession."

Lady Matsumae sputtered in fury. "The nerve of you! Have you no manners? You act like a cheap peasant girl."

"Save your insults," Reiko said. "They don't hurt me. Nothing can, after what's happened."

"What are you blabbering about now?" Lady Matsumae wiped her face with a wet hand and spat water into the tub in which she sat.

"My son is dead." Grief swelled within Reiko; her voice trembled. "He has been since before I got here."

Lady Matsumae's gaze was stupid with confusion. "How do you know?"

"I went to the keep. I saw the cage where they put Masahiro." The terrible memory almost undid Reiko. "I saw his blood."

"How did you get inside the keep?" Lady Matsumae said, as if that was the most important thing about what Reiko had said.

"That doesn't matter." Reiko didn't want to reveal that Wente had helped her; Lady Matsumae would punish Wente. "What matters is that your husband murdered my son. And I think it's your fault as much as his."

"My fault? How could it be? I never even saw your son. I didn't know he was here until you told me. If he's dead, I had nothing to do with it."

Reiko didn't believe her. "You started this whole disaster. You murdered Tekare. It drove your husband mad. You're directly responsible for all his crimes."

"I didn't murder her," Lady Matsumae said, impatient and offended. "I've already told you. I wouldn't lift a finger to kill one of those barbarian whores." Her tone was one she might use to say that stepping on ants was beneath her. "They're not worth the trouble."

"This one was, because you believe she murdered your daughter."

Dismay sagged Lady Matsumae's features. She clutched at her heart as if Reiko had struck her there. "Where did you learn that?"

"From Lilac. She told me how your daughter got sick and how Tekare performed a healing ritual. But your daughter died. And you think Tekare poisoned her."

"Lilac was a terrible gossip," Lady Matsumae said with disgust, but she didn't deny Reiko's claim. "I always said that her tongue would be the death of her."

"Maybe it was. Yesterday she promised me information about Tekare's murder. She'd already let me know that you wanted Tekare dead and why. What else did she have to tell?"

". . . I don't know."

"I think you do. I think Lilac saw you or your ladies setting up the spring-bow by the path. You found out that she knew. How? Did she try to blackmail you? Did she take money or gifts from you in exchange for her silence?"

"That's ridiculous."

Lady Matsumae was vehement, but Reiko continued, "When my husband started investigating the murder, that must have worried you. Here was someone who could give Lilac more than you could—a new life in Edo. You became afraid she would tell on you."

"There was nothing to tell about me!"

"You knew that if your husband found out you killed Tekare, he would put you to death," Reiko went on, relentless. "You needed to protect yourself. So you did away with Lilac."

Lady Matsumae drew herself up and declared, "I have nothing to hide from my husband. I had nothing to fear from a gossipy, conniving servant girl."

"This morning you followed her to the hot spring. You hit her on the head."

"I never left the castle until the funeral. I hadn't seen Lilac since last night. I never touched her!"

"You killed her," Reiko said. "Then you came to the funeral as if nothing had happened."

"Stop bothering me." Lady Matsumae's temper matched Reiko's. "Leave at once!" She pointed a dripping, shaky finger at the door.

Reiko folded her arms. "Not until you admit what you did."

"Then I'm going. I don't have to listen to your foolish accusations." Lady Matsumae rose, reaching for the towel and robe that lay near the tub.

Reiko snatched them and flung open the exterior door. Bright, freezing air poured into the bath chamber. As Lady Matsumae protested, Reiko hurled the towel and robe into the snow-covered garden outside. She faced Lady Matsumae.

Cowering in the tub, Lady Matsumae ordered, "Shut that door. I'll catch a cold."

"Don't expect me to care." Part of Reiko knew she was acting like a child having a tantrum, but it felt good in a nasty, shameful way. "You killed Tekare. You killed Lilac. You're responsible for my son's death. Admit it!"

Lady Matsumae shrank from Reiko. "You're mad!"

"Maybe I am. And people who are mad are dangerous. Your husband is proof of that. You'd better confess, or Lilac won't be the only one to die in a hot bath today."

"Help!" Lady Matsumae cried.

"I can kill you before anyone comes. Now talk!"

It didn't occur to Lady Matsumae to fight back against Reiko: She was physically passive, as were most women of her class. But her eyes gleamed with unexpected cunning. "What makes you so sure Lilac told the truth when she said she had more information?"

"Don't play games with me," Reiko said. "I'm running out of patience."

"She was dishonest," Lady Matsumae continued, although scared breathless. "She was just trying to get what she wanted out of you. She didn't really know anything."

Reiko put aside her own knowledge that Lilac had been stringing her along about Masahiro. Once a liar didn't have to mean always a liar. "I rate her truthfulness higher than yours. You're trying to save yourself. She's been murdered. That's evidence that she knew too much—about you."

Lady Matsumae suddenly repeated her earlier question: "How did you get inside the keep? Was it Lilac who took you?" Reiko's face must have given away the answer, because Lady Matsumae said, "So it wasn't." A mean, sly smile curved her mouth. "But I think I know who did. It was that Ezo concubine, the one you stopped me from beating."

"No," Reiko began.

"I suppose the little whore was grateful to you and wanted to return the favor. And you were ready to trust her because she seemed so pathetic, so simple." Lady Matsumae laughed disdainfully. "I warned you before that you don't understand the ways of Ezogashima. You outsiders think that what you see of the barbarians is all there is to them. But appearances are deceiving. Especially when you're so blind."

A cold, apprehensive sensation crept through Reiko. She was distracted even though she knew that was Lady Matsumae's intention. "What are you saying?"

"You've put your trust in the wrong place." Lady Matsumae was unafraid, her voice stronger now and laced with contempt. "Wente is Tekare's sister."

"I'm aware of that. She told me." But Reiko recalled her interrupted conversation with Wente yesterday. What would she have learned if they'd had the time to finish it?

"You don't seem aware that she and Tekare were on bad terms," Lady Matsumae retorted. "In fact, they were enemies. The other Ezo women had to keep them separated so they wouldn't fight. I suppose she didn't tell you that?"

Reiko was aghast at this information about her friend and upset because she'd had to hear it from Lady Matsumae. She woodenly shook her head.

Lady Matsumae laughed again. "Well, I'm telling you now. Maybe this time you'll listen to me. I saw a quarrel between the two of them, just a few days before Tekare died. They were slapping and clawing each other and shouting."

"What were they quarreling about?" Reiko hated to ask.

"I don't know; I don't understand Ezo language. But Wente had the last word. And I know a threat when I hear it." Lady Matsumae's smile shone with cruel triumph. "You should be accusing Wente instead of me."

Chapter Twenty-Four

"Who killed Tekare?" Lord Matsumae demanded. "Tell me who."

As Urahenka and the chieftain argued, it was obvious to Sano that someone was innocent and making a sacrifice, but he didn't know whom. He realized that he had one card left to play in this game of life or death, and timing was crucial.

Hirata said reluctantly, "I think Urahenka tried to kill me, that day we went deer-hunting. If one of them is guilty, it's him."

That was a card Hirata had kept to himself, Sano thought, probably because he'd been unsure of Urahenka's intentions and guilt. He'd just played it in favor of the chieftain. But the chieftain seemed dismayed, whereas Urahenka gave Hirata a look of gratitude and uttered a phrase that clearly meant, "It was I."

"Good enough," Gizaemon said. "No need to hear any more. Let's just execute him and be done."

Before Sano could willingly let that happen, he needed some idea of who was guilty or innocent. "Why not let the man have his say?" Maybe that would tell him which Urahenka really was. "Honor his last request."

Lord Matsumae tottered, clasped his head between his hands, and groaned. He stumbled around the storehouse, narrowly missing the fire. Tekare's persona rose up in him. Her features surfaced through his. They blazed with anger at Urahenka. "You killed me, Husband?" The voice was a bizarre combination of Tekare's and Lord Matsumae's, speaking native language in a high feminine register and Japanese in a low male one, both filled with incredulity.

It wasn't physically possible. Sano stared. But it was real. Although his men looked as shocked as Sano was, the Ezogashima folk seemed unsurprised: They'd seen it before. But Urahenka recoiled, his face gone pale. This was apparently the first time the spirit that possessed Lord Matsumae had spoken to him personally. "Tekare?"

"Yes, it is I. How could you do it?"

Urahenka sat speechless, transfixed.

"Answer me!"

When he spoke, Tekare's voice exclaimed in disbelief. Lord Matsumae's demanded, "Why did you need to get rid of her?"

Urahenka replied, and shock appeared on their two faces in one. Tekare blurted a question in native language, while Lord Matsumae said, "Her sister! You killed her so that you could marry Wente?"

Surprise hit Sano. Here was a motive he'd never uncovered. Although aware by this time that the natives were interconnected, he had never imagined a romantic affair between this man and Reiko's friend. Neither, apparently, had Reiko.

Urahenka spoke again, this time with defiance. Tekare shouted at him so loudly that she drowned out Lord Matsumae's weaker voice. Gizaemon said, "She's asking him how he could be in love with her sister, who's a dull, plain little mouse. She's nothing compared to Tekare. Tekare was the shamaness, the most beautiful woman in all the tribes. How could he want Wente instead?"

Sano wondered if this was another case of his misjudging the natives, thinking them too simple to engage in the tangled relationships that the Japanese had. Adultery must be common to all cultures, must provoke the same emotions in all the parties betrayed.

Tekare cursed at Urahenka. "She says he deceived her," Gizaemon said. "He broke their marriage vows. He's a miserable, worthless cheat." Lord Matsumae grabbed the whip from Captain Okimoto and began flailing Urahenka. The barbs tore at the native man, who flinched as he stuttered replies.

"She doesn't like his excuse that she treated him disrespectfully and left him for Japanese men," Gizaemon interpreted.

"Don't put the blame on Tekare!" Lord Matsumae yelled. "I don't care that you needed her sister to warm your bed at night!"

He pointed at Urahenka as Tekare ranted; he shook his head violently and clapped his hand to his chest. *You were my husband. And I never give up anything that's mine!* Sano didn't need a translation to understand. Urahenka shouted back at his wife, angry now himself. *That's why I had to kill you!* His motive was clearly the same as for a Japanese husband in his position.

"How dare you call her a whore!" Lord Matsumae cried while beating Urahenka, who continued trying to justify himself. Tekare's voice shrilled.

"She's angry because her husband says Wente is so good, so virtuous, everything Tekare isn't," Gizaemon said. "Urahenka says that when the chieftain decided to come to Fukuyama City and bring her home, Urahenka didn't want her back. He came planning to kill her." He flashed a triumphant look at Sano. "Seems it was him."

Sano had begun to think so. Maybe if he'd dug deeper into the natives' personal relationships he would have found out sooner about Urahenka. Maybe all those men wouldn't have died; maybe Lord Matsumae wouldn't have declared war. But it was selfish to feel guilt and regret on his own account. He should be glad that matters were being set right.

Lord Matsumae grabbed Urahenka by his beard. "Tell me how you did it." From Tekare came a low, poisonous croon. "Before I kill you, tell me."

Urahenka looked terrified enough that he would rather die on the spot than risk making his wife any angrier. He spoke. Lord Matsumae translated the words for himself as if trying to believe them—or to tear his own wounds open wider. "You sneaked away from camp every night. You waited near the castle for her to come out. You followed her along the path to the hot spring." He sobbed. "You got the idea to set a trap for her."

Lord Matsumae dropped the whip and pummeled Urahenka with his fists. He and Tekare howled, "Murderer!" as their personalities, voices, and languages blended. "You stole my life." "You killed my beloved." Together they cried, "Now you'll die!"

Giddy with hysteria, Lord Matsumae drew his sword. "Take him to the execution ground. I'll do the honors myself."

"Well, that's that," Gizaemon said, satisfied and relieved.

Stepping forward, he grabbed Urahenka by the ropes around his wrists and yanked him to his feet. Urahenka didn't resist; he had the grim look of a man whose fate is sealed.

"He hasn't said anything that proves he's guilty," Sano protested even though Urahenka had incriminated himself.

"It's over, Honorable Chamberlain," Gizaemon said. "Might as well admit you're wrong."

The chieftain, who'd been watching the interrogation with stoic forbearance, now asked a question. Lord Matsumae answered, in native tongue. Gizaemon laughed and said, "My nephew refused to call off the war. He doesn't care that the barbarians think he led them to believe he would. He wants them all to share their tribesman's punishment."

Awetok shook his head, defeated but as unsurprised as Sano was that Lord Matsumae had refused to make peace. The room filled with Tekare's laughter. She mocked the chieftain while Lord Matsumae's voice echoed hers: "You're so pitiful, so weak. When I was young, you didn't protect me from the Japanese who violated me. You were too cowardly to fight for our right to rule our own land."

Captain Okimoto pulled the chieftain to his feet, prepared to lead him to his death. Now was Sano's last chance to play his last card, to take one final stab at finding the truth.

"Tekare!" he shouted. "Listen to me!"

She and Lord Matsumae raged at her husband: "You didn't want me to better myself. If I had to die, so should you."

"Urahenka's not the only man you abused who wanted you dead," Sano told her.

Lord Matsumae raised his sword. "I'm not going to wait for an execution ceremony. I'll kill you now!"

Sano lunged and grabbed him. The troops grabbed Sano, pulling him back. He hung onto Lord Matsumae, who turned on him and fought him. Sano saw only one brilliant, fiery light in Lord Matsumae's eyes—Tekare's consciousness. When she snarled, Lord Matsumae's face belonged completely to her. His body had the soft, pliant feel of a young woman's. Sano was astounded to think that he was touching a ghost. When Tekare wrenched free of him, his hands felt scorched by her power. He broke loose from the troops and stood between Tekare and Urahenka.

"Get out of my way!" As Tekare spoke, Lord Matsumae's voice again echoed her words in Japanese. His hand waved the sword at Sano.

"Give your husband the benefit of doubt," Sano said. "The real killer could be someone you're overlooking."

The troops hurled themselves at Sano, recaptured him, and dragged him away from Urahenka. But Tekare frowned, her attention engaged at last. "Overlooking? Who?"

"You're inside him," Sano said.

Tekare raised Lord Matsumae's eyebrows in surprise. She glanced down at the male human body she'd taken over, then laughed. "Don't be ridiculous. Lord Matsumae was in love with me." She lifted his hand and caressed his face. The act evoked a disturbing presence of the two lovers together. "He worshipped me."

"At first," Sano agreed, "until you mistreated him."

"Who says I did?"

"This does." Sano pulled out the book he'd been carrying with him. "It's Lord Matsumae's diary. It tells the truth about his relationship with you. Listen." He paged through the book, reading passages: " 'I notice how other men look at Tekare. Does she smile at them? Do their eyes hold a moment too long?' "

The troops unhanded Sano and listened with rapt, unnerved attention, as if the voice of their master spoke through him and he was vested with Lord Matsumae's power. But Gizaemon demanded, "Where did you get that?"

"From Lord Matsumae's room." Sano noted how surprised Gizaemon appeared. Had he not known how things were between his nephew and Tekare? Or had he only been unaware that Lord Matsumae had kept a diary? But it wasn't Gizaemon's possible motive for murder that concerned Sano right now.

" 'My worst fears have been realized,' " he continued, paging through the diary. " 'I saw Tekare and the young soldier.' 'They dared to couple right in front of me, as if I were not there!' 'She smiled at me as I lay helpless and horrified.' "

"But it was just a game we played." Tekare sounded surprised that Lord Matsumae should have minded. "Jealousy excited him. He liked it."

"Not according to this." Sano read on: " 'I raged at her.' 'I threatened to send her back to her tribe unless she behaved herself. But she said that if I did, I would never see her again. And I know that my threats are no good. I am at her mercy.' Does that sound as if Lord Matsumae liked your game?"

"He loved me." But Tekare was shaken, uncertain this time.

"In his own words: 'I now fear and revile Tekare as much as I love her. She has cast over me an evil spell that has reduced me to a pathetic shadow of myself.' 'I must destroy her before she completely destroys me.' "

"He wouldn't have hurt me." Tekare gazed at Lord Matsumae's hands, flexing them, as if she couldn't believe he'd used them against her. "He couldn't."

"You didn't have as much control over him as you believed. Here's what he said." Sano read, " 'At night I lie awake, plotting her death.' 'Perhaps I should poison her food. Or set a spring-bow trap along a path she walks.' "

Sano emphasized these last words, then repeated, *"A spring-bow trap."*

Amazement dumbfounded the troops; evidently the idea had never occurred to them. Hirata's eyes filled with hope. They turned toward Chieftain Awetok, who listened as though he'd understood everything Sano had said and wasn't surprised.

"You're talking nonsense," Gizaemon said.

"That can't be!" Tekare exclaimed in outrage. "Lord Matsumae didn't write that book!"

"Don't take my word for it. Let's ask him." Sano called, "Lord Matsumae, are you there?"

Tekare stiffened as though a current of lightning had run through her. Her face went blank. A second, faint spot of fire ignited in each of her eyes.

"What do you have to say for yourself?" Sano asked Lord Matsumae.

The man's masculine cast and posture returned, but before he could answer, he shouted at himself in Tekare's voice: "Is that book yours?"

He beheld the diary in Sano's hand as if afraid that it would bite him. ". . . Yes."

"Did you write those things?"

"Yes. No," he stammered.

"Which is it?" Sano said, at the same time Tekare asked, "Did you hate me that much?"

"No! I was just confused, scribbling foolish notions. I loved you with all my heart."

"You were planning to set a trap for me. Did you?"

Lord Matsumae's gaze was full of fear directed inside himself. "I—I don't know."

"Of course he didn't." Gizaemon said to Sano, "After he's been driven mad by grief over the woman, after he's let you investigate her murder, how can you accuse him?"

"Grief isn't the only thing that drives people mad. Guilt can, too." Sano had wondered if Lord Matsumae had sought to relieve it by punishing someone else for his crime.

Tekare leaned forward, menacing the man she possessed.

The two spirits inside him created an illusion that his body had divided into two separate physical entities. "How can you not know? Did you or didn't you kill me?"

Lord Matsumae backed away in a futile effort to escape her. "I mean, I don't remember!"

"You deliberately forgot you killed Tekare because you didn't want her to know." This theory made as much sense to Sano as anything that happened in Ezogashima. "You were afraid of what she would do if she found out."

Gizaemon spat out his toothpick in disgust at Sano. But rage suffused Tekare's features that masked Lord Matsumae's. "It was you!"

Lord Matsume stumbled as he recoiled from the adversary within him. "It wasn't, my beloved. I couldn't, I wouldn't—"

"Did you kill me?"

"No!" But Lord Matsumae's denial weakened as his will eroded.

Sano urged, "Be an honorable samurai. Take responsibility for your actions. End this madness now." If he couldn't kill Lord Matsumae with his own hands, he would settle for coercing him to commit ritual suicide.

Lord Matsumae began slapping his own face. Tekare's voice spewed invective. "You killed me! Murderer!"

His fists beat his chest, his stomach. As everyone else stared in shock, he fell and writhed while the spirit of Tekare screamed, "You'll pay for my life with yours! Die!"

He closed his hands around his throat, strangled himself, and banged his head against the floor. His body bucked; his legs kicked. He gasped for air and choked.

"Stop him!" Gizaemon yelled at the troops as he ran to his nephew's aid. "Before he kills himself!"

Chapter Twenty-Five

Reiko tiptoed down a passage in the women's quarters and stopped outside a door that led to the section where the native concubines lived. Through it filtered their voices, conversing in their language. Reiko banged on the door, then shoved it open without waiting for an answer.

Their conversation halted. Reiko paused on the threshold of a chamber furnished with mats on the walls, thatched curtains over the windows, a table that held wooden spindles, and a loom partially filled with woven cloth. The concubines sat around a hearth, wooden bowls on their laps, spoons in their hands, eating a meal that smelled of dried fish and pungent seasonings. Mouths full, they gazed at Reiko. She was so blinded by anger that their tattooed faces looked identical; she couldn't tell which belonged to the person she'd come to see.

"Wente!" she called.

One of them set down her food and rose. Wente's shy smile faded as she perceived that Reiko hadn't come in friendship.

"Why didn't you tell me that you and Tekare were enemies?" Reiko demanded.

Fright appeared on Wente's face. She looked at her companions, seeking safety among them. Eyes averted from Reiko, she said, "How you know?"

"Lady Matsumae told me that you and Tekare used to fight. Your friends had to keep you apart."

The other women clearly didn't understand what she and Wente were saying but sensed danger in the air, for they scrambled to their feet and exited the room. Wente made a move to follow, but Reiko stepped in front of her. The two of them were alone in the smoky, firelit room that was like a native hut far from any place familiar or comfortable to Reiko.

"No have time," Wente mumbled.

"There was plenty," Reiko said, although she remembered that she'd been in a hurry to find Masahiro. Her mind veered away from the memory of hopes shattered, from grief. She buoyed herself up with the anger that had fixed on Wente. "It would have taken only a moment to tell me the truth about Tekare."

Wente bit her lips. "You ask me about Lady Matsumae."

"Forget Lady Matsumae." That woman had blown a big hole in Reiko's certainty that she was a killer. Reiko now acknowledged how rashly quick she'd been to trust Wente, to believe her grief for her sister was genuine and to sympathize with her. "You're the one I'm interested in now. You had a quarrel with Tekare shortly before she died. What was it about?"

"Why you care?" Wente sounded timid yet resentful of Reiko's prying. "Why you care who kill my sister?"

"Never mind that." Anger at herself for her negligence doubled Reiko's anger toward Wente. "Now why did you and Tekare quarrel?"

Wente's resistance crumbled. Probably the habit of obeying the Japanese was too strong to break. She sighed, then said, "She ruin my life."

Reiko felt the clear wind of truth sweep away the atmosphere of deception. "How?"

Extreme hatred came over Wente's face, disfiguring it so much that Reiko barely recognized it. "When she come castle, she want me by her. I no want leave village. But she say I have to, even though—" She struggled to find Japanese words to explain. "Not concubine, no can live here. So Tekare find soldier want Ainu woman. He bring me."

Now she was so eager to vent her grievance toward Tekare that she forgot Reiko was looking to pin the murder on her, neglected caution. "I no want him. But he take me." Bitterness saturated her voice. "And she happy."

Reiko absorbed the ugly meaning of this tale. Wente had been forced to become a concubine in order that Tekare could have her company at the castle. Tekare had paired Wente up with a Japanese man, regardless of Wente's feelings. Wente had suffered doubly, from sexual enslavement and her sister's cruel, selfish connivance in it.

"So you fought with her because of that?" Reiko asked.

Wente nodded, then shook her head: What Tekare had done was the root of the argument but not its topic. "I want go home. She no let me."

Reiko perceived that she'd stumbled up against another situation beyond her limited understanding of Ezogashima. "But once you became a concubine, wasn't it up to the man to say where you can go?" That was how the situation worked in Edo. "What authority did your sister have?"

"Soldier tired of me, say he send me back to village. But Tekare say she ask Lord Matsumae let me stay. He do anything she want him do for her." The hatred exuded from Wente, foul as rot. "I beg her, but she no give in."

Reiko wondered if Tekare's side of the story had been different. "Maybe she was scared to be by herself at the castle. Maybe she was homesick and needed someone from her family, someone she loved, with her."

Wente burst out indignantly, "She no scared. Always, 'Wente do this, Wente do that.' 'Wente, bring me food, rub back, brush hair.' She no love me!"

It sounded to Reiko as if Tekare had treated her sister as nothing but a servant, adding insult to abuse.

"Same at home," Wente continued. "When we children, I do all work—gather food, cook, sew, wash. Tekare do nothing. She shamaness. She special. I just plain girl." Reiko heard old disgruntlement as sharp as a knife blade in Wente's tone. "She always treated best. Get best things."

Wente touched her clothes, her bead necklace. "When not enough food, she eat. Village need her. I go hungry. She take everything. Leave nothing for me. And she happy."

Reiko got a picture of a girl who'd been led to believe she was better than the other villagers. The Empress of Snow Country, who'd enjoyed her privileges, who'd provoked her ordinary sister's jealousy.

"All my life, I wait to get away from Tekare. I older, I marry first, have own house. We grow up, and I find man. He strong, handsome, good hunter. He best man in village." Wente's eyes shone with the memory. "We fall in love." Tenderness softened her voice. "We—"

She fumbled for words, and Reiko said, "Became engaged?"

Although Wente nodded, her expression went black. "But *she* want him. Can't bear I have something she no have. She do magic rituals, make him love her, forget me. He marry *her*!"

Reiko pitied Wente, having her sister steal her fiancé. But she hardened her heart against Wente. This history only strengthened her cause for murder.

"In village, I try not see them, not look at him. But I still love. And she no care about him. She want rich Japanese. When she get Lord Matsumae and she bring me to city, I think I never see Urahenka again."

"Urahenka?" The familiar name jarred Reiko. "Isn't he one of the men at the camp?"

Wente nodded. Now Reiko remembered her watching him at the funeral. But she'd not bothered to wonder why; she'd been too preoccupied with her own feelings to perceive a love triangle.

"Men come for Tekare, want take her home. But not Urahenka. He come for me. He say marry Tekare, mistake. He no love, no want. He love *me*." Wente touched her bosom; she radiated delight. "He say when we get back to village, he no more Tekare husband. We marry."

"That's why you wanted to go home, and why Tekare wouldn't ask Lord Matsumae to let you," Reiko clarified.

"She didn't want to give up Urahenka even though she didn't want him." Her greed must have infuriated Wente all the more. "That was why you quarreled, why you threatened to kill her. She stood in your way." But now Reiko realized that Wente hadn't been the only one whose hopes Tekare had dashed. "What about Urahenka? What did he do because Tekare kept you here?"

Wente was quick to sense the accusation implicit in Reiko's questions. "He not hurt Tekare! No matter how she treat him, he too good, too—" She grasped for an adjective and found one she must have heard often in the samurai domain. "Honorable."

But honor often took second priority to love. Urahenka wouldn't have been the first man who'd wanted to rid himself of one woman so he could have another. He had as much reason for murder as Wente.

"He could have killed Tekare," Reiko said. "I think it was either him or you. Tell me which."

Maybe Wente would confess now in order to protect Urahenka. But she declared, "Not him. Not me."

For the first time, Reiko considered the possibility that there was more than one killer, that the murder had resulted from a conspiracy. "Maybe it was both of you. You told Urahenka that Tekare used that path to the hot spring at night. He set the trap. She walked into it. If Lord Matsumae hadn't gone mad and taken everyone in Fukuyama City hostage, you and Urahenka would have been free to go home and marry."

Wente repeated, "Not him." She had the look of a hunted, cornered animal. "Not me."

"But that's too complicated," Reiko said. "Often the simplest answer is the correct one. It's more likely that you acted alone. Urahenka doesn't know you killed his wife, your own sister. But I think Lilac did. She saw you. She blackmailed you. And you killed her."

Now Reiko grew furious on behalf of Lilac, Urahenka, and many others in addition to herself. "Lord Matsumae will kill your people in a war because of what you did. Many

Japanese will die, too. If you have any decency at all, you'll confess. Maybe it's not too late to save them."

Woe clouded Wente's eyes. "Mistake," she pleaded.

"You're still saying Tekare's death was an accident? I suppose Lilac's was, too? And my son's?" Reiko laughed sarcastically. "Spare me your nonsense." She was ready to hold Wente responsible for Masahiro's death, to believe that the loss of her son stemmed from Wente's selfishness. "I should kill you for everything you've done!"

Wente stiffened in terror of Reiko, of the Japanese who held the power of life and death over her. She extended a trembling hand toward Reiko. "Please," she whispered. "Believe."

Her appeal begged the favor of Reiko's mercy in exchange for favors Wente had granted. It called on Reiko to remember the brief yet intense relationship that had sprung up between kindred souls thrown together in harsh circumstances. But Reiko turned her back on Wente. She wasn't absolutely sure that Wente had killed Tekare or Lilac, but she was certain that true friendship must be based on trust. This relationship was over.

Chapter Twenty-Six

Lord Matsumae lay on his bed, wrapped from chin to toes in a quilt tied with ropes wound around his body. He groaned and writhed as Tekare ranted curses at him out of his own mouth.

"Is he going to be all right?" Gizaemon asked anxiously.

"I don't know," said the physician. He tried to stick acupuncture needles in Lord Matsumae's head as it tossed from side to side. "Not if he keeps trying to hurt himself."

Guarded by troops, Sano watched from the place across the room where Gizaemon had ordered him to stand out of the way. When Tekare had attacked Lord Matsumae, Sano and Hirata had helped restrain him, get him to his room, and wrap him up. Afterward, Gizaemon had sent Hirata back to the guest quarters. Now Sano locked eyes with Gizaemon.

"Look what you've done," Gizaemon said bitterly. He looked aged ten years by worry. "This is all your fault."

Sano wasn't sorry. "Lord Matsumae killed Tekare. He deserves to suffer. It's fitting that the spirit of Tekare kills him."

"He didn't kill her," Gizaemon insisted angrily. "He's innocent."

"He's guilty of everything else that's happened since the murder." Sano thought of Masahiro. How much had he suffered?

"You're so sure you're right. But suppose for the moment that you're wrong. What happens to my nephew?"

Soldiers held Lord Matsumae's head. He snarled, tried to bite them, and howled while the doctor inserted the needles.

"I honestly don't care," Sano said.

But now that he'd had time to think, he was forced to admit to himself that the case against Lord Matsumae was far from closed. Lord Matsumae had never actually confessed, and the other suspects had never been cleared. Sano was disturbed by his own rush to judgment. The death of his child had destroyed his objectivity. But he must separate the murder of Tekare from Lord Matsumae's other crimes. Honor required him to see justice applied justly.

"I'll find out for certain who killed Tekare," he said. "If it's not Lord Matsumae, that should save him from her." *But not from me.*

Gizaemon beheld Sano with contempt. "You think you're going to continue your investigation? It's already made things worse for my nephew." As the doctor twiddled the needles between his fingers, stimulating the flow of energy through Lord Matsumae's body, Lord Matsumae screamed as though under torture. "Whatever you do next will probably kill him. Forget it."

Sano had lost count of how many times an investigation of his had been hindered or shut down. He was determined to continue this one because the killer had set off the events that had led to Masahiro's death and was therefore just as responsible as Lord Matsumae was. Sano wanted revenge on everyone involved. It was the only thing that might bring him and Reiko peace. But he knew better than to expect that argument to convince Gizaemon.

"It's my duty to Lord Matsumae," Sano said.

Gizaemon said with a sarcastic chuckle, "As if he's in any shape to care about that now."

"We have a deal," Sano reminded him.

"I just broke it."

"What gives you the right?"

"Now that my nephew is out of commission—thanks to you—I'm in charge."

A moment ago Sano wouldn't have thought anyone could be a worse ruler than the mad Lord Matsumae, but Gizaemon was. Stubborn, narrow-minded, plus mean added up to a spark in the powder-keg that was Ezogashima. Besides, if Lord Matsumae wasn't the killer, then Gizaemon was still a major suspect.

"I outrank you in the Tokugawa regime," Sano said, even though he knew that mattered little so far from Edo. "I'm taking over."

"You and your little band of men? Don't make me laugh." Gizaemon jabbed a finger at Sano. "Your investigation's over. And you're not needed here." He nodded to the troops.

The haste with which they pushed Sano toward the door made it clear that Gizaemon had already established himself as ruler. Sano said, "You can't cure your nephew by keeping him tied up. If he's left as he is, he'll die. You need my help."

"More of your help will finish him off." Gizaemon swelled with new, malignant authority. "You're forbidden to come near him again."

As Sano resisted the men dragging him away, Gizaemon added, "Lord Matsumae let you get away with too much. I won't. And don't bother threatening me with your army, the shogun, or Lord Matsudaira. Your army is far away, and if the shogun and Lord Matsudaira cared about you, they'd never have sent you here."

Troops marched Reiko up to the guest quarters just as others arrived bringing Sano. One of the soldiers with Reiko said, "Your wife has been causing trouble, Honorable Chamberlain." He shoved her at Sano. "Keep her under control."

After Reiko had cornered Lady Matsumae in the bath chamber, the woman had complained to the guards, who'd found her in the native concubines' quarters and removed her. Now Reiko was relieved to see that Sano was safe, but the huge weight of her grief for Masahiro crushed happier emotions.

Sano moved his lips in what failed to pass as a smile. "Are you all right?"

"Yes," Reiko said, although that had never been less true.

She felt as if they inhabited separate worlds moving farther apart. "And you?"

"Yes."

She could see that he didn't want to burden her any more than she wanted to burden him, but lines of fatigue and sorrow carved his face. Reiko had a vision of what he would look like in twenty years—if they lived that long. She tried not to imagine that much time without Masahiro, time she'd planned to spend watching him grow into a man, marry, and give her grandchildren. She forced herself to concentrate on the moment, on putting one foot in front of the other along the course toward vengeance, her only, harsh comfort.

The troops locked her and Sano in the building, which was as cold inside as outside. Reiko and Sano removed only their boots in the entryway and kept their coats on. As they headed toward their room, Reiko said, "I have to tell you what I've learned."

The door of the room where Sano's men were staying opened, and Hirata appeared. "What happened?"

"I'll tell you in a moment." Sano accompanied Reiko into their room. It was freezing; their beds were not put away, and no food was left for them. "It looks like the servants have quit us."

He opened the braziers and put in coal. Reiko knew he needed to keep busy for the same reason she did, but she couldn't help feeling annoyed at him because his actions were so practical, so trivial. "Must you do that now?"

"Don't you want me to warm this place up?" Sano lit the coals and used his glove to fan up the fires.

"Yes, but I need you to listen."

"I can listen while I work." An edge sharpened his voice.

They'd often done this sort of ordinary bickering, but Reiko found that although grief diminished positive emotions, it intensified negative ones such as resentment toward her husband for not paying her enough attention. "Just stop for a moment. This is important."

Sano replaced a lid on a brazier with exaggerated care and dusted off his gloves. "All right. I'm listening."

"I think I know who killed Tekare and Lilac."

"Oh?"

Disappointed by his lack of enthusiasm, Reiko said, "It's either Lady Matsumae or Wente." She described her conversations with both. "Well? Which one do you think it is?"

"Either sounds as good as the other," Sano said wearily.

Reiko couldn't understand his attitude. "Don't you care?"

"It's not that." Sano drew her down to sit with him beside the brazier that emitted faint, inadequate heat. "The situation has changed." He told her that he'd confronted Lord Matsumae about the diary and how Lord Matsumae had reacted.

Reiko was amazed by the idea that the spirit inside Lord Matsumae had tried to kill him. "You believe Lord Matsumae killed Tekare?"

"As much as I can believe anyone else did," Sano said, "but the spirit of Tekare didn't give him a chance to confess. And Gizaemon has taken over. He's shut down the murder investigation. Who really killed Tekare, or Lilac, is beside the point."

Reiko was devastated because her efforts had come to nothing, and angry because she didn't agree with Sano one bit. "Maybe it doesn't matter to you, but it does to me."

"I didn't mean it doesn't matter to me. I'm just saying—"

"You're saying that no matter who killed Tekare, the truth is useless because even if we find it, you can't make anybody here do anything with it."

Sano exhaled. "If you must speak so bluntly."

"Well, I still want to know who the murderer is, and I have a good use for the information. He or she instigated what happened to Masahiro. I want that person punished. I want revenge." Reiko's voice shook with rage and grief. "It's all I have left."

"I know how you feel," Sano said. "I feel the same."

"Do you?" Reiko tasted the acid in her words. She didn't see how the death of a child could possibly hurt the father as much as the mother who had borne him.

"Of course," Sano said, clearly wounded by her implication. "Masahiro was my son, too."

The pain of hearing him mentioned in the past tense boosted Reiko's desire to lash out at someone, and Sano was the only person available. "Then stop acting so defeated. Let's figure out who started this whole disaster!"

"It's not that easy," Sano explained. "I have even less freedom to question suspects, look for witnesses, and find clues than I did before. There won't be any more guided tours around the castle and city for me or Hirata-*san*. We're locked in here. My hands are tied."

Reiko understood, but his helplessness angered her even more. "That would seem to be your own fault. If you hadn't accused Lord Matsumae, he might still be in charge and willing to cooperate with you."

Visibly angry himself now, and stung by her rebuke, Sano said, "I agree that was the worst mistake in my life, even though it seemed like a good idea at the time." He shook his head in bewilderment. "What is it about this place? Good ideas always turn out wrong here." He rubbed his eyes. "I wish I'd never found that despicable diary or confronted Lord Matsumae with it."

His self-reproach pained Reiko, but she took a mean pleasure in hurting him. "You're always so concerned about justice. What about justice for your son? What about your samurai duty to avenge him? If you cared, you'd find a way."

"Shut up!" Sano exclaimed. Making an effort to calm himself, he put his hands on her shoulders and deliberately lowered his voice: "I know how upset you are, but don't take it out on me."

Reiko lost her own self-control. "Let me go!" She fought Sano, hitting him, savage with grief and fury. Part of her dimly realized that this was how Lord Matsumae must have felt when Tekare had died. Now she was going mad, too.

"Stop that," Sano ordered, as he struggled to restrain her, "before you hurt yourself. Don't let this turn us against each other."

But Reiko fought harder, sobbing wildly. The precious, beloved fruit of their union was gone, and so was their love for each other. Their marriage had died with their son.

"We have to stick together," Sano persisted. "We have to live through this."

"Why?" Reiko cried. She welcomed death, which would end the suffering.

"Because we have another child at home." Sano's voice was intense with urgency. "In case you've forgotten Akiko."

Reiko almost had. Masahiro's death had left her few thoughts to spare for Akiko. But now the mention of her daughter silenced Reiko like a stab to the heart. Akiko didn't compensate her for the loss of her firstborn, but Reiko suddenly longed for the baby she'd left behind in Edo. She realized with a shock that the situation was even worse than she'd imagined.

Gazing up at Sano in horror, she whispered, "We're never getting out of here, are we? We'll never see Akiko again."

"Don't say that," Sano said, equally horrified and afraid that her prediction could make itself come true.

She could see in his eyes that he didn't have much faith in their ever returning home, either. "Gizaemon isn't going to honor Lord Matsumae's promise to set us free if you find the killer. He won't let us go back to Edo and tell tales about what's happened here. As far as he's concerned, we're better off dead. It's just a matter of time before he figures that out."

Sano was silent. A deep frown of despair carved his brow. Reiko sat with him amid the wreckage of their life, their marriage, their family. Outside, war drums boomed. Cheers rose from soldiers drunk on wine, celebrating today's massacre, rallying for battle. The sounds reminded Reiko that she and Sano and their comrades weren't the only ones doomed. The natives were about to lose their lives, their society, their existence as a people. There seemed nothing she or Sano could do to save them, either.

Then Sano spoke in a voice hushed with enlightenment: "If all is lost, we have nothing left to lose." His face wore an expression Reiko had never seen before. It was ravaged yet strong, bleakly resigned to defeat yet luminous with purpose. "If our hours are numbered, then let's make the most of them."

Reiko imagined that this was how a samurai looked when embarking on a mission bound to end in his death. She sensed a fervor in Sano, a contagious energy. Her spirits rose in spite of herself. "By doing what?"

"What you said we should. Avenging our son's death."

Reiko felt a spark of the ardor she'd once felt toward her husband. Even though they were fated to die, there was something left between them. Suddenly breathless with anticipation, she said, "How?"

"I don't know yet." Sano's tone was without fear or lack of confidence. "But I swear on my ancestors' honor that I'll right all the wrongs that have been done here in Ezogashima. I'll think of a way before this night is over."

Chapter Twenty-Seven

After an eternal night, the sun thrust up from behind the hills above Fukuyama City, round and glowing red in the pale sky, crossed by wisps of violet cloud, like a giant battle standard. Outside the castle, the heads of the massacred natives stood frozen on their pikes. Inside, a bonfire in the main courtyard had burned down to smoking ashes. The barracks were filled with soldiers sleeping off last night's revelry. All was quiet as Ezogashima poised on the brink of war.

Inside the guest quarters, Hirata crept through the silent darkness that immersed the building. His trained senses compensated for his lack of eyesight. The faint sound of his own breathing echoed off the walls, forming an auditory picture of the empty corridor. He moved soundlessly down it. Pausing outside the room where the guards were, he felt their heartbeats, a slow, steady pulsation that meant they'd fallen asleep on their watch. They hadn't overheard the whispered conversation that had gone on between Sano, Hirata, Reiko, and the detectives all night. They were sitting ducks.

Hirata eased their door open. Smoky heat wafted from charcoal braziers. He felt rather than saw the four human figures curled motionless on the floor. Hirata tiptoed over to each man, pressed a finger against his neck, and delivered a burst of energy. The sleeping men fell into deeper slumber. Their pulses slowed to the minimum required to pump blood through their bodies. They would stay unconscious for several hours. Hirata took their swords, a long and a short from each man, then hurried back to the room where his comrades waited.

"First mission accomplished," Hirata said, and passed out the weapons.

Sano, Marume, and Fukida drew the long swords from the scabbards and examined the blades by the light of the oil lamp. "Good enough," Marume said.

"Thieves can't be choosers," Fukida said.

Reiko held out her palms to Hirata. He laid a dagger across them. Her face was solemn and fierce. A chill ran through him. He'd seen that look before, on samurai who'd come to Edo Castle to register vendettas against their foes. But he'd never before seen it on a woman.

The detectives headed out of the room; the Rat reluctantly followed. Hirata, Sano, and Reiko lingered. Sano bowed to Hirata and said, "A million thanks for your faithful service."

The words had a gravity that said he meant his thanks not just for now, but for all the years they'd been master and retainer. He had spoken them because he might not have a chance later.

"It was nothing," Hirata insisted with a vehemence that said they wouldn't fail in their mission, wouldn't die and never talk again. A lump formed in his throat. Unable to look at Sano or Reiko, he bowed and walked out to meet the destiny he'd come seeking in Ezogashima.

Reiko and Sano were alone for what might have been the last time. Sano said, "You don't have to do this."

"I must," Reiko said.

She saw him studying her for signs of fear, but she felt none. Her spirit had moved beyond fear and grief to a place of still, perfect calmness. Her body was a tool for revenge, her sense of purpose untouched by emotions.

"Don't go alone," Sano said with pleading urgency.

"It's what we decided." Rather, Reiko had decided, against his strenuous objections. Her voice was even, untroubled. She knew she would succeed in the mission she'd charted for herself. She didn't care what happened to her as a result.

"Come with me," Sano said. "We've always worked well together." His words alluded to the crimes they'd solved in the past, the dangers they'd faced and surmounted, the whole history of their unconventional marriage.

"We've also worked well separately."

"I remember the times you struck out on your own, and I worried about whether you would come back to me safely."

Those times merged with this instant. Even as Sano was ready to object again, Reiko said, "You have your task. I have mine. This is how it must be."

Sano inclined his head, conceding. "Reiko-*san* . . ." He sought words to express his love for her, to commemorate their marriage in the brief time they had left.

Reiko placed a finger on his lips to silence him. She could not let him revive her emotions. She needed all her strength and concentration for the challenges ahead.

Sano caught her hand. "We may not have another chance."

"We will," Reiko said with sublime confidence.

Even if they didn't survive this day, they would see each other again—when death reunited them and Masahiro. Then they would have an eternity to say all the things they hadn't gotten to say while alive.

"Then I suppose we're ready to go." Sano's voice was resigned, but strong with his own sense of purpose.

They joined their comrades in the entryway. Hirata opened the door. The ruddy dawn illuminated their alert, serious faces. Reiko spared a thought for the years that they'd worked together, which ended now. Hirata listened a moment, then said, "All clear."

One by one they exited the building. They silently fanned out in separate directions, Sano joined with Marume, Fukida, and the Rat, while Hirata and Reiko each went alone, across snow that the rising sun stained red as blood.

The castle awakened. The intoxicating breath of war pervaded the air, rousing the soldiers from their drunken stupor. As they hurried about, hauling weapons and provisions, they sparred and joked with one another. The palace was battle headquarters. Commanders streamed in and out, gave orders to troops. Busy with preparations for their raid on the nearest Ainu villages, they didn't realize they were under surveillance.

Sano, Marume, Fukida, and the Rat crouched behind a stone lantern. As they watched the activity at the palace, Marume said in a low voice, "Too many troops around Lord Matsumae."

"It'll be hard to get close enough to kill him," Fukida said.

"Let's forget it, then," whimpered the Rat.

But Sano had confidence born of sheer determination. "One or another of us will manage."

The last phase of his plan called for slaying Lord Matsumae as his punishment for Masahiro's death. Sano, Marume, Fukida, Hirata, and Reiko would attempt that, after they'd completed their initial tasks.

"Which of us do you think it will be? I'm taking bets." Marume spoke with great joviality. They were all aware that they would be captured and killed sooner rather than later, and he'd decided to enjoy the rest of his life.

Sano knew that Hirata, with his secret martial arts skills, would make a formidable assassin. So would Sano, Marume, and Fukida, now that they'd cast off the constraints of duty and turned renegade. As for Reiko, not even the gods could stand between her and the man she blamed for her son's death.

"Even odds," Sano said. "But first things first."

He had to find out who'd killed Tekare and set off the chain of events that had led up to this moment. Then he would slay the murderer. If it turned out to be Lord

Matsumae—as he believed—that would simplify his task. His favorite suspects were off-limits, but one branch of the investigation remained open to him: Lilac's murder.

He, Marume, Fukida, and the Rat stealthily made their way across the castle grounds. They tried to stay behind rocks, trees, and buildings, but they couldn't avoid all the open spaces in view of the watch turrets. Once they heard footsteps coming down a passage and ducked out a gate just before troops passed them. Fortunately, the soldiers were too busy with their war preparations to notice anyone around who didn't belong there. Sano and his comrades arrived outside the maids' barracks attached to the women's quarters. They took shelter behind a snow-covered bush to assess the situation.

Maids came outside, draped bedding over the veranda railings to air, and emptied chamber pots into night-soil buckets. The war hadn't affected their daily routine.

"Someone's going to see us," the Rat whispered. "Let's go back to our rooms now, and maybe everything will be all right."

"If you want to go back, then go by yourself," Marume said. "Otherwise, shut up."

Too big a coward to leave on his own, the Rat moaned as he followed the other men up to the barracks and in through the door. In a large space divided by bamboo screens, some fifty women were dressing, chattering, washing their faces, and combing their hair. When they saw the men, they shrieked and hurried to cover themselves.

"It's all right," Sano said, alarmed because the commotion could bring the guards running. "We're not going to hurt you."

They kept shrieking so loud that the Rat stuck his fingers in his ears. They rushed to hide, knocking over screens, spilling water basins. Marume drew his sword.

"Shut up!" he ordered. "Nobody move!"

Young and old, plain and pretty, the women fell to their knees, clinging to one another in terrified silence. Sano said, "Who killed Lilac? Does anybody know?" Nobody answered.

When he looked at the women one at a time, they averted their gazes and shook their heads. He couldn't tell if they really didn't know anything or were just too intimidated to talk. "Which of you was closest with Lilac?"

He heard nothing except their rapid breathing. The room stank of feminine sweat. Marume ordered, "Speak up!"

A low, frantic murmur swept through the maids. They pushed forward an older woman, her thin hair streaked with gray, her full cheeks red and mottled like an apple. She looked as frightened as her companions, but she spoke boldly for them.

"Lilac kept to herself. She thought she was too good to be friends with us."

That fit what Reiko had said about Lilac, the girl with big dreams. Sano persisted, "Had she talked to anybody in the few days before she died?"

"Probably Lady Matsumae. Or the soldiers." Disgust tinged the woman's voice as she added, "People she thought could do something for her."

"Did she say anything at all to you or the other maids?"

The woman looked around the room. Her companions all shook their heads, except for one, a husky girl with a strong-featured face, who looked as if she had native blood. She whispered to the older woman, who told Sano, "Lilac said she was working on something big. She'd found someone to take her to Edo."

It could have been Reiko, but maybe another person—her killer. Sano asked, "Did she say who?"

The woman conferred with the mixed-blood girl, then said, "No. Lilac always talked that way. The other girls never paid her much attention."

"Did you see Lilac yesterday, before she went to the hot spring?"

"Yes. She was the first one up, which was strange, because she was lazy and always slept late. She said she wanted to get away before the funeral started. She said she had important business."

This interested Sano. He wondered if Lilac had gone to meet her killer. "Did she say what it was? Or with whom?"

Again the maids shook their heads. Sano felt time speeding away. The Rat looked nervously at the door, and Marume's eyes signaled Sano that they needed to move on. Sano realized that the only person who could tell him about Lilac was Lilac herself, and since she was dead, the things she'd left behind must speak for her.

"Show me where Lilac lived," Sano said.

The woman led him through the quarters, past mattresses and quilts still spread on the floor amid dressing tables that held mirrors, combs, hairpins, and other feminine paraphernalia. Cabinets stood open, revealing clothes and shoes crammed inside. She stopped in a corner of the room that was bare, uncluttered.

"There's nothing to see." She opened a cupboard to show Sano an empty compartment. "We sent all Lilac's things to her family in town."

Sano gazed at the cramped space that seemed barely adequate for a human to live in. Although the other maids could have used more room themselves, they hadn't taken over Lilac's spot, probably shunning it for fear that her bad luck would rub off on them. He saw coarse, grayish salt crystals sprinkled on the floor, to chase away evil spirits. Sano could understand why Lilac had wanted to leave Ezogashima, why she'd tried to latch onto Reiko. But he found no clue to who had killed the girl.

"What now?" Marume asked.

His face reflected the disappointment that Sano felt. As Sano tried to think where to turn next, he paced Lilac's corner, and something caught his attention. Salt crystals had collected in a crack between two floorboards, a crack slightly wider than elsewhere. Halting, Sano noticed that one board was shorter than the rest, about as long as his hand. He stepped gently on the short board, and it gave under his weight.

"A secret compartment?" Marume said, intrigued.

"I hope." Sano knelt. He tried to lift the board, but couldn't get his fingers inside the crack. He spoke to the maids who'd gathered around to watch: "Fetch me a hair-pin."

One was handed to him. He inserted it in the crack and pried up the short board. Underneath he found a narrow space between the floor joists and a wad of brown cloth. When he picked it out, it was heavier than it looked, due to small, hard objects wrapped inside. He shook into his palm four irregular, gleaming yellow lumps.

"Is that gold?" Marume put a lump in his mouth, bit it, and said, "In my amateur opinion, yes."

The maids murmured with awe at the sight of more money than they could earn in years. The older woman said, "Lilac always had good things. She was like a squirrel, hiding them away."

"Where could she have gotten this gold?" Marume asked.

"I think I can guess." Sano asked the woman, "Did Lilac know Daigoro the gold merchant?"

The woman shook her head, but the half-blood girl tugged her arm and whispered to her. "She says she once saw Lilac talking to him in town."

Sano's investigation rebounded to the suspect that Hirata had interviewed, which they'd not pursued because they hadn't had time, and other suspects had seemed likelier culprits. Now Sano had made a connection between Daigoro and Lilac. He weighed in his hand the gold nuggets she must have extorted from the merchant. Daigoro was back in the picture, a new chance for Sano to solve the murder case just when he'd thought he'd exhausted his options.

"It's time for a talk with Daigoro," Sano said.

"My thoughts exactly," Marume said, "but how do we get out of the castle?"

Chapter Twenty-Eight

Dagger in hand, Reiko pressed her back against the wall of a building inside Fukuyama Castle. Soldiers carrying armloads of guns hurried near her through the courtyard. When they were gone, she sped along passages. She glanced sideways and backward, alert for threats, but kept her mind focused straight ahead. The world outside the castle had vanished from her consciousness. Normal, human life had ended for her. She didn't feel the cold. She had no past nor future; she existed solely in the present moment. All her physical and spiritual energy pulsed through her with concentrated intensity. She was a human arrow, burning flames at both ends, fired toward a single purpose.

She didn't bother spying on Lord Matsumae. He could wait. If Sano and Hirata failed to assassinate him, she would succeed. She would slash his throat and gladly watch him die for what he'd done to Masahiro. Her sense of purpose blazed away self-doubt as well as fear. But she had other matters to take care of first.

Slaying Lord Matsumae wasn't enough to satisfy her. Although he'd have made the decision to kill her son, a samurai lord didn't dirty his own hands. He wouldn't have tended to Masahiro in that cage, treating him like an animal. Other men had done that. Reiko wanted their blood, too. They must pay for Masahiro's suffering. She didn't know who among all the troops they were, but she knew where to start looking.

Reiko headed for the keep. She easily evaded the troops

busy preparing for war and the servants trudging on their daily routine. She felt invincible.

The tower was a black monolith against the orange sunrise. It appeared on fire, the cloud wisps like smoke. Reiko hurried up the hill, retracing the path she'd taken yesterday, an eternity ago. As she ran in the open door, her heart pumped with wild, erratic rhythm. She could taste blood from her own innards lacerated by grief, from those about to die by her hand.

All her senses and instincts were preternaturally alert. They tested the atmosphere in the tower and found only dead, empty air. Nobody was inside. Disoriented, she stumbled outside, down the hill. She paused at the gate to rethink her plans and catch her breath. The violent energy charging through her made her dizzy. Black waves licked her vision. She couldn't remember how long it had been since she'd eaten or slept. Her body might give out on her before she was finished with it. She was aware that she'd gone as mad as Lord Matsumae. There must be something in the air in Ezogashima that drove people to extreme actions. The madness was destroying her as it had done him. Reiko clutched the gate for support and willed her strength to endure.

As she breathed deeply, her forehead pressed against the cold stone wall, the blackness retreated. She could see the wall's rough, grayish plaster surface. Tiny black markings flecked it. They resembled crudely written characters. Reiko blinked, and they popped into focus. They actually were characters. She could read them.

Mama Papa
I escaped from prison
I will come home to you
Masahiro

A cry burst from Reiko. She dropped to her knees in the snow beside the wall. She yanked off her glove and touched the characters, afraid that she was hallucinating this message from her son. But she felt the rough edges where they'd been scratched into the plaster with some sharp object. The black color was charcoal ground into them. It rubbed off on her fingers. The message was real.

Reiko pictured Masahiro carving the words on the wall with a rock. Somehow he'd gotten himself out of his cage, out of the keep. He'd known that she and Sano would come for him, but decided to make his break for freedom in case they arrived too late to save him. He'd wanted to tell them he was making his own way home. He'd written the message where they might possibly find it, where his captors wouldn't. Reiko saw Masahiro rub a piece of charcoal against the characters so that they would be visible, then run out this very gate. She clasped her hands and sobbed. Her brave, resourceful boy! The full implications of her discovery struck her.

Maybe Masahiro wasn't dead after all.

Maybe he'd managed to get out of Fukuyama Castle, the Matsumae troops had never executed him, and the blood on the blanket wasn't his.

Maybe he was still alive.

The hope she'd forsaken surged anew in Reiko. Her body trembled violently from its force that exploded the plans she'd made, shattered her unnatural state of calm, disciplined insanity. Her mind shifted focus, away from vengeance, to the new possibility of reuniting with Masahiro. She laughed for joy as mad as her grief had been. She noticed that the sun had risen, dazzling and gold. But her laughter quickly faded.

How long ago had Masahiro escaped?

What had happened to him since then?

Merciful gods, where was he now?

Reiko staggered to her feet and looked around for some clue about what had become of Masahiro. But she saw nothing except the empty compound, the deserted keep. As she tried to think what to do, she heard footsteps from the other side of the wall. A male voice said, "Old Gizaemon is working us so hard, I'll be exhausted before the war even starts."

Another, similar voice said, "Me, too. Let's take a rest in here. Maybe he won't notice we're gone."

The gate opened. Two young soldiers were beside Reiko before she had a chance to hide. "Hey, who are you?" one said. His friend asked, "What are you doing here?"

Reiko took in their almost identical pudgy faces and stocky builds, their belligerent expressions. She recognized them as the two guards she'd seen on her first trip to the keep, the men she'd come hunting. She wasn't so far past her obsession with revenge that she'd forgotten it; she hadn't forgotten her anger toward her son's jailers. She still wanted to kill them.

She lashed her dagger at the soldiers. They leaped away, too surprised to fight back.

"Hey!" one of them exclaimed. "Why are you attacking us?"

"This is for what you did to my son!"

"I know who she is," the second said. "She's the chamberlain's wife."

Reiko carved wild swaths in the air with her blade. The men dodged. The first drew his sword. She slashed at his hand.

He yelled and let go of the weapon, a cut on his hand dripping blood. "She's crazy!"

"I'm going to kill you!" Reiko shouted.

The second man grabbed her from behind. She stomped on his feet and banged her head against his face. He lost his grip on her, and she lunged at his comrade, who stumbled and fell on his back in the snow. Reiko bent over him, her dagger at his throat. The other pulled his sword.

"Throw that sword as far as you can, or he's dead," Reiko ordered.

The fallen man lay pop-eyed with fear, arms spread, hands and heels dug into the snow. His comrade hesitated in confusion. Reiko said, "Is this your brother?"

The man gulped. "Yes." He flung his weapon away.

"The other one, too."

He obeyed. "Please don't hurt him."

Reiko would have liked to kill them both, but she wasn't so consumed by her anger that she didn't realize they were worth more to her alive than dead. "Where is my son?" she demanded. When they looked dumbly at her, she said, "The little boy you kept in the cage. Where is he?"

"We—we don't know," said the soldier on the ground.

"Did he get out of the castle?"

The brothers traded glances. A different fear shone in their eyes. The man standing said reluctantly, "I guess we have to tell her."

"Tell me what?" An awful idea stabbed Reiko. "That he didn't get away? That you killed him?"

As the arc of her hope plunged downward, Reiko sucked in a deep breath, ready to cleave the soldier's throat.

"No!" he cried, squirming desperately. "We let him go."

"What?" Reiko stared at him, then his brother.

"We felt sorry for Masahiro," said the brother. "He was a nice little boy. He was always polite to us, even though we locked him in the cage."

Reiko drank in this news of her son. Her heart warmed because the soldier's description of Masahiro was so in character. Masahiro was not only nice and polite, he was clever enough to have befriended his captors.

"Lord Matsumae ordered us to put him to death," said the soldier on the ground, "but we couldn't bring ourselves to do it."

"So we told Masahiro we were going to set him free," said his brother. "We took him out of the keep. He wanted to leave a message for you and his father. We gave him a knife and a piece of charcoal to write with." The man pointed at the words on the wall. "I guess you found it."

Reiko's jaw dropped in surprise that these soldiers she'd come to kill had helped Masahiro escape. If he was alive, she owed it to them. Hardly daring to breathe, she said, "When was this?"

"About twenty days before you got here."

Reiko trembled as her hope soared anew. "Where did you take him?"

"Out the gate. After that, he was on his own," the brother said.

Reiko was horrified. "On his own? An eight-year-old boy, in a strange land?" And the northern winter would have already begun. "Did you give him food to take, or money, or warm clothes, or advice on how to get home?"

"I wish we could have, but there wasn't time," the fallen soldier hastened to excuse their actions. "We had to get him out fast."

A wail rose from within Reiko. The idea of Masahiro turned loose to fend for himself! Anything could have happened to him since he'd left the castle. She let her weapon dangle. The soldier eased away from her and stood. He and his brother regarded her with sympathy as well as caution. They took turns continuing their tale.

"We told Lord Matsumae we'd killed him. He believed us. But our lieutenant asked to see the body. Of course we couldn't show it to him. So we made up a story that Masahiro had broken out of his cage."

"The lieutenant sent us and some other troops out searching for Masahiro. He wasn't in the castle, so we went into town."

"My brother and I ran ahead of the others and found Masahiro before they did. He was at the harbor, trying to talk some fishermen into taking him across the sea in their boat. But then the others came. All we could do was tell him to run."

"They chased him out of town and lost him in the woods. That was the last we saw of him."

"We went out every night for the next few days, looking for Masahiro, but we never saw him again. We don't know what's become of him."

Both men said humbly, "We're sorry."

Reiko couldn't blame them; they'd saved Masahiro's life. But that didn't change the fact that he was gone, or let them off the hook. "I'm going to find my son," she said, "and you're coming with me!"

Reiko knew with bone-deep certainty that Masahiro was alive. She couldn't believe she'd ever thought him dead. How misguided by fears and false clues she'd been! There was no mistake now. She clutched at the two young soldiers with the same fervor with which she'd almost killed them.

They looked sadly at her. "We're sorry," said one. The other said, "We can't leave our posts."

Reiko saw that there was no use arguing. The soldiers' duty was to the Matsumae clan, not a stranger in need. Her knees buckled, and she leaned against the wall. Masahiro had been out there in the wilds of Ezogashima, cold and hungry, lost and alone, for twenty days—during the last of which she had been trapped in the castle.

"What am I going to do?" she whispered.

Her first idea was to tell Sano and Hirata. They would think of something. But she didn't know where they were, and even if she could find them while evading the Matsumae troops, what could they do? They were unfamiliar with the terrain. No matter their intelligence and strength, they were city men; they would be as lost and helpless in the forest as she. Reiko knew of only one person to call on. Someone whose friendship she'd rebuffed, who'd generously given aid but might not be willing this time. Someone whom Reiko still suspected of murder.

Wente.

"If there's anything else we can do for you . . . ?" one of the soldiers said anxiously.

Reiko's mind raced through ideas and strategies, obstacles and threats. From them she devised a plan. "Yes, there is." She told the men what she needed from them. But her plan's success ultimately depended on Wente.

Chapter Twenty-Nine

Hirata hid in plain sight as he traversed the castle grounds, walking noiselessly a few paces behind groups of soldiers. He damped down the energy that his body gave off, and they didn't sense his presence. When they passed other people, he hid behind them, his human shields. Nobody noticed him, but he could detect each person before they came within his sight or hearing. They emitted energy that shone like beacons to Hirata's inner consciousness. When he felt soldiers approaching from his rear along a path, he darted into a doorway and waited for them to pass him. Then he followed them, their silent shadow.

His journey took him by the storehouse where the natives were imprisoned, its walls stained orange by the rising sun. He could feel their energy inside, two faint pulses. Hirata was tempted to break in and rescue them. It would be so easy, but the hard part would be getting them out of the castle, then defending them and their people from the whole Matsumae army. Not even the best martial artist could do that alone. And Hirata's first duty was to Sano. No matter how lured by other interests he felt, he would always choose Sano because his honor depended on how faithfully he served his master who was also his dearest friend. Solving the crime and assassinating Lord Matsumae were Sano's top priorities and thus Hirata's. And there were clues that nobody except Hirata could hope to find.

Hirata headed for the castle gate through which the funeral procession had passed. He approached it along the wall and stopped. Twenty paces farther, a sentry paced in front of the gate. Hirata backed away from the wall, crouched, drew a deep breath, and concentrated his physical power in his legs. He flexed a spiritual muscle within his mind and sprang.

A burst of energy fired along nerves and tendons through him. It launched him in a high, fast arc. He landed on his feet atop the wall, with a soundless impact that the guard didn't notice. There he squatted, looking down the other side. The hillside and path were empty, the woods dark as night except for the treetops, which glowed in the rosy dawn. Hirata jumped down from the wall and ran for the woods. As he followed the path that the funeral procession had taken, he blotted out his sensory impressions of the trees and snow, birdsong, the air's coldness in his lungs. He kept a small part of himself anchored to his surroundings; the rest walked in another dimension.

This dimension was a black void illuminated by traces of energy left by human emotions in the past. His hours spent meditating and attuning himself to the cosmos had developed his skill in detecting them. Along the path Hirata saw sizzles of light—the grief, anger, and dread experienced by the funeral party. He took the fork in the path that led toward the hot spring. Ahead, the energy flared into sparks and fountains where the Matsumae troops had massacred the natives. Hirata slowed his steps, looking downward, searching.

He didn't know the precise location of the murder scene, but he stopped at a tangle of luminescence that lay on the snow. Here Tekare had fallen, struck by the arrow from the spring-bow. He read her pain, her terror. Sano hadn't found any clues here, but since Hirata had come to Ezogashima he'd discovered a new realm of existence. On the hunting trip, Chieftain Awetok had opened him to a glimpse of its power, its potential to reveal information heretofore secret. Now Hirata hoped to use his new perception to solve the murder case, for the natives' sake as well as Sano's. The truth might yet save Awetok, Urahenka, and their people.

As he had during the deer hunt, Hirata immersed himself in a meditative trance. Again came the sensation of escaping his body, the propulsion into a rich, vast, unfamiliar world. The spirit of Ainu Mosir flowed through Hirata. He was a dust mote tossed by its power, awash in the energy from the earth, the wild creatures, forest, and sky that comprised its mighty self. Their voices barraged him. Deafened by messages he couldn't interpret, feeling completely lost, Hirata clasped his head in his hands. Even if the world of nature did harbor clues about Tekare's murder, how would he sort them out from this chaos?

He instinctively reverted to the breathing techniques learned through long years of training. Their rhythm steadied him, slowed the deluge of sensations. Hirata found himself balanced between two realms—the human world and the natural—as if on a raft on a turbulent sea beneath a stormy sky. Two disciplines—samurai art and Ainu magic—worked together within him. Hirata gasped with sheer, joyous exhilaration. This was the breakthrough he'd been seeking. Arduous training had prepared him for it, but only in Ezogashima could he have found it. But this breakthrough was a station on the way to his ultimate destiny. He had work to finish before he could move on.

He revolved beneath the brightening sky, in the shadows that dispelled as day came. From a tall pine an owl took flight, heading to its nest after a night of hunting. Around the owl, around every branch and pine needle, and along the earth, pulsed a limpid green energy field that hummed with nature's life-force. The light where Tekare had fallen and the sparks from the massacre blended with the radiance of the nonhuman world. Hirata called upon yet another discipline, the skills he'd learned as a police detective. He looked for something in the picture that didn't belong—a clue.

The green energy field wasn't uniform, its hum not continuous. There were interruptions with jagged edges. He spied one in the forest and stepped off the path to examine it. He discovered a hole on a leafless tree, the interior eaten away by insects. The tree was dying, its voice a moan of pain. Hirata listened harder. Sharp noises, like metal impinging on stone, led him to a snow-covered mound. Brushing off the snow, he found a rock about the size of his head. Small white scratches marred the rock's flat gray surface. Hirata recognized them; he'd seen their like at the archery range in Edo Castle, on the stone wall near the targets. Sometimes novice archers missed their shots by a wide margin, and their arrows hit the wall. These scratches were arrow marks.

Hirata gazed in a straight line from them, through the place where Tekare had fallen. The spring-bow had been set somewhere along the line, in the woods on the path's opposite side. The killer had tried out the weapon before the murder, had sprung the trap to see where the arrow flew. Hirata examined tree trunks near the rock. Caught in the rough bark of a pine tree were tiny fibers from the string that had triggered the spring-bow. They made a barely audible, trilling vibration in the field. Hirata envisioned and followed the string across the path, into the woods. He found more fibers on two more trees. The killer had experimented with different positions and angles, determining which was best. This told Hirata that the killer had a methodical mind—but did not reveal his identity.

The green energy glow diminished; Hirata couldn't sustain forever the trance that allowed him to see it. The sound of a temple bell ringing interrupted nature's voices. Hirata strained his perception, listening with all his might; his head ached with the effort. As the glow disappeared, he felt an *otherness* in the woods, from some small, foreign object.

The voices went silent. He was back in the ordinary world. The sun was shining, the sky blue above the trees, the forest's mystical dimension closed to him. His feet were numb from the cold, his senses deadened. He searched frantically for the foreign object, but he couldn't see anything that stood out.

His teacher, Ozuno, spoke in his memory: *Reality isn't just what you see on the surface, you fool! It has layers beneath infinite layers. When the truth eludes you, dig deeper!*

Hirata sighted on the fibers in the bark of one pine tree. He dug in a circle in the snow around its base. Reaching the earth, he found nothing except twigs and leaves. He tried the other pine, digging rapidly with hands stiff from the cold. The object was visually indistinguishable from the debris on the forest floor, but Hirata's keen nose detected a sweet, spicy, familiar scent that was out of place. He sifted through the debris and held up a short, thin sprig of sassafras wood.

A toothpick.

One of many Hirata had seen chewed, spat out, and littering the ground in Ezogashima. The harmless but now incriminating habit of one person.

Gizaemon.

Victory elated Hirata. He pictured Gizaemon tying the string around the tree, toothpick in his mouth. Before he walked across the path to tie the other end of the string to the spring-bow, he spat the toothpick onto the ground. He'd probably done it unconsciously, his habit so ingrained that he hadn't even thought to remove the toothpick. And until this instant, his carelessness hadn't mattered.

Nobody else had noticed the toothpick. But now Hirata had the evidence that connected Gizaemon to the murder, evidence that Gizaemon couldn't explain away by saying he'd dropped the toothpick when he'd discovered Tekare's body. It had been nowhere near where she'd died. There was no reason for him to have been loitering in the woods by those tree trunks—except to rig the crime.

Hirata stowed the toothpick in his glove. He ran down the path, heading for the castle. He had to find Sano and tell him the news that Lord Matsumae wasn't the only person they wanted dead. Gizaemon must be punished for the murder of Tekare and its disastrous consequences.

A peaceful morning graced the women's quarters. In the garden, the trees' bare branches resembled black embroidery decorating an azure sky striped with white puffy clouds.

Blackbirds pecked crumbs strewn on the snow. Gaily patterned quilts aired on veranda railings. To look at this scene, one would never know that a war was imminent, Reiko thought. But as one of the guards from the keep sneaked her up to the building and the other kept a lookout nearby, she heard distant gunshots from the troops testing weapons and ammunition. Men cheered after each blast.

Crouched on the veranda of the building where the native concubines lived, Reiko knocked on a window shutter until Wente held up the mat inside. Wente's expression was unfriendly: She remembered too well their last encounter.

"I'm sorry about yesterday," Reiko said. "I shouldn't have treated you like that. Will you please forgive me?"

"Why I should?"

"Because I was wrong to accuse you of killing your sister." Reiko would say anything necessary to regain Wente's good will. "I didn't mean it."

Wente gazed at Reiko with suspicion, but she nodded, accepting the apology. Her eyes shone with even more terror than was due to the war that threatened her people.

"Has something happened?" Reiko asked, sparing a moment of concern for the other woman.

"Nothing." Wente shook her head, the gesture more a refusal to confide than a denial. "Why you come?"

"I have news. About my son." The joy in Reiko bubbled over in smiles and tears. "Masahiro is alive."

As Reiko explained what she'd discovered at the keep, a visible torrent of relief assailed Wente. The woman closed her eyes for a moment; she muttered in her own language, in the universal cadence of prayer. A radiant smile of vicarious joy, far above what Reiko had expected, transformed her face. She reached toward Reiko, and they clasped hands.

"Where?" Wente asked eagerly.

"That's the problem. I don't know." Reiko described how the soldiers had chased Masahiro into the woods. "I have to ask you for another favor. Will you help me hunt for Masahiro? I promise this will be the last time." Her voice trembled because should she fail this time, Masahiro would surely die.

At first Wente didn't answer. Thoughts flickered in her eyes; emotions evolved in their dark brown depths. Finally she said, "All right. We go now."

Chapter Thirty

"The wall's too high to climb," the Rat said, bright with hope that Sano would give up on his dangerous plans.

"Don't worry, we won't try," Sano said.

They hid with Marume and Fukida in a thicket of pine shrubs against the castle wall. Sano peered through the pine needles at the closest gate, some twenty paces away. It had taken them hours of sneaking and avoiding troops to get near the exterior wall, and he'd given up hope of escaping the castle undetected. By the gate, two guards stood over a fire smoking in a metal urn. There was no way out except through them.

Marume scooped up some snow, packed it into two balls, and leaped out of the shrubs. The guards turned. He hurled the snowballs and hit the men square on their noses. As they exclaimed in surprise, Marume charged them. He grabbed them, banged their heads against the wall, and dumped their unconscious bodies into a snowdrift. Sano and the other men hurried to join him at the gate, which Fukida unbarred.

"They'll come to before they freeze to death," Marume said.

"When they do, they'll report that we escaped," Fukida said. "We'll have a hard time getting back inside the castle."

"Never mind that now," Sano said. "Let's go."

Outside, they cut through the woods and followed a rough track that was deep in snow, with a narrow rut tamped down the middle by not many footsteps. They entered Fukuyama

City through its inland fringes. This was clearly the poor side of town, with tiny shacks huddled together, the snow fouled by ashes, cinders, and wastewater frozen in ditches. The few people outdoors had a grimy, primitive appearance. An old man tended a heap of burning trash. When Sano asked him the way to the gold merchant's shop, he muttered directions and pointed.

Sano and his comrades trudged through the few alleys into the main part of town. As they passed a shrine, a movement beyond its weathered *torii* gate caught Sano's attention. He glanced into the shrine and stopped. A little boy, bundled in a fur coat and hood, tiptoed around the brass gong. He aimed a child-sized bow and arrow, hunting imaginary game. Sano's heart began to thud as the boy turned toward him.

It was Masahiro. He smiled and waved at Sano. Astounded, Sano waved back. Masahiro vanished.

"What's the matter?" Fukida said.

"Nothing." Sano didn't want to explain. What he'd seen must have been the spirit of his dead son. He didn't want his men to think he was as mad as Lord Matsumae.

They located the gold merchant's shop. Upon entering, they ignored the clerks who greeted them and made straight for the passage at the back. A clerk ran after them, saying, "That's private. You can't go there."

"Watch us," Marume said.

Sano and his men hurried down the passage and burst into the office that stank of dead things. Daigoro sat on a bearskin rug beneath a display of mounted animal heads, masturbating. A book of erotic Ainu prints by a Japanese artist lay open on the desk in front of him. When he saw his visitors, he jumped in surprise.

"Hey!" He stuffed his erection into his loincloth, closed his fur coat, and slammed the book shut. "How dare you barge in here?" Recognition stunned him. "Chamberlain Sano?" He pasted an obsequious grin over the fright on his face. "What can I do for you and your friends?"

"You can answer a few questions," Sano said.

"Oh? About what?"

Sano dumped Lilac's pouch of gold nuggets on the desk. "Did these once belong to you?"

Daigoro's eyes took on a hungry, acquisitive gleam as he looked at the nuggets. "Maybe. A lot of the gold in Ezogashima passes through my hands."

"They were found in Lilac's room."

"Who?" Daigoro drew back from them as if they might burn him.

"Lilac. The girl who died in the hot spring yesterday," Marume said.

"Why did you give them to her?" Sano asked.

"I didn't. I never even knew the girl."

"Yes, you did," Fukida said. "Don't lie to us."

"I'm not lying," Daigoro huffed.

"She blackmailed you," Sano said, fed up with the runaround he'd been getting ever since he'd started his investigation. "About what?"

"Nothing! Whoever told you that was mistaken."

"Did you kill Tekare?" Sano demanded. "Did Lilac find out? Did you pay her to keep quiet?"

"No! You've got it all wrong."

"Oh, come on, don't waste our time." Impatient, Marume pulled his sword, then grabbed Daigoro's hand and held it flat against the desk. "Start telling the truth, or I'll cut off your fingers one by one."

Daigoro squealed and struggled. "No! Please!"

Sano ordinarily didn't approve of torture, but this time he would make an exception. Even if Daigoro wasn't a double murderer who deserved to lose his head, never mind his fingers, he was a beast who preyed on native women, and Sano thought he was also hoarding information. Sano nodded to Marume.

Marume raised the sword. Sano braced himself for bloodshed. He felt as though he was crossing a line and compromising his principles, but this was Ezogashima; here, ideals didn't matter.

"All right!" Daigoro cried. "Stop! I'll tell you if you let me go!"

"Talk first." Marume kept his grip on Daigoro, and the sword poised to chop. "We'll see if what you say is worth sparing your fingers."

Daigoro strained away from the blade. "Lilac was blackmailing me, but it wasn't about Tekare. It was about—" He moaned. "If I say, I'll get in trouble."

"Trouble doesn't get any worse than this," Marume said. "Spit it out."

Daigoro blurted, "I lend money to Lord Matsumae's retainers. Whenever they can't pay it back, they steal supplies from his storehouse. I accept them in lieu of money and sell them in town. Lilac saw me with some soldiers, taking bales of rice from them and cutting a deal. She threatened to tell Lord Matsumae. I paid her not to."

This was a petty crime, but if Lord Matsumae had found out, he would have put Daigoro as well as the thieves to death as an example to other would-be criminals. Sano could understand why Daigoro had been reluctant to confess, why he'd succumbed to Lilac's blackmail.

"So Lilac asked you for more gold, and more," Sano surmised. "She bled you dry. So you murdered her."

"No, no. That was the only time she asked. She was satisfied. The little fool didn't know I'd have paid ten times more to shut her up. I didn't need to kill her. It wasn't me."

This sounded like the truth, and Sano was not only disappointed by the letdown, but consumed by fury. The air in Ezogashima seemed full of mischievous spirits goading him to violence.

"Kill him," Sano told Marume.

Marume, Fukida, and the Rat looked astonished by the savagery in Sano's voice, but an order was an order. Marume shrugged. "Here goes."

He seized Daigoro in a tight hug and put the blade to his throat. Daigoro wriggled and shrieked for help. None came; his employees were probably too scared. He clawed at Marume's arm, trying to pry it off his chest, his eyes goggling with fear.

"Wait!" he screamed. "Don't kill me. If you want to figure out who killed Tekare, I'm worth more to you alive than dead."

"Why? Do you know who did?" Sano said in spite of distrusting Daigoro and understanding that this was his last-ditch effort to save himself.

"Not exactly." Feral with desperate cunning, Daigoro said, "But I have a good idea."

"Because it was him that killed her," Fukida said. "Don't let him manipulate you, Sano-*san.*"

But Sano wasn't so possessed by desire for violence that he'd lost his instincts, and they said not to kill Daigoro yet. "How is that?"

"I was there. When Tekare died."

Sano said to Marume, "Let go of him, but keep that sword handy." Marume obeyed; Daigoro slumped and groaned in relief; Fukida looked askance. Sano turned to the Rat. "Start counting from one to a hundred."

"What for?"

"Convince me that you were there," Sano told Daigoro. "If you haven't by the time he's finished, you're dead."

"One . . . two . . . three . . . ," the Rat began.

Daigoro gulped and spoke rapidly: "That night, I went to the castle to collect on a debt. My man met me at the back gate and paid me with a bag of tobacco he'd stolen from Lord Matsumae."

The Rat continued counting. Daigoro hurried to say, "I started back to town, along the road that goes down the hill behind the castle. I stopped to urinate, and I'd just finished when I heard someone coming. It was two women. They were arguing. One of them ran past me, into the woods. I didn't turn around fast enough to see who it was. The other came running."

"Thirty . . . thirty-one . . . thirty-two . . ."

"Her I did see. It was dark, but there was a full moon. It was Tekare. I hadn't seen her since she moved on to Lord Matsumae, but I still wanted her. When she passed me, I thought, *Here I am, there she goes, tonight's my chance.* I followed her."

A dirty gleam of lust appeared in his eyes; saliva pooled in his grin. Sano was revolted. As the Rat counted past fifty, Sano said, "You don't have much time left. What happened?"

"I could hear Tekare running and panting ahead of me. Then suddenly she screamed. There was a thud. It sounded like she'd fallen. I kept going until I saw her. She was on the ground. She was moaning and flipping around. I didn't know what to make of it. She screamed again. Then she stood up and staggered toward me. I was scared. I backed into the woods to hide." He saw Sano frown. "What?"

Tekare had obviously been hurt, and Daigoro hadn't even thought to help. Sano said, "Never mind. Go on."

"She fell again. She thrashed and made awful noises. Pretty soon she stopped, though. She just lay there. I tiptoed over to her." Daigoro swallowed a retch. "And oh, merciful gods."

"One hundred," said the Rat.

Sano raised his hand, signaling Marume to wait.

Daigoro said, "There was blood all over her. I knew she was dead. So I got out of there. I ran all the way home."

"Well, I have to say that sounds just like him," Fukida said to Sano.

Marume said, "I think he's finally telling the truth."

So did Sano, but he was furious at Daigoro. "You not only neglected to mention this to Hirata-*san* when he came to see you about the murder, but you never told anyone else, either."

"After how Tekare treated me, I was glad she was dead," Daigoro hastened to excuse himself. "When I found out she'd been murdered, I figured someone had done me a favor. Why turn them in? I thought I'd better not say I'd been there because Lord Matsumae might think I did it. And I didn't want him looking into why I'd been at the castle that night. Later, when he went crazy—" Daigoro paused, then said with a shamefaced grin, "Well, I was too scared."

These excuses failed to placate Sano. He grabbed Daigoro by his fur coat. "If you'd reported it at once, maybe none of this would have happened. Lord Matsumae wouldn't have gone mad. He wouldn't have murdered my son." Almost choking on his rage and grief, Sano said, "He wouldn't have declared war on the natives. This is as much your damned fault as the murderer's!"

"I beg to disagree," Daigoro said haughtily. "Who's to say what would or wouldn't have happened if I'd told? I didn't kill Tekare. What I saw wouldn't have helped Lord Matsumae. I don't know who did it."

"But you have a good idea, as you said yourself. That other woman you heard lured Tekare to the spring-bow. She must have set it." Sano shook Daigoro so violently that his head whipped. "Who was she?"

"Hey, you're hurting me."

"Want me to start counting again?" suggested the Rat.

"Was it Lady Matsumae?" Fukida asked.

"If you want me to say any more, you have to let me live," Daigoro bleated. "You have to pardon me for stealing from Lord Matsumae."

Marume slapped his face. "You're in no position to bargain."

"So then kill me. When I'm dead, you'll be sorry."

Sano was not only running short on time, he was sick of Daigoro, a small fish compared to the one he wanted. "Oh, all right." He gave the man a last, hard shake, then released him. "Now talk."

Daigoro giggled with triumphant relief. "The women were speaking Ezo language."

"Then she was a native," Sano said. "Who was it?" He'd already guessed the identity of the woman most at odds with Tekare, whom Tekare would have followed into the night. But he needed to be sure.

"I never saw her. She just disappeared."

She'd hidden in the forest until she heard Tekare scream and fall, which had told her the trap had sprung. Then she'd returned to the castle as if nothing had happened.

"But I can tell you what I heard," Daigoro said. "I understand Ezo. She said something like, 'You always make me do everything for you. You take everything from me. You won't even let me have somebody you don't want. Well, I'm not going to put up with your selfishness anymore!'

"Tekare said, 'Oh, yes, you will. I'm the shamaness. I'm Lord Matsumae's mistress. You have to do what I say.' The other one said, 'You'll have to catch me first.' "

You always make me do everything for you. You take everything from me. Sano remembered Reiko saying that Tekare had received the best clothes, jewelry, and food in the native village, whereas lesser mortals, her kin included, had been forced to serve her.

You won't even let me have somebody you don't want. "Somebody" meant Urahenka, the man Tekare had married and her sister loved.

It was Wente who had murdered Tekare.

Accompanied by the two guards from the keep, Wente plodded across the back courtyard of Fukuyama Castle, leading four dogs harnessed to a sled laden with a big, lumpy bundle covered by a blanket. "Hey," the sentry at the gate said to her, "where do you think you're going?"

Wente bit her lips, too frightened to speak, so one of the guards answered for her. "She's going out for a ride."

"Oh, no, she's not," the sentry said. "Nobody leaves the castle, on orders from Gizaemon-*san*."

"I have Lord Matsumae's personal orders to let her go," the guard bluffed.

Reiko, curled under the blanket on the sled with provisions that the guards had given her and Wente for their journey, felt her heart seize with fear. If she and Wente couldn't get out of the castle, how would they rescue Masahiro? There was nothing she could do except stay hidden in the cramped darkness under the scratchy blanket. If the sentry found her trying to escape, all was lost. Hugging her knees to her chest, Reiko listened and tried not to breathe.

"Well, all right." The sentry sounded unconvinced yet afraid to disobey his lord.

Reiko heard the gate creak open and felt weight depress

the sled as Wente sat in front of her. The sled began moving, slowly at first, scraping and bumping on iced-over snow. Then they were skimming fast, faster. The dogs barked gaily. Reiko clung to the sled, which zoomed downhill, veered around trees. Bumps jarred Reiko's body. Soon her legs went numb. After what seemed like hours, Wente shouted to the dogs. The sled coasted to a stop.

"You come out now," Wente said.

Reiko flung off the blanket. Icy air frosted her face. Patches of white sunlight and vivid blue shadow blinded her. She squinted as she staggered to her feet. Tingles cramped her legs. She was on the crest of a low, sparsely forested hill. The city and castle were gone. The only signs of them, of civilization, were thin smoke spires that rose from the distant south. In the other directions stretched winter forest and snowy plains. To the north, hills climbed toward lavender blue, ice-capped mountains. Reiko felt awed by the beauty of the landscape, horrified by its vastness that dwarfed her hope of finding Masahiro.

Wente was beside her. "Give me boy's things."

Reiko handed Wente the toy horse in the leather pouch. Wente offered it to the dogs. They sniffed the pouch that Masahiro had handled many times. Their breath steamed off their tongues as they panted. They raised their heads, barked, and raced off, spurred by the scent of their quarry.

Wente jumped onto the sled and grabbed the reins. Reiko barely managed to climb on and sit behind her before she and the sled and dogs sped away. "Hold on!" Wente cried.

Chapter Thirty-One

Sano, Marume, Fukida, and the Rat fanned up the hill toward the castle, hiding behind trees so the sentries in the watch turrets wouldn't spot them. Marume carried a coil of rope they'd stolen from a shop in town. Some twenty paces from the wall, Sano raised his hand to stop, and they lay flat. He pointed to a section of the wall screened by spindly pine saplings. Marume tied a slip-knotted loop in the rope, crawled up to the trees, and hurled the loop at the iron spikes that topped the wall. He missed; the rope fell.

"It's not going to work," the Rat said, less worried than hopeful.

Marume tried and failed again.

"Maybe we should go back to town," the Rat said, "and try to hitch a boat ride home."

"Shut up," Fukida said.

On the third try, the loop fell over a spike. Marume tugged the rope, tightening the knot, then turned and beckoned.

"I'll go first and be the lookout," Fukida said.

He joined Marume, took hold of the rope, braced his feet on the wall, and shimmied up. It was slow going with his heavy boots, clothes, and sword. He crouched between the spikes, looked into the castle, then dropped down the other side of the wall. Marume followed even more slowly, hindered by his greater bulk. Then he was over.

"Our turn," Sano said.

The Rat hung back. "I'm scared."

"Come with me, or fend for yourself." Sano crawled up the hill. The Rat groused, but scuttled after him. Sano handed him the rope. The Rat climbed, nimble as his namesake. Then Sano hauled himself up. His muscles strained; too much desk work had left him out of shape. His wounded arm ached; his feet skittered on the wall. He was making so much noise that he expected to hear an uproar at any moment. But he reached the top and saw the other men waiting below him in a passage between the wall and a building. Sano dropped, and they started moving.

He was still bent on revenge. Wente deserved to die for committing murder, for all the trouble she'd caused even if inadvertently, but he was sorry the killer had turned out to be one of the natives. He'd wanted to think of them as more noble than the Japanese who'd mistreated them. Now he had to admit that they were just as capable of jealousy, hatred, and violence as anyone else. He had qualms about executing a woman, especially one who'd tried to help Reiko. But he must slay Wente. Then would come Lord Matsumae's turn to die for murdering Masahiro.

Crossing the castle grounds, Sano caught his first glimpse of the troops, and he immediately knew something had changed. They were still busy running around, but they seemed less organized, more agitated. They paused to chat in groups, and as they talked, their gazes roved. Crouched behind a bush with his men, Sano cursed under his breath.

"They know we're out. It's us they're looking for."

"Well, that means we don't have much time," Marume said, just as someone shouted, "Hey! There they are!"

A pack of troops chased them. Bows zinged; arrows whizzed and pelted the snow around their feet as they ran. The troops called more men to join the chase. Sano and his comrades burst into the palace's back garden. Looking for a place to hide, Sano spotted a loose strip of lattice askew at the base of the building. He and Marume pried it back. They and their comrades crawled under the building. He pulled the lattice shut just as troops arrived.

"Did they come in here?" asked a soldier.

Lying on their stomachs on the cold, hard earth in the dim space, Sano and his comrades held their breath and didn't move a muscle.

"I don't see them, but we'd better check," came the answer.

Legs stalked past the lattice. Sano willed the men to give up and go. Then a low voice said in his ear, "They're gone now."

Sano jerked with surprise as he found Hirata lying next to him. The Rat startled so violently that he banged his head on the underside of the building. Hirata had stolen up on them so quietly that they hadn't heard him.

"You almost scared me to death," Marume said.

"Not so loud!" Fukida whispered. "Someone will hear us."

"This is excellent timing," Sano said. "We've found out who killed Tekare."

"So have I," Hirata said. "It's all right to talk. There's nobody in this part of the building."

"Good work," Sano said. "Now we can team up to deliver Wente and Lord Matsumae to justice."

Hirata frowned. "Wente? But she's not the killer."

Sano saw that their separate investigations had led them to different conclusions. "Who do you think it is?"

"It's Gizaemon." Hirata described how he'd searched the scene of Tekare's murder; he showed Sano the sassafras toothpick. "This proves it."

"But I've proved it was Wente." As Sano related what the gold merchant had told him, enlightenment struck. "My version of the story and yours aren't mutually exclusive. They're both true."

Hirata nodded. "Gizaemon set the spring-bow. He must have known how Tekare treated Lord Matsumae—I doubt if anything much around here ever escaped his notice. He'd have wanted to punish Tekare and get her out of Lord Matsumae's life. But someone needed to make sure Tekare sprang the trap."

"That was Wente's job," Sano realized. "She quarreled with Tekare and provoked Tekare to chase her along the path."

Hirata marveled, "It was a Japanese-Ainu conspiracy."

Two people from different cultures historically at odds had joined forces. Their interests had intersected in murder. And Sano saw what this meant for him.

"So now we have two people to kill besides Lord Matsumae," Fukida said. "Which do we tackle first?"

Sano weighed Wente's simplicity and kindness to Reiko against Gizaemon's ruthless cunning. "I don't think the scheme was Wente's idea. It smells of Gizaemon. He's the leader of their conspiracy." He was also the force behind the war, now that Lord Matsumae was indisposed, and Sano's greatest adversary. "I choose Gizaemon."

"That may be a problem," Hirata said in the tone of a chief retainer duty-bound to contradict his master's bad decision. "Gizaemon is a tough prospect, surrounded by troops. Something might go wrong. If it does, we'll lose our chance at Wente."

"The woman should be easier. We should get her out of the way first," Fukida agreed.

"All right." Sano thought how bizarre this was, discussing which murder to commit first, as matter-of-factly as deciding which dish to order at a food stand. It occurred to him that he would probably never eat again. Even if they succeeded in killing all three targets, they wouldn't live much longer until the troops ganged up on and slaughtered them. "Wente it is."

"Follow me," Hirata said.

He slithered across the ground under the palace. Sano trusted that he knew where he was going; maybe he could sense the native women's energy. Sano and the other men crawled less gracefully after him. They'd traveled long enough for Sano's knees and elbows to grow sore, when Hirata stopped. He pointed upward, then at the lattice at the bottom of the nearest wall. He inched over to the lattice, peered outside, then heaved his shoulder against it.

The wooden grid broke loose. Everyone emerged into the garden outside the women's quarters. Troops called to one another, but none were in sight. Sano and his men ran up the steps, through the door, then down the corridor. Sano heard the concubines speaking in their language. Marume halted outside a sliding door, cracked it open, glanced in, and nodded to the others. They all invaded the room.

Women were kneeling grouped together, their tattooed mouths wide, staring at him and his men. Sano saw their ancient fear of his kind. The room was a shambles, with clothes and furniture flung around, ashes from the fire pit scattered on the mats, a loom broken. The women looked so much alike that Sano had to study their faces closely. He noticed fresh bruises, bleeding lips, and swollen eyes, but the person he wanted wasn't among them.

"We want Wente," he said. "Tell us where she is, and we'll leave you alone."

The oldest, a woman with a strongly beautiful face, uttered a brief phrase. The Rat translated, " 'Wente's gone.' "

"Gone where?" Sano said, impatient.

As the woman spoke, the Rat said, "She left the castle. She took dogs, a sled, and food." The woman pointed at Sano, and surprise altered the Rat's expression. "She took your wife."

"Reiko?" Sano's impatience turned to puzzlement. "Why?"

A torrent of words issued from the woman. "She doesn't know," the Rat said. "None of the concubines do. But Reiko and Wente were going on a long journey. They took enough food for several days."

Sano shook his head, trying to make sense of this. Things were changing too fast. What had diverted Reiko from her original plan and sent her off on a trip with Wente? A possible answer alarmed Sano.

"Maybe Wente pretended she'd found out that Masahiro escaped from the castle and he's alive," Sano said. "Reiko would have been desperate to believe in miracles and easily tricked. She would go to the ends of the earth with anyone she thought could give her back our son."

"Anyone, including a murder suspect," Marume said. His and the other men's faces showed dismay as they caught Sano's meaning.

"Reiko could have stumbled onto evidence that incriminated Wente," Sano said. "Maybe Wente was only afraid Reiko would. But whatever the truth, Wente must have lured Reiko out to the wilderness, to silence her permanently."

He didn't think Wente would use outright physical violence against Reiko. That seemed not in character for Wente, considering her part in Tekare's murder. More likely, Wente would take Reiko far enough from town that she couldn't make her way back alone, then abandon her to die of the cold. Wente's devious cruelty shocked Sano. The thought of Reiko, innocent and vulnerable, alone with the murderess!

The native woman shouted something at Sano, waving her hands to get his attention. It sounded like a warning. The Rat said, "She says your wife and Wente are in danger. Gizaemon knows they left. He's gone after them."

Misfortune piled on top of misfortune. Reiko was at the mercy of one killer and under pursuit by the other. "How did Gizaemon find out? When was this?"

As the woman spoke, the Rat anxiously translated: "Wente and Lady Reiko left about three hours ago. Gizaemon came here just before us. He was looking for Lady Reiko."

Sano realized what had happened while he and his men had been out solving the crime. The guards in the guest quarters had regained consciousness, had reported that the prisoners were missing. Gizaemon had launched a hunt for them and searched for Reiko in the women's quarters.

"He asked these women if they'd seen her," the Rat continued. "They said no. Wente had sworn them to secrecy. But he guessed that they were lying." The woman gestured at the tumbled furniture and clothes. "He got mad and wrecked the room. Then he noticed that Wente wasn't here. He asked where she was. He seemed even more upset about her being gone than about Lady Reiko. He beat the women until they gave up and told him Wente had taken Lady Reiko away."

Sano put together the rest of the story. "After Tekare's

murder, Gizaemon would have ordered Wente to keep quiet." Gizaemon had thought himself safe because she knew that incriminating him would incriminate her as well. "But when I started investigating the murder, he became afraid that Wente would crack." Now Gizaemon was less concerned that Reiko, Sano, and their comrades were at large than threatened because Wente had escaped his control. "He can't let her go free to tell anyone about his part in Tekare's death; he can't risk that Lord Matsumae might hear. He has to cover his tracks by doing what he knows he should have done sooner."

"Eliminate Wente," concluded Marume.

Sano's horror multiplied as he realized what that meant for his wife. "When Gizaemon kills Wente, he can't leave a witness. If Reiko is there to see, she'll figure out why he did it. She can't be permitted to live and tell. Gizaemon will kill her, if Wente hasn't yet." The situation altered drastically once more, as did Sano's plans. "We have to get to Reiko and Wente before Gizaemon does."

"All right," Marume said. "We'll go after them. But what about Lord Matsumae? Should we forget about him, or kill him first?"

Sano's attitude toward Lord Matsumae shifted to fit the new reality. Lord Matsumae hadn't murdered Tekare. And although Sano wasn't willing to forgive him for everything else, including Masahiro's death, there was a reason to keep him alive. Sano thought of Reiko and Wente somewhere in the vast, winter wilderness of Ezogashima. He and his men lacked the equipment and skills to find the women. They would surely get lost and freeze to death before they could save Reiko, and Gizaemon had a big head start.

"No," Sano said, "we shouldn't forget Lord Matsumae, but we won't kill him—at least not yet. We need him."

Chapter Thirty-Two

Sunset painted brilliant copper bands across the sky. Reiko and Wente rode the sled through a meadow whose snow glowed with fiery, reflected light. They and the dogs trotting ahead of them were alone in the wilderness landscape that spread as far as Reiko could see.

They'd spent the long day following a trail that Masahiro must have stumbled onto when he'd run from the soldiers who'd chased him. Before the snow it would have been visible; now it was buried. They'd met no one, seen no human footprints. At first Reiko had spied small villages in the distance, settled by Japanese traders and farmers, but in late afternoon they'd crossed into Ainu territory.

Now Reiko felt as if she'd truly broken loose from everything familiar. Ainu territory was the loneliest place she'd ever been. She experienced a city-dweller's fear of nature untamed by man and the fear that she wouldn't find Masahiro. All that connected her to him was an invisible trail of scent. She clung to Wente as the sled bumped over ice. Her body was stiff from the cold. The full moon rose; the sky darkened into cobalt that quenched the sunset. More stars than Reiko had ever seen glittered like crystals. The cold intensified. How would she and Wente survive a night in this frozen kingdom?

Woods abruptly immersed the sled. The moonlight on the snowy trail didn't penetrate the thick shadows among the trees. The trail was a tunnel roofed by the starlit sky, a road to nowhere. Reiko was beginning to dread what she would find at its end, when a clearing opened ahead of her. Wente called to the dogs and dismounted from the sled as it coasted to a stop. The dogs barked at a hut that had materialized as if by magic. Reiko clumsily rose as Wente ran to the hut.

"What is this place?" Reiko could hardly believe that a man-made structure existed here.

"Men come here when hunt," Wente said.

The hunting cabin was padded with thatch and blanketed with snow, a shelter from the cold. All day Reiko had refused to acknowledge the probability that the dogs would find Masahiro's dead, frozen body. Now relief rushed through her. She staggered toward the hut, calling, "Masahiro! Masahiro!"

Wente lifted a mat of thatch from the wall. The dogs, still tethered to the sled, lunged at the doorway she uncovered, frantic to reach the quarry they'd tracked all day. Wente looked inside, then turned a somber face to Reiko.

"Not here," Wente said.

Disappointment wounded Reiko even as she refused to believe. "He must be! He has to be! Masahiro!" She scrambled into the hut. In the dim moonlight that shone through the doorway she saw dirt mounded against mat-covered walls, a fire pit filled with cold ashes. The hut was vacant. Reiko sagged to her knees, too anguished to cry.

Wente brought the dogs into the cabin, and they eagerly sniffed around. Kneeling by the fire pit, she sifted ashes through her fingers and smelled them. "Hunters not gone long."

Reiko supposed she could tell how recently they'd burned their fire, but what did it matter? Masahiro wasn't here. The dogs barked and growled, worrying at something they'd found in a corner. It was a stack of floor mats.

"They smell boy," Wente said. "He sit there, sleep there."

That didn't comfort Reiko. "But where is he now?" she cried. Against her will, she pictured him lying in a snowdrift, eyes closed, motionless. Yet she imagined his chest rising in slow breaths. The stubborn hope of saving him refused to die.

Wente left the cabin, and Reiko hurried after her. "We have to keep looking. Let's go!"

But Wente untied the bundle of provisions on the sled and carried it into the cabin. "We stay here tonight. Morning come, we go."

"We can't wait that long," Reiko said, aghast.

"Night cold, dangerous." Wente unpacked the food, the bedroll. "We need warm, eat, sleep."

"I don't care!" Although chilled to the bone, Reiko said, "I must find my son before it's too late!"

"Tomorrow." Wente's manner was sympathetic but firm. "Dogs need rest."

The dogs lay on the cabin floor, huddled together, exhausted. Reiko gave up because her life depended on their good health. She helped Wente fetch sticks from the forest to build a fire. Wente struck an iron fragment against a quartz stone. Sparks ignited wood dust. She lit a wick in a ceramic oil lamp and set the lamp on the edge of the fire pit. Desolate, Reiko stared at the floor. The lamp's flame illuminated grimy black patterns on the mat, from spilled ashes. They looked almost like written characters . . .

Wente started to walk across them. Reiko cried "Wait! Don't!" and pointed at the floor. "It's another message from my son. He wrote it in ashes." She read: "Mama, Papa, I met some nice native hunters. I'm going home with them to their village. Masahiro."

A huge, blissful relief overwhelmed Reiko. Her nightmarish picture of Masahiro dying in the snow changed to a happy scene of him fed, protected, and accompanied to a safe place by natives. He'd cheated death again!

"Village not far," Wente said. "We get there tomorrow."

She built a little fire and fed the dogs, who soon fell asleep. Reiko and Wente drank hot herb tea and ate soup made from lily-root starch dumplings and dried salmon. The food, the bright, crackling fire, and the snoring dogs soothed Reiko, as did the certainty of seeing Masahiro tomorrow. Although the cabin was far from warm enough, she fell into a snug, contented doze. But Wente was restless; she kept going to the door and peeking at the night.

"What's the matter?" A danger that hadn't previously

occurred to Reiko now scared her fully awake. "Are there bears outside?"

Wente shook her head and sat down, but she had a tense, listening air. A moment later she was up again for another peek.

"Something is wrong," Reiko said. "Tell me what."

Sano, Hirata, Marume, Fukida, and the Rat lay in a row under the palace, peering through the lattice. Nightfall had diminished the activity inside Fukuyama Castle, and the grounds were empty except for two soldiers walking up the path to the front entrance. Fukida whispered, "How about these?"

"Too low in rank for our purposes," Sano said.

"Pretty soon it'll be too late to get anybody," Marume warned, but in a few moments along came Captain Okimoto. "Aha, that's more like it."

Marume burst through the lattice. Sano and the other men followed, swords drawn, and charged at Okimoto. "Hey, what—," Okimoto said, as he halted in surprise.

Sano and his men surrounded Okimoto. Hirata seized him from behind, stripped off his swords, and pressed an arm tight across his throat.

"Let me go!" Wheezing, Okimoto grappled with Hirata's arm; he kicked the air while Hirata held him effortlessly. The sentries at the palace door came running to his aid.

"Everybody drop your swords or he dies," Sano said. Weapons hit the snow: The men were friends of Okimoto's. "Good. Now open the door."

The sentries reluctantly but promptly obeyed. Marume and Fukida ran up the steps. Hirata propelled Okimoto, who dragged his feet and choked out, "What do you want?"

"To speak with Lord Matsumae," Sano said. "You're going to help us get to him." Backing through the door, he called to the sentries, "Don't even think of following us."

He and his men marched Okimoto through the palace. They met soldiers who exclaimed, drew weapons, and blocked their way until Sano shouted, "Stand back! We've got your captain." Hirata squeezed Okimoto's throat harder. Okimoto made strangling sounds. "Let us pass, or we'll kill him."

They breached the chamber where Lord Matsumae howled in his bed, still wrapped in the quilt and rope. Two male servants held his head. His face was covered with blood that ran from his mouth in red trickles. He snarled and growled at the servants as they pried his jaws apart. The doctor stood by, holding a ceramic cup.

"What's going on?" Marume said.

The doctor looked more worried about his patient than frightened by the sudden arrival of the escaped prisoners. "Lord Matsumae tried to bite himself to death. We're trying to give him a sedative potion."

He poured liquid from the cup into Lord Matsumae's mouth. Lord Matsumae roared and spat out the potion. His lips and tongue were cut. Tekare obviously hadn't given up trying to kill him.

Okimoto cried out, "My lord!" Hirata released him, and he knelt by Lord Matsumae and broke down in tears. Sano saw that this mean, tough man truly cared for his lord, whose dire condition had shocked him. He said to the doctor, "Can't you cure him?"

The doctor shook his head regretfully. Sano said, "Let me try." He motioned everyone else away from the bed and crouched by Lord Matsumae. "Tekare, listen. I've found out who killed you."

She snarled, baring bloody teeth at Sano. "I already know. It's him!" She chomped on Lord Matsumae's lip. His voice screamed as more blood flowed.

"No," Sano said. "He's innocent of everything except punishing other people for your death. It was your sister who murdered you."

"Wente?" Scorn laced Tekare's voice. "She's too weak and timid. She'd never have dared lift a finger against me."

Sano had at least distracted her from her attack on Lord Matsumae; now he had to convince her. "She was with you the night you died. She ran into the forest and you chased her."

"Yes. How did you know?"

"Your old friend Daigoro told me. He was there. He saw. Do you want to know why Wente ran?"

Tekare frowned, confused. "Because she was upset. Because she wanted to get away from me."

"That's what she wanted you to think, but it's not the reason. She was luring you to your death."

Even though Sano could see that he'd shaken her, Tekare said, "That's ridiculous. Wente isn't smart enough to think of using a spring-bow."

"She didn't need to be smart," Sano said. "She had an accomplice who was. They conspired to murder you. One to set the trap, one to make sure you triggered it."

"No!" Convinced now, Tekare wailed in outrage. The sister she'd thought inferior, whom she'd tyrannized all their lives, had defeated her. As her body convulsed inside the quilt and strained at the ropes, her hold on Lord Matsumae lapsed. His voice said, "See, my beloved, it wasn't me. I'm innocent."

"Would you like to know who Wente's accomplice was?" Sano asked.

Tekare sobbed and cursed. "She won't get away with this. I'll haunt her into her grave!"

"Who?" Lord Matsumae surfaced to ask the question.

"It was Gizaemon," Sano told him.

Lord Matsumae's spirit reclaimed his features from Tekare. They went blank with shock. "My uncle? He would never hurt anyone who mattered to me."

Captain Okimoto also looked shocked. "He would never betray our lord."

Hirata held up the toothpick. "You all know this belongs to Gizaemon. He dropped it when he was setting the spring-bow. I found it. He's guilty."

"My uncle. He was like a father to me. I trusted him with my life." Lord Matsumae had the expression of a child who'd been skipping along a path when suddenly a sinkhole opened under him. His voice echoed up from a well of loss. "And he took from me the woman I love." Fury enflamed him. "He'll answer for what he's done. Bring him to me at once."

"I'm afraid that's not possible," Sano said. "He's gone."

"Gone where?"

Tekare resurfaced. "Where is Wente? I demand to see her."

"Wente ran away this morning," Sano said. "Gizaemon wants to kill her so she can never tell anyone that they conspired to murder Tekare. He went after her." Sano didn't mention his wife; Lord Matsumae and Tekare wouldn't care about Reiko. "My men and I will hunt them down. But we need your help. We need sleds, dogs, and troops."

"We also need guides," Hirata said. "Let the two native men come with us."

"Whatever you want," Lord Matsumae said. "But I'm going with you."

"So am I," Tekare said through him.

Sano didn't like the thought of them running wild. "That's not a good idea. It may be a long journey. You're in poor health."

"If we don't go, neither do my troops, my sleds, my dogs, nor the barbarians," Lord Matsumae declared. "And you won't get far by yourselves."

If Sano wanted to save Reiko, he had little time to waste arguing and even less choice. "Very well."

"If anyone's going to deliver those two murderers to justice, it'll be me," Lord Matsumae said.

"Me," Tekare's voice echoed.

"We'll leave at dawn," Lord Matsumae said.

"Dawn is too late," Sano protested.

"Traveling through Ezogashima in the dark is too dangerous," Lord Matsumae said. "We must wait until daylight. In the meantime, we have preparations to make. Untie us."

"I afraid they come find us here," Wente said.

"Do you mean Lord Matsumae's men?" Reiko asked.

Wente nodded.

That fear had diminished for Reiko the farther they'd

traveled from Fukuyama City. "We didn't see anyone following us. Maybe they don't even know we've left the castle. Or maybe they don't care."

Reiko thought it possible that the troops didn't consider two women worth chasing. The only person certain to care about her was Sano. She felt a pang of sad yearning for him. He probably didn't know she was gone, and she had no idea what had happened to him.

Heedless of Reiko's reassurances, Wente paced the cabin, twisting her hands. Reiko began to feel nervous herself. "What makes you so sure they're coming?"

Wente hesitated, clearly torn between her wish to keep a private matter private and the temptation to unburden herself. She sighed. "He no want I get away."

"Who?"

"Gizaemon."

"Why would he be after you?"

Kneeling by the fire, Wente bowed her head and spoke in a barely audible voice: "So I no tell."

"Tell what?" The fire had burned down to sullen red embers, but the sudden chill Reiko felt didn't come from physical coldness.

"That he kill Tekare."

"Gizaemon is the murderer?" Reiko was more confused by Wente's revelation than stunned by it. The man had been Sano's favorite suspect; that he should turn out to be guilty didn't come as a shock. "You knew?"

Wente nodded mutely.

"Since when?"

"The night Tekare die."

Reiko's confusion turned to incredulity. "And you didn't say anything?" She moved closer to Wente, who avoided her gaze. "Do you realize how much trouble you could have prevented if you'd told back then?"

Miserable, Wente hung her head. "I sorry."

"Sorry isn't good enough!" Yet even as Reiko wanted to harangue her friend and vent her frustration, she sensed something more to the story, something bad. She probed for the rest. "How do you know Gizaemon killed Tekare? Did you see him set the spring-bow?"

"No," Wente whispered. The air around her seethed with secrets, like flies around rotten meat.

"Then how?"

"It was mistake," Wente said in a plaintive tone.

That was what she'd said when Reiko had first asked her about the murder. Now Reiko knew Wente didn't mean she'd thought Tekare's death had been an accident. "Tell me what happened. This time I want the truth."

Gazing into the fire, Wente muttered, "One day I fight with Tekare. Japanese ladies no like noise, tell Gizaemon. He make us stop fighting."

The sticks in the fire pit were burned white, shaped in a hollow like a rib cage. In this, among smoke tendrils that twisted around red sparks, Reiko saw an image of Wente and Tekare punching and clawing and shouting at each other, and Gizaemon forcing them apart.

"He hear what we say," Wente continued. "He understand I mad at Tekare because she treat me bad. Later, he come see me. He say we can fix it so Tekare never hurt me again. I say, how? He tell me, just do what he say."

A breath of astonishment rushed from Reiko. Not in her most far-fetched dreams could she have imagined a Japanese plotting the murder with a native. Certainly not a conspiracy between that surly, tough samurai and this meek, gentle woman who had nothing in common—except the desire to be rid of the same person. Horror stole into Reiko.

"Next day he tell me bring Tekare outside castle after dark," Wente said, "to path in woods. Say make her chase me toward hot spring. He say I not go all the way to spring, should stop by big oak tree. Hide in woods until she pass me. Then I run home. That's all."

Wente's tone reflected the surprise she'd felt that her problems with Tekare could be solved with so little effort on her part. Reiko was surprised because the story wasn't playing out as she'd expected. The idea of murder didn't seem to have been discussed by the conspirators.

"So I do what Gizaemon say. Tekare make it easy. While we eat dinner, she scold me, argue with me. I go outside castle. She follow. I bring her to path, I run. Happen just like Gizaemon say. But next morning—"

Memory spread a shadow across Wente's face. "Tekare dead. Then I know why Gizaemon make me bring her to path." She turned an anguished gaze on Reiko. "So he can kill her!"

"You never suspected?" Reiko said, amazed.

"No!" Wente pounded her fists on her knees. "I think he just meet Tekare in woods, talk to her. Maybe scare her, she leave me alone."

"You didn't wonder why Gizaemon would bother to help you?"

"I think he feel sorry for me," Wente said, as if mere pity could have induced Lord Matsumae's uncle to put himself out for a member of the race he despised. She insisted, "It was mistake."

Her mistake, which had proved fatal to her sister.

"I just want be free of Tekare! I no mean for her die!"

Reiko realized that Wente bore far less responsibility for the crime than Gizaemon did; she was more guilty of naïveté than murder. But Tekare was dead whether Wente had intended it or not, and Wente's actions had contributed to the awful consequences of the murder.

"You should have told!" Reiko said, furious at Wente. "You owed that much to your sister. However badly she treated you, she didn't deserve to die. You deserved to be punished!"

Wente cringed, humiliated by Reiko's lashing. "I want tell. Gizaemon say if I do, he kill me. I try make up for what I do." Remorse and pleading filled Wente's eyes. "I try help you find son."

Reiko finally understood why Wente had been willing to take the risk, to befriend her. It wasn't just because Reiko had protected her from Lady Matsumae. Wente blamed herself for what had happened to Masahiro; she wanted to atone for that as well as her sister's murder. The lost boy and his desperate mother had given her the chance. But Reiko suspected her of another, less noble motive.

"You didn't bring me out here just for my sake and my son's," Reiko said. "You were scared of Gizaemon, especially after Lilac died. You must have guessed that he'd killed her."

The chagrin on Wente's face was her answer.

"That's why you were in such a hurry to leave," Reiko said. "He's afraid you'll break down and confess. You wanted to get away from him before he could kill you, too. Now I understand why he's after us." Now Reiko became aware that Wente wasn't the only person in danger from Gizaemon. If he found them, she herself would be caught in the middle, another witness for him to eliminate.

"I sorry," Wente whispered.

But Reiko couldn't forgive, even though Wente had been good to her. Had Wente turned herself and Gizaemon in at once, Lord Matsumae might have punished them and been satisfied; he might not have gone mad or closed off Ezogashima. Anger churned in Reiko as she built her chain of speculation. Masahiro wouldn't have been sent here and taken captive. Neither he, Reiko, nor Sano would be in this predicament now. Reiko moved to the opposite side of the fire pit and glared at Wente across the cooling, hissing ashes.

After a while, Wente said timidly, "We leave when sun rise, better sleep now."

Reiko was too upset to sleep, but she was also exhausted; she needed rest. She fetched a mat and lay down on it.

Wente spread mats and unrolled the thick, down-filled quilts they'd brought. "Come sleep with me."

"No, thank you." Reiko couldn't believe Wente would suggest such intimacy after what had just happened.

"Must," Wente said. "Alone, cold. Together, warm."

Reiko saw that the small fire Wente had been able to build wouldn't heat the room all night. Already shivering, she reluctantly walked over to Wente.

"Take off clothes," Wente said as she stripped off her boots, coat, and robe.

Reiko stared in offended dismay. She wasn't sexually attracted to women, and she abhorred the idea of touching this one. Wente had blood on her hands, even if not by intention.

"Clothes off, warmer," Wente explained with matter-of-fact authority. "Leave on, freeze."

Realizing her mistake, Reiko decided that if she wanted to survive, she'd better do as Wente said. She undressed as fast as she could. Shivering violently, she curled up on the quilt-covered mat beside Wente. She flinched as their naked backs touched. Wente pulled more heavy quilts over them, heads and all. Their bodies warmed the dark, stuffy space under the quilt. Wente soon fell asleep. Reiko listened to her soft breathing, smelled her ripe, female odor. As Reiko drifted into sleep, amazement resounded through her. She was in the middle of nowhere, flesh to flesh with a murderess upon whom her life and her reunion with her son depended.

Chapter Thirty-Three

As afternoon tipped the sun from its zenith, a long parade of dogsleds raced across a snowfield in Ezogashima's native territory. Urahenka and Chieftain Awetok led, riding so effortlessly that they seemed to fly behind their dogs. Sano hung onto the reins while his sled careened. Hirata, beside him, appeared to have mastered this new form of transportation, but Sano heard curses behind him, looked over his shoulder, and saw Marume tumble off his sled. Fukida stopped to help him back on. The forty soldiers jeered. Lord Matsumae stood upright on his sled, leaning forward, like a figurehead on a ship. He balanced expertly, his body controlled by Tekare, who'd been born to sail the snows.

Ahead, Sano could see the tracks they'd been following since dawn. Long furrows striped the snow. In some places they ran parallel; in others they merged and braided. The tracks left by Gizaemon and his troops had run over those from Reiko and Wente. This morning Sano and his comrades had spotted the remains of a bonfire where Gizaemon had camped overnight. It wasn't far enough from the Ainu hunting cabin where ashes from another recent fire indicated that the women had stayed there. Gizaemon was hard on their trail. Even if Wente hadn't killed Reiko, maybe he'd already caught them. As he and the rescue party sped onward, Sano prayed they wouldn't be too late.

Reiko and Wente rode along a stream that curved through hilly, forested land. Below them, rapids sparkled in the sun.

Dry golden reeds protruded from the ice near the banks that sloped upward through snowbound vegetation to meet tall pines and cedars whose boughs were heavy with icicles. In the distance rose snow-flanked mountains. The air was so clear that they looked close enough to touch. Majestic white clouds floated in turquoise blue heavens. The beauty of the scenery awed Reiko. She thought about how this land had belonged to the Ainu since time immemorial and now they stood to lose it. Sorrow for them coexisted in her heart alongside her eagerness to see Masahiro. She wished she had someone with whom to share her thoughts, but there was only Wente.

Even though Reiko clung to Wente, her knees hugging the other woman's body, they hadn't spoken since last night. Wente's confession had raised a barrier as impenetrable as a glacier between them. Reiko supposed she should forgive Wente's mistake, especially after everything Wente had done for her, but she was too angry. Wente brooded, afraid to provoke Reiko by talking. Only the sounds of the river, the wind, the dogs trotting and panting, and the sled scraping the snow filled their silence, until Reiko heard another noise. It sounded like weird, dissonant, yet cheerful music.

Wente flashed a smile over her shoulder. "Village," she said, pointing ahead.

The music grew louder. The dogs barked excitedly and broke into a gallop. The sled veered around a curve in the stream and the village came into view, a group of perhaps ten huts with shaggy thatched roofs and walls, on a plateau above the river. Wente halted the sled at a trail flattened in the snow by footsteps that had trodden back and forth between the village and the water's edge. She untied the dogs from their harnesses, and they raced up the trail. Reiko ran with Wente after them. They all arrived breathless in the village.

It appeared empty even though Reiko could now distinguish voices singing to a tune plucked on stringed instruments and the rapid beat of drums. "Where is everybody?" Reiko looked around at the houses screened by hedges made of willow sticks shaved to form mops with long, vertical handles and heads of curly peelings, at privy sheds, at storehouses raised on stilts, at wooden racks hung with fish and skinned deer.

Wente and the dogs headed for the woods beyond the village. Reiko followed. In an open space under the trees was a crowd of several hundred natives. Over their deerskin coats, fur leggings, and fish-skin boots they wore patchwork robes with geometric patterns. Men beat drums and plinked at what looked like Ainu versions of the samisen; women played bamboo strips held between their teeth to make a humming sound. It seemed to be a party, with a wild, noisy action at its center that Reiko couldn't see through the crowd.

"What are they doing?" she asked.

"Iyomante," Wente said, "bear ceremony." Her face shone with happiness. "We honor god of bear, send home to spirit world. Tribes come from other villages, feast."

Tattooed women and burly, whiskered men flocked to welcome her home. She exchanged fond greetings with them until they noticed Reiko. Disconcerted, they beheld the Japanese trespasser in their land. Wente spoke, explaining her presence, introducing her to them. But Reiko roved away through the crowd, seeking the only person who mattered to her.

"Masahiro!" she called.

She emerged into the center of the action. A brown bear lumbered on the packed snow. Twenty or thirty men restrained him with heavy ropes. The bear growled, fierce yet playful. Scores of dogs barked and lunged at him. The crowd sang, clapped, and cheered. Mothers scolded a group of children who edged too close to the bear. Suddenly one boy detached himself from the group. He raced toward Reiko, shouting, "Mama!"

It was Masahiro. The sound of his voice pierced Reiko with a happiness so powerful it was agonizing. As Masahiro ran to her, he extended his arms, and she opened hers wide. The light around him scintillated, obliterating everything else. He seemed an illusion born of her yearning for him, but then he was in her embrace, solid and real. Gasping as though she'd pulled him out of an ocean that had almost drowned them both, Reiko hugged him fiercely, then held him at arm's length and feasted on the sight of him.

He wore the same native clothes as the other children; he could have been one of them. He was thinner than Reiko remembered, his hair long and unruly, but his face was radiant. His eyes sparkled. "Mama, you came! Did you get my messages?"

"Yes." Reiko felt her face bloom with the first genuine smile since he'd vanished. It thawed muscles frozen by misery. "They guided me to you. You're such a clever boy!"

She'd wept many tears for Masahiro, but none so violent as these. Sobs exploded from deep within her. They choked her, sank her to her knees, convulsed her body in painful spasms. For so long she'd suppressed her fear that Masahiro was dead; she'd pushed it down inside her and sealed it there with her stubborn hope that she would see him again. Now it erupted, and her spirit released it as though ridding her of fatal poison. She pressed her face against Masahiro's, inhaling his sweetness. She felt as though she hadn't breathed since she'd lost him, and now she could.

"Mama," he said, patting her back, "don't cry. Everything's all right."

When her weeping subsided, pure, blissful tranquility filled Reiko. She rose and wiped her eyes. The tears on her cheeks didn't freeze in the cold air; her whole body glowed with warmth, a spiritual fire rekindled. Reiko smiled at Masahiro. She would never stop smiling. The scene around them was bright with sun and the natives' robes, jewelry, laughter, and music—a world reborn to color and life.

"I want you to meet my friends," Masahiro said, gesturing at two boys who stood nearby. One was about his age, the other an adolescent, his face stubbly with new whiskers. They regarded Reiko with shy curiosity. "Their names are Totkamaru and Wnotok." Masahiro spoke to them in their language: He'd already picked it up. "I told them you're my mother." They bowed to Reiko. "They were hunting with their fathers the day I ran away from the castle. They found me wandering in the woods. They took me with them. And look what they gave me."

He showed Reiko a little bow and quiver of arrows that he wore. "So I could hunt with them."

Reiko turned her smile on the boys. "Thank you," she said with fervent gratitude. "I'm forever in your debt."

Realizing that she owed as many thanks to someone else, she looked around for Wente. No matter her sins, Wente had at least partially atoned for them by reuniting Reiko with her son.

Wente was talking to a group of men and women, gesticulating frantically. Reiko supposed she was telling them that Lord Matsumae had declared war on them and his army was on its way. They reacted with surprise, disbelief, and questions. As they hurried off and spread the word, music and celebration stopped; fright swept the crowd.

"Mama, what's happened?" Masahiro asked.

Old men who wore crowns made of woven wood fibers—the tribal elders, Reiko presumed—shouted orders. Women gathered up children. The men leading the bear hauled him toward a big wooden cage. Wente ran up to Reiko, said, "Must hide," and pulled her toward the forest.

"I'll explain later," Reiko told Masahiro as she towed him along with her, after the fleeing mothers and children.

But now she heard dogs barking in the distance, coming closer, from seemingly all directions. Dismay struck her because Gizaemon had caught up with her and Wente. He and his army had made much better time than they. The village dogs growled and keened, sensing the approach of enemies. As the women fled, those in the lead stopped so suddenly in the forest that the others ran smack into them. They screamed. Men yelled in Japanese: "Stop!"

The horde reversed direction. Women and children streamed past Reiko, Wente, and Masahiro. A mob of soldiers, accompanied by dogs on leashes, charged at them.

"Run!" Wente shouted.

She and Reiko and Masahiro raced back to the village. There, more soldiers were rounding up the natives, walking in a tightening circle around the houses, cutting off escape. The bear roamed free while village dogs faced off against the soldiers' in a frenzy of yowling. Reiko saw the elders arguing with Gizaemon and his commanders, wanting to know what they'd done to deserve a war. Gizaemon barked questions at them while his gaze searched the scene.

"No let him find us," Wente urged.

She yanked Reiko so hard that Reiko's hold on Masahiro's hand broke. Reiko cried "Masahiro!" and saw him caught up in the crowds that the soldiers herded together. She tried to pull free of Wente. "I can't lose him again!"

But Gizaemon and his commanders were heading in their direction. Wente pushed her into a hut already full of frightened women, babies, and children. Reiko and Wente squeezed in among them. Outside, Japanese men called Wente's name and demanded that the villagers bring her to them. Then came the noise of them tramping from house to house. Reiko felt Wente grip her arm. She realized that even though Wente was technically a murderess, she didn't deserve to die at her coconspirator's hands. That wasn't justice, especially if it meant Gizaemon would get away with his major share of the crime.

Soldiers tore off the mat over the doorway. Daylight exposed the women, who cringed. The soldiers yelled "Come out!" and began yanking the women from the hut. Reiko groped along the wall, found the mat that covered the window, and lifted it. "This way!" she called to Wente as she climbed out the opening.

But she heard the soldiers stamp into the hut and Wente scream as they seized her. Reiko hid behind the hut, peered around the corner, and saw two men struggling with Wente, propelling her over to Gizaemon. Natives watched in confusion, but Reiko didn't see Masahiro among them. Gizaemon called to his troops, "You can stop searching. We've got her."

The soldiers forced Wente to her knees and pulled back

her head to expose her throat. Gizaemon drew his sword. A gasp swept the villagers. Wente shrieked and pleaded. Native men charged, brandishing knives, swords, and spears at Gizaemon. But soldiers intercepted and attacked them. The natives battled fiercely, but they were outnumbered. Japanese blades slashed them. They fell as their women wailed and horror overcame Reiko. Their blood stained their ceremonial robes and crimsoned the snow. The bear roared, driven wild by the carnage.

Gizaemon swaggered up to Wente. Contempt for her showed in his eyes; her eyes were closed, her lips moving in silent, desperate prayer. He was going to slaughter her as if she were an animal. There was no one to save her, except Reiko.

Reiko felt torn in different directions. Common sense told her to run and hide, the mother in her wanted only to find Masahiro, but her honor dictated that she couldn't stand idle while Wente died. She moved out from behind the hut and called, "Gizaemon-*san*!"

All eyes turned toward her. Gizaemon paused. "Ah. Lady Reiko." He sounded pleased to see her, not a good sign. Wente beheld her as if she were a savior.

"Don't kill her." At least maybe Reiko could postpone the inevitable.

"You can't stop me," Gizaemon said scornfully.

Improvising as fast as she could, Reiko said, "Wente shouldn't be punished for smuggling me out of the castle." She couldn't let Gizaemon know that she knew his real reason for wanting Wente dead. "It's my fault. I talked her into it." Reiko resisted the impulse to look for Masahiro in the crowd; she kept her eyes leveled on Gizaemon. "Please don't hurt her."

Gizaemon studied Reiko with hostile suspicion. She could feel him wondering if she was as ignorant about his conspiracy with Wente as she pretended to be. "This is none of your business. Stay out of it."

Wente's eyes were glazed. Immobilized by panic, she'd ceased struggling. Urine stained the snow under her.

Desperate, Reiko said, "All these people are going to see you kill her. They'll be witnesses."

Gizaemon sneered. "Too bad."

He flicked his sword at Wente. The blade slashed her throat. She uttered an awful, gurgling shriek. Blood sprayed from the cut in an obscene red geyser. Gizaemon stepped backward to avoid it. The soldiers let go of Wente. She collapsed onto the snow, her body twitching.

"Wente!" Reiko rushed to kneel beside Wente. She cradled her friend's head and moaned as she pressed her glove to the wound in a futile attempt to stanch the bleeding. "I'm sorry!"

It was too late for apologies. Wente's body stilled. The spirit faded from her eyes. Reiko wept for the woman who'd been her loyal friend until the end. Wente finally deserved forgiveness for her part in her sister's death. She'd paid for her jealousy, her hatred, and her gullibility with her life.

A cold shadow fell upon Reiko. She looked up and saw Gizaemon standing over her, his figure black against the sun.

"The barbarians won't dare tell, and they don't matter anyway. The only witness I care about is you, Lady Reiko." Gizaemon's tone said he understood that Wente had confessed everything to her. "But you won't live long enough to talk."

Chapter Thirty-Four

Two soldiers grabbed Reiko. She thrashed with all her might, beating her fists on the men, kicking their stomachs, legs, and groins. They yelled for their comrades to help them. Four, five, six men wrestled with her. Her gloves came off, and she raked her fingernails at the men, but they held her arms and legs immobile even as her body bucked and she tossed her head.

"We'll take her into the forest, where she'll never be found," Gizaemon told the men.

As they bore her away, Reiko couldn't even scream for help lest her son rush to her rescue and be killed with her.

The sled tracks abruptly ended at the bottom of a trail that led up from the river. Sano and his group jumped off their sleds below the village where Reiko and Wente must have gone. Sano's heart sank at the sight of troops milling around the huts. Gizaemon had beaten him.

Sano, Hirata, and the detectives climbed the path ahead of Chieftain Awetok and Urahenka. Reaching the village, they found strewn across the ground the dead bodies of native men. Other natives stood surrounded by troops. Horror flooded Sano because Gizaemon's army had attacked the village. What had become of Reiko and Wente?

The troops turned at the sound of his party's approach. Sano yelled, "Where's Gizaemon? Where is my wife?"

They stood dumbfounded by his unexpected arrival. Their surprised gazes shifted beyond him, to their fellow Matsumae troops stampeding up the path behind Sano. They raised their swords and prepared to fight, but Lord Matsumae staggered breathless into the village and ordered, "Stop!"

His hair was wild, his eyes burning in his haggard face, but he'd gained strength during the journey. Vengeance was at hand for him and Tekare. "Lower your weapons! Let us through!"

Shocked to see their master, they moved aside for Sano, Hirata, and the detectives, who hurried through the village with Lord Matsumae and his troops. Sano almost stumbled over the lone dead woman lying with her throat cut, in bloody slush, among the corpses.

It was Wente. Gizaemon had already eliminated his accomplice. Now Sano divined that he was after Reiko, who must have figured out he was the killer and was the only person left to bear witness against him.

Lord Matsumae gaped at Wente's body. Tekare's savage aspect darkened his face. He started kicking Wente and cursing her in native language: Tekare was upset because she'd been cheated out of her revenge on her sister. Sano forged onward through the crowd of natives until he glimpsed Reiko in the hands of four soldiers carrying her toward the forest. Gizaemon was with them.

"Gizaemon!" Sano called.

The man turned. Displeasure knitted his brow as he recognized Sano. When he spotted the troops accompanying Sano, shock rearranged his features. He halted; the men carrying Reiko slewed around. Her expression went from terrified to ecstatic.

Although overjoyed to see her, Sano focused his eyes on Gizaemon. "Tell your men to let her go."

"How in hell did you get out of the castle?"

"Lord Matsumae freed us."

As Gizaemon's face went blank with astonished disbelief, Lord Matsumae stepped past his troops and stood beside Sano. "Yes, Uncle, it's true."

"Nephew." Gizaemon swayed as if shock had punched him. "Why?"

Lord Matsumae addressed the soldiers who held Reiko: "Put her down."

"No, don't," Gizaemon sharply countermanded.

The soldiers compromised by lowering Reiko to her feet but holding her arms. She fixed on Sano a look in which hope vied with fright.

"Chamberlain Sano has solved the crime." Lord Matsumae's voice shook with anger. "He's fulfilled his duty to me. Setting him free was the least I could do in return."

Gizaemon's complexion paled to an ashy gray as understanding sank in. "What are you doing here?"

"You killed Tekare. I've come to make you answer to me," Lord Matsumae said.

"Chamberlain Sano told you I killed her? That's nonsense." Beneath his scorn Gizaemon was clearly distraught. "He's lying."

"Evidence doesn't lie. You left one of your toothpicks in the woods where you set the trap for Tekare," Lord Matsumae said. "You ought to be more careful where you drop them."

"I must have dropped it when we were looking for Tekare after she disappeared." Gizaemon's jaw shifted as he scrambled for more excuses. "Or Chamberlain Sano planted it. To make me look guilty. To turn you against me."

"No, Uncle." Even if Lord Matsumae hadn't already made up his mind to believe Sano, he'd read the signs of guilt in Gizaemon's behavior. "*You* turned against *me*." He hurled his pointing finger at Gizaemon, then pounded his fist on his chest. "How?" he demanded in a voice ragged with injury. "How could you betray me by murdering the woman I love?"

This accusation of disloyalty, the worst charge a master could level at a samurai, appeared to shatter something inside Gizaemon. "I would never," he whispered.

"No more lies! You're going to tell me the truth if I have to force it out of you!"

Lord Matsumae gestured to his men. They drew their swords and advanced on his uncle. Gizaemon flung up his hands in a gesture of entreaty. "It was for your own good. To protect you from that barbarian whore who was ruining you."

"Don't you dare call her a whore!" Lord Matsumae said.

"Me a whore," Tekare's voice echoed.

"You asked for the truth, now face it," Gizaemon said in the tone he must have used to discipline his nephew as a child. "That's what she was. She used men. She used you."

"She loved me!"

"She blinded you with her charms." Gizaemon spoke with bitter resentment toward Tekare, with pity for his nephew's delusion. "She was like a lot of barbarians, hated the Japanese for the wrongs she thought we'd done to her and her people. I saw it in her eyes whenever she looked at any of us. She blamed you, the lord of Ezogashima. She made you pay every time she had another man right under your nose."

Lord Matsumae said, "You're wrong!" even as his expression registered dismay at what he saw in the mirror that Gizaemon had held up to his affair with Tekare.

"That love potion she gave you was poison that made you sick and weak. I know—I tested it on a dog. He had a fit, went wild, and died. Same thing would have eventually happened to you if I hadn't taken action."

Sano saw that Gizaemon was trying to turn Lord Matsumae's anger at him onto Tekare. Maybe it would be a good thing if uncle and nephew made up, even it if meant Gizaemon would escape justice. Sano would excuse Gizaemon for the murder and its consequences if only Gizaemon would let Reiko go. Sano saw these thoughts occur to her and raise the hope in her eyes.

Lord Matsumae said, "I don't care! I'd rather have died by her hand than lived all these months without Tekare!"

"You're better off without her."

"You had no right to make that decision!"

"It was my duty as a samurai," Gizaemon said. "To rid my master of an evil influence even if he didn't want to be rid of it. That's the Way of the Warrior."

Sano couldn't condone the murder that had wrought its own evil influence upon Lord Matsumae, yet the warrior in him approved of Gizaemon's action. Honor had motivated Gizaemon; he'd had his lord's welfare at heart, even if he hadn't foreseen the consequences.

"How was I to know that Tekare would manipulate you even after she was dead?" Gizaemon's defensiveness crumbled into anguish. He reached his hand toward Lord Matsumae. He looked older than moments ago, as if his body had petrified around the secret he'd kept, and now that the secret was out he was mortal, decaying flesh once again. "If I'd known what would happen—"

Remorse eroded new wrinkles in the tough hide of his face. "All your life I've guided you, watched over you. You're more than a son to me, you're my life. I never wanted to hurt you. I'm sorry. If I could take back her killing, I would."

His words melted his nephew's antagonism. Lord Matsumae whispered, "I know, Uncle." He staggered forward, his hand extended to grasp Gizaemon's.

Sano was moved despite his reluctance to see a crime excused. He saw Reiko relax and felt the tension ease in the other people witnessing the scene. All was well that ended peacefully, if not satisfactorily.

Then Lord Matsumae's body whipped like an eel hooked by a fisherman. Tekare's features, incensed with anger, reclaimed his. "Well, I don't," her voice spat from his mouth. "And you can't take back what you did to me."

Gizaemon recoiled from her as she railed at him, "Who are you to criticize me for using Lord Matsumae? It's you and your kind that have used my people. You've taken the fish we catch, the animals we hunt, and the things we make, and you've paid us a pittance. Your men have used me for their pleasure. And you stole my life!"

She swerved and said, "Are you going to let him get away with it, my lord?"

Uncertainty puckered Lord Matsumae's face.

Loath to have her stir up more trouble, Sano said, "It's

over, Tekare. You've already punished enough people for your murder. Leave us now."

Lord Matsumae rounded on Sano. "You stay out of this!" He punched Sano on the jaw. Sano went reeling; Hirata caught him.

"You said you wanted to avenge me," Tekare challenged Lord Matsumae. "You say you love me."

". . . I do."

"Then prove it! Give me a life for the life that was taken from me. Kill him!"

Lord Matsumae stared aghast at his own hand that pointed at Gizaemon. "But—but he's my flesh and blood. He only wanted what was best for me. I can't—"

"Coward! You're the lord of Ezogashima, but you're afraid of that man because he's bossed you around all your life." Tekare's curses spewed from Lord Matsumae. "If you can't kill him, let your soldiers!"

Helpless against the vindictive spirit that possessed him, Lord Matsumae groaned. "All right, if it will make you happy, my love." He beckoned his troops. "Kill my uncle."

Swords drawn, reluctant yet game, they advanced on Gizaemon. All his troops but one, who held onto Reiko, leaped forward to defend him. Gizaemon shouted, "Touch me, and Lady Reiko dies!"

The soldier rammed his blade against her throat. Panic splayed her hands, froze her eyes wide and her mouth in a grimace. Sano shouted, "No!" Lord Matsumae's troops lashed their swords at Gizaemon's, trying to get at Gizaemon. His troops lashed back, shielding him. Sano, Hirata, and the detectives plunged into the battle and dragged Matsumae troops out. Lord Matsumae thumped his fists on Sano and his men. He and Tekare shouted, "Go away! Let them execute him!"

"I outrank your master," Sano told the Matsumae troops. "I override his orders. Stand back!"

Whether the troops respected his authority or they didn't really want to kill comrades with whom they'd served the same clan all their lives, they obeyed Sano. Lord Matsumae shrieked in Tekare's voice, "I'll kill him myself!"

He rushed at Gizaemon. Detective Marume grabbed Lord Matsumae. Even though Marume was bigger and stronger, Lord Matsumae almost broke loose. Fukida helped restrain him. Tekare cursed and clawed at them.

Furious, Sano drew his sword on Gizaemon. "Let my wife go."

"Sorry. She's my way out of this alive." Gizaemon jerked his chin at the soldier who had Reiko, at his other men. "Come on. We're leaving."

They backed into the forest behind Reiko, their shield. Sano said, "Where do you think you'll go?"

"Plenty of hiding places in Ezo territory for someone who knows how to survive here. I do."

Sano saw that Chieftain Awetok and Urahenka had sneaked up on Gizaemon from the rear. They poised bows and arrows to shoot. Other native men held the bear on a leash. "Pardon the natives if they think you've worn out your welcome in their land." Sano nodded in their direction.

Flicking a glance backward, Gizaemon said, "My men and I can hold those brutes off long enough for us to reach the coast." His army had assembled, their sleds and dogs ready to go; they pointed bows, arrows, and lances at the natives. "We'll hop a ship."

"To where?" Sano asked. "You'll be a wanted man everyplace in Japan."

"Then I'm damned whatever I do." Sardonic and reckless, Gizaemon said, "Might as well make a run for it."

"Surrender, and I'll pardon you for both murders and everything else that's happened," Sano said.

"Even if I trusted you, which I don't, a true samurai never surrenders," Gizaemon declared, as Sano had guessed he would. "Now listen: If I don't get out of this village alive, neither does your wife."

Despair paralyzed Sano because he couldn't move against Gizaemon without dooming Reiko. But if he let

Gizaemon go, Gizaemon would only kill her later. The natives stood firm, ready to shoot. Lord Matsumae howled and fought the detectives. Sano saw the troops getting restless. This stalemate was too volatile to hold. Reiko's eyes begged Sano to do something, anything. Never had he felt so helpless.

A twanging sound shivered the air. A loud thump followed. The man holding Reiko screamed. He let go of her, dropped the sword, and clutched his right eye. From it protruded a short arrow with a feathered end. Blood poured down his face. He wobbled, then fell dead.

As exclamations of astonishment swept the spectators, Sano looked in the direction from which the arrow had flown. On the roof of a hut stood Masahiro. He held his bow aloft. He laughed in triumph.

A huge, weighty blackness lifted from Sano. Light rushed back into the world; his being pulsed with joy. His son was alive! He wanted to fall to his knees, weep, and thank the gods. But he had no time for that, nor to marvel at how Masahiro had made such a perfect shot. Reiko, set free, ran toward Sano. Gizaemon yelled, "Catch her!"

His troops chased Reiko. As she dodged them, Sano ran after them and hacked at them with his sword. Hirata and the detectives joined in with him. Lord Matsumae's troops battled Gizaemon's. Native men and women wielded spears, clubs, and knives against any and all Japanese troops. The bear marauded, growling and snapping at whoever crossed his path. Masahiro fired more arrows, as did native boys on other rooftops. The forest resounded with war-cries, colliding blades, and agonized screams.

As Sano fought to reach Reiko, she slipped on ice and fell. Gizaemon threw himself at her, and she rolled away just in time. She sped away, but a soldier grabbed her from behind. He lifted her off her feet and spun while she kicked and her arms beat the air. Sano lashed out his sword. It cut the soldier across the knees. He howled, dropped Reiko, and collapsed. She ran, but a pack of other troops headed her away from Sano, into the war raging amid the village. Lord

Matsumae shouted incoherent orders in his own voice. He shrilled curses in Tekare's and cut down his own troops with his sword. Gizaemon came barreling toward Sano.

Fury locked Gizaemon's face into an ugly grimace. Eyes crazed with desperation, he looked madder than Lord Matsumae ever had. He swung his sword wildly at Sano. They slashed and parried so fast that their swords were a cyclone of blades through which they moved. Hirata and the native men joined forces and attacked Gizaemon's army. Native women banded with Reiko and fought the soldiers pursuing her. Gizaemon's men dropped dead from arrows fired by the boys. Sano barely noticed the chaos. In the space between cuts, there was no time to think. His body lunged, ducked, and pivoted, operating on sheer instinct. The din of metal clanging on metal deafened him. He never saw the critical misstep that decided the outcome.

One instant Gizaemon was savagely fighting Sano. The next, Sano felt his blade cleave flesh and bone. Gizaemon roared. He clutched his right wrist, which spurted blood; the hand was gone. Sano had sliced it clean off. It lay in the snow, fingers still gripping Gizaemon's sword. Gizaemon stared at his amputated hand in horror.

The sudden victory shocked Sano. His heart was still thudding wildly, his lungs heaving, his muscles still tensed for combat. But all around him the combat fizzled as Matsumae troops noticed that Gizaemon was done for and couldn't divide their loyalties any longer. Hirata and the Ainu men surrounded Gizaemon. He dropped to one knee in a circle of their swords and spears pointed at him. He gazed up at Sano, defeated yet too proud to beg for mercy.

Sano felt himself roughly elbowed aside by Lord Matsumae. Lord Matsumae brandished a sword already red with blood from Japanese men that Tekare had killed. Her aspect masked his face, clearer than ever. Sano could even see her tattoo around his mouth.

"He's mine," she said.

Gizaemon beheld his nephew with a tragic, despairing expression. He was already pale from blood loss, half dead. Lord Matsumae swung his sword and decapitated Gizaemon.

As blood spewed from Gizaemon's neck and his head hit the ground, Lord Matsumae uttered a high-pitched, ululating cry. His back arched, and a horrible grimace of pain twisted his face. His muscles spasmed; his sword dropped. His toes pointed and sprang him up from the ground. A human shadow wrenched free from him. It had the shape of a naked woman. A cry went up among the spectators. Lord Matsumae fell limp, unconscious. The shadow gained substance and detail until Tekare appeared in the flesh.

Sano stared in amazement. She was glorious, brown-skinned, with full lips like an exotic flower in the intense blue tattoo, long, wavy black hair, and dark, deep, knowing eyes. Her nipples were erect, her muscles as strong as a man's yet sleek, supple, and feminine. Tekare surveyed Gizaemon and smiled with private satisfaction: She'd had her revenge at last.

She swept a triumphant gaze across her audience that stood entranced, silent, and motionless. Then she turned and walked toward the forest. The trees ahead of her shimmered like a painting on a sheer silk curtain blown by the wind. A thunderous crack shook the earth as the portal opened to the spirit world. Tekare walked through the shimmering trees. She disintegrated as if composed of a million particles of light that winked out rapidly one by one. The shimmer abruptly ceased; the world was quiet. Everybody gazed at the forest, where Tekare had vanished.

Captain Okimoto cried, "Lord Matsumae!" He rushed to his fallen master, shook him, and patted his face. "He won't wake up."

Troops flocked around Lord Matsumae. Joined by their fear that he was dead and they were masterless samurai, they'd forgotten that they'd been fighting to kill one another. Sano knelt, put his ear by Lord Matsumae's nose, and felt his neck. "He's breathing, and his pulse is strong."

Chieftain Awetok spoke, and the Rat translated: " 'When the spirit of Tekare left him, it was a shock to his system. He'll sleep for a while. Then he'll be fine. Take him home.' "

A few troops loaded Lord Matsumae onto a sled. Others gathered up their slain and wounded comrades, some twenty in all. Natives knelt beside and mourned their dead. Urahenka sat with Wente cradled in his lap. Sobs shuddered through him. The air filled with the sound of weeping.

Sano took charge. He said to Chieftain Awetok, "On behalf of the Matsumae clan, the Tokugawa regime, and myself, I apologize for what your people have suffered. I'll see that you're compensated. In the meantime, I'm calling off the war."

Chieftain Awetok nodded in acceptance if not forgiveness. Sano looked anxiously about the village and heard his son's voice call. He saw Masahiro and Reiko running toward him, hand in hand. Masahiro broke loose from Reiko. He launched himself at Sano. Sano picked him up in his arms. They both laughed with joy. Tears blurred Sano's eyes. It didn't seem fair that so many people had died and suffered today and he was so happy. But the balance of fate could tip tomorrow. For now he just celebrated his miracle.

"Papa, I knew you were in Ezogashima. I knew you would come," Masahiro said.

Sano was touched because his son had such faith in him. "How did you know?"

"I saw you."

"Oh, you did?" Sano smiled fondly, thinking what a good imagination Masahiro had, glad that it had comforted him. "Where?"

"I was out hunting in the woods with my new friends yesterday. And suddenly you were in front of me. You were with detectives Marume and Fukida and the Rat. Don't you remember?"

An eerie sensation tingled inside Sano as he remembered the vision he'd had in Fukuyama City.

Masahiro playfully punched his chest. "I waved at you, Papa. You waved back. You saw me, too."

Chapter Thirty-Five

In his chamber in Fukuyama Castle, Lord Matsumae lay in bed, his gaunt body swaddled in thick quilts, a nightcap on his head. He stirred and yawned. His eyes, gummy with sleep, blinked open at Sano, who knelt beside him.

"Welcome back to the world," Sano said.

"Chamberlain Sano." Lord Matsumae sounded confused but lucid. "Where am I?"

"At home."

Lord Matsumae raised himself on his elbows and squinted at his surroundings. "The last thing I knew, I was in a native village. Let me look outside."

Sano rose and opened the window. Another huge snowstorm had buried the garden up to the veranda railings. Masahiro was having a snowball fight with Reiko, the two guards who'd helped him escape, the detectives, the Rat, and the Ainu concubines. They laughed as they pelted one another. The precarious harmony between the natives and the Japanese had been restored—at least temporarily. The deaths on both sides were forgotten for now.

The sunlight bleached Lord Matsumae's whiskered face. "How long have I been asleep?"

"Five days."

". . . Merciful gods. What's happened?"

"You don't remember?"

Alarmed recollection deluged Lord Matsumae's gaze. "I killed my uncle Gizaemon. Because he killed Tekare." He gasped. "Tekare. Where is she?"

"She's gone," Sano said, "to the spirit world."

"Gone." With an expression that combined bereavement and relief, Lord Matsumae sat up and examined himself, flexing his arms and hands that he alone now controlled. He touched his face that belonged only to him.

"Yes," Sano said. "She's at peace."

Lord Matsumae echoed, "At peace. As I wish I could be." A breath of despair gusted from him. "I'll love her and miss her all my life. But I'm glad she's gone. Uncle Gizaemon was right about her. When she was with me, I did terrible things that I didn't want to do but couldn't help myself." Shame colored his woe. "I disobeyed the shogun's laws, forsook my duty, and let my domain go to hell. I massacred innocent natives and declared war on them. I've treated you abominably, and I put your son to death." He regarded Sano with puzzlement. "After what I've done to you, how can you sit talking calmly with me? Why don't you kill me?"

"Fortunately your men thought better of following your orders to kill my son. There he is." Sano pointed out the window at Masahiro. "As you can see, he's alive and well."

"No thanks to me," Lord Matsumae said, still guilt-ridden. "I must atone for what I've done. I'm turning my domain over to the shogun. Please allow me a few days to settle my affairs and say good-bye to the men who've served me faithfully even when I was mad. Then I will commit seppuku."

Sano saw that his remorse was genuine; Lord Matsumae was his decent, rational self again. But those weren't the only reasons that Sano said, "Ritual suicide won't be necessary. I'm going to advise the shogun to pardon you and let you stay on as lord of Ezogashima." He didn't know how much influence he still had over the shogun, but it was worth a try.

"But I must take responsibility for my actions." Lord Matsumae sounded adamant instead of ready for an easy way out.

"You weren't responsible. Tekare was."

When Sano had first come to Ezogashima and discovered

what Lord Matsumae had done, when he'd watched Lord Matsumae in action, he'd never imagined wanting to pardon the man. A big part of Sano hadn't believed in spirit possession even though he'd personally seen evidence of it. But after he'd watched Tekare cross over to the spirit world, after he'd learned that his own vision of Masahiro had been real, his mind had accepted that Ezogashima was a place where the impossible happened. Now he was convinced that Lord Matsumae had truly been possessed, his actions beyond his control, and was innocent by reason of temporary madness. And Sano had another reason for keeping Lord Matsumae in control of Ezogashima.

"But I'm at fault for letting Tekare gain control of me while she was alive," Lord Matsumae protested. "People have suffered because of my mistake. I shouldn't be allowed to escape with no consequences."

"You won't," Sano assured him. "You'll pay restitution to the families of the people you killed. You'll give better trade terms to the natives. You can also give them more freedom and protect them from Japanese who prey on them." Should someone else take over the domain, heaven help the natives. A new lord would exploit them worse than ever.

"Very well," Lord Matsumae said, uncertain yet grateful. "I'm forever in your debt. If there's anything I can give you, just name it. A banquet? A hunting trip? A ship to take you home? All the furs, gold, and medicinal herbs in my storehouses? Can I persuade you to stay for a tour of Ezogashima in the spring?"

A lord beholden to him was enough reward for a man in Sano's shaky political position, and Sano had been away from Edo too long. "I won't say no to the ship."

Three days later, a blue sky graced Fukuyama City. Sunlight sparkled on an ocean flecked with tiny whitecaps. In the harbor, Matsumae sailors inspected the ship while troops carried supplies aboard. Peasants in rowboats, armed with axes, chopped away the ice that had frozen the waters close to shore. The castle astrologer had predicted that the favorable weather would hold long enough for Sano and his party to reach home.

Detectives Marume and Fukida walked up the gangplank. "When we get back to Edo, I'm going to jump in a hot bath and stay there until spring," Fukida said.

"I'll join you," Marume said. "We'll add a few girls, a little music, and a lot of sake to liven things up."

The Rat followed them, loaded down with a bundle of native goods he'd purchased in town. "I'm never coming back here again. The next time Chamberlain Sano needs a translator, let me know, so I can make myself scarce."

On the dock a crowd had gathered to see the ship sail. Commoners from town mingled with Fukuyama Castle troops and servants. Apart from them, Hirata stood with Chieftain Awetok, who'd accompanied him back to the city.

"Thanks to you and your master for solving the murder and making peace," Awetok said.

Hirata remembered the many natives killed, the families in mourning, and the Ainu who'd lost both the women he'd loved. "I'm sorry for everything. I hope Urahenka will be all right."

The chieftain frowned as they thought of the young man they'd left at the village. "He's like a blade trying to cut a stone wall. Either he learns to control his anger toward your people, or it will destroy him. Time will tell what becomes of him, and all of us."

The Ainu had escaped extinction, but Hirata feared that the day would come when they wouldn't. He felt sad for them, for the richness of their culture that was threatened by his own kind. "I want to thank you for your lessons. They've opened a whole new world to me. If only I didn't have to leave." But he felt pulled toward Edo and knew his ultimate destiny waited for him there. "I wish I could stay and learn more."

Amusement crinkled the chieftain's stern face. "You can

leave Ainu Mosir, but Ainu Mosir won't leave you. She's part of you now. She will teach you."

Nearby, Lady Matsumae and her attendants bowed to Reiko. Lady Matsumae said, "We wish you a safe trip."

Reiko could tell that Lady Matsumae wouldn't cry if the ship sank and she drowned. "Thank you. It was kind of you to come and bid me farewell."

They exchanged looks as frigid as the northern sea. Reiko thought Lady Matsumae had probably come to make sure she really left. Nothing that had happened had changed Lady Matsumae. Still bitter about her daughter's death, she still blamed Tekare. Her bitterness was a poison that couldn't hurt Tekare but would ruin her own life. Reiko supposed she had a lesson to learn from Lady Matsumae even as she disapproved of the woman's attitude. She looked toward the ship that would bear her away from Ezogashima.

Masahiro scampered around the deck, chattering to Sano, who leaned on the railing and smiled at him. Stuck in Reiko's heart like a barbed fishhook was her anger at Lord Matsudaira for kidnapping her son and sending him to a narrowly avoided death. As she boarded the ship, Reiko felt the same need for revenge that Lady Matsumae did, that Tekare had felt toward the Japanese. Where it would take her remained to be seen.

Masahiro said, "I can't wait to get home and tell my friends everything that happened. Do you think they'll be impressed to hear that I was in a real battle?"

"Yes, indeed." Sano wondered what lay in store for himself in Edo. How much political ground had Lord Matsudaira gained at his expense while he'd been gone? Sano knew for sure that they were overdue for a showdown, and he was looking forward to it.

"I shot five enemies," Masahiro boasted, skipping around the deck.

Reiko joined Sano. She had a worried look on her face. "I wish Masahiro weren't so happy about killing."

"He's a samurai," Sano said, rueful yet proud. "War is his heritage."

"He's only eight years old!"

"He's our son." Sano's tone alluded to the fact that he and Reiko had also spilled blood. "And he lives in our world."

Reiko nodded in reluctant acceptance, but said, "I wish he hadn't been through the things he has. I wish there were someplace where nobody had to kill to survive. Someplace we could live in peace."

"We've come to the frontier of Japan and not found it," Sano pointed out. Human strife tainted even the beautiful wilds of Ezogashima. "I don't think there's such a place anywhere."

Reiko watched Masahiro climb the rigging, agile as a monkey. "What will become of him?"

"He's strong and smart. He'll live to carry on the family name." Sano's mind drifted to issues more immediate than his son's future.

"What's bothering you?"

"The part of the mystery that we didn't solve."

"Do you mean who killed Lilac?" Reiko said, "It must have been Gizaemon. I've figured out that Lilac saw him set the spring-bow. She didn't say anything at first. She waited to see how she could make the most of what she knew. When you started investigating the murder, she promised the information to me. But she also blackmailed Gizaemon. She didn't trust either of us to give her what she wanted, so she negotiated with us both. Somehow he found out she was talking to me, as well. Maybe she bragged to somebody who told him. He arranged to meet her at the hot spring and give her money to go to Edo. Instead he killed her so she couldn't tell me or anyone else that he'd murdered Tekare." Reiko sighed. "Lilac's cleverness was her downfall."

"That sounds right," Sano said.

"Of course, we'll never know for sure," Reiko said.

"But the question of who killed Lilac wasn't the one on my mind."

"What other one is there?" Reiko thought a moment, then asked, "Who attacked you in the castle?"

"Yes. I've questioned the Matsumae troops and found one that swears Gizaemon was with him during the attack on me. I think he's telling the truth. Gizaemon didn't do it. And I haven't been able to find out who did."

"Maybe one of his troops who died in the battle in the village and isn't around to confess?"

"Maybe," Sano said doubtfully, "but why would they attack me?"

"To protect Gizaemon?"

That had occurred to Sano as a reasonable theory, but he had a hunch that it was wrong. "I think the attack had nothing to do with the murder case. I think it was another in the series of events that brought us here."

"The acts of sabotage against you and Lord Matsudaira?"

"None other. And I've become convinced that he's not responsible for the ones directed at me any more than I am for those directed at him."

"Then who is behind the sabotage?" Reiko asked.

Sano was beginning to get an idea, but it seemed impossible. Reiko wouldn't believe him if he told her.

All the travelers were aboard the ship now. A channel had been cleared through the ice toward open sea, and the sailors cast off the mooring ropes. The spectators on the dock waved as the rowers below deck propelled the ship southward.

"When we get back to Edo," Sano said, "I'm going to find out."

Keep reading for a sneak peek at Laura Joh Rowland's next Sano Ichirō novel

THE FIRE KIMONO

Available soon from St. Martin's Minotaur

Prologue

A fierce windstorm swept the hills outside Edo. Lightning seared bright white veins down the gray sky while distant thunder reverberated. A Shinto priest hurried along a path through the forest. He clutched his black cap to his head and staggered as the wind buffeted him. His white robe flapped like a swan in mad flight. Dirt and leaves swirled around him in cyclones that stung his face, blinded him. He stumbled faster uphill toward the shrine, where he could take shelter.

The trees swayed, creaked, and thrashed. The wind's howling force knocked the priest to the ground. As he struggled to regain his feet, he heard an ominous cracking noise, as if the world were splitting. He saw a huge, dead oak tree pitch toward him. Crooked, leafless branches reached down like monstrous hands to grab him as the tree toppled, its massive trunk a black battering ram aimed to kill. The priest flung his arms over his head and screamed.

The tree crashed with a thud that shook the world. Branches scraped the priest, enmeshed him. He was stunned but miraculously alive. The wind's fury ebbed. Untangling himself from the branches, he saw that the heavy tree trunk lay close beside him. The gods had spared his life.

Dazed, the priest climbed the hill, gawking at the fallen corpse of the tree. The roots had torn loose from the dirt. They'd left a yawning hole in the forest beside the path. Something in the lumpy earth just below the surface level at the edge of the hole caught the priest's attention.

The object was brown from the soil, with a rounded top the size of a small melon. The priest squatted for a closer inspection, and recoiled in dismay. Empty eye sockets stared and bare teeth grinned up at him. It was a human skull.

Chapter One

Lady Reiko rarely left home, and never without an army for protection.

In the past few months, the strife between her husband, Chamberlain Sano, and his rival, Lord Matsudaira, had escalated drastically. Their troops brawled in the streets of Edo, eager for war. No one was safe; anyone could be caught in the violence.

Riding in a palanquin through the city, Reiko peered through the window shutters. Her mounted guards blocked her view of the high walls and roofed gates of the mansions in the official district. All she could see were armored legs astride moving horse flanks. Her bearers marched in time with the steps of the foot soldiers in her entourage, which numbered fifty armed men in all. Reiko leaned back on the cushions and sighed.

Not a glimpse of the city's color and bustle or breath of spring air could reach her. Yet these precautions were vital. Last winter, Lord Matsudaira had served notice that Sano's family wasn't off-limits in the power struggle. He'd had Sano and Reiko's eight-year-old son, Masahiro, kidnapped and sent to the far north. Knowing that she might be the next target, Reiko left Sano's estate inside Edo Castle only on the most serious business.

Her aunt had died, and although they hadn't been close, the woman had been kind to Reiko during her childhood. That fact, plus family duty, had obligated Reiko to brave venturing outside to attend the funeral. Now her procession suddenly slowed. Guards at the front ordered, "Get out of the way!"

She risked opening the shutters a crack and saw two oxen yoked to a cart filled with lumber blocking an intersection. Such carts, owned by the government, were the only wheeled vehicles permitted in Japan. Forcing everyone to travel by horse or by foot prevented troop movements and insurrection—at least in theory. Soldiers behind her called to the others, "Keep going, don't stop!" The front guards yelled, "Move it now, or die!"

A jarring thud hit the top of the palanquin. Reiko gasped as her bearers wobbled under the extra weight. One of them shouted, "There's a man on the roof!"

The man must have jumped off the wall. While her guards shouted and jostled around her palanquin, she felt another thud as another man landed.

"Ambush!" shouted the guards.

The doors of the palanquin burst open. Reiko screamed. Her attackers—two young samurai with knives gripped in their teeth—swung upside down from the roof at her. As she drew the dagger she wore in a sheath strapped to her arm under her sleeve, they flipped into the palanquin, transferring their knives from teeth to hands.

"Help!" Reiko shrank into the corner and lashed her dagger at her attackers.

Her blade cut their arms. They seemed not to care. Blind savagery glazed their eyes as they slashed at her. Their hot breath and pungent sweat filled the palanquin. Reiko saw the crests stamped on their kimonos. They were Lord Matsudaira's men, no surprise. She frantically parried against their blades. One grazed her face. Outside, swords clashed while her guards fought off more Matsudaira troops who'd joined the attack. The combatants' bodies thumped against the palanquin. Horses whinnied as the battle raged.

"Turn around!" her guard captain shouted. "Head back to the castle! Somebody get those bastards off Lady Reiko!"

Reiko heard her chief bodyguard, Lieutenant Asukai, call her name. As her attackers pinned her arms and she kicked at them, he lunged into the palanquin and seized one of the men. The palanquin veered in a jerky about-face. The bearers broke into a run.

Lieutenant Asukai dragged the man outside. They tumbled into the street under the horses' skittering hooves and the feet of the battling soldiers. The attacker still inside threw himself on top of Reiko. He clutched the wrist of her hand that held the dagger. His weight immobilized her. She desperately thrashed and writhed, beating at him with her free left hand. His blade strained toward her throat. Reiko could see her terrified face reflected in the shiny steel.

"Hold on, Lady Reiko, I'm coming!" Lieutenant Asukai shouted.

He grabbed her attacker's legs. Reiko struck at the man's face and sank her fingernails into his eyes. He screamed, let go of her, and reared up. Lieutenant Asukai yanked at his legs until he flew backward out of the palanquin, bleeding from the eyes, knife raised, mouth yowling.

Reiko saw the portals of Edo Castle ahead, promising sanctuary. The castle was neutral territory in the conflict between Sano and Lord Matsudaira, by tacit, mutual agreement. They both lived inside it; neither wanted war on his own doorstep. The sentries stared in amazement at Reiko's palanquin hurtling toward them and the battle that trailed it like unruly streamers.

"Let us in!" Lieutenant Asukai shouted, running beside Reiko.

The sentries swung open the huge, iron-banded gate. Winded and puffing, the bearers staggered carrying the palanquin through it. The gates slammed shut. Reiko sighed in relief.

"That was too close a call," Sano said.

He crouched on the floor beside Reiko, in their private chamber, watching grimly as the doctor dabbed medicinal ointment on the cut on her cheek. First his son kidnapped, now his wife ambushed. Lord Matsudaira had gone too far. Sano tasted fury as raw as blood.

Reiko managed a brave smile. "It's just a scratch. I'm fine, really." The doctor finished, gathered up his medicine chest, and departed. Reiko spoke to Masahiro, who knelt near her. "I don't look half as bad as you do."

Masahiro, nine years old, had come running when he'd heard about the attack. His white martial arts practice uniform was dirty from wrestling on the ground; he sported cuts and scrapes on his hands, arms, and knees. A fading purple bruise surrounded his left eye. Ever since his abduction, Masahiro had pursued his martial arts studies with punishing vigor, the better to defend himself. This was no longer just a game he was good at, but a matter of life and death.

Now he said, "Don't joke, Mama." His tone was serious, reproving, and adult. "You could have been killed."

Sano hadn't wanted Masahiro to know about the attack, had wanted to shield him from adult problems. But Masahiro had a way of finding out what happened; his sharp ears and his nose for information rivaled those of any spy in the government intelligence service. And he'd matured a lot during his experience in Ezogashima. Having survived it by his own wits and courage, he'd earned himself a new place in their family. Sano beheld his son with a mixture of love, pride, and sorrow.

He could see Reiko in the shape of Masahiro's eyes, and himself in the set of his jaw; but Masahiro was his own, unique person, and he was growing up too fast. There was little room for childhood in their harsh world.

"Masahiro is right," Sano said to Reiko. The boy sat straighter, gladdened by his father's approval. Sano remembered looking up to and aspiring to be like his own father, now dead eleven years. How long before Masahiro became aware of his failings and the hero-worship ended? "You can't go out again."

"Yes," seconded Masahiro. "You have to stay home."

Reiko had opened her mouth to object, then closed it, taken aback by his authority. Sano hid a rueful smile. She would need to get used to having two men telling her what to do. This time she conceded. "For how long?"

She spoke as if she didn't expect Sano to answer, and he didn't. He only wished he knew how long this feud with Lord Matsudaira would go on.

Unhappiness shadowed her beautiful face. "What are you going to do?"

"I'm going to see Lord Matsudaira," Sano said.

"Are you going to declare war on him?" Reiko asked.

Excitement charged the air as she and Masahiro waited for Sano's reply. They thirsted for a showdown as much as Sano did. But Sano knew the odds better than them, and he said, "No."

Indignation appeared on their faces. Reiko said, "Not even after what Lord Matsudaira did to my son?"

"And to my mother?" Masahiro said.

"It's not the time for me to challenge Lord Matsudaira in battle," Sano said. "His troops outnumber mine by too many."

Sano's army had shrunk drastically since last autumn. He'd come home from Ezogashima to discover that he'd lost entire regiments during his absence. Without Sano here to keep them in line and their morale up, Lord Matsudaira had easily won them over. That was just as Lord Matsudaira had planned when he'd kidnapped Masahiro and Sano had gone to Ezogashima to rescue his son.

"And I can't afford to run a war for more than a few months." Sano had also lost key allies among the *daimyo,* the feudal lords he'd counted on to fund a military venture.

"It can't be that bad," Reiko said. "You still have many allies." She named some, all wealthy, powerful *daimyo* with large armies. "You can win."

"Let's declare war!" Masahiro's face shone with zeal and confidence in Sano. "You're not afraid of Lord Matsudaira."

Sano dreaded the day when he would see Masahiro begin to doubt him. Now he needed to give Masahiro a lesson as difficult to teach as to learn.

"Of course I'm afraid," Sano said, even though he hated admitting fear. "A samurai who isn't afraid of a dangerous enemy isn't a hero; he's a fool." More and more often, Sano heard his own father's words coming out of his mouth. "A truly courageous samurai masters his fear."

Impatient, hardly listening, Masahiro jumped up and paced back and forth, Reiko's habit when excited. "I'll ride into battle with you. Together we'll defeat Lord Matsudaira."

Sano ached with pride in his son's spirit. Reiko looked aghast. "You can't go to battle. You're not even fifteen yet!"

Fifteen was the age at which samurai boys officially became adults, when the forelock that Masahiro wore tied above his brow would be shaved during his manhood ceremony.

"A war could last six more years until he is," Sano pointed out. "The wars that ended with the Tokugawa on top went on for almost a century."

"I'm almost as tall as a lot of boys who are fifteen," Masahiro said, standing still and drawing himself up to his full height. "And I'm a better fighter."

"You're also too modest," Reiko said, tart in her fear for him. She turned to Sano. "All right, I don't want a war, either." She'd clearly lost her appetite for it now that she saw her son headed for the front lines. "But if you're not declaring war on Lord Matsudaira, why go to see him?"

"To propose a truce. To make peace if I can."

Reiko stared in disbelief. "You mean you're going to let him get away with what he's done?"

"He deserves to be punished!" Masahiro clenched his fists.

"The country doesn't," Sano said. "If we go on like this, there will eventually be war, and Japan will suffer. War involves more than the two top men fighting it. Should it spread beyond Edo, cities and villages everywhere will be destroyed. Thousands of innocent people will die."

"I don't care," Masahiro said stubbornly.

He was too young for the consequences of war to seem real to him, Sano thought. Despite the maturity forced on him, Masahiro was a child, with a child's limited understanding.

"As the shogun's second-in-command, I have to care,"

Sano said. "It's my duty to protect the country and the people. And when you inherit my position, it will be your duty."

Masahiro nodded, swelling with pride at the thought that he would someday succeed his father. Hoping he could hold his position long enough to pass it on, Sano rose to go.

Sano summoned Hirata—his chief retainer—and Detectives Marume and Fukida, his two top personal bodyguards. Accompanied by a squadron of troops, they went to the special compound inside Edo Castle where the Tokugawa branch clan members lived. Lord Matsudaira, the shogun's cousin, had the largest estate. Sentries were posted outside its gate, at intervals along the high stone walls, and in the watch towers. When they saw Sano's party coming, their hands flashed to their swords.

"I want to see Lord Matsudaira," Sano told the four gate sentries.

Their leader said, "With all due respect, Honorable Chamberlain, you have a lot of nerve coming here. After what you've done today."

"After what *he's* done?" Hirata said. "What are you talking about?"

Noting the mystified expressions of Sano and his companions, the man smirked. "Looks like you and your people have lost your memories, Chamberlain Sano. Well, don't worry; Lord Matsudaira will fill in the blank spaces."

He sent a runner to tell Lord Matsudaira that Sano was here. As other guards opened the gate and escorted Sano's party inside, Sano exchanged perturbed glances with Hirata, Marume, and Fukida. This was a strange reception that didn't bode well for their peace mission.

They moved through courtyards and passages lined with armed, hostile soldiers. If not for the prohibition against violence inside Edo Castle, they would have attacked Sano. The air smelled of gunpowder.

Sano found Lord Matsudaira waiting in his reception room. Flanked by bodyguards, with troops stationed along the walls, Lord Matsudaira stood on the dais. His posture was arrogant, his expression murderous. But he was thinner, and visibly older, than when Sano had left for Ezogashima only six months ago. The strain of building his army, juggling allies, and battling treachery had carved new lines in his strong-featured face. The fire in his eyes verged on fever.

"What in hell do you want?" he demanded.

"I have a proposition to make," Sano said even as his hatred toward his enemy flared. He hadn't started this quarrel; he'd been willing to work with Lord Matsudaira to serve the shogun, their master. It was Lord Matsudaira who wanted to be shogun himself, who saw Sano's power as a threat. "I'll excuse your attack this morning, if you'll agree to a truce."

Astonishment raised Lord Matsudaira's eyebrows. "A truce? Are you insane? And I didn't attack you this morning."

Infuriated by the denial, Sano said, "Your men ambushed my wife and tried to kill her. Or have you forgotten you sent them?"

Lord Matsudaira seemed as much confused as scornful. "I didn't." He pointed a finger at Sano. "It was *you* who just sent *your* men to kill *my* wife."

Sano thought of what the sentries had said. Consternation filled him. "You'd better explain what happened."

"Playing innocent, eh?" Lord Matsudaira's face darkened with anger. "I suppose you came to gloat over what you've done. Well, all right, I'll show you. Come."

Beckoning, he stalked outside. His troops herded Sano's party after him, into the garden. More troops patrolled amid azalea bushes in bright red bloom. Increasingly baffled, Sano followed Lord Matsudaira to the heart of the estate, a group of low buildings connected by covered corridors. One lay half in ruins, walls broken, the tile roof collapsed. The ruins were covered by black soot. Servants labored, cleaning up the mess.

"These are the women's quarters," Lord Matsudaira said, gesturing angrily. "My wife was inside. She has burns all over her. It's a miracle she wasn't killed. One of her attendants was." He glared at Sano. "Don't say it's not your fault."

"It isn't," Sano said, as disturbed as sincere.

"No more lies! Two of your men sneaked into this estate and threw jars of kerosene plugged with burning rags into the windows. My men caught them running away from the explosion. See for yourself."

Lord Matsudaira led Sano to a blanket spread on the charred grass near the ruins. He flung back the blanket, exposing two young samurai who lay dead and bloody.

"They're not mine. I've never seen them before in my life." Sano turned to Hirata, Marume, and his other men; they shook their heads.

"You have so many retainers that you don't know everyone who works for you," Lord Matsudaira said. "Look at the crests on their clothes." He pointed at Sano's flying-crane insignias. "They're yours, all right."

Sano didn't see any point in arguing; Lord Matsudaira would never believe him. "Well, I have two bodies of men that my troops caught and killed after they tried to stab my wife. They're wearing your crests."

"I had nothing to do with that," Lord Matsudaira protested. "Whatever business I have with you, I would never attack your woman." His tone scorned that as cowardly, dishonorable, beneath him. "This is the first I've heard of it."

His shock and dismay seemed genuine. A familiar uneasy sensation trickled through Sano. He said, "This isn't the first time that people on your side have been attacked and *I* wasn't responsible, or that people on mine have been and you've claimed you weren't."

During the past six months, Sano's troops had been ambushed, had been the target of firebombs and snipers. So had Lord Matsudaira's. The frequency of the attacks had increased since Sano had returned from Ezogashima. Each rival had blamed the other, with reason based on evidence as well as motive. But Sano knew he wasn't to blame, and he was ready to acknowledge that perhaps neither was Lord Matsudaira.

"Something is going on," Sano said.

He'd had ideas about what it was, yet they remained unproven. Although he'd investigated the attacks, he'd found no substantiating clues as to the person behind them. He'd never mentioned his suspicions to Lord Matsudaira, who would only think Sano was trying to trick him.

"Of course something is going on, and I know what," Lord Matsudaira said. "You've been faking attacks against yourself, to make me look bad and justify attacking me. Now you've violated protocol against attacking inside Edo Castle." Lord Matsudaira bunched his fists and shook with fury. "Merciful gods, you'll stop at nothing to destroy me!"

"The two of us should stop our quarrel," Sano said, although he realized it was futile to hope he could convince Lord Matsudaira. "Agree to a truce. Then we can get to the bottom of these attacks and work out a peace treaty."

"Take your peace treaty and shove it up your behind," Lord Matsudaira said. "Now leave before I throw you out."

As they glared at each other, Sano felt the war he wanted to prevent rushing on them like a tornado. The sensation was as exhilarating as it was dreadful. When he and his men turned to depart, Lord Matsudaira warned, "Remember that your home is a target, too."

A servant came running up to them. "Excuse me, but I have an urgent message."

"What is it?" Lord Matsudaira barked.

"The shogun wants to see you. And Chamberlain Sano. At once."